A Vancouver Mystery
by

Rosey Dow & Andrew Snaden

PROMISE PRESS

An Imprint of Barbour Publishing

Face
Value

ISBN 1-58660-589-5

This book is a work of fiction. Names, characters, places, and incidents are either products of the author's imagination or used fictitiously. Any similarity to actual people, organizations, and/or events is purely coincidental.

For more information about Rosey Dow and Andrew Snaden, please access the authors' web sites at the following Internet addresses:
www.roseydow.com
www.andrewsnaden.com

Acquisitions and Editorial Director: Mike Nappa
Editorial Consultant: Rebecca Germany
Art Director: Robyn Martins

Cover Design: LookOut Design

Published by Promise Press, an imprint of Barbour Publishing, Inc., P.O. Box 719, Uhrichsville, Ohio 44683, www.promisepress.com

 Member of the
Evangelical Christian
Publishers Association

Printed in the United States of America

We'd like to dedicate this series to Jehovah-rapha,
the Lord who heals. Exodus 15:26

—RD & AS

Prologue

With a single hacking cough, Peter Martin hunched his grizzled neck deeper into his yellow slicker and shivered. A wet September day in Abbotsford, British Columbia, had never felt more miserable.

Scowling, he muttered a choice word at Samson, his prize Hereford bull. A red livestock trailer sat with its open door against the narrow wooden loading chute. The dank odor of soggy manure and rotting straw hung over the barnyard.

A couple of jolts with the cattle prod usually had the bull inside the cattle trailer without a problem. Today, Samson had his massive white head pushed against the chute toward Peter, his eyes rolling wildly, his nostrils flaring.

The farmer jabbed him on the rump. "Get up there!"

The bull bellowed and held his ground.

Dropping the prod, Peter stood on the second-to-bottom rail of the fence and gave the animal's meaty side a powerful slap. Samson snorted and lunged into the fence. Peter jumped back just in time. The entire length of posts quivered.

Shaking his head, Peter said, "Watch yourself, old boy. Cash isn't the problem it used to be. Much more of this nonsense and maybe I'll take you to Julien's butcher shop instead of to stud with Harrison's heifers."

Sliding the trailer door shut with a screeching clang, Peter strode into the holding pen and yanked open the gate on the back end of the chute. He coughed again, then said, "Come on back, Boy. If you don't want to go today, you ain't going."

Two white puffs of hot air shot out of the bull's wide nose as he swung his head back and forth, touching each side of the chute in rhythm.

Impatient to get back inside the house for a cup of hot coffee, Peter called, "Come on back, you old fool!"

Tossing his short horns, Samson slowly backed down the chute and burst into the holding pen. The bull trotted past the gate, then suddenly spun around and charged the man.

Peter Martin's stout legs tangled with the Hereford's cropped horns. In an instant, the bull lifted the old farmer and tossed him six feet in the air. He landed hard and flopped on the muddy earth like a beached whale—trying to suck air into his lungs, struggling to get up—but his legs refused to move.

He glimpsed a slim figure in red beyond him at the fence. It was his wife's ward. Reaching for her, he shouted, "Amy, help me!"

The girl twisted her long blond hair, her face pale, her mouth tight. She stared at him and didn't answer.

Samson's thundering hooves drowned out his second cry.

Chapter
One

The operating room was decorated in soft blue tones, and a Mozart CD played quietly in the background. Dr. Dan Foster leaned over the table to smile into the sun-seamed face of Beth Martin.

"How are you feeling?" he asked.

Her gray eyes glazed from preop medication, a loose grin crinkled Beth's weathered cheeks. "I feel. . .fabulous. What did that nurse give me?" She nodded toward the lithe, green-clad form of Allison Hursley. Allison smiled at the patient as she unrolled a packet of instruments onto a shiny steel tray near the top of Beth's head.

Dr. Foster winked at Beth and said, "It's a trade secret. Ready to go to sleep now?"

Beth nodded. Her green surgical cap crinkled against the pillow. "Make me beautiful again, Danny," she murmured.

Dan glanced across the table at anesthetist Steve Logan, who sat on a rolling stool beside Beth's left shoulder. Dr. Logan was a blond tennis-star type minus the tan.

As Dan straightened, Steve leaned closer. His voice had a clear, precise tone. "Mrs. Martin, I want you to count backwards from one hundred, please."

Mumbling, she droned, "One hundred, ninety-nine, ninety. . ." Her voice faded. Beth Martin was out.

Fifteen seconds later, the endotracheal tube slid into place, and Steve switched on the oxygen. With his eyes on the monitor, Steve said, "She's all yours. . .*Danny.*" He glanced at Dr. Foster. "Is she a long-lost auntie or something?"

Squinting slightly, Dan's gaze swept across Beth's lined brow to the deep crow's-feet beside her eyes. "Beth's been my bookkeeper for the past three years. She has a habit of making everyone into a relative after she's known them for two weeks."

Allison looked at Beth's face. "I can't believe she's only forty-five."

"Let that be a lesson to you," Dan said. "You are looking at the result of too many hours in the sun. Twenty-five years ago, this woman made the guys do a double take whenever she walked by."

Allison scrunched up her nose. Light freckles sprinkled across her fair cheeks. "She doesn't look like a bathing beauty to me," she said.

"Not now, she doesn't," Dan said. His gloved hands moved across the sleeping woman's face, feeling the muscle structure below the skin. "Beth married a farmer and worked beside him in the fields from dawn to dusk. Believe me, she's earned every one of these wrinkles." He gently tugged the skin to see the effect.

"I take it she's going for the full-meal deal," Steve said.

"Can you blame her?" Picking up a blue marker, Dan deftly drew a line at the scalp starting behind one ear, over the brow, and ending behind the other ear. Allison handed him a syringe filled with epinephrine, and the procedure began.

Dan continued to talk while he worked. He'd performed this same surgery so often that his fingers moved automatically, like someone tying shoes. "The way I see it, Beth deserves a treat. Her husband was Scrooge incarnate. She had to do book-keeping on the side just to keep herself in decent clothing and to get her hair done every now and then."

With the hands of a delicate artist, he worked the Metzenbaum scissors to loosen the skin from underlying tissues.

"Why's he shelling out money for this operation now?" Allison asked, her words covering the soft beeps of the monitor. "Did he finally get a life or something?"

Dan leaned forward, intent on his work. "He didn't get one. He lost one. Her husband was Peter Martin. He got trampled by his bull a month back." He lifted the instrument and glanced at the nurse. "In spite of all his faults, he carried a decent life insurance policy. Our dear Beth is pretty well off, and I'm glad for her. She deserves to get her beauty back."

"Speaking of beauty," Steve said, "how's Jessica Meyers?"

Dan paused. "Fine. Why do you ask?"

A knowing chuckle came from behind Allison's mask. Dan ignored her and continued his careful snipping.

His eyes active above his mask, Steve shot a glance at Dan. "No reason. I saw both of you last night. You were sitting at a cozy table for two near the front window of the Glover Street Café. I suppose you were 'counseling' her for post-traumatic stress syndrome. At eleven P.M."

Dan took his time over Beth's left temple. "We met at the hockey game and decided to have a snack." He laid down the scissors. "Look, don't make a case out of it. She went through a very scary experience and has some lingering issues. I do have training in psychology, you know. She needed a friendly ear, and I let her borrow mine."

Steve adjusted a knob. "That friendly ear hasn't hurt your client base any. Cruch is starting to complain about you pulling in all the big names. In the past, high-profile patients have always asked for him."

Dan paused to let the comment register. Jessica Meyers had been the doctor's big break. Two years ago, he'd been covering a shift for a friend at Vancouver General Hospital when paramedics rushed Jessica into Emergency. Her face had been mangled in a nasty car accident. At first glance, Dan hadn't recognized the face all Vancouver knew. Using a publicity photo from the TV station, Dan worked miracles that night. Today, Jessica had minor scarring that makeup could hide. Without Dan, her TV career would have been over. And she wasn't shy about spreading that fact around to her friends.

"You shouldn't listen to office gossip." Dan laced the first fine suture. "Last week Dr. Cruch and I had a friendly talk over lunch. We both want this clinic to offer premium care. I told him he could check up on my work anytime."

"You did?" Allison asked.

"Sure. He's the senior surgeon in this clinic. I value his input."

"Yeah, right," Steve said.

"Let me translate that for you, children," Dan said. "I don't need him mad at me, so I thought I'd best be a little humble."

"Now you're speaking English," Steve said.

Twist and pull. Tug and clip. The sutures went in with precision and grace in time with the beeping monitor. Dan's large hands had an easy nimbleness that made him a natural at this type of delicate surgery. Dan Foster was a master craftsman.

"What do you think of the Giants' chances against the Cougars on Friday?" He veered the conversation toward safer topics as he moved down to tighten Beth's sagging neck. The conversation stayed light until the last stitch lay in place.

Pulling off his gloves, the surgeon stepped back, satisfied. "Take her to recovery," he told Allison after she withdrew the tube. "I'll check on her in an hour or so."

Dan left the operating room and entered the empty doctor's

lounge. He pulled off his scrubs, bundled them into a ball, and slam-dunked them into the laundry hamper. He went to his locker, pulled on his street clothes, and snatched a bottle of pills from his locker shelf, dropping it into his coat pocket.

Two minutes later, he stepped out of the heavy door that barred the public from the surgery wing, on the way to his next appointment. His long legs stretching out, Dan headed down the hall to the three-story office section of the clinic. A portly man dressed in white coveralls held the elevator door open for him.

"Going up, Doctor?"

Dan glanced at the man in the elevator and shook his head. "No thanks, Sam," he said, heading instead to the left toward the staircase. After bounding up three flights to the third floor, he pushed open the solid oak door to his office. He smiled at his receptionist, a brunette with dancing green eyes.

"Hi, Connie," he said, not the slightest bit winded from his jog up the stairs.

Connie smiled. "Your appointment is in Room B."

Dan picked up his office laptop from its shelf, tucked it under his arm, and strode to the examining-room door. He swiped a sheet of paper from a plastic tray bolted there, scanning down the form to glean medical history and other pertinent details. This was the first time he'd seen this girl. Interestingly, she had the same rare blood type as he did: O negative.

He pushed open the door to see a rail-thin girl about four-teen years old sitting rigidly on the short examining table. Her gangly legs barely touched the step at the end of the black table. She had stringy blond hair, and her narrow lips formed a straight line. Lumpy scar tissue covered the right side of her face. The paper said that her face had been burned when she was five years old. Whoever had done the emergency care should have been sued.

Next to the window, a massive woman in a blue polka-dot tent dress draped herself over a blue plastic chair. Her gray hair was pulled tightly into a bun; dark-rimmed glasses framed a round face. She stood when Dan walked in. "Dr. Foster," she said, holding out pudgy fingers. "I'm Marion Burke, Chelsea's foster mother." Dan shook her hand. "Please, sit down," he said. Foster mother? Social services didn't pay for plastic surgery. He glanced at the page again and saw his brother's name listed as the referral. *Another charity case*, he thought. *Cruch will have kittens.* Oh well, they'd talk money after he examined the girl.

He held out his hand to the patient. "Hi, Chelsea. I'm Dr. Foster."

She rolled her eyes to look up at him but kept her chin planted firmly on her chest. "Hi," she mumbled and took his hand in a listless grip.

Dan wasn't sure which he was more concerned about, her face or her size. She wore a tight, belly-out T-shirt that showed the clear outline of a few ribs. Chelsea had to be at least ten pounds under weight, a possible sign of an eating disorder.

He placed the laptop on the counter and opened its lid. For the next few minutes, the doctor asked questions and typed information into Chelsea's new file. Finally the history was finished, and he stood up.

"Mind if I take a look at your cheek?" he asked.

Chelsea didn't answer.

Dan gently touched her chin and turned her face to a better angle. Using his penlight, he carefully examined the scarring. He touched the jagged ridges of flesh bordering the burn and ran his fingers along the fiery skin. Other than the burn, she had fine features and should have been a nice-looking girl. But her face was an emergency-room hatchet job followed up by a careless surgeon. Still, Dan could fix it. He'd fixed worse.

"Thanks, Chelsea," Dan said a moment later. "How about

taking a seat in the hall while I talk with Marion?"

She slid off the table and shuffled across the white tile to the door. Her fingers lightly around the door handle, she paused and turned toward him. A tear rolled down her scarred cheek. "I don't want to be ugly anymore."

Dan smiled. "Just wait outside."

Chelsea left the room.

He leaned against the examining table and turned to Ms. Burke. "What's her story?" he asked.

Ms. Burke's face tightened with suppressed emotion. "I've had Chelsea since she was five years old. I picked her up at the hospital after she was treated for that burn."

"How did she get it?" Dan asked, moving back to his rolling stool.

Marion's voice sounded stiff. "Her mother was drunk and angry. She branded Chelsea with an iron."

Dan forced his face to remain cool and professional, but inside he seethed.

"That was just the beginning of Chelsea's pain," Marion continued. "Since the first day she stepped into kindergarten, Chelsea has lived with cruel teasing. It's gotten worse since she became a teen. . .so bad that. . . "

"Go on," Dan said.

Marion Burke took a deep breath. "Two weeks ago Chelsea tried to slit her wrists. I caught her just in time." She looked up at him, her face set. "Chelsea and I barely get by from paycheck to paycheck, but if we can work out a payment plan, I'll pay whatever is needed over time. Chelsea needs help."

"Have you asked Social Services for assistance?"

Marion turned up the corner of her mouth. "Oh yeah. All they're willing to do is pay for counseling to help Chelsea *cope* with her situation. But I'm sorry, counseling just isn't going to cut it."

Dan put his hand to his chin. "I see my brother Mike referred you to me. How do you know him?"

"We go to the same church."

The word "church" struck a sour chord. Though he knew the answer, Dan couldn't resist asking. "Have you asked the church for help?"

Marion bit down on her lip, and her jaw tightened. "Yes."

"And what did they say?"

"The pastor said plastic surgery is controversial and he'd rather not make an open appeal."

Dan smirked. "In other words—nothing." His saintly aunt Elinor had the same opinion of plastic surgery and never missed an opportunity to point out he was wasting his God-given talents.

"Oh no," Marion said. "The pastor donated five hundred himself, and he's by no means a rich man. Another two hundred came from an anonymous donor."

That took a bit of wind out of Dan's sails, though he had a pretty good idea his brother was the anonymous donor.

Dan sat on the stool and rolled within a couple of feet of Marion. "Those funds will cover Chelsea's personal expenses during her surgery. You keep it for that."

Marion's jaw dropped. "Really?"

"Yeah," Dan said. "Really."

"Why are you doing this?"

Dan looked at the closed door leading to the waiting room. "I have my reasons." He turned to Marion. "So, who gives her the good news? Me or you?"

"You do it."

Dan opened the door and looked to the left, where Chelsea sat in the wide hallway. "Chelsea," he called, "come in, please."

She shuffled into the room, turning her head to hide her face from him as she passed. She'd probably spent every day since her tragedy walking with her face obscured. Dan touched her shoulder, turned her around, and lifted her chin toward him. "What are you doing for the Christmas holidays?" he asked, smiling gently.

She refused to look up at him. "Nothing."

"Good," Dan said. "Because that's when we're going to start working on your face."

Her eyes wide as saucers, Chelsea's gaze met his. "Really?"

"Absolutely," Dan said. "I have to warn you, though. This is going to take some time. I may have to do some grafting and finish the work with a laser. More than likely, with the help of makeup, no one will be able to tell one side of your face from the other when we're through."

Chelsea stared at him, her mouth hanging open.

"My office manager will call you," Dan said. He picked up the laptop and strode out. Outside, he paused at Connie's desk. "Book the operating room for whenever the kids get out of school for Christmas break. Ask Steve and Allison if they'll volunteer to assist."

"Yes, Doctor," Connie said.

Dan slid his slim computer into its cubbyhole and headed back toward the surgery wing. Beth Martin should be awake by now. He had to check on her. He quickstepped down the stairs and headed for the recovery room.

In the hall outside the recovery room door, Dan saw the back of a slender woman with long, shimmering blond hair. It was Amy Creighton, Beth's ward. At Beth's urging, he'd taken Amy to dinner a few times, but nothing ever came of it.

When he reached her, Amy flinched and jerked around. Fear clouded her blue eyes and drew back her full lips.

Dan touched her elbow. "Are you okay? Maybe you should sit down."

Blushing, she drew away, her face down. Her words came

breathy and fast. "I'm sorry, Dr. Foster. I'm a little jumpy, I guess. Maybe I'm worried about Aunt Beth."

Amy had lost her parents in a car wreck fifteen years ago. Peter and Beth Martin had taken her in and raised her. After so much trauma at age thirteen, losing Peter had probably revived old fears.

"Beth's doing fine," Dan told her, smiling. "Once the swelling goes down, she'll be a new lady. You won't be able to hold her back."

"I hope so," she said.

"You've both had a rough time lately. I hope this surgery opens a new chapter for each of you."

"Is it okay if I come in while you talk to her?"

"Please do. You should hear the postop instructions so you can help her."

"If she'll let me," she said. "You know Aunt Beth; she helps everyone else, but no one helps her."

Dan pulled open the door, and Amy passed through. Closing the door, he turned to see Beth across the room. Six beds lined the walls, but only two were occupied. Beth's narrow bed had its top end elevated to forty-five degrees. Twin ice packs lay on each side of her face.

Dan passed the bed of a Japanese woman whose husband had a video camera going nonstop to catch every angle of her swollen face.

Dan drew near Beth's side. "How are you feeling?" he asked, raising the ice packs for a glance. She looked like a boxer on the losing side of a bout.

Her voice sounded muffled. "Like I've been run over by a tractor."

Gently replacing the ice packs, he said, "You'll have to take it easy for a couple of weeks until the swelling goes down. Come back next Wednesday so I can take a peek at your progress. The stitches should have dissolved by then." He jotted something down on her chart.

"You'll be in some discomfort," he continued. "I'd suggest Tylenol or Advil for pain. Stay sitting up for a couple of weeks, even when you sleep. The worst thing that can happen is for blood to pool under the skin and form a hematoma to distort the work I've done. Use that comfortable old recliner you've got in your living room."

"It's gone," Beth said. "It was Peter's chair."

Dan lifted his eyebrows. Usually a widow held onto her husband's most-loved possessions. Then again, with the way Peter had treated her, his death might have come as a relief.

"We'll get a new recliner," Amy said, saving Beth the trouble of talking.

Dan dug into his coat pocket for the bottle of pills from his locker. "I want you to take this antibiotic as a preventative measure. The directions are on the bottle. You're not taking any other medication, are you?"

"Just allergy medicine," Beth said.

"That won't be a problem." He set the bottle on her stand and glanced at his watch. "You've got my home number if you have any questions."

Beth nodded and let her eyes close.

With a nod to Amy, Dan hurried from the room. Two steps into the hall, Amy called from behind him, "Can I talk to you?"

Just then, Dr. Cruch passed by them. The elderly doctor nodded briefly toward Dan but didn't break his stride as he unlocked a nearby supply room and disappeared inside.

Dan turned his attention to the smooth oval face of the young woman beside him. "What is it, Amy?"

She looked up at him. "Why don't you. . .and um. . .your brother and aunt have Thanksgiving dinner with us?" she asked. "Beth would want me to invite you."

Dan touched the penlight in his shirt pocket. Thanksgiving in the United States was a celebration of American heritage held in late November. In Canada the holiday was held in October and meant to be a time set aside to thank God for his blessings—though it had long since lost that religious meaning to most people. Still, Dan liked the Canadian version of the holiday; celebrating it in October seemed to stretch out the festive season until Christmas just a bit longer.

"Let's see. Aunt Elinor said something about going away to visit friends for the holiday. That means the choice for Mike and me is frozen dinners alone at home or turkey dinner with you and Beth. And that's a no-brainer. We'll be there."

"Great," she said, her eyes lingering on his face for a moment before turning back to the recovery room.

Smiling, Dan hurried to his next appointment.

Chapter
Two

Wearing faded jeans, filthy sneakers, and stained sweatshirts, Corporal Mike Foster and Constable Bernie Thorpe joined a mob of skytrain riders waiting for the elevated train traveling from Surrey to Vancouver. They looked like Mutt and Jeff with about fifty extra pounds on each of them. Mike's weight made his Canucks sweatshirt bulge around the biceps, shoulders, and chest. Bernie's pounds lapped over his belt.

Mike's thick and wavy red hair reached his shoulders. He always had three days' growth of amber stubble on his rugged face. The only hint that he was an officer was his solid build, but he might as well have tried to hide an elephant in a pea patch as try to hide his physique. Bernie had a straggly beard and a shiny bald head under his dirty cap. The men looked dull and shiftless, but they'd completed seven arrests between eight o'clock and ten o'clock that evening.

"Look at those idiots," Bernie murmured, glancing left toward the main thoroughfare, a dingy hallway with brilliant florescent lights at close intervals. The skytrain track stretched as far as one could see. At this time of night, this area was only moderately full.

Mike scratched his head, stealing a brief look at a skinny

white kid and his tubby friend. Everything they wore shouted a designer label. Each boy's jeans hugged his lower pelvis and pooled around his ankles. The fat one called out at regular intervals to passing patrons, "Want some good stuff?"

Mike said, "I'd say they're about sixteen. Under the Young Offenders Act, the worst they're going to get is a frothy glass of cold milk and a box of Oreo cookies from one of their kind uncles down at the station house. With a stern warning for dessert."

"Think we should bother with them?" Bernie asked, fingering his greasy beard.

Mike grinned, a reckless gleam in his eye. "Why not?"

The elevated train silently whooshed into the station, and Bernie angled toward the exit doors to block any fleeing suspects. Mike ambled toward the young entrepreneurs. As he moved, Mike slipped on the black leather jacket that had been hanging over his arm.

A moment later he stood directly in front of the targets. "You guys know where I can score some crack?" he asked, his voice holding just the right amount of contempt.

Tubby opened his mouth, but Skinny gave him an elbow in the side before he could answer. "You a cop?" Skinny demanded.

"Huh?" Mike said, his eyes half open, imitating the glazed stare of a drug user.

"You a cop?" the kid insisted.

"Aw, c'mon." Mike sounded bored. "I'm just looking for some crack."

"Don't have no crack, just pot," Tubby volunteered.

Skinny glared at him.

Mike dove in. "It'll have to do. I've got to have something now."

Skinny bit down on his lower lip, considering Mike for two seconds. "Okay. Follow us."

From the corner of his eye, Mike spotted Bernie moving down the stairs from the platform, lining himself up to follow them. Skinny pulled Tubby in front of him when they reached the steps. Halfway down the stairs, he gave Tubby a shove.

"Run! He's a cop."

At the bottom of the steps, Tubby split left, and Skinny split right. Mike made eye contact with Bernie and signaled to let them go, then Mike stood on the stairway, jaw hanging open, shocked and stupid.

Skinny sprinted like the wind, but Tubby had a dilemma. Every fifth step, he had to reach back and yank at his belt to keep his pants up, giving him a gait like a galloping goat. Twenty yards away, he lost his grip, and his jeans slid to his knees, revealing an expanse of red boxers with white hearts on them. Tubby fell like an oak. He heaved a couple of breaths, got to his feet and repaired the damages, then ran again. Watching him, Mike had to chew his inner cheek to keep from howling.

Fifty yards down the brightly lit terminal, Skinny slowed, turned, and headed back. A minute later, Tubby followed suit.

His vacant stare still intact, Mike met the teens at the bottom of the metal stairs.

"I thought you said he was a cop," Tubby said, gasping. His round face gleamed with sweat. He had a bruise on his left cheek.

Skinny answered, "If he was, he would've chased us. We've got to be careful." He elbowed his friend. "Show him what we've got."

Tubby reached into the pocket of his jean jacket and produced a dented cigarette pack. He opened it to reveal about twenty joints. "How many you want?"

"Everything you've got," Mike said, reaching into his back pocket for his wallet.

Bernie had already moved behind the kids.

Instead of the wallet, Mike produced his badge. "RCMP,

you're under arrest for trafficking in narcotics."

Skinny turned into the arms of Bernie, who had him on the ground and cuffed in five seconds. In a momentary flash of brilliance, Tubby simply turned and put his hands behind his back. No more running for that boy. Mike cuffed him. Watching his prisoner, Mike pulled out his portable radio and said, "Members at Surrey Place skytrain station require transport for two males."

"Ten-four," crackled the radio. "A patrol unit is on the way."

Mike and Bernie led their prisoners to a green metal bench. "Hold still while I go through your pockets," he said.

Tubby behaved, but Skinny squirmed. Only Bernie's powerful grip on the boy's shoulder kept him still. From the boy's jean jacket, Mike drew out a wallet, some loose change, and a keyless remote for a car. Gazing lovingly at the remote, Mike smiled. "I think we'll hang on to this."

Panic flashed across Skinny's eyes. "What for?" he asked.

Mike smirked. "Just because."

"Give it back! You've got no right." He tried to lunge at Mike but fell back, helpless, at a nudge from the big officer's shoulder.

"You'll get it back later," Mike told him. "Care to tell me where the car is?"

Skinny curled his upper lip. "I'm not saying nothing."

"Suit yourself," Mike said. He pulled out his notepad. "What's your name?" he asked Skinny.

The boy glared and didn't speak.

Mike flipped open the young man's wallet. "Let's see. . . No ID." He turned to Tubby. "How about you? Got a name?"

Skinny's stare silenced him.

Mike seemed pleased. "That's fine. You can sit in detention cells until you recover from amnesia."

A white patrol car pulled up to the curb. Mike and Bernie

handed their two prisoners into the custody of two gnarled constables.

"They don't remember their names or have any ID to confirm their ages," Mike told them. "Lock them up with the adults. There's no proof they're juveniles."

"You got it," the driver answered, enjoying the moment. He pulled the shift lever into drive.

"Wait a minute!" Tubby called out from the backseat. Mike ignored him and waved the patrol car away.

"Five minutes in the adult holding cells should get their names out of them," Bernie said, hands on meaty hips. "That was nice work, Foster." He glanced at the small bit of black plastic in Mike's hand. "We going on a tour?" he asked.

Mike held it up. "You bet."

Bernie grinned. "What are we waiting for?"

They cruised the area in Mike's '96 Camaro, clicking the remote at row after row of parked cars. Twenty minutes later, they spotted flashing lights on a side street behind the Surrey Place Mall.

"Bingo!" Bernie cried out, laughing. "This is better'n Christmas."

The officers drove up to a gleaming silver-toned BMW. At the push of a button, the driver's door lock slid open. Leaving the Camaro double-parked, they made a systematic search. Nothing in the trunk or under the spare. Nothing beneath the seats or in the engine compartment. Then Mike jerked out the plush backseat and hit pay dirt.

"Take a look at this, Partner," he called.

Bernie peered over Mike's shoulder and swore.

Mike shot him a look.

Bernie grinned. "Sorry, Mike. Sometimes it just slips out." He took a second look. "There's got to be fifty pounds of home-grown there."

Letting the seat fall back into place, Mike straightened and slammed the door. "Let's call for a cruiser to watch this baby while we have another talk with those kids."

Jessica Meyers sat in the spacious bedroom of her high-rise apartment, staring at the wide makeup table before her. After a moment, she lifted a long brunette wig from its box. She'd pinned her strawberry-blond hair tightly to her scalp, so the wig slipped easily into place.

"Why did I agree to meet this woman?" she asked the mirror. "She wouldn't give me her name or what she had to tell me. I should have turned her down flat."

Investigative journalism was no longer Jessica's thing since her promotion to the anchor's chair. But when the girl had called the station, she'd said enough to get the old reporter instincts churning again. This was one appointment Jessica intended to keep. There was no use analyzing why she felt that way. She just did.

She opened a jar of foundation makeup. Normally pale, tonight she chose a compound that gave her a tanned appearance. She gave extra attention to the shadow of a scar that ran from her left cheekbone back to her jawline. It disappeared nicely. Applying some powder, she paused over the little bump where her nose turned up at the end.

"Why didn't you take that bump off while you were there?" she'd asked Dan Foster when he visited her private hospital room two days after her accident.

He pulled up that warm smile of his. "Every beautiful face needs distinctiveness to set it apart from the crowd. Yours is that little bump. It adds to your beauty." His voice took on the barest hint of something more. "Believe me, Ms. Meyers," he said. "You're still a lovely woman."

Jessica picked up a tube of lipstick and twisted it open. Stretching her lips, she applied dusty rose. Dan Foster was an unusual man. He was always willing to talk, yet he'd never made a move on her.

Too many men in Vancouver had taken Jessica out just so they could later blab to their buddies every detail—most of which was untrue—of their date with a star. Dan was different. He just listened.

Finished with the makeup, she brushed out the long wig and smiled at her reflection. Passersby would think she looked vaguely familiar but wouldn't make the connection with her TV persona.

Now, what to wear?

Her outfit must not say *Jessica Meyers*, not even a hint. She dug into some drawers near the floor of her walk-in closet and found a rumpled pair of faded blue jeans her sister, Carol, had left behind when she'd visited from Kamloops. Fortunately, Jessica and Carol shared the same size-eight figure, and the jeans fit comfortably. Over a navy T-shirt, she pulled on the University of British Columbia sweatshirt she'd worn back in her journalism days. It smelled a little musty, but that was all the better.

Forcing her way toward the back of the closet, she flicked aside hanger after hanger until she finally came to a plain blue windbreaker. It was the humblest thing she had. Slipping it on, she swung her purse over her shoulder and headed for the door.

At ground level, Jessica strode out of the elevator, a woman with a mission. Ignoring the doorman, she stepped out onto Denman Street. She flirted with the idea of taking her little red Porsche Boxter to the meeting. It had been her parents' graduation present when she finished at the University of British Columbia and was now parked in the apartment's garage. But the Porsche was too distinctive. Jessica hailed a cab.

"Where to?" the East Indian cabby asked, his accent thick.

"The Cranfield Restaurant in Richmond."

She slammed the door behind her, and they pulled out into the Friday night traffic. Twenty minutes later, she handed him a bill, then waited for her change and a receipt. WTV was going to pick up the tab for this little adventure.

When Jessica entered the brightly lit restaurant, a tired-looking woman with a European accent asked, "How many in your party?"

Jessica searched the center section of the dining room and spotted a young woman wearing a Colorado Avalanche cap. "I see my friend's already here," she told the hostess and moved forward.

A small Chinese waitress met Jessica at the table and set a menu in front of her. "Coffee?" she asked, pen in hand.

"That would be nice. Thank you."

The girl in the cap glanced up when Jessica sat down, then kept her face half hidden in the long menu. In that brief glance, Jessica knew she was in her early twenties. She had a thick mop of glossy blond hair sticking out from the back of the ball cap.

"Did you come alone?" the girl asked.

"Of course," Jessica said. An Asian couple passed them, returning from the hot bar with loaded plates.

"Are you recording this conversation?"

Jessica leaned forward, her eyes on the young woman's face. "I've done everything as we agreed. Now, what's this all about?"

"Remember the farmer who got killed by his bull awhile back?"

"Yes," Jessica said, nodding. "The Martin accident."

"It was no accident."

Jessica nodded, waiting.

"He was murdered," the girl said.

"And the murder weapon was?"

The girl shrugged and looked away. "I don't know. The bull, I guess."

"What? Are you saying someone drugged the bull so it'd kill Martin?"

The girl looked down. "I can't say."

"Who did it?"

She kept her head bowed and didn't answer.

Jessica reached across the table, took the girl's chin in her hand, and lifted her face. "Listen, you phoned me about a drug ring that killed someone. Now you're telling me Peter Martin was murdered by his bull. You don't know how, and you won't tell me who." Jessica let go of the girl and started up from the table saying, "You're wasting my time."

She grabbed Jessica's arm. "Please, don't go. You don't understand."

Jessica lowered herself back into the booth. "Then perhaps you can help me understand?"

"The guys who did this are into grow-ops. Big time."

"When you say 'grow-ops,' you're referring to hydroponics marijuana?"

"Yeah. They have several houses throughout the lower mainland and the Fraser Valley. Peter Martin was on to them. So they killed him."

"Killed—for pot?"

"For millions of dollars in pot. Most of this stuff goes across the border into the United States."

Jessica's eyes narrowed as she looked into the girl's frightened face. "And how do you know this?"

"I can't tell you. Just report on the news that he was murdered. Is that so hard?"

"I'm afraid it is. I need verification. I need details. Where, when, how, what, and why?"

The girl shot up from her seat. "That's all I can say." She

hurried out of the restaurant.

Staring after her, Jessica sat in a daze for a full minute. What was that all about?

In Interrogation Room Three at police headquarters, Mike Foster slammed the tiny black remote onto the metal table. "Tell me where the car is, Punk!"

Skinny—who finally admitted that his name was Billy Wickum—sneered. "Call me a lawyer."

Mike flung a chair across the room and added another scratch to the hundreds on the plastered wall. He shoved his red face inches away from Billy's. "Tell me where the car is, or you'll need an undertaker, not a lawyer."

"Get a life," Billy snapped back.

Spinning hard on his heels, Mike stormed out, leaving the teen alone with his thoughts. Bernie was grinning when he stepped into the hallway after his partner.

Mike tossed the remote to a nearby constable. "Keep him here for fifteen minutes, then release him and the other kid with their stuff."

The two RCMP officers headed out of the station to Mike's car. The night was clear. With street lamps, the city was completely lit.

They took twenty minutes getting back to the BMW. The drive only took ten, but they stopped off at Tim Horton's for two extra-large coffees and a box of honey-dipped donuts. They were veteran stakeout artists and came prepared. Mike wedged his Camaro between two parked cars, and they settled in to watch the BMW sitting half a block away.

"Music or sports talk?" Mike asked, reaching for the radio knob.

"Well, I'm not a big fan of that religious stuff you play, so how about sports talk?"

"You got it." Mike tuned his radio into the show. On the program a caller was bemoaning the recent loss of the Vancouver Canucks hockey team to Los Angeles. They passed some time listening to fans gripe.

Sometime later, Bernie glanced at his watch. "It's been three hours. I wonder what's taking so long."

"Billy's brother probably spent at least an hour screaming at him for taking his car. I bet the little punk doesn't even know what was hidden in it. Now he's probably trying to decide if we know where the car is and what's in it. He'll show up to claim his goods. He can't afford to abandon that car."

The words were barely out of his mouth before a dark sedan pulled up beside the BMW. A lanky white man got out of the passenger side. Mike and Bernie hunched down. A flash of headlights showed the car alarm had been deactivated.

"Looks like Larry Wickum is going to take a chance," Bernie whispered, one eye above the dash for an instant.

The BMW slowly cruised past them. Bernie ducked down, and both men waited fifteen seconds. With headlights turned off, Mike pulled out of the parking space and did a U-turn to follow the BMW.

Bernie spoke into a walkie-talkie. "Which way?"

"He turned left toward King George Highway," a voice crackled from the speaker.

Mike wheeled his car to the left. Ahead he saw the taillights of the BMW disappear to the right. He flicked on his headlights and gunned the Camaro to the traffic light. Turning sharply, he fell into the busy traffic. The BMW was six car lengths ahead of him.

They followed the car, keeping back at least three car lengths. At a red light by Fraser Highway, blue smoke burned out of the back of the BMW as it turned against the light.

"Think he's made us?" Bernie asked.

Mike said, "Maybe we should let him run a bit and see what he does."

The decision was taken out of Mike's hand when the blue and red lights of a patrol car filled the night. Mike thumped the steering wheel. "Why'd he have to pull that stunt in front of a patrol car?"

With the patrol car in pursuit, siren blaring, there was little point in concealing themselves any longer. Bernie mounted a portable flashing red light on the dash, and Mike hit the switch for the siren. It didn't take long for Mike's high-performance Camaro to catch up to the patrol car and pass it. The BMW was a couple of hundred yards ahead.

Out of the corner of his eye, Mike saw Bernie double-checking his seat belt.

"If it's any comfort, I had a passenger airbag installed."

"It isn't," Bernie answered.

The Camaro sailed each time it hit a bump on the road, their speed occasionally approaching a hundred miles an hour. A white WELCOME TO LANGLEY SIGN flashed by. Mike called out, "Notify Langley RCMP we're involved in a high-speed pursuit in their jurisdiction."

Bernie immediately got on the radio to notify the Langley detachment and request a roadblock on the Fraser Highway.

The chase settled down—the BMW driving eighty miles an hour with Mike and the other patrol car following several car lengths behind. Occasionally, they had to dodge late-night traffic. Five minutes later, brake lights flashed on.

Mike slammed to a stop. Bernie lurched forward and held on. The BMW did two 360s before powering down a side road that led into the woods. Mike downshifted and took the corner, his left wheels almost lifting from the ground.

"I don't care to die tonight," Bernie yelled. "I've got a wife and kids."

"I'll keep that in mind," Mike said. Just before he could ease up on the accelerator, the BMW's taillights spun to the right. The car flipped end over end and disappeared over a bank. Mike jammed on his own brakes and downshifted, his car spinning in circles. An explosion. His face stung. The car came to a creaking stop.

"What happened?" Bernie moaned.

Mike shoved the deflated airbag out of his face. "We hit something. You all right?"

"Nothing's broken except my worn-out nerves."

The patrol car's siren wound down as it skidded to a stop behind them. Flashlight in hand, Mike jumped out of his Camaro. He had to steady himself as a wave of nausea hit. After a few seconds, his head cleared some.

He stumbled to the front of his car and groaned. The front bumper crunched back against the radiator on the left side. The left fender looked like a broken accordion. As he circled the car, his flashlight beam caught the lifeless form of a deer in the ditch ahead of them.

"The BMW must've hit the deer first," Bernie said, joining him. "The deer flipped over that car for us to hit it again."

Mike shone the flashlight over the crumpled BMW. Its roof was almost at door-handle height. Turning, he shouted, "Call an ambulance!" to two patrol constables who were picking through low-lying brush on their way to the accident scene.

Mike pulled his Smith & Wesson, and Bernie did the same. They approached the BMW from opposite sides, weapons at the ready. When he got to the driver's side, Mike lowered his gun. "Poor kid," Mike said.

Bernie came around. "Hey, one less drug dealer."

"Maybe so, but he still had a soul."

"Yeah, right," Bernie said.

"Well, Hotshot," Mike said, his volume rising, "if you don't care about that, we still don't know where that pot came from or where it was going."

Bernie flashed his light in Mike's eyes. Mike squinted and bellowed, "What are you doing?"

"Are you all right, Man?"

Mike held up his arm to shield his face. "Get that light down!"

Bernie lowered the beam. "You're all white."

"I'm fine," Mike said, his voice gruff. He started toward his damaged Camaro when the ground rushed up and hit his face.

Half an hour later, the phone rang in Dan Foster's dark bedroom, waking him out of a deep sleep. He groped for the receiver and knocked his alarm clock from the nightstand. Finally he found the phone. "Dan Foster here."

"Dr. Foster, it's Amy."

Dan sat up, blinking and trying to focus. "Amy, are you all right?"

"It's Mike. They brought him to emergency a few minutes ago."

Dan came wide-awake. "What happened? Is he okay?"

"He was in a car accident. He seems to have a concussion. They're doing tests now."

"I'll be right down."

Without waiting to hear her good-bye, Dan dropped the phone into its cradle. He was dressed and on the road in five minutes.

Langley Memorial Hospital was only ten minutes from his home, and Dan didn't spare the horses. Mike was all the close family Dan had left. Out of breath, his hair uncombed, and his pajama shirt stuffed into his jeans, Dan arrived at the ER door seven minutes later. His heart pounded as he rushed into the emergency ward. Knowing him, the staff waved Dan right in.

He stopped suddenly when he saw his brother lying in a bed, wearing a weak smile. Amy stood near the IV stand. She smiled awkwardly and turned away to check the instruments.

"What happened?" Dan demanded.

Mike moved his head to look at Dan and winced at the effort. He had deep blue circles around his eyes. "I hit a deer," he said.

Dan grabbed the medical chart. The initial diagnosis was shock. It wasn't uncommon for the internal organs to take quite a beating, though the outside seemed fine. He quickly examined his brother's face. No damage except a few small cuts.

"They going to keep you overnight?" Dan asked, dropping the chart into its rack.

"Yeah, but I feel fine, besides some nausea. I told them you're a doctor and you could look after me, but that didn't seem to matter."

Dan cocked his head. "I have better things to do than nursemaid you. Amy seems to be doing a good job. You should stay here where she can keep an eye on you."

"That's right," Amy said.

Mike grinned again. "I hear we're invited for dinner on Thanksgiving."

"Right again, Sherlock," Dan told his brother. He smiled at Amy, then looked back at Mike. "The way you look right now, she may just change her mind."

"Not in my profession," she said. "I've seen much worse than a couple of black eyes."

Dan stayed long enough to speak to the attending doctor. Satisfied that Mike had no signs of major problems, he headed home at four-fifteen. All Mike needed was twenty-four hours of observation time in the hospital, and he'd be released.

At the front step of the house he shared with his brother and his aunt, Dan aimed for the keyhole, but the door swung open. Sixty-eight-year-old Aunt Elinor stood before him in a thick lavender robe with matching slippers, her short, spiky hair pointing in a dozen directions at once.

"Where did you go at two o'clock in the morning?" she snapped. "I've been waiting for almost three hours for you to come home."

Dan stepped inside and pulled off his light jacket. "Mike had an accident. He hit a deer and crunched his car. He's okay, though."

"Where is he?"

"He's in the hospital." He turned and dutifully kissed her delicate cheek. "He's only there for observation. Tomorrow, he'll be here making both of us miserable. I tried not to wake you up. I didn't want you to worry."

She put her hands on her hips. "Well, I did wake up, and I did worry. My mind just flew in all sorts of directions. Plastic surgeons don't get called out in the middle of the night like real doctors."

Dan put up his hand. "Aunt Elinor, let's not go there. I'm tired, and I just want to go back to bed."

She took a deep breath and pushed it out. "So was I. Now I'll have to take a melatonin pill to get back to sleep." Turning toward the hall and shaking her head, she said, "You boys will be the death of me yet."

Dan chuckled. "You know we're keeping you young!" he called after her. Elinor disappeared into her apartment built onto the back of the house.

Dan headed wearily up the stairs, wondering why his brother hadn't chosen a sane profession like garbage collecting.

Chapter
Three

At ten o'clock on Sunday morning, Dan Foster entered Mike's bedroom to find his younger brother buried under the blankets on his king-size bed. Since he'd come home from the hospital two days ago, Mike hadn't been his usual energetic self. The accident had taken more out of him than he was willing to admit. Still, Mike had made Dan promise to wake him up in time for church.

Dan gave him a healthy shove. "Wake up, Sunshine!" he called.

Their mother had called Mike "Sunshine" because of his red hair. He hated it when anyone else used that term.

"Get lost," Mike murmured. He pulled the blue comforter over his head.

"Fine with me," Dan said, standing back. "Church is your thing, not mine."

Mike slowly pulled the blankets down, revealing four wide bruises on his muscular torso. "Thanks, Bro. I forgot it was Sunday." He blinked at Dan. "You coming with me?"

Dan held up both hands and hustled toward the door. Turning back, he said, "Like I said, church is your thing, not mine."

Mike sat up and ran his hand through his red mop. "I

don't have any wheels. You aren't going to make me take a cab, are you?"

Dan stepped to the doorway. "I'll drive you," he said, then moved across the hall.

Mike shouted after him. "You might as well stay since we've got to be at the Martins' for dinner. Why drive me to church, then come back to get me?"

"I'll go somewhere for coffee," Dan called back. He moved to his wide closet and slid back the door.

Mike got to his feet and came to the hall. "Don't be so stubborn. You'd rather sit alone in a café than come with me?"

"I won't be alone," Dan said.

Grinning, Mike moved to Dan's door. "Ah, the plot thickens. Meeting Jessica?"

"She called this morning. Wants to talk."

"She'd be good for you, Bro," Mike said.

Dan waved him away. "We're just friends. Now hurry up and get ready." He glanced at the red stubble on Mike's face. "You really need to shave."

If Mike was anything, he was quick. In twenty-two minutes he'd showered, shaved, dressed in his suit, grabbed a muffin, and was ready to go. He winced when he lowered himself into the leather seat of Dan's car.

"Sure you don't want to stay home?" Dan asked.

"You mean eat a bologna sandwich instead of dinner at the Martins'?" Mike asked. "That doesn't sound like a plan to me." He slammed the door closed. "Let's go."

It took ten minutes to drop Mike off at Langley Faith Centre and another five to get to Denny's. Dan spotted Jessica's red Porsche parked in front of the restaurant and wheeled his blue Marquis in beside it. He got out, stretched the kinks out of his tall frame, and headed into the busy restaurant. Looking over the heads of people waiting for a table, he made out Jessica in a booth beside the windows. The brilliant morning sun brought out red highlights in her hair. As usual, her makeup was impeccable, giving every advantage to a face that needed none. She wore designer jeans, a cream-colored silk blouse, and a maroon blazer.

"How's it going?" he asked, sliding into the bench seat across from her.

She gave him a dazzling smile. "Great!"

"Wonderful," he said, surprised at her enthusiasm. "No nightmares?"

Jessica brushed a strand of hair from her face. "I haven't had one since Friday."

He lifted the menu. "I thought you'd travel to your folks' house for the holiday."

She shrugged. "Mom's not the traditional type. She'd rather spend the holiday having friends in for after-dinner cocktails. They'll sit in front of the fireplace and discuss the stock market until midnight. That type of thing doesn't interest me, so there's no reason to go. When I leave here, I'm starting a movie marathon featuring Cary Grant and Katharine Hepburn."

Dan looked up at her. "You actually like those old movies?"

"Absolutely. I love classic chick flicks. *Holiday* is my all-time favorite with Hepburn playing Linda." Her lips formed a rakish smile. "She's a poor little rich girl with a yen to break out of the mold."

He slowly nodded, watching her carefully. "I can see why you'd like her," he said. "But you didn't call me to discuss Hepburn, did you?"

Her hazel eyes were dancing. "I got a tip on something, and it brought out all my investigative-reporter instincts. I'd forgotten how much I loved that job. I thought you might be able to help me with my story."

Dan cocked his head. "Me?"

"Didn't you mention that you knew the farmer who was killed by his bull awhile back?"

"Sure. Peter Martin. His wife is my bookkeeper. What about him?"

Her voice dropped a few decibels. "Before we start, you must promise that you'll treat our conversation as confidential as you would any doctor-patient relationship."

He shrugged, wondering where she was heading. "Fine."

"What would you say if I told you Peter Martin was murdered?"

Dan chuckled. "I'd say whoever gave you that idea is off their rocker. Imagine telling the cops the murder weapon was a bull. They'd laugh you out of town."

"It sounded off the wall to me, too. . .at first. But my source was pretty convincing. Would you keep your ears open and let me know if you hear anything that could tie into this? I have a feeling that this could be big."

Dan leaned back as the waitress set down their coffee mugs. "Sure, but it's not likely anything will come up."

They ordered breakfast and enjoyed casual conversation over the meal. Finally Dan glanced at his watch. "I gotta go." He touched a napkin to his mouth. "I'm going to be late."

"Already?" Jessica asked.

"I dropped my brother off at church, and I have to pick him up in five minutes." He stood and picked up the bill.

She plucked it out of his hand. "Hey," she said, "this was my invitation, and it's going to be my treat."

"Have it your way." He grinned. "But I reserve the right to return the favor on Friday night at eight."

She watched him, surprise and pleasure on her face. "It's a date."

Pushing open the restaurant door, he thought, *Believe it or not, Dan Foster, that's exactly what it is.*

On the drive to Beth Martin's house, Mike stared out the window at wide fields, horses, and scattered rolls of hay.

"I used to think that the country was a safe, clean place," he said to Dan, "where nothing bad ever happened. I guess my job has made me cynical in some ways. Knowing too much can be a burden sometimes."

"What do you mean?" Dan kept his eyes on the road and his hands smoothly guiding the steering wheel.

"When a person thinks of the country, he usually thinks of wholesome food, good people, and clean fun. But then when I see a house with foil reflecting off a basement window, my mind immediately goes to grow-ops. It spoils the whole atmosphere for me."

Dan slowed for a curve. "You think there's a hydroponics operation around here?"

"Maybe," Mike said. "There are certain signs to look for: aluminum foil on the windows, condensation on the glass. . ." He droned on for the next five minutes.

Turning into Beth's driveway, Dan said, "You have the right job, Bro. You thrive on the hunt. Just talking about a case brings your adrenaline level up." He shook his head. "That's where we're on different tracks. I get the shakes just thinking about facing people with guns or walking into the middle of a bunch of lowlifes. As hard as it was when we decided on separate careers, we definitely chose the right professions."

Two minutes later, Amy opened the door to them and gave them a welcoming smile. Then she noticed the medical bag in Dan's hand.

"I thought you were coming to dinner," she said.

Dan said, "I figured I might as well remove Beth's bandages now and save her a trip into the office."

"Well, come right in, gentlemen," she said, smiling. Even in a full-length apron, her hair pinned up, and her face flushed from a hot stove, Amy's good looks were still very evident. Nothing could hide those delicate features and that flowing mane of hair. Dan glanced back and noticed Mike watching her face like a deer caught in the headlights. Amy seemed oblivious.

Dan stepped aside to allow his brother to enter first. Mike moved slowly, and Amy picked up on his awkward movements. "Are you all right?"

Mike nodded. "I'm still a little sore," he said, trying to make light of it and failing.

"After what I saw of you in the ER last week, I'm not surprised."

The smell of roast turkey with all the fixings was a welcome greeting to Dan's nostrils when he and Mike entered the farmhouse. Amy led them into the living room. Staring at an aged TV on a low stand, Beth lay propped in a royal blue recliner, the only piece of furniture in the room that didn't look like a yard-sale reject. She lifted her hand when they came in. Her voice sounded weak. "Thanks for coming," she said. "I was hoping my new furniture would have come by now. They promised to deliver by last weekend."

"We didn't come to look at the furniture," Dan said. "We came to see you."

Mike added, "Thanks for the invitation. Otherwise it would have been a Thanksgiving of bologna sandwiches."

"It's our pleasure," Beth said.

Amy sat on an overstuffed stool while Dan and Mike took seats on opposite ends of a lumpy brown couch. A rolltop desk in thick dark wood stood in the corner.

Amy asked, "Mike, do you have any leads on the guy you were chasing when you totaled your car?"

A buzzer from the kitchen stopped Mike's answer.

"I'll have to take care of that," Amy said, getting up. "The corn casserole is ready."

Dan spoke to Mike. "Why don't you go in and update Amy on your great adventure while she finishes up? I'm going to check Beth's progress."

Mike pushed himself to his feet. "I'm pretty handy in the kitchen," he told Amy. "Maybe I can fill water glasses or something."

After they left, Dan grabbed the stool and sat beside Beth. Opening his bag, he removed some scissors. "Might as well take off those bandages and have a look."

"Amy was sure thrilled you'd be coming over," Beth murmured while he snipped.

"We were just as thrilled." Dan's hands worked carefully.

"No, Dan," Beth said. "Amy was thrilled that *you* were coming over."

Dan paused and looked into Beth's eyes. "I don't understand. What do you mean?"

Beth smiled. "Just open your eyes, and you'll see for yourself. Now get back to work."

Dan frowned. "Okay." He lifted the gauze and didn't like what he saw. The facelift itself was in good shape, but red puffiness followed the stitch lines. "Are you taking the antibiotics?" he asked.

"Of course. Why?"

"Looks like you have the beginnings of an infection. You're sure you've been taking them?"

"Yes." She raised her hand to chin level as though she wanted to touch the incision but was afraid to. "The incision has been aching. I thought it was just from the surgery."

"We'd better keep an eye on this swelling. If it gets worse, I want to see you right away."

Amy stepped into the living room. "Dinner's ready. Shall I bring it in here?"

"No," Beth said, reaching for the lever beside the chair.

"I'm sick of sitting in this chair. If Dr. Foster has no objections, I'd like to sit at the dinner table."

"No objections whatsoever," Dan said, clipping his bag shut and standing.

Amy looked at her watch. "I thought Rocky was coming."

"Rocky?" Mike asked from the doorway.

"My nephew," Beth answered. "I'm sure he'll show up when it suits him. He's not the most reliable fellow." Moving in slow motion, she came to her feet. Dan took her arm.

"He'd better be reliable today," Amy declared. "He's supposed to bring dessert."

"Hey, from what I've seen in the kitchen, no dessert's necessary," Mike chimed in. "This dinner looks great."

When they were seated, Amy served Beth's plate and cut her food into small bites. Mike spent most of his time trying to make conversation with Amy, but Dan noticed Amy seemed to spend her time stealing glances at him. Did she have some kind of crush on him? She said she agreed they weren't a good fit after they'd dated. Had she lied? Dan hoped not. Especially since he'd come to know Jessica.

Half an hour later, Dan finished his second cup of coffee. He leaned back and patted his stomach. "I'm stuffed. I think I'll go outside and take a little walk."

"Hopefully Rocky will be here with dessert by the time you get back," Amy told him. She pushed back her chair. "I'm going to clear this table."

"I'll help you," Mike told her, standing. "Moving around will do me good."

Outside, Dan drew in a chest full of crisp air. He wandered toward the barn and stopped beside a pen where Samson, the bull, was happily munching hay. Dan perched one foot on the bottom rail and leaned against the top rail, watching the animal. Was this meek animal the same one that had trampled Peter Martin?

From behind him, a rough voice said, "It never would've happened if he'd listened to me."

Dan spun around. "Kurt. I didn't hear you coming."

Small and wiry, the grizzled old man spat out some chewing tobacco, then wiped his mouth with the back of his hand. He had two front teeth missing, one on the top and one on the bottom.

"Who wouldn't listen to you?" Dan asked.

"That very morning I told Mr. Martin he should let me load the bull. It was misting rain and him with a cough; I thought he'd best stay in the house. But he figured he could do it anyway as though wearing a flimsy slicker would keep out the cold and damp." The old man shook his head. "Something must have riled old Samson here. He's usually gentle as a kitten."

His rheumy gaze wandered over the bull. He murmured, as though talking to himself, "Nothing would have happened if he'd listened to me." He dug into his pocket for a foil pouch. "Oh well, it's all for the best, I guess."

"How can you say that?"

Kurt's grizzled cheeks stretched into a grin. He leaned closer to speak confidentially. "I've never seen Miz Martin so happy." He winked. "I don't think they got along all that well."

"Dessert!" Amy called from the house.

Glad to find a reason to excuse himself, Dan said good-bye and headed for the pumpkin pie.

Inside Dan saw a young man with a black ponytail and a gold stud earring. He sat next to Beth at the table.

Beth asked, "Dan, have you ever met my nephew, Rocky?"

Dan reached out to shake hands.

Rocky had a firm grip. He wore a wide silver ring with diamond chips forming his initial. Slight and angular, Rocky had little resemblance to his aunt. He looked appreciatively at Dan.

"Doc, you've made Aunt Beth look fifteen years younger. You're a real artist."

"Rocky brought us some flowers," Amy said. She held an arrangement that was predominantly red roses.

"Those are for Aunt Beth," he said, smiling at Beth. "I brought some wine and cheesecake for dessert," Rocky added. "Take a glass, Doctor?" he asked, reaching for the bottle.

"No, thanks," Dan answered.

"May I have some, Doctor?" Beth asked.

"A glass or two won't hurt you," he told her, "but no more."

"I thought you were going to bring a pumpkin pie," Amy said.

Rocky shrugged. "The Superstore was all out, and I didn't have time to go anywhere else." He lifted his glass. "Cheer up, Amy."

With Rocky present, dessert was much livelier than dinner. Dan frowned when he saw Beth reach for a third glass of wine, but he held his tongue. He would definitely speak up if she went for a fourth.

Half an hour later, Amy put her hand to her forehead. "Boy, I'm exhausted. I didn't realize how tired I was until just now. How do you manage this year after year, Beth?"

"Maybe the men can help you with the dishes," Beth said.

"I'll dry," Mike said with the exaggerated voice of a martyr.

Amy smiled. "Thanks, Mike." She looked at Rocky. "You can wash." She took off her apron. "Dan, I'd like to go for a short walk to cool down. I'm roasting after working over that stove all morning. Care to join me?"

"Uh, sure." He got to his feet. He didn't feel good about this.

A moment later, they stepped outside and ambled along a road that evenly divided the farm's three hundred acres.

"Thanks," she said when they reached the edge of the barn-yard. "I don't like to be alone outside, and I needed to get away.

I try to be nice to Rocky when Beth's around, but he gives me the creeps." She scuffed her sneaker at a stone in the driveway.

"What does Rocky do for a living?" Dan asked.

"Who knows? He claims to be an entrepreneur, but he's never started any business that I've ever seen."

They walked on for a ways. The cool breeze lifted Amy's hair, fluffed it, and set it down.

"So, what do you think of Mike?" Dan asked.

"I think he's a boy who refuses to grow up," Amy said.

"Really. Why?"

She stopped and turned toward him. "Do you know he thinks it's funny that he almost got killed last week. He boasts about it as if it were some rite of manhood. He's definitely not my kind of guy. I like the quiet type that figures going down a waterslide is a great adventure."

Stepping around a puddle, Dan said, "Believe it or not, that sounds like Mike. Except for his undercover work, he's a pretty tame guy. He goes to church on Sundays and again on Wednesday nights if he's not working."

Amy looked at Dan. "Mike goes to church?"

Dan nodded. "And did you know more construction workers and loggers are killed every year than policemen?"

"I didn't know that," Amy said. "But then, they aren't my type, either."

When they reached the house twenty minutes later, Mike sat on the sofa reading a magazine. Rocky lay back in the lounge chair with his eyes closed.

Dan's voice roused them. "Where's Beth?" he asked.

"She said she had a headache," Mike told him, his attention on his magazine. "She went to her room to lie down."

Dan frowned. "Why didn't you call me?"

"Why?" Rocky asked. "It was just a headache and a little nausea. Maybe she ate too much."

"Nausea?"

"Yeah, she said she felt sick to her stomach."

Alarm bells sounding off in his brain, Dan rushed to Beth's bedroom. The door stood ajar. He knocked. "Beth?" She didn't answer, so he looked inside.

She lay slumped to one side on the bed. Some of her pillows lay on the floor. "Amy!" he shouted out the open door. "Amy! Get in here!"

Dan rushed to Beth and gently pulled her upright on the elevated mattress. Her skin burned to his touch.

Amy flew into the bedroom. "What's wrong?"

"Get my bag!"

Her training taking over, Amy disappeared. Dan pressed his finger against Beth's neck, feeling for a pulse. Nothing. Her motionless chest told him she wasn't breathing. Mike and Rocky arrived in the bedroom.

Dan barked, "Mike, help me get her on the floor. Rocky, call 911!"

Mike and Dan lifted Beth onto the hardwood floor. Her head lolled like a rag doll's. "Tell me you still remember your CPR," he said to Mike.

"You bet. Want me to breathe or thrust?"

"Thrust."

Every five thrusts, Dan breathed into Beth's mouth.

Amy returned. "What's happening?"

"Cardiac arrest," Dan said, then blew in another puff.

After a minute, Dan motioned for his brother to stop, then he placed his ear against Beth's chest. Five seconds later, he said, "Start again."

Sweat poured from both brothers as they worked to keep Beth alive. The welcome sound of a siren reached their ears, and two male paramedics—one young and blond, one old and bald—charged through the door. One of them carried a massive medical kit. Dan immediately backed away, letting them do their work.

Mike moved to a corner. Amy stepped close to Dan. Instinctively, he put his arm around her. She clung to him and pressed her face against his chest. Every few seconds, she sent a fearful glance toward Beth's still form.

The younger paramedic took a defibrillator from their case.

"Clear!" the bald one shouted.

His partner lifted his hands away. Amy moaned when Beth's body arched from the charge of the electricity. The blond man placed a stethoscope on Beth's chest, listened for a few seconds, looked at his partner, and shook his head.

"Clear!" Once more Beth's body arched.

The men continued to fight, but as time crept by, Dan knew Beth was not coming back. Finally, the bald one flipped off the defibrillator and shook his head. "Sorry," he said. "There's nothing more we can do."

Amy collapsed against Dan. He half-carried her to the bed. Mike was rubbing his eyes. Only Rocky seemed unfazed by the tragedy.

Amy put her fist to her mouth. "How could this happen? She was all right at dinner." Tears streamed down her cheeks.

The bald paramedic told Dan, "We've put in a call requesting the coroner to come out since she just had surgery."

"I understand," Dan said.

"Uh, mind if I use the washroom?" he asked.

"Go ahead," Dan answered.

"She's all I had," Amy choked out, her head still against Dan's chest. "She took me in because she was my mother's friend. No questions asked. She helped me through nursing school. . . ." A fresh wave of tears came over her.

When the paramedic emerged from the washroom, he had a puzzled look on his face. He held up an open prescription bottle containing shiny orange pills. "Was she taking these?"

"What are they?" Dan asked.

"I'm not sure. The pills have P-D 270 stamped on them."

Dan felt a jolt. "Let me see those!"

The paramedic poured one into his hand and held it out for Dan.

The blood drained from Dan's face. "That's Nardil."

"She have high blood pressure?" the paramedic asked.

"No. She shouldn't have been taking this at all." Dan turned to Amy, who stared at the bottle. "Where did she get those pills?"

"That's what you gave her," Amy stammered. She hugged her arms close to her waist.

"I didn't give her this. I gave her amoxicillin."

The paramedic wiped his forehead. "The coroner's sure gonna want some answers about this."

Dan's mind went into a daze. Combined with alcohol and antihistamines, those orange pills were deadly. Everyone was going to assume that his negligence had killed Beth Martin.

Chapter
Four

In his glassed-in office in the center of WTV's massive newsroom, News Director Roger Pronger gulped, then almost spewed his coffee across his desk. His beefy hand snatched a tissue from the box near his elbow. He swallowed and dabbed at his lips, his jowls jiggling as he laughed aloud.

"This is serious," Jessica said, shifting to the edge of her chair. "This girl says Peter Martin was murdered because he was involved in some kind of drug gang."

Pronger touched his eyes with the tissue and forced a straight face. "They used his own bull to ice him?"

"Yes." Jessica knew the idea seemed farfetched, but something about her informant had stuck with her since their meeting. Jessica wanted to follow through on this.

"And just how do you go about getting a bull to murder someone?" Another grin crept across Pronger's round face. "Hypnotize it, maybe?"

Jessica stood, straightened her green plaid skirt, and shook her head. "If you're not going to take me seriously. . ." She took a step toward the door.

With a wide wave, Pronger motioned for her to return to her chair. "Aw, come on, Jessica," he said. "Cut me some slack.

This is really off the wall. You can't expect me to jump at it."

She stared at him and her voice grew strident. "And what if this turns out to be true, Roger? What if there is some way to get a bull to kill a person? Think of what a story that would be."

Pronger leaned back in his massive leather chair. "It'd be a great story," he said. "But I'm not prepared to waste the talent of my number-one anchor on a million-to-one chance." He glanced at his watch. "Who, by the way, has to do a newscast in fifteen minutes."

Jessica took a deep breath and sighed. "Tell you what," she said. "On my own time, I'll do some digging. If I can figure out how someone could get a bull to commit murder, what would you say then?"

Pronger leaned forward and clasped his pudgy hands together. "I'd say run with it."

"It's a deal then," she said and turned toward the door.

Just then, Fred Carley from the news desk burst in with a sheet of paper in his hand. The lanky man was as much a fixture at WTV as Pronger's fifty-year-old desk. Fred wore a broad smile, and his wrinkled cheeks glowed. When he saw Jessica, he stopped short, instantly sobered.

"What is it, Fred?" Pronger asked.

Fred's eyes darted toward Jessica. His hand stroked his red tie, and he stammered, "I thought Al was doing the Thanksgiving broadcast."

"Al has a family," Jessica told him. "I agreed to cover for him."

Fred twitched his lips and flicked his paper with a thumbnail.

"What have you got?" Pronger asked.

Fred handed the page to Pronger. Pronger scanned the document, frowned, then glanced up at Jessica. "Well, Jessica, maybe I owe you an apology."

Jessica glanced from the paper in Pronger's hand to his

face, where deep furrows creased his broad forehead. "What is it?" she asked.

"Lightning struck twice at the same place. Peter Martin's wife died a couple of hours ago."

Jessica gasped. "You're kidding."

"I wish I were," the news director murmured. He ran his finger down the page. "This says she died from surgery complications. The surgery was done by. . .uh-oh."

"What?" Jessica moved closer. Pronger pursed his lips but said nothing. Jessica snatched the page out of his hand.

"Dr. Dan Foster," she whispered. The report went on to say that the coroner's initial assessment leaned toward a mix-up in medication, and that Dr. Foster might have been responsible.

Jessica went cold. If this were true, Dan was guilty of malpractice. She felt a migraine coming on. There was no way this could be true.

"We going to run with this?" Fred looked hopeful.

Pronger gazed at Jessica. "We have to." When Jessica opened her mouth, he cut her off saying, "I know what Dan Foster means to you, but we are a news station." He looked at his hands clasped on the desk. "Besides, with what you told me earlier, this takes on new significance."

"This can't be true," Jessica said. "Dan's incredibly careful."

"Maybe so," Pronger said, "but every news agency in Vancouver is going to run this story. We can't afford not to."

"But it'll ruin him," Jessica said. "Even if he's cleared, the story will stick to him. You know that."

Pronger held out his hands. "So, what do we do? Let everyone else break the story while we keep silent? Is that our job?"

Jessica turned to Fred. "What does Dr. Foster say? You got his reaction, right?"

Fred shook his head. "I called three times. His brother always answers the phone and won't give any comment."

Jessica locked eyes with Pronger. "Look. Let me call him and get his side of the story. If there's an explanation, let me add it to the story. It's the least I can do."

Pronger hesitated, then nodded.

Jessica pushed past Fred Carley's long, lean form and out of Pronger's office. She rushed down an aisle between a dozen computer stations to her office in the back corner of the newsroom, another glassed-in affair with a clear back door that opened into the TV production set.

Plunking down in the chair behind her black acrylic desk, she glanced at the clock. Ten minutes. Clerks had already keyed that broadcast's stories into the teleprompter. She dialed Dan's home number and got a busy signal. After the second tone, a message from the phone company came on the line. It was a computerized voice offering to keep trying the number in exchange for a charge. Jessica accepted the offer.

While she waited, Jessica scrolled through the news copy on her computer. Fred had the Foster story leading. She winced as she read the copy.

The silver clock on her desk showed five minutes to news time. Fred Carley stood about ten feet away from her glass wall, anxiously looking in at her. The phone rang. Jessica snatched it from the hook.

"Foster residence," Mike Foster said.

"Mike, it's Jessica," she said, breathless. "I need to speak with Dan. . .quickly."

"I'm not sure that's a good idea," Mike said. "You are the media."

"I'm also his friend," Jessica said. "I need Dan's comments to balance the story we're running. You know me, Mike. I'd never hurt Dan. Never."

"Hang on," he said.

Jessica tapped her long, tapered fingernail on the blotter.

The newsroom director—a slim man with a shiny head and a black moustache—stood beside Camera 1. He stared at her, scowling.

"Hi, Jessica." Dan's deep voice came through the receiver. He sounded drained.

"Dan, I've got four minutes until news time," she said. "Tell me one thing. Did you prescribe the correct medication for Beth Martin?"

"I didn't prescribe any medication," he said. "I gave her the pills from my own stock. I am absolutely positive I gave her amoxicillin. I have no idea how she ended up taking Nardil."

"You're sure you'll be cleared? There are no ghosts in the closet or anything like that?"

"There are no ghosts in my closet whatsoever," Dan said.

The director headed for Jessica's door, face red, mouth set. Only a minute to go.

"Thanks, Dan," Jessica said. She dropped the receiver, jumped from her desk, and charged into the blue-and-orange newsroom. Taking her seat at the news desk, she held her face toward a man with a greasy ponytail and a silver earring. He held a makeup sponge in one hand and a soft brush in the other. She clipped in her earpiece while he dabbed at her nose, chin, and forehead. The makeup man scurried away as a small red light glowed on Camera 1. In one smooth movement, Jessica lifted her paper copy from the desk and smiled into the lens.

She ignored the teleprompter. "Today in Abbotsford," she began, "Beth Martin died of a drug reaction after minor surgery. The coroner is investigating." She turned toward Camera 2. "On the political scene, British Columbia's provincial government restored bus passes for seniors."

She could hear shuffling in the background, but Jessica plugged on. Ten minutes later, the floor director gave a signal, and they cut to a commercial. Jessica looked up to find

Pronger in her face. His eyes were wide, his face was flushed. "What are you doing?"

Jessica looked at him and spoke calmly. "I'm reporting the news."

"You missed three-quarters of the Foster segment," he said. "Your job is to read, not edit."

Jessica paused for a moment, then said, "I just did this station a big favor. You'll thank me a week from now."

Pronger raised his coarse eyebrows. "Oh, really?"

"Yes, really," she said. "Dan Foster gave me absolute assurance that he is not responsible for Beth Martin's death. When the truth comes out, we'll be the only news station that can say we waited for the facts."

Pronger straightened and glared at her. "Did it ever occur to you that Foster might have lied to you?"

Jessica shook her head. "Dan Foster would never lie to me."

Already wearing his blue bathrobe at two minutes to six, Dan placed the phone on its cradle. Exhausted by the strain of Beth's crisis and the following questions by paramedics and the coroner, he'd come home, showered, and dressed for comfort. He looked at Mike, who was lying back in the tan lounge chair beside him, and shrank under his brother's insistent stare.

"There are no ghosts in your closet?" Mike asked, sarcasm in his voice.

"That's long buried," Dan told him. "Don't worry about it." He stretched one of his legs along the seat of the black leather sofa as he leaned against its corner. "Flick on the TV. Jessica's broadcasting."

Mike picked up the remote. Jessica's oval face filled the massive screen in the center of the black entertainment center. Fifteen seconds later, Dan let loose a sigh of relief.

"PTV isn't going to be so easy on you," Mike told him.

"I know," Dan said. "But eighty percent of the province watches Jessica. As long as I have her in my corner, I've got a chance of getting a fair shake from the media."

"Until she finds out about what happened before."

"The record was expunged!"

Mike reached for his can of ginger ale on the small table at his elbow. "They always find out. If I were you, I'd get right on that phone and tell her the truth before someone else does. I hate to be glib, but honesty is the best policy."

Dan glared at him. "I don't believe your self-righteous attitude. You're an undercover cop who goes to church on Sunday and lies every other day of the week."

Mike set down the can and lowered the chair's footrest. He leaned toward Dan. "Listen, you never completely recovered from your last incident, Bro. You've got a psychology degree. You know this is too much stress for you."

"I'm doing pretty good, considering," Dan said, avoiding Mike's eyes. "I haven't had any more spells, if that's what you're wondering. All I feel is profound sadness." He tried to force some spirit into his voice. "I'm okay. Honest."

Mike didn't let up. "Are you sad because of Beth or. . . ?"

Dan looked up at his brother. "Beth mostly," he said. "I know I didn't make a mistake on that medication. Beth was murdered when she had her first chance at a good life. What's worse, your police force is treating it like malpractice when they should be investigating a murder."

"They're not restricting their investigation to you."

"Why did they take my fingerprints? Why did they tell me not to leave the area?"

"That's routine," Mike said. "Believe me, you're not the only suspect. I've talked to Anna Carrington, the lead investigator. She's looking at other possibilities."

Dan Foster's shoulders sagged against the back of the sofa. "I talked to Anna Carrington, too. She thinks she's got an open-and-shut case of medical malpractice. This is high profile, and she's looking to score some career points at my expense. That woman is going to let a killer get away unless I do something."

Mike stiffened. "What are you going to do?"

Dan held up his hands. "I don't know. Look at the Martin family's dirty laundry, check on the pills. Maybe find the killer."

"You'll do no such thing," Mike said. "If Beth was murdered, the Serious Crimes unit doesn't need any amateurs fouling up evidence and endangering themselves in the process."

Dan shot to his feet. "See! Even you don't believe me. *If* she was murdered! She *was* murdered! I gave her amoxicillin, and someone switched it for Nardil. And if this is just a simple case of malpractice, why is the Serious Crimes unit involved?"

Mike held up his hand. "Sorry, bad choice of words. The reason Serious Crimes is involved is because that's the unit Anna Carrington is assigned to. She just happened to be in the area when the call came in, and being senior member, took charge. I wouldn't be surprised if she passes it off to someone else. Either way, stay out of it, Dan. If you stay clear, I'll park on Anna's case, or whoever takes it over, and make sure they don't get tunnel vision on us. Deal?"

Dan Foster stared at his brother for a long moment, then nodded. "I guess so," he said.

The phone rang.

"I'd turn it off," Dan said, "but it could be an emergency call."

Mike got up from the chair and snatched the phone from the thick maple table beside Dan. "Yeah, what do you want?" he barked. The next second he winced. "Oh, sorry, I thought you were another reporter."

With a sheepish look, he handed the phone to Dan.

"Dr. Foster speaking," he said. "Oh, hello, Dr. Cruch. . . Uh huh. . .but I had nothing to do with it. It's all going to be cleared. . . . Well, don't you think that's up to the board?" He paused for fifteen seconds.

"This is a big mistake." He looked at the dead receiver and set it down. "The clinic's board of directors had an emergency meeting by teleconference. At Dr. Cruch's recommendation, they suspended my contract until this is cleared up."

"What are they doing? The coroner hasn't reported yet."

"It's a private clinic," Dan said. "From the board's viewpoint, only what's right for the clinic matters. My rights have nothing to do with it."

"Does Dr. Cruch have something against you?"

"Not that I know of. After I rebuilt Jessica's face, high-profile clients started asking for me. He called me in for a conference, and we had a good talk. I gave him permission to check on all my work. As far as I could tell, he seemed okay with that."

"Nice guy," Mike said.

"No kidding. You'd better put a fire under Anna Carrington, or my career is toast." Dan rubbed his hand across his face. "Oh no!"

"What?"

"I promised Chelsea I'd do the first procedure on her face during the Christmas holidays."

Mike sank back into his chair. "Oh man, I never thought of that," he said. "Chelsea is so fragile right now. Marion told me that after her visit with you, the kid was full of hope. This could. . ."

"Drive her into deep depression," Dan finished.

"Isn't there another clinic or a hospital where you could work?"

Dan shook his head. "No clinic or hospital is going to grant me privileges while I'm under suspicion."

"How about another surgeon? You must know someone else who'll help you out with this."

Dan looked doubtful. "I'll ask around, but Christmas is a tough time to get plastic surgeons to work, never mind for free."

"We'll pray you find someone," Mike said.

"While you're praying," Dan said, "what do we tell Chelsea?"

"I don't have a clue," Mike said.

Chapter
Five

Jessica Meyers arrived at the newsroom at half past eleven on Monday morning. Since Monday was the legal holiday after Thanksgiving, the place was quiet.

As she approached her office, Jessica spotted an East Indian man with picture-perfect features. Ted Dhillon, the afternoon anchor, was at his desk, scanning something on a computer monitor. His office sat next to Jessica's with an entrance into the production set as well. As though feeling her gaze upon him, he looked up and frowned.

"Hi, Ted," she mouthed through the glass partition with a little wave.

He nodded but avoided eye contact and returned to his monitor. Jessica felt uneasy. Ted usually came out to flirt with her.

Before Jessica reached her own office, Roger Pronger's office door whipped open. With his head down like a bull ready to charge, Pronger filled the doorway. "Get in here."

Jessica moved toward Roger's office, her shoulder bag tapping against her brown leather skirt. She felt like a kid caught smoking behind the school building. From the look on Roger's beet-red face, this wasn't going to be pretty.

He stepped back to let her enter. As always, Pronger's office smelled of coffee and stale donuts. She stood watching him as he came around the desk and thudded into his swivel chair. He tossed a piece of paper at her. "Read that," he said.

Jessica hesitated to pick it up. She had a bad feeling about this whole situation.

"Read it," Pronger repeated.

She picked up the printout. It was a transcript of a PTV news broadcast. As she read each line, she felt sick. Their competitor had scooped them. How could she have been so wrong?

"Don't we look like fools?" Pronger asked. "PTV broke that this morning. I'm sure you won't mind if we report the full story this afternoon."

"Of course not," Jessica whispered. The sick feeling in her stomach melded into anger. Dan had made a fool of her. He'd told her a blatant lie.

Pronger said, "So much for the big favor you've done us. Why should people watch WTV when we only report what we like?"

Jessica squeezed her eyes shut, trying to keep control. How could Dan have done this to her? He'd counseled her, comforted her, then lied to her. Jessica's hard-fought professional reputation was on the line because she had stuck her neck out for him.

Pronger relaxed his stance. "I don't know what to say," he said. "One day you're my best news anchor, pulling no punches, hammering out the stories. Next day you're on about killer bulls and killing stories. I know Foster saved your career, but that was his job. He was paid to do it. You owe him nothing."

"I guess you're right," Jessica said. But did she believe that? She'd talked to the nurses afterward. They'd said they'd never seen a surgeon work as hard as Dan Foster had that night. And what about afterwards when the nightmares came? Not once had he ever complained about wee-hour calls. Not once had he refused to meet her for a late-night snack. Part of her wanted to slap his face, but the other part desperately wanted to talk to him, to find out why he lied.

"I need my old Jessica back," Pronger said, "the one who reports the whole story."

"You've got her," Jessica said. *And the first thing I'm going to do is get the whole story on Dr. Dan Foster.*

Shifting in his bed, blinking at the bright sunlight coming through the windows, Dan tried to go back to sleep. He rarely slept in, but what did that matter now? It was the day after Thanksgiving, but all his days were holidays now. Tomorrow, he'd go to the office to clear up some details and refer all his patients to the other doctors in the clinic.

Maybe one of them would agree to skip his Christmas trip to Rio so a young teen could get a new future, but thinking through the list of his colleagues, Dan had little hope. Other than Steve Logan, none had shown any interest in doing even one charity case. He made a mental note to talk to Chelsea and reassure her that she would get her surgery—just not by Christmas.

Pulling off the wool blanket, Dan rolled to a sitting position on the edge of the bed. He sucked in a deep yawn followed by a stretch. A rich coffee aroma filled the house, evidence that Mike must have gotten up and around. Dan glanced at the clock. He really had slept in; it was almost noon. He pulled on a robe and shuffled across the hall to his brother's room.

Dan knocked lightly, then opened the door. All he found was a made-up bed. He headed left, calling Mike's name at the top of the stairs. No answer. *Maybe Mike went out to buy muffins or something,* he thought as he stumped down the stairs. In the kitchen he spotted the glass coffee carafe half full.

Good old Mike. He knew how to take care of his brother. The pot was probably four hours old, but Dan could drink coffee in almost any condition. He grabbed a mug from the tree on the granite countertop and filled it. When he reached for the fridge door to get some cream, he found the note.

Got a call from work. Probably going undercover.
Talk to you when I can.

—Mike

Dan groaned. This wasn't the first time Mike had left him a note like this, and it always bothered him. He felt responsible for Mike. Both their parents had passed away within a year of each other shortly after Mike had graduated from high school, and as older brother, Dan felt a need to watch out for Mike. He hated not knowing where he was, what he was doing, or how much danger he was in. Though he never said it out loud, he couldn't bear the thought of losing his little brother.

At least Aunt Elinor wasn't at home to worry about him. She'd left the day before to visit an old friend for the Thanksgiving holiday. What she didn't know while she was in Denver wouldn't hurt her.

Dan glanced at the picture above the note. It was Jesus holding out His hands. Under it a caption said, "He's got the whole world in His hands." This was where Mike and Dan parted company. They'd lost both parents, and then Dan had lost. . .

His throat tightened. If God had the whole world in His hands, people were falling through the cracks.

Pushing back dark memories that still haunted him, Dan opened the fridge door and took out the cream container. He poured a healthy dose into the coffee cup and set the cardboard carton back in the fridge. When he sank a spoon into the cup to stir, he suddenly lost his breath. His knees felt weak. He stumbled to the kitchen table and dropped into a chair.

Setting the mug far back on the table, Dan leaned forward to press his hands across his face. "Denise," he whispered, "I'm so sorry."

Jessica's impulse to slap Dan Foster's face had faded by the time her Porsche reached his house. Dan had lied to her, but she wasn't about to throw away their friendship because of it. Everyone had secrets. For some reason Dan had kept this one. She had to know why.

Compared to Vancouver, Langley was country. Sure, it had its share of malls, office buildings, and condos, but it still had lots of nice neighborhoods, not to mention plenty of farms. Dan lived in one of the middle-class housing developments.

Jessica got out of her Porsche, clicked the remote, noting the familiar chirp that indicated the security system was armed. She glanced down the road where a dozen kids were taking advantage of the sunny day by playing street hockey. A few parents in lawn chairs looked on. Someday Jessica would love to live in a neighborhood like this, maybe watching her own kids playing outside. She sighed. At thirty-two years old, those dreams were just as far away as when she was eighteen.

She walked up to the door and rang the bell. Silence. She rang again. If he had answered his phone when she called him this morning, she wouldn't have to show up unannounced like this. She couldn't blame him, though, the way reporters had been hounding him. Keeping his mouth shut was probably the best plan.

As seconds ticked away, it occurred to Jessica that Dan might not want to talk to her. She *was* part of the media. She rang the bell again and wondered what to do. Walking down the sidewalk in front of the house, she took three steps down to the garage door. She peered through the high glass window and saw Dan's Grand Marquis. He had to be at home.

Jessica skipped back up the steps. She rang the doorbell for five straight seconds, then pounded the door. "Dan! It's me, Jessica," she called out and followed her words with a couple more raps.

Finally, she heard steps on the other side of the door. It swung open, and Jessica gasped.

The good doctor's eyes were puffy. He had wide red streaks down his cheeks. His bathrobe hung half open, and his short dark hair stuck straight up on the left side of his head. If she didn't know him better, Jessica would have thought he was on a drinking binge.

"I take it you've seen the news," she said, resisting the urge to tighten his terry-cloth belt and smooth his hair.

"Huh?" He rubbed his face and tried to focus on her.

"The news," Jessica said. "You saw it?"

"No." He yanked the door fully open, turned his back to her, and wandered down the darkened hallway.

Jessica's jaw sagged. He hadn't heard the news, so what had happened? He looked like someone had just died. She stepped inside. Maybe Mike had been in another car accident?

She closed the door behind her and rushed after him. Dan sat at the kitchen table, staring at a cup of coffee wedged between his hands. She pulled a chair close to him and put her hand on his arm.

"What's happened?" she asked. "Was there another accident? Is Mike in the hospital? Is it Aunt Elinor?"

He looked up, and his gaze rested somewhere on her forehead. "Huh?"

"Dan, what's going on here? You're scaring me."

He blinked twice and shook his head. "Jessica," he said.

He spoke like he'd just realized she was there.

She touched her hand to his forehead. It was cool and clammy. No fever. "What's the matter?" she asked.

A sorry attempt at a grin curved his mouth. "It's nothing. I'm just upset about everything that's going on lately."

Jessica didn't buy it. Eight years as an investigative reporter gave her a keen sense for honesty. Her internal lie-detector scale moved into the red. "Want to try again?" she asked.

He shrugged. "A patient I cared about has died, and everyone thinks I'm to blame."

"I thought you might be upset about this morning's news."

He gave her a deadpan stare. "What now?"

"PTV broke the story that Beth Martin wasn't your first drug mix-up. It's happened before."

The color drained from his face.

"I don't suppose you remember telling me that there were no ghosts in your closet?"

He kept his head down, his chin resting on his palm. "I remember."

Jessica leaned forward and spoke right into his face. "Because of what you said, I buried most of yesterday's story. You realize how foolish that makes me look?" Staring at him, she sat back in her chair and folded her arms tightly against her middle.

He stared dumbly at his coffee cup.

"Aren't you going to say anything?" she asked.

He slowly raised his head. "I'm sorry. I should've told you."

"It's true then? This has happened before?"

Dan got up and took his coffee mug to the sink. He dumped it out and poured himself another cup. "Want some? It's pretty old. I could make a fresh pot."

"I want an answer, Dan," she said.

He scratched his whiskers. "Yeah."

He poured cream into his cup, taking his time. Jessica

stared at him. What was he doing? Trying to come up with a story that would satisfy her? She thought she knew Dan Foster, but obviously she had been wrong.

He returned to his seat and said, "During my residency at the Prince George Regional Hospital, I gave penicillin to a woman who was allergic to it."

Jessica had a sinking feeling. She'd hoped the PTV story was wrong.

Dan took a sip of his coffee and went on. "I had just returned to the hospital after a. . . ," he swallowed and struggled to speak, ". . .after a personal matter that affected me greatly. I'd come to the hospital to ask for time off to pull myself together.

"While I was there, a bus carrying a girls' volleyball team collided with a fully loaded logging truck. Before I had a chance to talk to the administrator, kids on stretchers flooded the emergency room. We had a decent-sized ward, but this was overwhelming. They needed everyone they could get. I shouldn't have been treating anyone, but I ended up working anyway."

He took a deep breath. "There were so many kids that we couldn't even fly them out. There weren't enough resources. It was horrible. Broken limbs, gaping wounds—the ward was pandemonium. I was caring for half a dozen girls. My most serious case was a tall redhead named Sharra. She had a piece of metal stuck in her chest." His stare wandered toward the sink.

"In the midst of that mess, there was a vagrant woman who was having coughing spasms. She kept screaming for a doctor." He glanced at Jessica. "She was low on the priority list, Jessica. I mean, we had girls who were going to die." He rubbed his eyes. "I had just gotten Sharra stabilized when this woman started yelling again. I figured it would be worth the peace and quiet to treat her and get her out of there."

Dan's jaw tightened. "She was rude. Instead of thanking me,

she swore at me. I took a look down her throat and saw a rip-roaring infection. I had barely opened her chart when a nurse yelled that Sharra had gone into cardiac arrest. I handed the chart to a nearby nurse and ordered the vagrant woman a course of penicillin. I said to get her out of there." He glanced at Jessica. "I never did read her chart."

Jessica let out a long breath. "She was allergic to penicillin. Is that it?"

Dan nodded. "It was on the chart."

"So what happened?"

"The lady reacted, but we treated her in time with no long-lasting effects. The hospital held a review of my conduct, and I was cleared. When all the circumstances were taken into account, it was concluded that the whole situation was an accident waiting to happen. In fact, the panel concluded that it was a miracle nothing worse had happened. My record was expunged."

"What happened to Sharra?" Jessica asked.

"I'll show you. Wait here." Getting up, he disappeared up the stairs and came back holding a picture frame. Standing in RCMP dress uniform was a striking redhead. "This is Sharra," he said.

Jessica took the frame from him. "Obviously she lived."

"That's one of the rewards of this job," he said. "Sharra sends me E-mail all the time. Keeps me up-to-date on her life."

Staring at the photograph in her hands, Jessica wondered if she wasn't any more special than Sharra. Jessica Meyers, just one of the many former patients that Dan kept up with.

"You all right?" he asked.

"Sure," Jessica said, forcing a smile. "It's great that you can stay in touch." She handed the picture to him, and he laid it on the table.

"Yeah," he said. He took another sip of coffee. "Look, I'm

really sorry I didn't tell you about this. I figured that since there was no record, it didn't matter."

"If the record was expunged, how did PTV find out?"

Dan shrugged. "Someone must have told them."

"They found an informant." She leaned toward him. "Look, Dan, off the record and the absolute truth. Did you mix up Beth's medication?"

He shook his head. "Not a chance. I don't even have Nardil in my office. That's blood pressure medication. There's no reason for me to have the stuff."

"Exactly what is Nardil? How could it have killed her?"

Dan picked up his mug and held it between both hands. "Nardil is a monoamine oxidase inhibitor. It's a group of particularly nasty drugs that can have terrible side effects. Normally it's used to control high blood pressure or depression."

"And Beth had neither condition?" Jessica asked.

"Not a chance," Dan said. "Her blood pressure was fine, and she was in great spirits, looking forward to a brand-new life."

"Is there any chance she saw another doctor and didn't tell you about it?"

"There's always a chance," Dan told her, "but after what happened in Prince George, I do an especially thorough preop exam and questionnaire. She was only taking antihistamines. Her blood pressure was perfect, Jessica. She was my book-keeper. I never saw any evidence of depression in Beth Martin."

"If Nardil is a prescription drug, how could it be so dangerous. . .so deadly?" Jessica asked.

"Nardil isn't fatal on its own, no matter what your medical condition," Dan said. "It's only fatal when it interacts with some other drugs and certain foods. Some of the drugs include cocaine, antihistamines, and lidocaine. Nardil can also react with cheeses, certain sausages, beer, and wine. On Thanksgiving Day, Beth Martin had wine and cheesecake. She was taking antihistamines. It was a recipe for disaster."

Jessica searched his eyes and saw absolute sincerity. "Then someone else gave her Nardil," Jessica said. "Someone killed her."

Dan held his hands out in a pleading gesture. "That's what I keep trying to tell everyone, but all eyes are still focused on me. There's a killer out there who's probably sitting back and laughing because he's going to get away with this."

"Or she," Jessica said.

"Who knows," Dan replied. "Either way, I'm taking the blame, and I don't like it. My brother promised he'd make sure the cops don't restrict their investigation to me, but now he's gone undercover. He's the only one who believes I'm innocent."

Jessica put her hand on his shoulder. "Hey, relax," she said, giving him a gentle shake. "First of all, your brother isn't the only one who believes you."

"I appreciate that," he said, "but the cops are the ones that count. They think I'm guilty."

"We have to prove you aren't," she said. "I was an investigative reporter, remember? A little detective work doesn't intimidate me."

Dan looked at her. "Mike told me to keep out of it."

"Mike can tell you whatever he wants," Jessica said. "My best friend has been framed for killing Beth Martin. On top of that, I've got a source that says Peter Martin was murdered as well. I think the two are linked. I'm going to dig into this, no matter what your brother thinks." She smiled. "Besides, he isn't here."

A slow grin creased the lines of Dan's face. "Hey, that's right." He relaxed for the first time since she arrived. "Since you're the expert, how do we prove I'm not the incompetent buffoon the media is making me out to be? How can we catch a killer?"

"We start where it all began," Jessica said. "Your clinic."

"Let's go," Dan said, standing.

She grinned. "You might want to get dressed first."

He looked down at his robe. "That might be a plan."

Dan strode out of the kitchen, direction in his steps for the first time that morning.

"Hey," she said just before he disappeared up the stairs, "any idea what Mike is working on?"

Dan shrugged. "Not a clue. Probably some drug case. That's his thing."

Chapter
Six

S howered and shaved, Dan reappeared twenty minutes later. They took Jessica's Porsche to the clinic in Langley. Dan glanced at Jessica, who was confidently handling the smooth machine.

Every book on doctor-patient relations advised that a physician should never get emotionally involved with his clients. Only twice had he failed to heed his training in that area. Sharra had been the first time. Jessica had been the second.

Five hours after Jessica's reconstruction surgery, he'd walked into her hospital room to check on her, and she'd awakened screaming. Her panic echoed into the depths of his soul. Only once before had he heard such a scream, and it had come from the lips of his beloved. After that, Dan could never refuse Jessica when she needed him—even if it was only to talk.

The Porsche cruised down the street to the clinic—a white three-story building nestled in the center of a black-asphalt parking lot. Because of the holiday, Dan expected the lot to be empty. He was wrong. Three police cars and a police van were parked in front of the building.

"Great," he muttered.

"It might have nothing to do with you," Jessica said, slowing and flipping on her turn signal.

"You really believe that?"

"No." She parked close to the police cars. "Maybe we should do this another time," she said, moving the shift lever into park.

Dan stared at the glass entrance doors where a green canvas awning stretched twenty feet out from the building to the edge of the parking lot. The thought of entering that place filled him with dread.

"Maybe we ought to wait," he said.

Jessica shifted into reverse. Dan put his hand over hers. "Hold it," he said. "I've spent more than a decade getting to where I am today. I'm not going down without a fight. If the police are here because of me, I want to know why."

Jessica killed the motor, and Dan climbed out of the Porsche. He waited for Jessica to get out and around the car before heading toward the building. He pulled at the door handle. It rattled but didn't open. Dan took his wallet from the back pocket of his slacks and got his keycard. He swiped it in the reader and the door clicked open.

"At least they haven't locked me out," he said.

"Yet," Jessica added.

Dan held open the door, and Jessica walked in ahead of him. The lobby was deserted. Beside the elevators sat a high information desk. On a normal business day, a slim worker named Robbie sat there showing his perfect white teeth at regular intervals. His job consisted of making sure that well-heeled clients didn't get lost at New Spring Surgery Clinic.

The lobby's pink walls held a dozen heavy frames filled with contemporary artwork. Dan preferred paintings that looked like something, but according to Dr. Cruch, a plastic surgery clinic should project an image that's always on the cutting edge. Of course, Cruch never used the word *cutting* in front of the patients.

Jessica headed toward the elevators and pressed the button. Dan stopped short. She looked back at him. "Coming?" she asked.

"Actually," Dan said, "I'd prefer to take the stairs. It's only three flights, and I need all the exercise I can get."

Jessica stared at him. "What do you mean you need all the exercise you can get? No one gets a physique like yours by taking the stairs. You work out plenty."

Dan wet his lips. "More is better," he said, trying to sound light, but the quaver in his voice threatened to betray him. "This way," he said, opening the door to the stairs.

Still wondering, she glanced up at him as she walked past.

The stairs were wide, so they could walk up side by side. "Any idea what you're going to say to the police if they are here about you?" Jessica asked.

Dan shrugged as they turned the corner and started up another flight. "I'll probably say something like—don't you guys have something better to do, like find whoever murdered Beth Martin?"

Jessica touched his elbow, and they stopped midflight. "Dan, you realize there's a chance you could be charged with manslaughter?"

Dan felt a chill. "I thought losing my medical license was the worst that could happen—and that's bad enough."

Jessica wiped a strand of hair from her face and said, "Maybe we should slip out of the building and go somewhere to talk before you take on the police."

Dan stood firm. "I'm not running, Jessica," he said. "I did nothing wrong. I can't prove that by hiding." He reached for the banister, and Jessica followed him.

When they arrived on the third floor, a thickset constable stood in front of Dan's office door. When the metal door clanked shut behind Dan and Jessica, the officer spun on his heels and disappeared into Dan's office. Dan hustled down the hall, his long stride leaving Jessica behind.

When he reached the door, Corporal Anna Carrington stepped into the doorway. For an instant they stood nose to nose. She was a tall, heavy-boned woman with a dark curly mop of unkempt hair. Despite his rage, Dan couldn't help but think how he could soften her features by scaling back her nose a bit and shortening her cheekbones.

Corporal Carrington calmly stared at him. "May I help you, Doctor?"

Dan's fists came up to waist level. "You'd better have a search warrant."

Carrington dug into the pocket of her bulky uniform jacket and produced a folded document. She handed it to him. Heels tapped on the floor behind Dan, and Carrington turned to see who was approaching. Immediately her expression tensed.

"Hello, Corporal Carrington." Jessica's normally soft voice contained an edge.

"Ms. Meyers," the corporal said, "the media isn't permitted in here. You'll have to leave."

Dan suddenly had the scary feeling that he stood between two lionesses about to lunge.

He stepped aside. Carrington definitely had the weight advantage, but Jessica's eyes were smoldering and her jaw was tense. On second thought, he had it wrong. This was like a bear and a wolverine about to duke it out. Jessica's hazel eyes had changed to a dark brown. "I'm not here as media," Jessica countered. "I'm here as a friend."

Carrington gave her a hard look. "Oh, that's right. Dr. Foster is the miracle worker who rebuilt that china-doll face of yours. I guess you'd do anything for him. Even bury a story."

Jessica squared her shoulders and placed her feet for balance.

Carrington was on thin ice. Jessica spent three nights a week at a women's self-defense club. Speed kills, and Jessica was fast.

Jessica raised her arm and pointed at Carrington's long nose. "That's right. I'm willing to help Dan as much as I can. That's because I know him. You don't. My job is to make sure some promotion-crazy cop doesn't throw him in jail on a misguided hunch."

Carrington took a deep breath and scowled. Dan figured it was time for him to lower the temperature before he had to break up a brawl. "Mind if I go into my office?" he asked.

Anna Carrington broke her stare at Jessica and turned on him. "After we're done."

"He has the right to observe the search," Jessica said.

Carrington raised her thick eyebrows. "Oh, are you a lawyer now?"

"I know enough to understand that your actions are an attempt to interfere with Dan's legal rights. Not a smart move during a police investigation, don't you think, *Corporal?* And speaking of rights and lawyers, maybe we should give Dan's lawyer a call. You probably know him. Arthur Stoll."

Carrington's scowl stiffened. Her chin raised a fraction while she stared at Jessica. Obviously she did know Arthur Stoll. Too bad Dan didn't know him.

"Fine," Carrington said, stepping back. "Come in, but stay out of the way." She turned and disappeared down the hall toward Dan's study.

Dan entered his waiting room and reined up short when he saw Dr. Cruch sitting in a gray cloth-covered chair, flipping through a fishing magazine.

The elderly surgeon looked up at Dan and frowned. "Dr. Foster," he said, "you seem to be causing this clinic a lot of trouble. And this is a holiday, besides. Do you know the police pulled me off the golf course so I could let them into your office? I was having a pretty good round, too. At least now that you're here, I can go."

Dan's mouth dropped open as the chief of the clinic brushed past him and started down the hall without another word. Dan stepped into the hallway. "Dr. Cruch? Wait a moment, please."

The elderly physician turned. "Yes?" He took a few steps back toward Dan.

Dan stepped up to him. "Uh, I have a favor to ask you."

The older doctor's bushy eyebrows lowered. "A favor? Are you kidding?"

"It's not for me," Dan said. "It's for someone else, a fourteen-year-old girl. I scheduled her for skin grafting and laser work over the Christmas holidays. Obviously, I won't be able to do it."

"Don't worry about it," Cruch said. "I've already talked to the other doctors. We'll cover your patients for you. We'll reschedule her for after Christmas when everyone is back to work." Cruch turned back down toward the elevator.

"Dr. Cruch, it's not that simple."

Cruch turned on his heels, waiting.

"I was going to do it for free."

Dan heard Jessica approaching behind him.

"Free? Why on earth would you agree to do it for free?"

"She's a ward of the province. There's no way she can pay." He noticed Jessica standing beside him but slightly back.

Cruch shrugged. "When she grows up, she can get a job and pay for it. This clinic isn't a private charity hospital."

"She's a special case," Dan said. "She got a face burn at five years of age. The school kids have been extremely cruel to her. She's already tried to commit suicide because of them."

Jessica stepped up to the plate. "Her case could provide great public relations, Dr. Cruch. I'd make sure this got on the news."

Cruch shook his head. "Even if the clinic was willing to do

it for nothing—and I'm not saying it is—all the associates leave town for Christmas."

"I'm sure Chelsea won't mind waiting a little longer," Dan told him. "She just needs to know the surgery is going to happen."

Cruch paused, considering. "I'll see if anyone's interested in taking her case. But no promises."

"Thank you, Sir," Dan said.

Cruch stared at Dan for a couple of seconds. "You know, you've caused a lot of trouble for this practice. To be honest, I won't be sorry if they do pull your medical license."

"Wait a minute, Doctor," Jessica said. "You seem pretty convinced that Dan is responsible."

Cruch shrugged. "Who else would be?" Without another word, he turned and punched the white button to call the elevator.

When he disappeared behind the shiny doors twenty seconds later, Jessica said, "What a jerk!"

"He's got a right to be upset," Dan told her. "This is terrible publicity for his clinic. It's going to affect all the associates' patient load."

"Unless we clear your name," she said.

"Right," he said, not totally convinced. They turned back to his office and sat in his waiting room. "You and Anna Carrington seem to have some history," he said.

"Obviously," Jessica retorted.

"Care to tell me about it?"

She sat back, crossed her legs, and smoothed her brown leather skirt around her knees. "Corporal Carrington used to be Sergeant Carrington until I uncovered a story about how she had deliberately charged an innocent man so she could settle a score."

Dan raised an eyebrow. "And she still has her job?"

"As you're fast learning, in the media we don't need to convict beyond a reasonable doubt. We just have to reveal facts that fit the situation. Carrington's side of the story was somewhat different. She did catch the actual killer, so they reprimanded her by a demotion and paid the innocent guy an undisclosed sum of money."

"And now she hates you," Dan said.

Jessica nodded. "The feeling is mutual."

"So who is Arthur Stoll?"

Jessica gave him a broad smile. "Arthur Stoll is arguably the top criminal lawyer in the country. He was one of my law professors during my one year of law school. We've shared information on occasion. He is also the only lawyer who confused Anna Carrington so much while she was on the stand that he made her cry. No love is lost between the two of them." Her expression grew animated. "Actually, Dan, I think we should call him. I have his home number. He can make a whole lot of hurt disappear in no time." Jessica dug her cell phone out of her purse.

At that moment, Anna Carrington appeared in the inner hallway. "Dr. Foster, there's a locked steel cabinet in your office. Would you open it, please?"

Dan dragged himself off the couch. Jessica put her phone away, stood up with him, and followed them into his office. Dan held back a curse when he stepped inside. His personal files had been removed from the filing cabinet. They lay in haphazard stacks about the office. Two bulldog constables sat at his desk flipping through files.

"This is outrageous," Jessica said. "People's personal medical histories are in these files."

Carrington grinned, showing wide teeth. "Yeah, including yours."

Jessica's face flushed. Dan's blood was starting to boil

again. He'd never hit a woman before, but Anna Carrington was coming close to being the first.

Dan's eyes narrowed. "You read her file?"

Carrington smiled. "We're reading everyone's file to see if you've ever prescribed Nardil before. And to see if you've had any other goof-ups in medication. Besides the two we know about."

Dan took a deep breath. "I swear, if any details of what's in my files get out, I'll spend every last dime I have making sure you spend the rest of your career writing parking tickets."

Carrington smirked. "We know how to be discreet, Doctor. Now, please open the cabinet."

He turned to the steel box against the back wall and noticed pry marks on its door. Because he kept his drugs in there, Dan had bought a heavy steel cabinet that was really more of a safe. Anna Carrington did need his help.

"Use your crowbar," Dan told her. "I'm having trouble remembering the combination."

Carrington stiffened. "The search warrant requires you to assist me. If you don't open this cabinet, I'll charge you with obstruction of justice."

"The Charter of Rights also protects him against self-incrimination," Jessica said. "He can't be compelled to assist you in acquiring evidence against him."

Anna Carrington shook her head. "Look, Doctor, I will get that cabinet open. All you're doing is delaying the inevitable, making yourself look guilty, and making sure a perfectly good cabinet gets ruined."

Dan raised his hands, palm upwards. "Fine, I'll open it."

Blocking the dial with his body, he spun the combination and pulled the door open. He stepped back.

Carrington whistled. "That's a lot of drugs, Doctor. What's in those big bottles on the top shelf?"

"Antibiotics," Dan told her.

"The same antibiotics you say you gave to Beth Martin?"

He shoved his hands into his pockets. "Go to the head of the class." With gloved hands, Carrington removed a box filled with bottles. She cleared a space on his desk and dumped out the first bottle. For no reason, Dan suddenly feared that little faded-orange pills would spill onto his desk. What if Nardil really had been in the bottle and he was guilty? She opened the second bottle and repeated the process.

"You know we found your fingerprints on the bottle that contained the Nardil."

"Say nothing, Dan," Jessica said.

"It's okay, Jessica," Dan said. "Of course my fingerprints are on the bottle. I gave it to her."

Carrington watched him. "The bottle you gave Beth Martin contained amoxicillin, right?"

"You're batting a thousand," Dan said.

"And somehow Nardil magically appeared in the bottle?"

"Not magically," Dan said. "A murderer put it there. A murderer who's laughing while you waste your time on me."

"What I would like to know is, why did you give her the amoxicillin yourself? Why didn't you write a prescription and let her get it at the drugstore?"

"I used to do that," Dan said, "but patients feel so lousy after surgery that sometimes they don't bother filling the prescription right away. Then infection sets in, and that could ruin the surgery. It's cheaper for me to buy the pills and give them away than to fight an infection that didn't need to start in the first place."

"I see," Carrington said. She returned to the cabinet and pointed to boxes stacked on the bottom. "What are those?"

Dan shrugged. "I don't really know. The drug company rep is always giving me free samples. I just toss them down there until I go overseas."

Carrington arched an eyebrow. "Overseas?"

"Yeah," Dan said. "Every year or so I go to some third-world country and do charity work. Because medicine is so hard to come by over there, I take the samples with me and give them to the local doctors."

She sat cross-legged in front of the cabinet and started pulling out sample boxes, looking at each one, and tossing it on the floor. After twelve boxes, she paused. "Well, Dr. Foster, would you care to explain this to me?" She held up the box. The label clearly said Nardil.

Jessica gasped.

Dan felt cold. "Like I told you," he said, "I never look at the samples."

"Yes, you've told me a lot of things," Carrington said.

Dan ground out, "I did *not* give her Nardil. Look at the pills. They don't look anything like amoxicillin. There's not a chance on earth I could have mixed them up."

Carrington stood and came within inches of him. "That's what I'm thinking, too, Doctor. These pills are so different that you couldn't have mixed them up. Tell me, Doctor, do you still have blackouts?" She pushed the Nardil packet into his face.

Dan suddenly felt hot. The room went blurry with darkness around the edges.

"Blackouts?" Dan heard Jessica say. "What's she talking about?"

Dan pushed past Carrington. The room was closing in on him. He felt a gritty feeling in his throat. He had to get out. Now.

"Dr. Foster!" Carrington called after him, but he ignored her.

Coughing, his breath coming in short gasps, Dan rushed down the hall. He crashed against the steel bar of the door to the stairway and stumbled three flights down. His heart was pounding out of his chest. He didn't stop running until he got outside. Under the canopy, he slumped to the sidewalk and covered his face.

Chapter
Seven

I take it you didn't know about his blackouts." Corporal Carrington spoke in a flat, emotionless voice.

Moving in slow motion, Jessica shook her head.

The corporal's voice softened, and Jessica turned toward her. "You cost me big time with that exposé of yours, Meyers. But, I figure we women have to stick together if we're going to get anywhere in this man's world. Take it from me, if you're going to bet on Dan Foster, you're backing the wrong horse. There's a lot in his past he probably hasn't told you. I'm not coming down hard on him for the fun of it. I've got a reason for what I'm doing."

Jessica watched the corporal without answering. Anna Carrington had her own agenda, and Jessica was getting in the way. Jessica headed for the door and didn't look back. In the hallway, she stopped and took a few breaths. Despite Carrington's ulterior motives, she'd been right about one thing—Dan was hiding something. This morning he'd looked like a man on a drinking binge. Just now he had a panic attack. Her reporter's instincts ran up a red flag.

Pushing the button to call the elevator, she considered the

situation. There was no way on earth that she could be objective about Dan. Her feelings went beyond gratitude. Just how far beyond, she couldn't stop to analyze right now.

She stepped into the elevator and pushed the circle with an "L" on it. The doors closed, and her stomach felt that distinctive tickle from descending. Watching the blinking numbers overhead, she suddenly realized that she'd never ridden in an elevator with Dan. He always found an excuse for not coming to her apartment, even for a Christmas party. She lived twenty-three stories up. Too many stairs to climb?

When the elevator doors opened, Jessica crossed the lobby and pushed open the glass door that led to the parking lot. She found Dan sitting against one of the concrete pillars supporting the overhang. His face lay buried against his drawn-up knees. Jessica quietly walked over and knelt before him.

"You okay?" She touched his disheveled hair and saw a curved scar along his hairline that she'd never seen before.

Dan nodded, but he didn't look up.

"I think it's time for total honesty between us," Jessica said.

Dan nodded again.

She glanced at her watch. "How about an early supper?"

"Sure," Dan said. His voice sounded hoarse.

He stood up and swayed. His face looked chalky except for brilliant red spots on his cheeks. Jessica held his elbow and guided him to her car. He reminded her of an accident victim who was too shocked to understand what was happening around him. He was just going with the flow.

Jessica opened the door for him, and Dan slid into the Porsche. "Put your seat belt on," she said.

Staring forward, Dan did as he was told. Jessica fired up the Porsche and drove out of the parking lot. At a red light, she glanced over at Dan. Some normal coloring had returned to his face, but he didn't look at her or speak.

She guided the Porsche through Langley to the Denny's restaurant next to the Sandman Hotel. When she shut the motor off, she looked at Dan. "Are you okay?"

He nodded.

Jessica held the door open for him and followed him inside.

An attractive blond hostess met them inside. Her black nametag said *Wendy.* "A table for two?" she asked. She took a second look. "You're. . .you're. . ."

"Jessica Meyers."

"This is so cool," Wendy said. "Could I please have your autograph?"

Jessica glanced at Dan. "Maybe later." She looked across the dining room. "Is that table in the corner taken?"

"You can have it," Wendy said, her smile reappearing. She grabbed two long menus and led the way.

Jessica touched Dan's elbow, and he moved forward. Twenty paces later, she sank into the booth, relieved. Dan needed quiet, and she didn't want anyone else to recognize her.

"What would you like to drink?" Wendy took out her order pad.

"Coffee," Jessica said, pulling off her coat.

"And you, Sir?"

Dan said nothing.

"Coffee for him, too," Jessica said.

Wendy hurried away and returned in less than two minutes with two steaming mugs. Jessica made a mental note to get the girl's address and have publicity send her an autographed photo.

She reached across the table and touched Dan's hand. "Dan?"

He looked around at the restaurant, a wondering expression on his face. She decided to try acting normally. Maybe he would snap out of his stupor after awhile.

"You know, I skipped lunch today," she said, opening her menu. "I think I'll go for something heavier tonight. Maybe even a steak."

"Good idea," Dan said, reaching for his menu.

She concentrated on the list before her. The steak looked good, but she wasn't a big meat eater. Maybe she should go with chicken salad and a roll.

"I was engaged once," Dan said into the silence. "Her name was Denise. She died."

In a small conference room in Washington State, Mike Foster relaxed in a leather chair and picked up his coffee cup. He wore his undercover getup, complete with a three-day stubble on his chin. Next to him sat Inspector Phil Bernier, tall and thin with harsh facial features, the man in charge of the RCMP task force on narcotics. Across from them sat Mike's female counterpart in the operation, Louise Crossfield of the U.S. Drug Enforcement Agency. Chairing the meeting was Kent Olund, a middle-aged suit with a dark crew cut. Kent worked for the FBI.

Olund smoothed his red silk tie, opened a folder, and spoke. "Grow-ops in British Columbia have been supplying eighty percent of the marijuana to the Pacific Northwest for years. Some of the product has shown up as far east as Illinois. Their crop rivals Mexico's for dominance in the California market. Hydroponics marijuana is much more potent than anything the Mexicans can grow under the sun. Only their proximity to California keeps the Mexicans in the market at all."

"Maybe we should give the Mexicans the addresses of the Canadian growers and let them duke it out," Louise said, fingering the bottom earring of six that lined her left ear. She had a diamond stud at the left side of her nose with three gold circlets hanging above her upper lip. For all her tough image, her voice was soft and husky.

Ignoring Louise's attempt at humor, Olund turned a page

in his folder. "We've had fairly good success busting dealers on this side of the border, but it's a lost cause. They're like rats. You stomp one out, and two more show up to take his place. Canadian law enforcement hasn't been sufficient to deal with the supply end of the problem."

Mike looked up. "We're doing all we can with the resources we have." He looked over at Inspector Bernier, whose face held no expression. His boss seemed to have the same opinion as the FBI agent.

"Absolutely," Olund said. "I think the RCMP and Canadian municipal police have done an exceptional job. It's not your enforcement that's the problem."

Mike leaned back in his chair and lifted his right ankle to his left knee. "Then what is?"

"It's the legal system, Corporal Foster," Olund said. "You catch the growers, and nothing significant happens to them. The same conviction in the United States would carry a minimum of twenty years in a not-so-nice federal facility."

"Why are you telling us this?" Mike asked. "You should be lobbying the guys in parliament."

Bernier spoke up. "They want to lure the growers into their jurisdiction, Mike. That's why we're here."

Louise said, "Since Canadian growers never step into the United States, we want to set up an operation with so much money involved that the growers won't trust anyone else to handle it. Once we get the ringleaders onto our turf, we're going to slap them with so many charges that they'll leave prison in pine boxes."

"That's where you come in," Olund said. "Inspector Bernier tells me you're a natural when it comes to undercover work. We're going to certify you as a law enforcement officer in the United States and vice versa with Louise for Canada. The two of you are going to work as a team to set up the big buy. We've already got a local drug dealer who's going to help you get into the market."

"Why's he so willing to help us?" Mike asked. He didn't trust drug dealers—ever.

"He's just been charged with his third felony," Olund said. He paused to clear his throat. "He's a candidate for a life sentence. We're going to make the charge go away in exchange for getting you in. Louise is already known on the street as a dealer, so it won't be that hard to get you in, too." He paused, his dark eyes sizing up Mike. "Are you interested?"

"I'm in."

"Good," Olund said. "I'm sure you've already figured out that this could be a long assignment. If there's anyone you need to get in touch with, do it now. Once you go under, you stay put." He reached for his leather briefcase on the floor beside his chair.

Mike nodded. He knew the drill. He got up from the table and stepped into the hallway. Pulling his cell phone from the clip on his belt, he dialed home. . .and got the answering machine.

"Dan, it's Mike," he said into the phone. "I'm going to be gone for quite awhile. It's a really important case. You won't hear from me until it's done. Don't do anything stupid about Beth. Everything will work out." He paused. "And Dan. . .uh. . .take care."

He clicked the phone shut, started to put it away, then stared at it. He flipped it open and raised a finger to punch a number.

"I hope you're as good as they say you are," Louise said, coming up behind him.

"I do okay," Mike said, clicking his cell phone shut.

"Do us both a favor and keep two things in mind," she said. "One, you do exactly what I tell you. And two, remember this: Drug dealers down here don't mess around. If they think you're a cop, they'll kill you."

Shortly after Dan spoke the name of his fiancée, Jessica caught a movement to her left. Wendy had her pad and pencil out, coming to take their order. Jessica held up her hand, warning the waitress off. She didn't want anything to keep Dan from finishing what he'd started saying.

"Denise was so beautiful," he said. "So full of life. I loved her more than anything." He stopped, and Jessica saw his fingers trembling. She grabbed his hand and held it.

Dan took a deep breath. "She loved the outdoors. We both did. If we weren't working, we were out hiking or biking or just walking. There was only one hobby we didn't share." He stared out the window. It was clouding over. Rain would be coming soon.

"What was that?" Jessica asked.

His eyes were misty, his face haggard when he looked at her. "Cave exploring. Mike and I have been exploring caves since we were kids. We'd set up a trip to explore the Upana caves by Gold River on Vancouver Island. At the last minute, Mike got called away to work.

"It's dangerous to explore caves alone, so I needed someone to go with me. After a lot of pleading, I managed to convince Denise to come with me, to give it the good old college try."

Dan was looking into the distance, smiling. Probably remembering the young woman he had loved.

"She'd have done almost anything for me." His face clouded over.

"We hiked up to the entrance. Faced with walking into the dark cave, Denise got scared. It's one thing talking about going into a hole in the earth; it's quite another doing it.

Denise just couldn't take that step.

"I was pretty disappointed. We'd spent half a day getting to the site, and there the cave was right in front of us."

Dan's hand bunched into a fist. His Adam's apple bobbed as he swallowed deeply.

"I went in alone," Dan said. "I told Denise I'd only be an hour. First she tried to talk me out of it, but I wouldn't listen, so she agreed to wait by the cave mouth for me. If only she had waited." He sucked in a deep breath.

"Everything went well for the first half-hour. I saw some pretty cool stuff." His jaw tightened. "What an idiot I was. Caves are so damp and treacherous. I slipped, cracked my head, and knocked myself out."

His eyes locked with hers. "When I came to, I could hear Denise calling, but I couldn't see any light. I called out to her, and she called back. She told me she was lost, and her flashlight battery had died. When I switched on my spare light and looked at my watch, I discovered I'd been out for four hours."

Dan's chest started to heave. "I was just about to call to her, to tell her to stay put, when I heard. . ." He was trembling. "I heard her scream."

Jessica put her hand on his arm. "You don't have to tell me this."

Dan ignored her. "When Denise screamed, I tried to scramble to my feet. In the process, I dropped my flashlight and broke the bulb. I was in complete darkness. I called out to Denise, but she didn't call back. I had no idea what happened. I just knew I had to find her. I started searching the cave in the dark."

A sheen of sweat broke out on Dan's forehead.

"I don't know how long I spent inching through that dark void, feeling along with my hands, hoping to touch her, to know what happened. After awhile, the darkness seemed like it was swallowing me whole. I realized I was never going to find her, and I freaked out in there. I starting running in the dark and smashed into a wall. The next thing I knew, I woke up in an ambulance."

"That's why you won't go into elevators."

Dan nodded. "I can't stand confined spaces."

"And Denise?"

Dan breathed deeply, then forced himself to relax. "The Upana River runs through that cave. There's a guardrail, but vandals had broken it earlier. Denise slipped into the river." His breath caught in his chest, and Jessica wrapped her arms around him.

"And you've been suffering with this ever since?"

Dan pulled back. His jaw tightened. "Why shouldn't I? I was the idiot who went in alone. I didn't even have enough sense to tell her if I didn't come out, to go for help, not to come looking. The worst part of it is that in her death, she saved my life."

"How?"

"A couple of hunters found Denise's body downstream. It didn't take search and rescue too long to figure out what had happened, so they checked the cave and found me huddled against the cave wall, babbling like an idiot, in complete shock."

"I'm so sorry," Jessica said.

"I caused her to die, and she caused me to live. My brother calls it a Christ act."

"A what?"

"A Christ act," Dan said. "It's when someone dies to save someone else. That was supposed to comfort me or something. It didn't."

Jessica sat back and let Dan collect his thoughts as he stared out the window, watching the rain. She wished there were some way she could reach into his heart and take away his pain. Only time and love could heal him.

As though daydreaming, he said, "After the doctor released

me, I went to Prince George to arrange for a leave of absence. Her family lives in Red Deer, so the funeral was going to be there."

Jessica said, "That's when you got caught up in the ER crisis and had the drug mix-up."

"Right. That's why the review committee cleared me. It was amazing that I was able to function at all. For about six months after that, I suffered from blackouts."

Jessica shook her head, wondering. "You've always been so calm, so self-assured." She hated to ask but had to know. "Are you having blackouts again?"

Dan shook his head. "Not like before. This situation has dug up a lot of old pain. When Carrington started in on me back at the clinic, I felt like the room was closing in on me, and I felt that dry, gritty feeling in my throat like I felt in the cave. That's the way I used to feel when I was about to have a blackout." He looked at her, trying to make her understand. "I remember everything that happened today. Some parts of it I was on autopilot, but I knew what was happening."

Jessica dug her cell phone out of her purse. With everything Dan had just told her, there was one thing she had to do.

"Who are you calling?" he asked.

"Roger Pronger, the news director at WTV."

Dan's face paled. "Why are you calling him?"

Jessica smiled.

"WTV," a woman's voice said through the phone.

"It's Jessica. Let me talk to Roger."

A moment later a man's gruff voice came on. "Pronger here."

"Hi, Roger, it's Jessica."

"Jessica. Where are you? You know you're doing the late-night spot?"

"I can't, Roger. I'm onto something big here."

Dan tensed.

"What have you got?" Pronger demanded.

"Dan Foster is innocent, and I need the time to prove it. I've got six weeks of unused vacation and two weeks of sick time. I'm going to take off from work to follow through on this," she told him.

"What?" Pronger shouted.

"I'll be back when I'm finished with this story."

"Jessica, you know it doesn't work like that," Pronger said. "You can't disappear from the airwaves for two months just like that."

"Watch me," Jessica said. "My friend needs help, and I'm going to give it to him." She flipped the phone shut and smiled at Dan. It sure felt good to call the shots on Pronger for a change.

"Jessica, what did you just do?"

"I think I might have just quit my job," she said, dropping the phone into her handbag. She felt better every minute.

"Why'd you do that?"

Peering into his eyes, she leaned forward, her voice strong. "You are my very best friend, and I'm not going to let them lynch you. Whoever killed Beth Martin has messed with the wrong people. We're going to stick together until we get him. Or her."

Chapter
Eight

An hour later, piloting her Porsche out of Denny's parking lot, Jessica had an urge to run home and sprawl on her couch with a cup of sweet herbal tea, just so she could digest everything she'd learned. She'd have to postpone that luxury until later, though. Dan Foster was in no shape to be left alone.

She shifted the car up a gear. "What now?" she asked. "You want to catch a movie or something?"

Dan glanced at his watch. "It's just after six. Too early for a movie." He rubbed his hand over his chin. "Let's work our way over to Fraser Highway. There's something I need to take care of. Chelsea's sure to have heard what's happened to me. I need to tell her that someone will take care of her after Christmas."

Jessica sent him a small smile. "Don't be such a pessimist. We're going to uncover Beth Martin's murderer long before Christmas."

Ten minutes later they turned off Fraser Highway onto Potter Road. Two blocks away they spotted the flashing lights of emergency vehicles. Dan strained forward, trying to see what was happening.

"They're at 804," Dan said. "That's Chelsea's house."

Jessica parked in front of the yellow bungalow. As soon as

the wheels stopped turning, Dan was out of the car and down the sidewalk. Jessica hurried after him. In spite of her high heels and narrow leather skirt, she reached the front door seconds after he did. The brown panel door stood ajar, and sounds of a commotion came from inside.

A woman's shrill voice cried, "She's dead, isn't she? So much blood! Oh, Chelsea!"

Dan pushed inside the house and jogged down the central hall, looking into doors as he passed. He spotted Marion Burke in a small bedroom and dashed inside. At the adjoining bathroom door, two white-uniformed paramedics knelt beside Chelsea's pale form. A blue blanket covered her torso, and an oxygen mask covered her face.

Tears streaming down her cheeks, Marion rushed over to him. "Dr. Foster! Thank God!" She latched onto his arm. "Chelsea tried to kill herself. She's bleeding, and they can't get it stopped!"

He moved toward the emergency team. "I'm a doctor," he said, puffing a little from his sprint. "What's happening?"

A Hispanic paramedic with bushy black hair told him, "She cut her wrist, and she's bleeding out." The name on his badge said *Rodriguez*. Blood had soaked through the dressing he squeezed against her arm and puddled on the floor beneath her.

"Vital signs?" Dan asked, bending down near her hair. She was unconscious, her head lolling to one side.

"What have you got, Joe?" Rodriguez nodded toward the other paramedic, a clean-cut man with chocolate brown skin.

"BP one hundred over sixty," Joe responded. "Heart rate fifty-five and thready, respirations six and shallow. She was doing it right if you know what I mean."

Dan did know what he meant. There were two ways to slit your wrist—one way if you only wanted attention and another way if you meant business. Chelsea hadn't been fooling. He pulled down the girl's lower eyelid to check the color inside. Pale pink. There wasn't any time to lose.

Joe finished setting up an IV and lifted a saline bag that hung on his index finger. "Let's roll," he said.

"Wait a minute," Dan said. "How far is it to the hospital?"

"Fifteen minutes," Rodriguez answered.

Dan focused on the wound. At the rate she was bleeding, she'd be gone in another five minutes, ten at the most. "Do you have any surgical tools?" he asked.

"Just a basic kit," Rodriguez said. "It's in the box." He nodded toward his medical tool chest.

"Get it out," Dan said. "She won't make it to the hospital. I'm going to have to operate here."

Still holding the IV bag, Joe reached into the kit box and drew out two latex gloves. He handed those to Dan along with a rolled-up cloth. Dan pulled on the gloves and opened the sterile cloth kit. He placed it beside Chelsea's still form. A scalpel, a needle, and some sutures. Not fancy but adequate.

Joe handed Dan a length of limber rubber tubing. Dan wrapped it around Chelsea's forearm and pulled tight. "Okay, you can let go," he told Rodriguez.

The gash was jagged. With the dexterity of his craft, Dan cleansed the wound with water from another saline bag and repaired the artery. According to protocol, the external sutures would be applied at the hospital.

"Wow," Rodriguez said. "That was awesome."

Dan wasn't ready to break out the champagne and throw confetti just yet. Chelsea's face was the color of chalk, her breathing labored. "Okay, let's get moving," he said, standing. He peeled off bloody gloves and threw them into the metal bathroom garbage can.

"You got it," Joe said. He and Rodriguez moved Chelsea to

a stretcher, lifted it to engage the wheels, and whisked her out of the bedroom.

Dan hustled after them and drew up short when he saw Jessica with her arm around Marion Burke. "Follow us to the hospital," he said. "Bring Ms. Burke along, okay?"

"Sure, Dan," Jessica said. "We'll be right behind you." Jessica hurried after the stretcher with Marion wheezing along behind her, trying to keep up. By the time the paramedics had Chelsea inside the ambulance, Jessica fired up the Porsche. The hundreds of willing horses under the hood leapt forward, pressing the ladies back into their seats. Once they reached Fraser Highway, the speedometer crept up to one hundred and ten kilometers an hour, but Jessica held her foot steady. She was determined to keep up with the wailing vehicle in front of her.

Suddenly, dark clouds from the west let loose a torrent of rain as only a West Coast storm off the ocean could do.

Grim-faced, Jessica switched on the wipers. They batted sheeting water to one side, then the other. She eased off the accelerator.

"I shouldn't have gone out," Marion cried, holding a shredded tissue to her face. Her arms shook like she had a chill.

Jessica reached forward and turned on the heater. "What do you mean?" She flipped open her glove box, got out a package of fresh tissues, and handed them to the woman beside her.

Taking a moment to mop her face and blow her nose, Marion said, "When Dr. Foster promised to repair Chelsea's face, she was floating on a cloud. I warned her to keep it to herself, but she couldn't wait. She told the kids at school. She told everyone in the neighborhood."

Marion dabbed her eyes again. "Most of the kids were happy for her."

"Most?" Jessica asked, braking for another light.

"Hillary Johnson wasn't one of them. Hillary's mission in

life is to remind Chelsea that she is gorgeous and Chelsea isn't. Hillary phoned this morning to let Chelsea know that Dr. Foster had killed one of his patients, and Chelsea would be ugly forever."

Jessica gripped the steering wheel until her fingers turned white. She wanted to say something acid about Heartless Hillary, but she stifled the impulse. Jessica had her own ghosts.

"I was surprised at how well Chelsea took it," Marion went on. "She just shrugged and said that God would work it out. She went to her room to read a book and didn't talk about it again. No tears. No nothing.

"I checked on her every half hour, and she really was reading a book. When I asked her if she wanted to talk, she smiled and said everything was going to be okay, that God would look after her." Marion raised both hands and chopped them down. "How could I have been so stupid? She couldn't have been any clearer if she'd written it out for me."

"What did she mean?" Jessica asked.

"In heaven there's no pain, no tears. Chelsea was telling me she was going to go home to God where there's no more suffering. I thought everything was okay, and I went out to get some groceries." Another spasm of sobbing shook her.

Jessica squeezed Marion's arm. "You can't blame yourself."

Marion gasped. "God gave that child to me to look after. I failed Him."

"No one's failed yet. God brought Dr. Foster along at just the right time. God's still looking after Chelsea."

In the ambulance, Dan touched Chelsea's cheek. She was cold, her skin bleached. He checked her vitals again. Blood pressure was sinking fast. She needed blood in a hurry.

"How much longer?" he asked Rodriguez beside him.

"Three minutes by my watch."

Dan turned to the paramedic beside him. "She's got a rare blood type—O negative. Call ahead and have the ER check to see if they have any of that type on hand. If not, I'm also O negative, and I'm willing to donate. They should be prepared to take a sample for cross-matching when we walk in the door."

Rodriguez lifted his cell phone.

A five-foot-tall, needle-bearing technician met Dan at the emergency room desk. Dan recognized his scorching red hair instantly: Joshua Kelly, a former coworker.

"How's it going, Dan the Man?" Josh asked. He tore open an alcohol swab as Dan bared his arm. "This will hurt you more than it does me," he said, grinning. He reached for the needle and popped off the plastic top. "I hear you've been having your share of troubles lately," he said, his tone casual as he watched the vial filling up.

"Nothing serious," Dan said. "Mostly a misunderstanding."

Josh didn't say more, and Dan let the conversation die.

"Run, don't walk," Dan told him when Josh shoved the purple stopper into the tiny vial. "That girl needs blood stat."

Josh rushed away, his tray of vials and fresh needles swaying at his side.

At that moment, Jessica hurried in. Gasping for breath, Marion was five steps behind her. "Where is she?" Jessica asked.

Dan nodded toward Bay Six at the other end of the hall. Marion hurried past them to join Chelsea.

Dan told Jessica about the rare-blood shortage at the hospital. "They should have the results in five minutes," he said.

The phone at the nurse's station jangled, and a smooth-faced male nurse picked it up. He spoke and set down the receiver. "Dr. Foster," he said, "if you'll step down to Bay Six, the nurse is ready to start the transfusion."

Dan didn't wait to be told twice. He pulled back the green

curtain and darted inside as the angular nurse released the railing on a gurney next to Chelsea's bed and let the metal bar swing down.

She turned to Dan. "Hello, Dr. Foster," she said. "Please get on the gurney."

Dan climbed aboard the gurney and relaxed against the pillow. The nurse tightened a rubber hose above his right elbow and swabbed the area with alcohol. In minutes—and with surprisingly little pain—she had the transfusion going. Dan closed his eyes and felt life flowing from him to Chelsea.

In a few minutes, Chelsea's breathing returned to normal. Her cheeks turned their normal peach color. As he watched her return from the threshold of death, Dan knew that he would be connected to this girl for the rest of his life.

Jessica hung back during the transfusion. She strolled to the waiting room outside and found a comfortable seat in the corner. She had to talk to Chelsea when the girl was stable. Closing her eyes, listening to the beating of her own heart, Jessica faced her own battle with beauty in a whole new way, looking back instead of ahead.

Half an hour later, she returned to Bay Six and found Chelsea awake and sullen. Marion hovered over her, holding her hand and making soothing noises. Dan sat on the gurney looking pale and a little sick.

"Are you okay?" Jessica asked Dan. "You don't look too good."

"They're bringing me some orange juice and a cheese sandwich," he said. He tried out a smile. "Don't worry. This is a normal reaction. I'll be fine in a few hours." He slid off the gurney. "I'm going to find the little boy's room while the nurse brings the food." He trudged away.

"I'm awful thirsty," Chelsea murmured. "Can you get me a pop or something?"

"Sure, Honey," Marion said, stroking the girl's damp hair. "I'll get it right away." Lifting her tote-bag purse, she lumbered away.

"Hi," Jessica said, moving close to Chelsea's bed.

Chelsea stared for a moment, then recognition lit up her blue eyes. "You're Jessica Meyers." Her eyes widened with fear. "Was I on the news? Does everyone know?"

Jessica clasped the girl's limp hand. "No one knows. But it will probably be on the news sooner or later. There's not much anyone can do about that."

Chelsea grimaced.

"I'm glad you didn't succeed, Chelsea," Jessica said, "because I owe you an apology."

"Me?" Chelsea asked, staring. "I've never even met you before."

Jessica leaned against the safety rail, talking intently. "When I was in high school, I zeroed in on girls. . .like you. . . and made their lives miserable. There was one particular girl named Candace. She had horrible acne. I used to call her maggot face. It caught on, and before long everyone called her that." Jessica's eyes moistened. "Candace wasn't as lucky as you," she said. "No one found her in time."

Chelsea's mouth sagged for a second. "She killed herself?"

Jessica nodded. "I might as well have given her the pills myself. I can never apologize to Candace, but I can to you. I'm sorry there are girls like me out there who don't know what true beauty is. Marion Burke is beautiful, Chelsea. She loves you as though you were her own. Beauty isn't what we wear on the outside. It's what we are inside."

"I've heard that one a million times."

"It may sound shallow, but it's true. We show true beauty

not by how we look, but by what we do. Beautiful people care about others. Ugly people care only about themselves."

Chelsea turned her head away. "You don't have to live with this face every day."

Jessica walked around the bed and spoke to her again. "Dr. Foster will find a way to do your surgery, or someone else will do it. Have no doubt on that score. He'll pay for it himself if he has to. Dr. Foster is a beautiful person. When the surgery's over, you will be beautiful on the outside, Chelsea. The question is, will you be beautiful inside, too?"

Chelsea looked into Jessica's face, they made a connection.

"Marion Burke loves you more than her own life. When you tried to kill yourself, you drove a knife into her heart. Will you be beautiful enough to endure life's cruelties and love her as she loves you?"

Chelsea's face crumpled, and tears started to flow. Jessica took that as a sign that somehow or other, everything was going to be all right.

Chapter
Nine

Enjoying a bright and chilly Tuesday morning, Dan Foster cradled a travel mug of hot coffee between his hands and lounged against a pillar on his porch. He breathed deeply, enjoying the crisp smell of fall. Autumn was his favorite time of year.

The satisfaction from saving Chelsea's life lifted his depression. No matter what had happened earlier or what might happen later, today was a good day.

He glanced at his watch. Jessica told him she'd pick him up at ten, and it was already a quarter past. Dan was anxious to start some serious digging into Beth Martin's murder.

The throaty rumble of Jessica's car reached him from down the street. Dan smiled as the sports car stopped in front of his house. Jessica looked sharp, dressed in a tan suede blazer with a white turtleneck sweater and black wool slacks.

"What kept you? I was starting to worry."

A mischievous grin crept across her face. "Oh, I had a little errand to run." She shifted the car into gear and started down the street. "I had to stop by Chelsea's school. It took longer than I expected."

"Is Chelsea okay?"

Jessica chuckled lightly. "She's fine. I visited Ms. Hodgkins, Chelsea's principal. We had a little chat about Hillary."

Dan was all ears. "What happened?"

"Ms. Hodgkins has been very aware of Hillary and her relationship to Chelsea. Unfortunately, the way the schools are run nowadays, there's little the principal can do to make Hillary stop tormenting Chelsea. Ms. Hodgkins has tried detention. She's written notes to Hillary's parents. Nothing has worked."

"You mean you stood me up for a wasted trip?"

Jessica smiled like a silky cat caught with her paw in the birdcage. "Oh, it wasn't wasted. Ms. Hodgkins mentioned that Hillary wants to work in television. So we set her up."

Dan shifted in his seat so he could get a better look at her. "Now you're getting my attention."

Jessica swept a strand of strawberry-blond hair behind her ear. "The principal sent for Hillary and told her that I'd agreed to talk about her career goals, then Ms. Hodgkins left us alone."

"You didn't talk about her career, did you?"

"Oh, absolutely we did," Jessica said. "The girl is a knockout brunette. She has good poise, talks well, and she'd have no problem making it in broadcast journalism.

"I told her that Chelsea's a close personal friend of mine, and I knew that Hillary had been tormenting my friend. I made it clear that Hillary had better lay off Chelsea or she'd never appear in front of a TV camera. She had my personal guarantee."

She shifted down for a turn. "I figured for Chelsea's sake, you wouldn't mind if I was a little late."

"Not a bit," Dan said. "Now all we have to do is figure out who killed Beth Martin so I can make Chelsea's Christmas dream come true."

"Let's get started," Jessica said and piloted the Porsche to the Langley Bypass.

In Seattle, the lunch crowd at the Emerald Cafe was in full

force. Celine Dion's latest hit crooned in the background, almost drowned out by the lunchtime conversation. Lots of noise was good.

Louise Crossfield had a plate of chicken wings in front of her and was washing it down with draft beer. Mike Foster munched on a grilled chicken-breast sandwich, a tall root beer close by.

Ricky Federico, the reason for their Tuesday lunch meeting, was a two-time loser who promised to help Louise and Mike into the drug ring. Ricky wiped burger juice off his gaunt face with a napkin. His cheekbones jutted out above sunken cheeks. His bulbous eyes focused on Mike.

"Patti, I don't think I can get this guy in," Ricky said.

Patti was Louise's street name. Mike's alias was Arnie. Louise named him. She figured that since he was built like Schwarzenegger, the name fit.

"Why not?" Patti asked.

Ricky shrugged. His Mariners sweatshirt hung loose about his body. "He's got the face and clothes of a biker," Ricky said, staring at Mike, "but look at the way he eats. No booze, low-fat diet. What kind of pusher eats like that?"

Louise slouched back in her chair and looked directly at Mike. "He's got a point. You don't smoke, and you don't drink. They're going to spot you for a narc right off."

Mike finished chewing a piece of lettuce and set down his fork. "Let me tell you a story."

Louise's mouth twisted. "Not another one. Sitting with you is like being in Sunday school. I've heard enough sermonizing to last me twenty years."

"Hey, I like stories," Ricky said. He took one more bite of his half-finished burger and pushed his plate away.

"In Holland during the Second World War," Mike said, "there was a family named Ten Boom."

"Pretty explosive bunch," Ricky said, lifting his mug.

Ignoring Ricky's wisecrack, Mike went on, "Anyhow, this family hid Jews in their home. They had a hiding place behind a false wall upstairs. One day, the family's niece, Cocky, and her two brothers were visiting the Ten Boom home. Soldiers showed up looking for the boys. There was no time for them to get upstairs, so the boys hid in a trap door under the kitchen table. When one of the soldiers asked Cocky where the boys were, she said, 'They're under the table.' "

Louise and Ricky watched him as though doubting his intelligence.

"Why on earth would she do that?" Louise asked.

"She was a Christian. She thought lying was a sin, so she told the truth."

"How dumb can you get," Ricky said. "They caught them, right?"

"Nope."

"They couldn't find them?" Louise asked.

"The soldiers swore at her for being such a smart aleck, and they left."

Ricky took a swig of beer. "Cool story."

"What's your point?" Louise asked.

"Sometimes the best place to hide something is in plain sight," Mike said. "Lots of times I've been asked by drug dealers if I'm a narc because I don't use. I just laugh and tell them, 'Only a dope does dope. A smart guy doesn't use, he just sells.' It works every time. Do you think those drug lords in Colombia do drugs? Do you think they let their kids do drugs? Not a chance. Why should I be any different?"

Louise leaned forward. "Makes sense to me."

Ricky wiped froth from his mouth. "You don't always tell the truth, do you?"

Mike dipped his fork into the salad. "Wait and see."

Ricky shook his head. "You're going to get us killed, Man."

Mike clamped a hand on top of Ricky's shoulder. "You worry about your job, and I'll worry about keeping us alive—got it?"

Ricky squirmed under Mike's grip. "Hey, it's your ball-game, Coach."

"What do you think you're doing here?" Dr. Cruch stood at the recovery room door, staring accusingly inside.

Jessica stepped forward, her voice pleasant. "Dan's giving me a tour of the clinic."

Cruch glanced at Dan. "For what?"

"To find out what happened to Beth Martin," Jessica said.

"There's no mystery about that," Cruch said. He glared at Dan.

Dan's eyes narrowed. "Someone switched her pills. We're going to find out who."

Cruch pointed to a closed-circuit camera mounted on the wall above the entrance. "Everything's recorded on tape. I re viewed the tapes for the entire time Beth Martin was in recovery. No-body touched her pill bottle after you put it on the stand."

Jessica asked, "Would you mind if we look at the tapes?"

Cruch shrugged. "You can waste your time if you want to."

They followed the gray-haired doctor down the hallway past the nurse's station and into the main lobby. Dr. Cruch pulled out a fat ring of keys and opened a steel door on the far wall. He stood aside for Dan and Jessica to enter a small room. Just inside the door, they drew up short.

Corporal Carrington sat in front of a small TV screen. She pushed a button on a VCR, swiveled in her chair, and looked up at them. "Slumming again, Dr. Foster?" she asked.

"Yeah," Dan said, easing farther inside.

She turned her attention on Jessica. "I see you didn't take my advice."

"I can think for myself," Jessica said, following Dan.

"They'd like to see the tapes," Dr. Cruch told Carrington. "I have no objection if you don't have any."

Corporal Carrington gave a loose-wristed wave toward the only other chair in the room. "Please. Be my guest." Dan stepped aside, and Jessica took the seat. He stood behind her.

The door clanked shut as Dr. Cruch left. Dan's head jerked around at the sound. "It's going to get stuffy in here," Dan said and pushed the door open.

"I'm not too far into this," Carrington said, drawing Dan's attention to the monitor. "So far I haven't seen anyone touch the bottle of pills since Dr. Foster put them on the nightstand. I can go back if you want, or you can take my word."

"Let's go back to the beginning," Jessica said.

Carrington hit the rewind button and stopped the VCR at the point just before Dan placed the bottle of pills next to Beth. She pressed play. "You know, this can take forever at normal speed. Mind if we scan?"

Jessica looked up at Dan. "Sure," he said.

The three of them stared at the bottle on the small gray table. No one touched the bottle until Beth Martin dropped it into her jacket pocket and left the room.

Anna Carrington swung in her chair and faced them. "Well, Doctor, this is proof positive that no one had contact with that bottle from when you gave it to her until she left the hospital."

"Then the switch happened elsewhere," he said.

Carrington smirked. "Or you messed up and don't want to admit it."

"Or we missed something on there," Jessica said, nodding

at the VCR. "I'd like to watch the tapes again at regular speed."

Carrington said, "You're talking six hours of tape. I am not going to sit here all day."

"Make us copies then," Jessica told her. "Considering a man's career is being ruined here, that shouldn't be too much to ask."

Carrington shuffled some papers and stood. "Pick them up at my office in the morning," she said, lifting her shoulder bag by the strap.

"Thanks," Jessica said. She stood and turned toward Dan. "I don't know about you, but I'm starved."

"I could eat something," Dan said, a slight grin on his face. He pulled open the door, and Jessica stepped through.

"Usual place?" she asked.

"Sure."

Chapter
Ten

Outside the clinic, Jessica slipped her hand under Dan's elbow as they walked to her car.

"So," Dan said, "the tapes were a washout. What's next?"

"We follow the pills," Jessica said, her long stride matching his. "After Beth Martin left the clinic, someone switched the pills. I think it's a safe assumption that she went right home after being released, don't you?" She glanced at him. Easily five feet eleven inches, she still had to look up to Dan's six feet two.

He smiled at her. "Amy would know. She was driving."

"Who's Amy?"

"Amy Creighton, Beth's ward. She's a registered nurse. She lived with Beth."

"You're kidding," Jessica said.

Dan shook his head. "No. Why?"

"Dan, *hello*. The woman's ward is a registered nurse. A registered nurse could have easily snatched some Nardil and made the switch."

Dan shook his head. "Beth was like a mother to Amy. She took Amy in when her parents died. If you saw them together, you'd know Amy had nothing to do with Beth's death."

As they reached the car, Jessica asked, "How can you be so

sure about Amy's feelings for Beth?" She reached into her pocket for her key chain. "You've only seen her game face."

"Game face?"

"Sure," Jessica said, pulling the door open. "Everyone has several faces. Whenever you saw Beth and Amy together, you saw their public faces. Once they were alone, it could have been a completely different story. Haven't you ever known someone who you thought was a great guy only to learn later that he had beaten his wife?"

Dan nodded thoughtfully. "I see what you mean. Still, I can't believe it. Amy's a sweet kid."

Jessica slid into her seat, and Dan followed suit. "Dan, oh Dan, you are a wonderful surgeon but a terrible judge of human nature. Killers don't wear a red 'K' on their foreheads. Sure, the girl could be innocent. But at the very least, we should talk to her."

"Okay. I guess even if Amy wasn't involved, she could still help us trace that pill bottle. Maybe they made a stop on the way home. Maybe Beth had visitors. Amy's the only one who'll know now."

Jessica urged the car out of the parking lot. "Tell me, whose idea was it to have wine and cheesecake with Thanksgiving dinner when Beth died? Amy's?"

"Actually, no," Dan said. "It was Rocky's idea."

"Another mysterious person, eh? Who's Rocky?"

"Beth's nephew. Amy doesn't care for him much." Dan brightened. "If I remember correctly, Rocky was supposed to bring pumpkin pie for dessert. Instead he brought cheesecake and wine."

"No kidding," Jessica said. "He probably knew about Beth's allergies, too."

"Probably," Dan said. "I'll bet he switched the pills! When they didn't react with the antihistamines, he brought the cheesecake and wine to speed up the process."

She nodded and said, "If he inherits her estate, we've got ourselves a good suspect." She drove for a few minutes in silence.

"How would he switch the pills?" she asked after a moment. "You said yourself Nardil looks nothing like amoxicillin. Even if Beth didn't know the difference, surely Amy would."

Dan said, "Even if she didn't know what Nardil looked like, she'd surely know what amoxicillin looks like."

"Unless they're working together," Jessica said, her brain waves humming.

Dan shook his head. "Amy and Rocky? Not a chance. She loathes him."

Jessica turned into Denny's parking lot. "I'm starved. Would you settle for a hamburger?"

"You're on," Dan said. "I didn't eat any breakfast, and I can't remember if I had dinner last night or not."

"Say, you are in bad shape," she said, laughing. "I thought Aunt Elinor took better care of you than that."

"Ha!" he burst out. "In the first place, Elinor just got in from Colorado last night. In the second place, she isn't the motherly type. The only thing I've ever seen her cook is toaster pastries. And even those don't come out so great."

"Sounds like my kind of lady. I'll have to take her out to lunch sometime so we can get better acquainted."

They met twenty-five people coming out of the restaurant and had to wait on the sidewalk for the doorway to clear out—the end of the lunch crowd. When Dan and Jessica entered the dining room, they were practically alone.

Wendy appeared in front of them with two plastic menu holders in her arm. "Good afternoon, Ms. Meyers," she said, beaming. "This way, please." She led them to a corner booth.

"We don't need to look at a menu," Dan told the waitress.

"We'll both have the hamburger plate with fries and a giant cola."

"Coming right up," Wendy said. She hurried away.

As soon as the girl was out of earshot, Jessica leaned forward and said, "Dan, I've been wondering about Peter Martin's death. Is that case connected to this one?"

Dan gave her a slanted grin. "Slow down, Girl. You're giving me a headache." He tapped his empty shirt pocket. "I wish I had my notepad. I ought to be taking notes."

Wendy brought their frosty drinks, placed two straws on the table, and left.

He grew serious. "I wonder if Carrington has thought about any of this."

Jessica smirked. "Carrington's famous for her tunnel vision. I wish you hadn't drawn her for the member in charge."

"According to my brother, she should be passing this off to another member. I think she's got a grudge against me."

"That's all we need." Jessica's cell phone rang. "I bet that's Roger."

She flipped the phone open. "Jessica," she said.

Roger Pronger's voice boomed into her ear. "Am I glad I found you!"

"What is it, Roger?" she asked. She sent Dan a look that said, *I figured this.*

"It's Ted Dhillon," Pronger said. "He was in a car accident. He's in the hospital."

"Is he going to be all right?" she asked.

"Eventually," Pronger said. "His face is badly bruised, his right arm and leg are broken. He's going to be on sick leave for at least six weeks." He paused. "I guess you know why I'm calling."

"You want me to come back."

Panic tightened Dan's features.

Pronger said, "We're in a real bind here. Ted was going to move into your slot until you came back. We can't run with two rookie anchors, Jessica. You've got to help me."

"Sorry, Roger. I have to help Dan clear his name. The cops aren't going to do it, and he's innocent."

"Not a problem," Pronger said his voice smooth and considerate. "We only need you to read. As long as you make it to the station an hour before broadcast, we'll be fine. Surely two hours out of your day won't be too much. Jessica, come on, you can't leave us swinging like this. I'll give you full pay for two hours of work."

Jessica tapped the tabletop. "I'll call you back."

His booming voice came over the airwaves. "Jessica!"

She flipped the phone closed.

"The other news anchor was in a car accident. They want me to work for two hours a day. Would you be okay with that?"

"Hey, I'm thankful for any time you can give me. I don't have to be greedy about it. Besides, I can do some of this on my own. Point me in the right direction, and I'll do the legwork."

She waited to answer while Wendy delivered their food. "Since both people died there, I'd start at Beth Martin's farm. You've got to find out who had access to that pill bottle." She picked up the ketchup bottle, then paused. "Oh, that won't work at all, will it? Amy may not want to see you."

"Probably not," Dan said, "considering everyone believes I killed Beth." He lifted his burger for a giant bite.

Jessica applied ketchup to her fries and then flipped open her phone. "You know, even a rejection can tell you things."

Dan reached for his pop, sipped, and swallowed. "Like what? How it feels to be tossed out on your ear?"

"She might do that," Jessica said, "but then again she might not. It depends on how guilty she is. I'd love to see her reaction to you."

Dan stared at his burger. "What do I say? 'Hi! Thought I'd drop over and see if I can find any evidence about who really killed Beth—like you, maybe?' "

"You say, 'Hi, I came over to offer my condolences.' " She gave him a firm look. "You're not guilty. Don't act like it." She returned to her cell phone and punched in Pronger's number. "Soon as we're finished here, we've got to go. I have to drop you off, then go home, do my hair, and change." She lifted the phone to her ear. "You're a big boy. You can handle Amy Creighton."

Dan sighed. "I'm afraid she's going to handle me."

Jessica listened for the first ring. "Just keep one thing in mind when you visit her."

"What's that?"

"Don't let her pretty face fool you," she said. "Even sweet girls kill."

After Jessica's pep talk, Dan figured he'd best go ahead and face Amy. Just before three o'clock that afternoon, he traveled down Vye Road near the US-Canada border and approached the Martin farm. The closer he got, the more he felt like he'd downed a plate of Mexican jumping beans instead of a hamburger for lunch.

He slowed the Grand Marquis and turned onto the Martin lane. The entrance had a steel-bar gate that was rarely closed. Now was no exception. He drove his car through and heard the crunch of crushed gravel under his tires. Dan noticed that most of the other homes in the area had paved driveways, but Peter Martin never spent money on a luxury like asphalt.

His mouth grew dry as he coasted toward the single-story house. Its ragged cedar siding badly needed staining. Peter Martin had no use for anything related to outward adornment. That was probably why the old farmer had little use for Dan.

It must've galled him to know that Dan improved people's outward appearance and made more money than Peter could ever hope to make.

Best-case scenario, Amy would politely ask him to leave. Dan had a sudden vision of Amy inviting him in, then slamming the door as he stepped across the threshold so he'd end up with a broken nose.

Near the side door to the house, Dan shifted into park. He got out of the car but stopped before he closed the door. Why hadn't he thought of it before? He'd been so focused on his own nightmare that he hadn't considered what all this meant to Amy. She could be like a deer in a hunter's sights. And she didn't have a clue.

The jumping beans settled down. Amy could slam the door in his face if she wanted to. He'd keep on knocking until she heard him out. If someone had murdered Peter and Beth, Amy could be next.

Slamming the car door closed, he took the steps up to the door two at a time and banged on the chipped white paint. There was no answer. He knocked again, louder. No answer.

Maybe she saw him pull in. Maybe she was too angry to see him. Then again, she might not be at home. Maybe Kurt knew where she was.

Dan skipped down the steps and headed around the house. Behind it lay the barn, two sheds, and the farmhand's cottage. Dan glanced down at his gleaming Gucci loafers. Not exactly footwear for gravel driveways and farmyards.

The barn was a towering structure covered with steel siding and a steel roof. Its sides were a solid red, the roof bright white. No expense spared there. About a hundred yards south of the barn stood the hay shed, a massive structure comprised of posts thirty feet tall that supported a steel roof. Below lay dozens of round hay bales.

Off of the barn stood a corral built of heavy rough lumber. At the end of it, facing north, was the cattle chute where Peter Martin had died. Approaching the barn, Dan wondered about Jessica's killer-bull theory. He still had a hard time believing it. Farming was one of the most dangerous occupations in Canada. Peter Martin was probably just another farming accident.

A couple of hundred feet to the left stood Kurt's cottage. Like the house, paint was a stranger to it. With gray siding and asphalt shingles curled up at the ends, it was a sad affair. Dan suspected that Kurt had limited job skills if he'd put up with Peter Martin.

He started toward the cottage, then froze and slowly looked down. So much for his shoes. He thought of swearing, then chuckled. How did he imagine that he could be a great detective if he couldn't even watch where he was stepping? He rubbed his shoe sole in the grass and trudged on. The next instant a woman's scream had him racing toward the barn.

Finished with her first scan-through of that evening's news stories, Jessica glanced up at the clock. Still an hour before airtime. She picked up the phone and called Dan's home number.

"Foster residence," a shrill voice answered.

"Ms. Foster?" Jessica asked. "This is Jessica Meyers. Is Dan at home?"

"Why, hello, Dear. Dan hasn't been back since you picked him up this morning."

"I dropped Dan off at the house after lunch. You must have missed him."

"I've been painting in my room all day," Elinor said. "I just happened to be in the boys' kitchen when I heard their phone ring. So I picked it up." Her voice grew animated. "I've been meaning to ask you to have lunch with me at D'Evereau. They always hold a lunch table for me. We haven't had time for any girl talk yet, Dear."

"I'd love to, Ms. Foster, but I'm not sure about my schedule for the next few days. Dan and I are working on something. Can I let you know when I have time?"

"Call me Elinor," the older woman said, a smile in her voice. "Ms. Foster sounds like an old woman." She laughed. "We'll be in touch then, Dear. I'll let Dan know you called."

"Thanks," Jessica said. "Good-bye."

"No problem, Dear. Good-bye."

Jessica pressed down the receiver knob, then lifted her finger and waited for a dial tone. She called Dan's pager and left a numeric message. Dan had a cell phone, but he never turned it on. He only kept it to return emergency calls. He said if he used it, then the one time he really needed it, the battery would probably be dead.

She returned to her computer and pulled up the news stories about Peter Martin's death. The coroner's report was clear: Martin died from massive trauma to the chest after being trampled by a bull.

She scanned the copy. *Interesting that Amy Creighton found his body*, she thought. *That meant both Peter and Beth died when Amy was nearby.*

Jessica's bottom lip disappeared between her teeth. What did Amy do? Flash her pretty blue eyes at the bull and say, "Please trample Peter for me this afternoon"? Lots of beautiful women talked men into killing for them, but persuading a two-thousand-pound bull would be a first.

Jessica made a note. She had to start with that bull. Was there any way to get an animal like that to kill someone? Some drug, maybe? A veterinarian who dealt with farm animals would know. She remembered an old friend from her university days. If she remembered correctly, he grew up on a farm and had been studying to be a vet. What was his name? She couldn't bring it to mind.

Connecting to the Internet, Jessica retrieved the yearbook of her undergraduate class. Everything was on the Internet now. Just ten years ago, the same information would have taken a full day of legwork. Today she had it in minutes.

She scanned the pictures until she came to a freckly, red-headed guy with a pug nose: Eldon Lipke. She did another search and found a Lipke Veterinary Clinic in upscale Kitsilano. There were no farm animals in that part of Vancouver. Apparently Eldon's love for cows and pigs died somewhere along the way. She punched his number into the phone.

A young woman's voice answered, "Lipke Veterinary Clinic."

"May I speak with Eldon, please?" Jessica'd learned from experience—if you wanted to talk to a doctor, use his first name and maybe the receptionist would think you were a personal friend instead of a client wanting over-the-phone advice.

"May I ask what this is regarding?" the receptionist asked. Polite but firm.

"I'm an old college friend of his. Tell him Jessica Meyers is calling."

"Jessica Meyers as in WTV Jessica Meyers?" A hint of skepticism came into her voice.

"Yes, Jessica Meyers from WTV. He'll want to talk to me." She hoped.

"Hold, please."

Pop music came over the line.

Three minutes later, a deep male voice said, "Jessica! Is that really you?"

"Sure is, Eldon," she said.

"Wow. Great to hear from you. Got a sick puppy or something?"

Jessica chuckled. "No, Eldon. Actually, this is probably going to sound really dumb, but I was wondering if you could tell me something."

"Shoot," he said.

"Is there a drug that would make a bull aggressive?"

Eldon's laughter sailed through the phone lines. "We use drugs to calm them down, not charge them up."

"You mean there's no way to get a bull to, say, kill someone?"

"If you put it that way, I guess there could be."

Jessica tightened up on the receiver. "Really? How?"

His voice held a hint of something she couldn't quite identify when he said, "Meet me for coffee, and I'll tell you."

Chapter
Eleven

The scream came from the direction of the barn. Another high-pitched wail followed the first. It had an eerie tone that started shrill and ended with a howl. And it sounded like Amy's voice.

Dan charged toward the barn. Rounding the corner, he dashed through the open double doors. Just inside, he stopped short, his toes digging into the dust.

"You brute!" Amy shouted, her back to Dan. Wearing faded jeans and a green flannel shirt, she had a thin coating of dust over her, quite unlike the girl Dan Foster thought he knew. She stood on one foot next to a tractor and held the toe of her other stained sneaker.

Dan quickly scanned the barn's interior. Normally neat and trim whenever he'd been there before, it now showed signs of neglect. Tools stood propped against various posts and walls. A dented bucket lay on its side near the open silo door. Peter had kept the barn smelling of fresh straw and lime with a hint of corn silage thrown in. Today, it smelled acrid.

Dan could see no one but Amy inside the barn. The focus of her anger seemed to be the tractor tire beside her. The tire seemed to be doing fine. Amy's foot lost the battle.

Dan stepped forward. "Amy, what's going on?"

She jumped. "Dan! Oh my gosh, you scared me!"

"What's all the screaming about?"

"It's this. . .this. . . ," she pointed at the tractor, her mouth tight, her eyes flashing, ". . .this piece of *junk*."

Dan looked over the blue Ford tractor, a new hundred-and-fifty-horsepower machine with a closed cab. The tractor looked stoic as though protesting its innocence.

Dan moved closer to her. "What about it?"

Amy pushed hair from her face. Under a white cap, her long golden ponytail looked ragged and covered with dust. It had bits of straw in it. She thumped the fender with a small fist. "I can't get it started."

Dan looked in the open door of the cab. "Why are you trying to start it? Where's Kurt?"

Amy turned on him, her voice tight. "Kurt. . .that. . ." She bit down on her lip and forced calmness into her voice. "Kurt quit two days ago. The cattle need their evening hay, and I haven't got a clue about how to do it."

"Kurt quit?" Dan asked. "Why'd he do that?"

"He just up and quit. No reason, no notice, no nothing." She raised her hands. "I don't even know why I'm doing this. This isn't my worry. It's Rocky's. If he doesn't care, why should I?"

"Rocky owns the farm?" Dan asked. None of this was making sense.

Amy focused on him for the first time. "Everything's such a mess. I'm so glad you came out to help me."

Dan quickly said, "We need to talk." The last thing he wanted to deal with was an overwrought female.

Amy jerked her head toward the open doors at the end of the barn. "I've got to feed those cattle."

"Okay. I'll help you." Dan climbed into the cab and

plopped into the leather seat. The cab had air-conditioning and a sound system. The key was in the ignition. Amy hoisted herself up, resting her feet on the steps of the tractor, her back against the rear fender, watching his every move.

Dan pushed in the clutch and turned the key. The diesel motor rattled to life.

"What did you do?"

Dan shrugged. "I pushed in the clutch and turned the key."

Amy's eyebrows lowered, and she leaned into the cab, looking at the pedals on the floor. "Clutch?" she asked.

"You have never driven a manual transmission before, have you?"

She shook her head.

He pointed to the far-left floor pedal. "That's a clutch. It disengages the gears. If it isn't pressed in, the tractor won't start."

"I feel so stupid." Amy sighed. "The truth is, farming was their thing. The only part of it I liked was riding the horses."

"Well, climb in, and I'll show you how to run this beast," Dan said.

She entered the cab and perched close to Dan's seat, their sides touching. He shifted the tractor into gear and eased back on the clutch. The machine lumbered forward. Fortunately the round bale fork was already mounted on its front.

"Look here," Dan said. "This lever raises and lowers the fork."

Leaning forward against his shoulder, she said, "Actually, I don't really care. I think I'm going to take Kurt's lead and move out. Let's get the animals fed. I can't stand to think of them hungry all night. When I get back to the house, I'll call Rocky and tell him to come over and take care of his stock."

Picking up a little speed on the path to the hay shed, Dan asked, "Why is it Rocky's place? I expected that Beth would leave it to you."

"Beth had no choice in the matter. Peter made it quite clear to me that the farm would stay within the Martin bloodline whether he died first or not."

"Sounds like Peter," Dan said, easing the tractor around a wide curve. He and Amy bumped shoulders when the road grew rough.

Six-foot-high round bales lay on their sides before him. He easily speared one with the single-prong fork. The tractor lifted a bale, and Dan drove toward the field behind the barn.

"I'll open the gate for you," Amy offered when he stopped.

Moving with grace and speed, Amy climbed out and swung open the wide orange gate. When Dan drove through, she closed it behind him—a good thing, too. Bellowing cattle immediately hustled toward the tractor, converging on it from all directions.

Amy skipped into the cab with lightning speed. Gasping, she slammed the door behind her. "After what happened to Peter, I don't trust those beasts."

Fifty Jersey cattle in ages ranging from young calves to yearlings huddled around them, their white heads moving back and forth. Like calves who'd found their long-lost mother, the lowing cattle followed the tractor to a metal feeder. When Dan dropped the bale into it, they swarmed around it.

At the gate on the way back to the hay shed, Amy jumped out of the tractor to open the gate again. Instead of climbing back into the cab with him, she waved him on. She waited by the gate to open it for three more bale deliveries. After the last one, she followed the tractor to the barn.

Dan parked the tractor inside and climbed out. Amy waited by the open doors. He smiled as he approached her. "That went pretty good. I'm glad I came along at the right time." He grew serious. "Amy, we need to talk."

She looked scared. "About what?"

"About Beth."

Her lips formed a straight line. "Don't." She turned her back to him.

Dan touched her shoulder. She stiffened. "Amy, please hear me out."

She kept her back to him.

"The news media was right. I did make a mistake with medication once before. Because of it, I am extremely careful with drugs. I swear I gave Beth amoxicillin. I'm positive that I didn't make a mistake, so I know for sure. . ."

Amy turned. ". . .that someone else switched those pills?"

"That's right," he said.

Her shoulders sagged. "Beth murdered? But why? She never hurt anyone. She was good. . .the way she took me in and. . ." She swayed. Dan caught her before she collapsed to the barn floor.

Enjoying the soft Celtic music playing in the background, Jessica took a long sip of toffee cappuccino. Located near English Bay, the café was close to a popular Vancouver beach where a pod of orcas sometimes appeared. Old-timers claimed the whales used to frequent the bay, but development and shipping had pushed the creatures north to a few still-isolated inlets where they could find plenty of fish.

The massive dining room contained a life-size model of an orca hung by wires from its high ceiling. Giant pictures of whales covered the walls and the place mats. Prominently displayed coffee mugs—which patrons could purchase for five dollars—showed an orca breaking the water, soaring upward. This was one place no one mentioned whaling, even as a joke.

Jessica had arrived at the Orca Café half an hour early for her appointment with Dr. Eldon Lipke. She'd chosen a table near the back and sat facing the door.

It annoyed her that Eldon had managed to land a face-to-face meeting with her. She'd almost told him to get lost, but her calmer senses had prevailed. Jessica needed information. Eldon Lipke had it. What could a thirty-minute date over a cup of coffee hurt?

The glass doors of the café opened to reveal a tall red-haired man wearing a navy corduroy blazer. Jessica tried not to stare. Could that be Eldon? The guy she knew at the university had been lanky with a nervous walk. This broad-shouldered man strode confidently through the crowd. When he spotted her, he lifted his hand to show he'd seen her and went to the counter to purchase a cup of coffee before heading to her table.

"Jessica! Great to see you." He smiled and held out his hand. Jessica took it and noted his grip was firm but not crushing.

"Hello, Eldon."

He took the seat across from her. His freckles were only a shadow of what she remembered, and his pug nose now looked distinctive. His teeth were white and no longer crooked.

"It's good to see you," he said, grinning and at ease. "I mean, I see you almost every day on TV, but this is so much nicer."

Jessica kept her expression neutral. "I'm glad you're a fan of WTV."

"WTV? Not really. Jessica Meyers? Absolutely."

"Uh Eldon, I'm only here to. . ."

He held up his hands. "Sorry, Jessica. I'm making you uncomfortable." He sipped coffee and set down the cardboard cup. "As you've probably noticed, I'm not the same guy you knew at school."

"I'll say," she said. "It looks like a change for the better. What happened?"

He chuckled. "I call it an early midlife crisis. When I turned thirty, I was still single and hating every moment of it. It's not like I didn't have any chances to meet women. Working as a vet, I had lots of contact with young available women when they came to my office with their pets. I'd have no problem talking to the animal, but if the owner was an attractive woman, the cat really did get my tongue."

His grin turned sheepish, and for an instant Jessica saw the old Eldon. "Now I'm afraid I like the new me so much that I sometimes go too far and overwhelm my date. My personal trainer warned me this could happen."

Jessica stared. "Personal trainer?"

He nodded. "I figured the reason I was nervous around women was that I didn't have much to offer, so I decided to do something about it. I got my teeth fixed and hired a trainer. I'm talking too much. I guess I'm excited to see you, and I'm getting carried away."

Jessica resisted the urge to reach across and pat his hand. She'd been around the block a few times and had heard enough come-on lines to fill a dozen newscasts.

"I'm delighted for you, Eldon. I guess life really does begin at thirty for some people."

Still smiling, he nodded. "I guess it could begin at any age."

She lifted her coffee cup and took a sip. "I won't keep you long," she said, placing the cup carefully on the veneer table-top. "Let's get down to the main question. How could someone get a bull to turn into a killer?"

Eldon grinned like a bad boy caught with the cookie jar. "He'd use a cow in heat."

"What!"

"The one thing that drives a bull crazy is a cow in heat."

He paused, his mouth quirked. "Hey, this is for a story, right? I mean, there isn't someone you plan on. . ."

"No, no." Jessica shook her head and laughed. "It's definitely for a story."

"Okay," he went on. "If I wanted to get a bull to attack someone, I'd take the urine from a cow in heat and put it on his clothes."

Jessica crinkled her nose. "That's disgusting!"

He grinned. "Not to the bull."

In the farmhouse kitchen, Dan placed a cup of hot chocolate in front of Amy. "Here, drink this."

Amy took a sip. The warmth of the house had restored some color to her cheeks. The hot chocolate would give her energy to fight off shock.

In a moment, she said in a small voice, "It's like she died all over again. I mean, I'd come to grips with her accident. But murder?" She shuddered.

Dan took the seat across from her at the oak table. "Amy, I've got to find out who did this. Beth was a good friend to me. She didn't deserve this, and I want to make sure the jerk that's responsible goes to jail. I need to ask you a few questions. Do you think you can handle it?"

Amy's finger traced the handle on her cup. "Sure," she said, her gaze on the weathered tabletop. "What do you want to know?"

"We're trying to determine who had access to Beth's pill bottle after it left the clinic."

"We're?" Amy asked, looking up. "Are you helping the police?"

He let out a wry laugh. "Hardly. I'm talking about Jessica Meyers of WTV. She's a friend of mine, and she's helping me with the investigation."

Amy looked doubtful. "Dan, I'm not sure I want a reporter involved in this. They always blow everything out of proportion."

"I can assure you Jessica won't do that. She's the only one who's given me a fair shake in the media. Besides, I know nothing about investigating. Without her help, I'd be lost. Beth's killer would go free. You can trust her."

"What do you want to know?"

"I've got to find out when her pills were switched. No one tampered with the pills while they were in the clinic. A closed-circuit camera recorded everything in the recovery room. If the pills were switched, it happened afterward."

He searched Amy's face for signs of guilt. He didn't see any way she could be involved in a murder plot. This girl was truly torn up over Beth's death, but he had to ask. Jessica would be all over him if he didn't. He plunged ahead. "Amy, please don't get mad, but I need to know. Why didn't you realize the pills had been switched? You're a nurse. If you didn't recognize the Nardil tablets, surely you knew they weren't amoxicillin."

Amy's lips twisted into a sad smile. "Corporal Carrington from the RCMP asked me the same question." Her fingers tightened around the grip of the cup. "She made it sound as though I had something to do with Beth's death."

"What did you tell her?"

"I told her I never saw the pills." She looked at him, pleading with him to believe her. "You know Beth. She played nursemaid for everyone else, but no one could do anything for her. She stuck the pills in her pocket when we left the clinic, and that was that. I offered to take care of her medication, but she more or less told me to mind my own business. You wouldn't believe the trouble I had just keeping her in that lounge chair while the incisions healed."

"So, the pills came straight home with Beth?"

"Well, not straight home. We stopped at Overwaitea to get some groceries, but I went in alone. Beth stayed in the car." Amy paused. "You know, when I came back to the car, Beth was asleep. She hadn't locked her door. Do you think someone could have switched them then?"

Dan thought that through for a moment. "That sounds farfetched, but I suppose it's possible if someone followed you there. In any case, the switch happened before she took the first pill. I'm sure Beth would have noticed if she started out taking capsules and ended up with tablets. Whoever did this moved quickly. If not when she was asleep in the car, then here at home. Who has access to the house? Who was around when you got back?"

"Kurt has a key. Rocky visited shortly after we got home." She hesitated, then said, "Of course, there's me. I was with her constantly."

"When did Beth take her first pill?"

"As soon as we got home. I reminded her; she bristled, then went into her washroom. I assume she took them then."

"Was she ever alone?"

"About an hour after she went to sleep, Kurt asked me to help him feed the cattle. I did the same thing for him that I did for you. I held the gate. After we finished, I needed to clear my head, so I went for a short walk."

"You didn't see anyone or hear a car drive in?"

"No."

Leaning back in his chair, he hooked his elbow over the chair back. "I guess we have to figure out who gains from her death. You don't because you don't inherit the farm."

Amy looked down. "She was the closest thing I had to a mother."

Dan leaned forward to touch her hand. "I'm sorry about this, Amy. Just a few more minutes, and I'll leave you alone."

"That's all right," Amy said, clasping his hand and holding on. "I want to help."

"Does Rocky inherit everything?"

"As far as I know."

"And Kurt just took off without notice? Why would he do that, unless he was running from something?"

Amy shrugged. "He was a weirdo. I have no idea why he did anything, including why he worked for Peter all those years. He made almost nothing and had to put up with lots of abuse. Then when things started to ease up around here, he quit."

Dan pulled his hand away from hers and glanced at his watch. It was almost seven o'clock. "Look, it's getting late. I'm going to head home now. I'll talk to Jessica in the morning. She'll have some ideas about where to go from here. By the way, when is the funeral?"

Amy shrugged. "No idea. The coroner hasn't released Beth yet. I imagine it has to do with the circumstances surrounding her death."

"Probably does," Dan said. He stood, and Amy followed him to the door. Slipping into his aromatic shoes, Dan frowned at them.

"The hazards of farm life," Amy said, smiling a little.

"No kidding." Dan pulled open the door, stepped outside, then turned to face her. "Amy, I hate to mention this, but you need to be careful."

She straightened up. "Me?"

"We don't know the killer's motive or when he had opportunity. Beth may not be his only target."

Chapter
Twelve

"Cow urine! You've got to be kidding!"

Over breakfast at Denny's on Wednesday morning, Dan Foster choked and sputtered on his tea. He looked into his mug. What a morning to order tea instead of his usual coffee.

"That's right," Jessica said, digging into her ham-and-cheese omelet. The subject didn't seem to bother her at all. "My vet friend tells me there are pheromones in the urine. If it got on Peter Martin's clothes, the bull would go after him."

"You're suggesting that someone got some urine from a cow in heat and put it onto Peter Martin's clothes? Don't you think he'd notice the smell?"

Wiping her mouth with a napkin, Jessica nodded. "If he had certain clothes he wore to the barn, like a coat or something, a barn stench would've already permeated them. A little cow urine wouldn't make much difference one way or the other." She lifted her coffee. "We need to go over to the Martin farm and get the clothes he was wearing when he was killed."

"Doesn't the coroner have them?"

Jessica sipped and shook her head. "They don't keep those things unless there's a criminal case. Peter's effects would be returned to the family." She picked up her fork, then paused.

"What did you learn from Amy Creighton?"

Dan told her about his visit with Amy and ended with, "She's really shook up. I don't think she could be faking it."

"You'd be surprised," Jessica said. She lifted her hand to signal the waitress. "So, we have three suspects—Amy, Kurt, and Rocky."

Dan sipped his tea. "It's interesting that all three of them were on the property when Beth died. My money is on Rocky." He stabbed a forkful of pancake. "He inherits the farm, and he's slippery. The man is made to order."

"Hmm," Jessica said.

He paused with his fork near his mouth. "Hmm, what?"

"It's so tidy to have the least likely suspect pointing a finger at the most obvious suspect."

Dan shook his head. "You're barking up the wrong tree with Amy. You should've seen her when I told her that Beth was murdered. The kid went into shock. Besides, what does she gain? Nothing. She's not even in the will."

"True enough," Jessica said. She had her head tilted back, thinking. "Then again, you're a man. Men always want to believe a pretty girl."

"Hey," Dan said, "give me some credit. I've been around."

Jessica raised an eyebrow. "Really? Where?"

"You know what I mean," he said. "I'm not some hormone-charged teenager. Amy didn't pull a fast one on me."

"I'd like to meet Amy myself," Jessica said. "Let's drive over to the Martin farm and see about Peter's clothes. While we're there we could look through Kurt's place to see if we can find out why he ran. *If* he ran."

"What do you mean, if he ran?"

Jessica shrugged. "Maybe he's dead."

At a roadside bar near the Canadian border, Mike and Louise watched Federico saunter out. Two minutes prior, he'd introduced them to a biker named Garret, who sat at their table cleaning his fingernails with a hunting knife. Dressed in a black leather jacket, black T-shirt, and blue jeans, Garret was easily the size of Mike. The only difference was that Garret's chest sank in, and Mike had six-pack abs.

The bar sat beside the road to Mt. Baker. A few people occupied tables near the front of the room. Mike, Louise, and their new friend sat alone in a back booth with two beer steins and a glass of pop on their table. Loud country music covered up their conversation.

If Garret wasn't the direct source to the main pot supply, the trail definitely began with him. The drug dealer slid his knife into a sheath hidden in his boot. "So, you're looking for some BC Bud," he drawled, overly casual. His quick black eyes never stopped moving.

"That's right," Louise said. Before the meeting, she'd made it clear to Mike that she was in charge.

"How much are you looking for?" He pulled a metal toothpick from the back of his left leather glove and picked his tobacco-stained lower teeth.

"How much have you got?"

Garret shrugged.

"We were thinking a hundred kilos," Mike cut in.

Louise tensed. Mike ignored her. This was his element, and he felt good, like a ball player jogging onto the field while the crowd cheered.

"A hundred's not a problem," Garret said.

"To start," Mike said. He slouched against the corner of the booth, eyelids slightly closed.

Garret ran his hand over his slick black hair. "To start?"

"Right," Mike said. "We're breaking into a new market in

the Southern states. They're sick and tired of the seaweed that comes up from Mexico. We're going to distribute the first hundred kilos to check out the market. If it gets the response we think it will, we'll be looking for more. Lots more."

The biker cleared his throat. "How much more?"

"A thousand kilos."

Garret's eyes met Mike's for the first time. "A thousand?"

Mike leaned forward. "Too big a deal for you? If so, tell us now. We need a steady supply of quality BC Bud. If you're not our man, we'll find someone else."

Garret held up his hand. "Hey, I can do it."

Mike stood. By some miracle Louise followed his cue. "Make sure you do," Mike told him. "We may be the new kids on the block up here, but we're very well established down South. Mess with us, and you'll never know what hit you."

Mike turned and headed out of the bar with Louise close behind him. They stepped out into the cold air. Light snow fell around them. Hurrying across the tiny parking lot, they dived inside their car. When they were both seated, Louise grabbed the sleeve of his sheepskin jacket. Her solid grip surprised him.

Keys in hand, he turned to face her. "What's wrong? You don't look happy." White puffs came from his lips with every word.

Her eyes flashed. "This is my case. If I want you to talk, I'll tell you what to say. Got it?"

Mike smiled. "You're gorgeous when you're angry."

Louise clenched her fist, her face a mask of fury. "Don't be cute. You blew it in there."

"How did I blow it?"

"We didn't get a sample. And the idea was to make one big buy, not a small one, then a big."

Mike took a breath and let it out slowly. "We didn't get a sample because I wanted to let him know that we think he's small fish. Asking for a sample would have given him legitimacy. Now we've made it clear that we don't deal with anyone but the big players. At our next meeting, we'll see more than just him there." He shrugged. "Besides, he's an American. We need to get to the Canadians." He put the key into the ignition and turned it. The engine sprang to life.

Louise hugged her leather jacket close. "How do you know he's American?"

Mike grinned at her. "Because your average Canadian drug dealer can't help but say, *eh*, at the end of every question."

Louise glared at him. "Listen, *Cowboy*, from now on we go according to my plan."

"Sure," Mike said, putting the car in reverse. "But I've got to tell you that your plan stinks."

Staring out the front window, she drew in a long, slow breath. "I shouldn't be listening to you. . .but I am. What are you getting at?"

"These guys aren't stupid. They're going to stay in Canada no matter how much money you put on the table. There's only one way to get them across the border."

"What's that?"

Chuckling softly, he backed out of the parking space. "Let's get to someplace warm, and we'll talk it out. It's freezing out here."

Jessica wrapped her coat around her when they left Denny's restaurant. The sky was clouding over, the wind coming from the north. They didn't often get snow in the Vancouver area, but with this crispness in the air, the steely sky might dump plenty of white stuff on them, and soon. They'd come to the restaurant in her car, but it was entirely unsuitable for winter conditions.

Dan stared up at the clouds. "Maybe we should take my car," he said. "Drive me home, and we'll pick up mine."

"Good idea," she said.

They started crossing the parking lot when a voice from behind stopped them. "Dan Foster!"

Both Jessica and Dan turned to see a short, slight woman with curly blond hair. She was waving and rushing down the sidewalk toward them. Her face held heavy wrinkles.

"Friend of yours?" Jessica murmured to Dan as the woman waited for a passing car before she could cross to reach them.

"She doesn't look familiar. But from the looks of her, I could do wonders with her face."

The next moment, the woman stopped in front of them. "Boy, I'm glad I caught up with you."

"Do we know each other?" Dan asked.

The woman smiled, reached into her jacket, and produced an envelope. She shoved it at Dan. "We've never met. But you've been served."

She released the envelope, and it fluttered to the ground. "I'd pick it up if I were you," she said, then turned and walked briskly away from them.

Dan stared down at the yellow rectangle. He didn't move. The breeze lifted it, and Jessica trapped it with her black boot.

"You'd better pick it up, Dan. Ignoring it won't make it go away."

Dan reached down. Jessica released the envelope as soon as he had it in his hand. He held it by one corner.

"Open it," Jessica said, impatient. It was turning colder every minute.

Dan slid his finger into the corner and tore the envelope open. He pulled out an official-looking document. His expression tightened as he read down the page. "I don't believe this!"

"What is it?"

"Rocky Wiebe is suing me for the death of Beth Martin."

"Let me see that." Jessica took the summons from Dan's hand. There it was in black and white. Rocky had filed suit in the Supreme Court of British Columbia for the unlawful death of Beth Martin. "He doesn't want much," she said, handing him the page.

Dan's eyes widened. "Ten million dollars isn't much?"

"Hey, I was being sarcastic," she said. "The guy's dreaming. This is Canada, not the States. Even if he won, no court is going to give him that much."

Dan looked at the document. "I need a lawyer. Any suggestions?"

"I know just the man," she said. She dug her cell phone out of her purse and flipped it open. She punched in a number. There were a couple of rings before a mature woman's voice answered, "Arthur Stoll's office."

"This is Jessica Meyers," she said. "Is Arthur in by any chance?"

"Yes, he is," the receptionist said. "Hold for a moment, please."

Jessica looked up at Dan. "Let's get into the car," she said. "I'm freezing." They headed for the Porsche.

Dan held the door for her as a deep rough voice came on the line. "Jessica, nice to hear from you."

"You, too, Arthur," she said as she slid into the driver's seat. "I have a favor to ask. My friend, Dan Foster, is in a lot of trouble."

"Dan Foster?" he asked. "That's the doctor who helped you after your accident."

"Right." She glanced at Dan as he got into the passenger seat and closed the door behind him. "He's also the fellow the news has been smearing lately. They claim that he mixed up medications and killed a patient named Beth Martin. Three minutes ago a process server slapped him with a summons. Beth Martin's nephew wants ten million dollars."

Arthur's laugh reverberated in her ear. "Ten million? Where does this nephew think he is? California?"

"That's what I just told Dan. Can you see him today?"

A short pause. "Honestly, Jessica, I'm overloaded all this week and next."

Jessica glanced at Dan's worried frown. "Arthur, if it was me in trouble, could you find time?"

A nervous cough sounded in her ear. "Jessica, be nice."

"If I dug out my little book of favors, I think there are more debits than credits on my side."

"You nasty girl," he said. "Look, I do eat. Tell him to meet me at the Gallery Bar—Hyatt Regency—one o'clock."

"Thanks, Arthur," she said.

"Only for you, Jessica," he said. "But make sure you update your little book. I think I'm getting close to even."

Jessica chuckled. "Sure, Arthur. And thanks again." She flipped the phone shut and turned her attention to Dan. "He'll meet you at one o'clock at the Gallery Bar. That's at the Hyatt in Vancouver."

Dan looked at his watch. "That only gives me a couple of hours. We'll have to put off visiting the farm until later. Since you've got to do the news, I guess today is pretty much shot."

"Not necessarily," she said. "I can go to the farm while you meet Arthur."

"Don't you think we should both talk to Amy?"

Jessica's lips curved into a smile. "Actually, I think I'd enjoy dealing with Miss Amy one on one."

Fifteen minutes before one, Dan Foster stepped out from Jessica's apartment garage and hailed a cab. Concerned about the threat of snow, she'd asked Dan to take her car into the city and park it. She'd meet up with him later to return his car. It turned out to be a wise choice. The first few snowflakes fell as he reached the sidewalk. If it accumulated at all, the traffic in Vancouver would be a nightmare.

A yellow cab pulled up to the curb, and Dan climbed in. The Hyatt was close to Jessica's West End apartment, so the cab dropped him off at the hotel's front entrance five minutes later. Dan entered the lobby and headed toward the wide entrance to the Gallery Bar. The aroma of sizzling steak tickled his nose the moment he entered the restaurant.

The hostess, a young brunette, approached him. "Table for one?" she asked.

Dan paused to see if he could spot a heavy-set man with a bald head. "I'm here to meet Arthur Stoll. You wouldn't happen to know who he is, would you?"

The girl's dark eyes lit up. "Mr. Stoll? Certainly. Follow me."

She led him through the dining room toward a window where the patrons could enjoy a view of the street. Arthur Stoll sat at a corner table. He was an expansive man with jowls and a broad forehead. His dark blue suit shone like silk. When he saw Dan, he broke into a wide smile, stood, and offered his hand. "Dr. Foster, I presume?"

"Mr. Stoll." Dan shook the lawyer's hand. The ring finger and pinky on both of Stoll's hands sported gold rings clustered with diamonds. Dan hoped that wasn't an indication of the lawyer's billing structure.

Dan took a seat and noticed a menu lying next to a goblet with a folded teal cloth napkin standing in it.

"Anything to drink, Sir?" the hostess asked.

"Just coffee," Dan told her, shifting the menu aside. Since he'd received that summons, his stomach had been queasy. Besides, he'd downed three pancakes at Denny's that morning and wasn't hungry yet.

Stoll glanced out the window. "It's unusual to get snow this time of year. Looks like it's starting to get serious."

Dan looked outside. The flakes had become large and thick. Traffic would soon be snarled.

"The guys in personal injury won't mind this one bit," Stoll went on. "Lots of accidents mean lots of insurance claims."

"Actually, it's not bad weather for plastic surgeons, either," Dan said.

Stoll's gold caps gleamed in his mouth. "Really?"

"Sure. Accidents mean scarring. Since insurance is paying, guys like me get to repair the damage for a healthy fee. It's a funny world. One man's disaster is another man's blessing."

Stoll nodded. "I guess in our situation, it's my blessing and your disaster."

Dan shot the lawyer a wry grin. "That would be correct." Dan dug the summons out of the inside pocket of his wool overcoat and passed it to Stoll. "I got this a few hours ago."

Stoll slipped thin reading glasses out of his shirt pocket and put them on. He scanned the page like it was an old friend. Just like Dan's hands had sculpted hundreds of faces, this man's eyes had read thousands of such documents.

The hostess brought Dan's coffee. He added two packets of creamer while Mr. Stoll read.

After a couple of moments, Arthur Stoll lay the summons down. "I see Mr. Wiebe is represented by Zack Green."

"Is that bad?"

Arthur Stoll dropped his glasses into his pocket. "It's unethical for one lawyer to make a comment about another. Does that answer your question?"

It did. Doctors were under the same type of ethical code. "What should I do now?"

Stoll pointed at Dan's menu. "Decide on what you're going

to eat. Everything here is good." Stoll patted his stomach. "I have plenty of evidence."

Dan grinned and opened the menu. No sooner had he put the menu down than a blond waitress appeared to take their order. He suspected Arthur Stoll ate there often and tipped generously.

"I'll have my usual, Cara," Stoll told her.

"Yes, Sir." She turned her attention to Dan. "And what can I get for you?"

"Clam chowder," Dan said, "and a glass of ginger ale."

"You've had a rough go," Stoll said when the waitress hurried away. "Considering everything, you look to me like you're holding up pretty well."

"You haven't seen me at my worst."

Stoll leaned back in his chair and patted his girth. "Well, you've seen me at my worst. It's hard to believe that I was ever a trim hundred-and-seventy pounds. Hey, I don't suppose there's anything you could do to make all this go away or at least some of it?"

"You say you weren't always like this?"

He chuckled. "You should have seen me at thirty-five. For the past twenty years, it's been all uphill as far as the scales go."

Dan scanned the man's physique with a practiced eye, noting his trouble areas. "Have you been tested for thyroid problems?"

The lawyer nodded. "No problems there."

"Then I can help."

Stoll brightened. "No kidding."

"Sure. I can make several cuts in your body, vacuum out the fat, and do the same with your face. It's an expensive, painful, invasive procedure that's full of risks. After six months, you'll probably be back right where you are now." He paused, then slowly said, "There is another route, though."

"What's that?"

"Eat better and exercise."

Stoll laughed aloud. "I hear that advice morning and evening from my wife."

"You should take it."

"Getting down to business," Stoll said, "your whole case hinges on whether or not you gave that woman the wrong pills. Did you? And don't lie to me. I insist on the truth from all my clients."

"I didn't," Dan said. "I know I didn't."

Stoll rubbed his pudgy chin. "In that case, we'll need to follow the chain of custody on those pills. Who had them and when?"

Cara arrived with a tray, and the men waited for her to set their food on the table. "Anything else?" she asked, smiling at Stoll.

"Nothing now," he said. "Thank you, Cara."

She hurried away.

Breaking open a roll to apply butter, Dan said, "Well, of course, I had the pills first. They were in my locker."

"Are you sure the right pills were in your locker? Did you check inside the bottle?"

Dan nodded. "I always double-check medication." He propped his knife on the bread plate. "I dropped the bottle into my pocket. It stayed there until I delivered it to Beth Martin."

"Did anyone bump into you while they were in your pocket?"

"No. Why?"

"Pickpockets," Stoll said, sprinkling Parmesan cheese on his pasta. "A skilled pickpocket could have switched them, and you'd never suspect it."

"I would've known. I checked the bottle again before I gave it to her." He sipped a spoonful of chowder. Not bad.

"It didn't happen in the recovery room," Dan went on. "We have a surveillance camera in there. Jessica and I viewed the tape. The pills weren't touched."

"What happened after Beth Martin left the hospital?" Stoll asked, raising a forkful of pasta.

Dan gave him the details of his conversation with Amy.

Stoll frowned. "I'll have to be blunt, Foster. This doesn't look good. The only person who has a motive is the fellow who's suing you. Usually murderers avoid drawing attention to themselves. Of course, our defense will center around the fact that anything could have happened after Beth Martin left the clinic.

"Unfortunately, with your prior history of a drug mix-up, the judge is likely to give the benefit of doubt to the plaintiff. Good thing you have malpractice insurance. I doubt it covers ten million, but there's no way he'll get that." He forked in another mouthful of pasta and chewed. After he swallowed, he said, "The police have missed the real tragedy in all this."

Dan went still. "What's that?"

"If you didn't mix up the pills, then someone killed that poor woman."

Dan slammed the table. "Finally! Someone else sees that."

Patrons in the restaurant turned to stare. Dan lowered his face. "Sorry."

"Hey, that's okay. About once a year I deal with an innocent person who is facing jail knowing that a killer is going free. It's heart wrenching."

"More than likely, it's going to happen again," Dan said.

"What makes you say that?" Stoll lifted his coffee cup.

"Corporal Carrington."

The cup stopped in midjourney. He set it down. "Anna Carrington is in charge of this case?"

"That's bad, isn't it?"

"I'm afraid so. I don't think that woman understands that

it's not results but truth that matters." Stoll stroked the side of his bald head. "You know, this is a civil matter, and I was going to refer the case to one of my partners. But I don't think that's wise. I think I'd better handle this one myself."

Stoll looked directly at him. "Malpractice is nothing. You pay the money, face a disciplinary hearing, and you're back to practicing medicine. With Anna Carrington involved, I'm more interested in keeping you out of jail."

Chapter
Thirteen

Jessica skipped lunch and headed for the Martin farm-house. She knocked sharply on the door, then took a step back. Soon the door opened, and before her stood a young woman with the wholesome type of beauty often seen in a church choir or at a Sunday school picnic. No wonder Dan wanted to believe her.

"Amy Creighton?" Jessica asked.

The girl nodded, looking Jessica over.

"I'm Jessica Meyers, a friend of Dan Foster. I'm helping him find out what happened to Beth."

Amy's expression became guarded. "He mentioned you when he was here yesterday." Keeping Jessica on the step, she asked, "How do I know you're not just looking for a story?"

"I guess you don't, except that you have my word. I'm only interested in one thing—clearing Dan's name. I need your help to do that."

Amy slowly tugged the door open. "Come in." She sounded resigned.

Jessica stepped inside.

"The place is a mess," Amy said as she walked across the maple flooring in the hall. "Since Beth's death, I haven't had much interest in anything. Every time I start to clean, I see her. . . ."

Jessica followed Amy past a wide doorway that led to the living room. She paused to glance inside—the furniture was old, the wallpaper out of date. The only new furniture was a royal blue recliner, wide and deep with massive pockets on the sides for magazines.

Jessica nodded toward the room. "Mind if I have a look around in here?"

Amy paused at the end of the hall. "Why?"

"To be honest, I have no idea what I'm looking for. If I look around, I might see something that'll lead to a clue."

"That's the same furniture we had in there when she. . . died. I cancelled delivery on the furniture she'd ordered. I couldn't bear to have it here after. . ." She broke off and turned away. Over her shoulder, she said, "Look around all you want. I'll be in the kitchen." Three strides later, she disappeared through a swinging door at the end of the hall.

Jessica entered the living room. The hardwood floor had a path worn across the finish in high-traffic areas. The sofa cushions were lumpy, the fabric threadbare.

The center-most piano keys had the ivory worn off in some places. Jessica opened the lid of the bench seat and flipped through the music books. Nothing contemporary. She sat down and ran a few scales. The instrument was in tune.

Looking up, she studied the pictures hanging above the piano. Square patches of fresher-looking wallpaper told that some pictures had been removed. The remaining photographs chronicled Amy's growing-up years from riding a pony to starring as Lady MacBeth in the high school play.

Jessica left the living room and went down the hall to the kitchen. She found Amy standing by the sink watching the falling snow through the bare window. "At least that's one problem taken care of," the young woman said. There was an edge to her voice.

Jessica joined her by the window and looked outside. A semitrailer truck was backed up against the cattle chute, and the cattle were being loaded onto it. Light snowflakes made it an almost surrealistic scene. Puffs of vapor rose from the animals as they waited their turn at the loading ramp.

"Who are those guys?" Jessica asked.

"Beth's tenants," Amy said. "Rocky asked them to move the cattle to their place until the will is read. I told him there was no way I was going to keep feeding them."

"Tenants?" Jessica asked. "I thought only you and Kurt lived here."

"Peter had two other farms in the valley. He leased them out."

"How did the guy get to be so rich? Surely not from farming."

"He inherited a lot of land from his father who, I think, got it from his grandfather. The Martin family has been in this valley since forever. I think they used to own a lot more but sold chunks of it off over the years."

"Are the other places as big as this one?"

"I'm not sure," Amy said, as though it didn't matter. "Like I told Dan, the farming part of things never interested me."

Jessica watched the line of steers being loaded. "They're all steers. Didn't Peter keep any cows?"

"No," Amy said. "Peter found breeding a hassle. He'd much rather buy the unwanted male calves from dairy farmers, fatten them, and then sell them for meat. He said it was more profitable and a lot less work."

Leaning against the worn laminate counter, Amy peered out the window. "The ones they're loading now are the yearlings. They would have been taken off the farm soon anyway."

Jessica looked at her watch—more from habit than from being short on time. "By the way, when is the reading of Beth's will?"

"Tomorrow at one o'clock," Amy replied. She moved away from the window and perched on a chair at the table.

Jessica sat across from Amy. "Who's the lawyer?"

"Gary Barker."

"Would you mind if I tag along to the reading?"

"I'm not going."

"Why not? You should be there."

Amy's expression held anger and grief. "Like I told Dan. I get nothing. Peter said he'd make sure of it."

"Still, you should go," Jessica said. "After all, it's Beth's will, not Peter's."

"And give Rocky a chance to gloat? Not on your life!"

Running a tapered nail along the table's scarred top, Jessica chose her next words carefully. "Amy, I know this is a lot to ask of you, but would you mind telling me what happened the day Peter died? It may help me uncover some detail that would help Dan."

Amy looked out the window before turning her face to Jessica. "I was there. I saw it happen." She swallowed. "I never told anyone about it. Not even Beth. I just ran to the house and told her to call 911. I didn't tell her. . . ." She swallowed again and fought for control.

"Can I get you a cup of tea or something?"

Amy took a deep breath. "No, I'll be okay."

"What time did the accident happen?" Jessica asked.

Amy wet her lips. "It was around eight in the morning. I liked to walk outside early while Peter did his chores. I work four days for ten hours and have off three. The. . . accident. . . happened on a Friday, but it was my day off, so I was there."

"Start with when you woke up," Jessica said. "If you work

up to the accident, we may be able to spot something that was different than usual."

Amy nodded. "Okay. I got up at six like I always do. Aunt Beth was frying pancakes, and Peter had just come in from feeding three small calves he'd brought over the week before. He had to give them a special feed for a couple of weeks until they got used to eating grass."

"Was he in a good mood?"

"About the same as usual. He didn't talk much. That was his way. He was complaining about Kurt staying out too late the night before. Peter was always complaining about Kurt. I don't know why he kept him around." She paused. "He said he had to deliver Samson to Mr. Harrison down the road. He'd wanted Kurt to do it, but Kurt claimed he'd hurt his leg or something. So Peter ended up doing it.

"After breakfast, I helped Aunt Beth clear the table and went out for my walk."

"Where did you walk that morning?" Jessica asked.

Amy stood up to transfer a tissue box from a corner of the counter to the table. She pulled two out and blew her nose. "I put on my raincoat and walked down the drive to the pasture gate, around the back of the barn to the hay shed, and around the corral. It was misting some and chilly. Peter had backed the cattle trailer up to the loading corral. He was having trouble with Samson."

She shivered. "I never liked that bull. . .or any bull for that matter. Samson was the only one we had around. Usually, Peter handled him without any trouble, but that day Samson was kicking and bellowing something awful. I stopped on the other side of the holding pen to watch."

"Okay, Amy," Jessica said, "pretend it's a movie, and you've set the speed to slow motion. Think through exactly what happened and give it to me detail by detail. Start with Peter. Tell me how he looked and what he did."

"He was holding a long black cattle prod. I couldn't see it very well because his slicker kind of billowed out when he moved. He stood at the end of the chute, poking Samson and yelling for him to get up into the trailer. The bull started swinging his head around. He rammed into the side of the chute once, and I was afraid he'd get loose. I had just decided to go to the house when the bull turned on Peter."

She twisted a lock of her hair around and around. "I was so scared I couldn't move. I couldn't even scream." She gasped, drew in some short, quick breaths. Her face crinkled. "I didn't know what to do!" She bowed her head low and fell silent.

Jessica watched her carefully. Was this an act? If it was, Amy ought to be auditioning in Hollywood. She waited a few moments, then asked, "What can you tell me about Kurt?"

Dabbing her face, Amy looked at Jessica, surprised. "What about him?"

"Any idea why he took off? Any chance he could be involved in all of this?"

"No on both accounts. He was nowhere around when it happened."

"There's no chance he's in Beth's will? It's not unusual for faithful farmhands to get something."

Amy's face tightened. "If Peter was going to cut me out, I hardly think he'd leave anything for Kurt."

Jessica stretched to look out a back window opposite the table. She saw a cabin on the rear of the property. "That's Kurt's place back there, isn't it?"

At Amy's nod, she said, "Mind if I take a look around inside?"

Amy's expression darkened. "I told you, Kurt has nothing to do with this. Besides, it's probably illegal for you to look around in there without a search warrant or something."

"Police need a search warrant," Jessica said. "Reporters don't and certainly not owners. Until that will is read, you can grant permission. He abandoned the place, so you have every right to enter it."

Amy shrugged and turned away. "Go ahead."

"You want to come along?"

"No, thanks," Amy said. "It's cold and wet out there."

"Do you have a key?"

"I don't think he ever locked it."

Buttoning on her coat, Jessica went out the back door and stepped into a dusting of snow on the step. Thankful that she'd asked Dan to take her Porsche home, she fast-walked toward Kurt's cabin. By the time she got to the steps, her thin boots were soaked and her hair was dusted with snow. Getting back to Vancouver was going to be a chore. She stepped up onto the covered porch and turned to watch the men load the last of the cattle.

Shivering, Jessica opened the door and stepped inside. The main room was sparsely furnished and bitter cold. A lone rocker sat in front of a small TV on a coffee table. There were a few pictures on the walls—landscapes of western scenes. From the look of things, the place had been cleaned out.

Jessica crossed to the kitchen. She opened the pine cabinets and pulled open the drawers. Nothing. The fridge was as vacant as everything else. The only other door stood to her left. Jessica opened it and found a single bed with no bedding. A small chest of drawers stood between the bed and the wall. She went around the bed and pulled open the drawers. Nothing but dust.

She pulled open the closet door to discover—surprise—more vacant space. She looked down.

In the corner, camouflaged by dust, lay a white pack of matches. Jessica picked them up. She stepped back to catch the dim light from the window and brushed the dust off the cardboard cover. "Coyote Bar and Grill," she said aloud. "Your favorite drinking hole by any chance, Mr. Fletcher?"

Jessica's radar would never have picked up on Kurt Fletcher if he'd stayed at the Martin farm. The fact that he took off made him interesting. Rocky Wiebe still remained the number one suspect, but she wanted to talk to this Kurt fellow, too. If he wasn't involved, he might know something. Maybe something Amy didn't want her to know.

By the time Jessica left the cabin, snow was accumulating on the driveway. She had to get moving before the roads turned really bad. She opened up the back door of the main house to find that Amy had left the kitchen.

Jessica reached into her purse for her cell phone. It rang before she could take it out. She flipped it open. "Hello?"

"Jessica, Dan here."

"Hey, how did it go with Arthur?"

"Good," he said. "He thinks he can keep me out of jail." There was a touch of cynicism in his voice. "If we don't find out what happened with those pills, Rocky is going to get some dollars in that lawsuit. But look, I called to tell you not to come back into the city. Traffic is a mess. They say the highways are at a crawl. I tried to get a cab to take me home, and the guy just laughed. I'm staying at the Hyatt until the weather lets up."

"It's really that bad?"

"According to the news, the city will be shut down in another hour."

"But I've got to work tonight," she said. "I should at least try to come in."

"Jessica, don't," he insisted. "You know the chaos this city falls into when there's heavy snow. If you try, you just might become part of the news. What's it like out there?"

"Snowing, but just lightly."

"We must be getting the brunt of it out here," Dan said. "Trust me, you don't want to be anywhere near this place."

She sighed. "I guess you're right. I'll give Roger a call. I guess I'll have to look for a hotel out here."

"Hey, don't do that," Dan said. "Go to my place. Aunt Elinor came home on Tuesday, and she'd love to have you. She's going to be alone unless by some miracle Mike shows up, and that isn't likely."

"You're sure she wouldn't mind? I'm almost a stranger to her."

"Not a chance," Dan said. "She loves company."

"Okay, you've convinced me. I'll call her."

"Great! Talk to you later," Dan said.

"Have a nice night." Jessica flipped the phone shut, then opened it up again. She called Roger Pronger. He wasn't pleased, but he couldn't airlift Jessica into the station, so there was nothing he could do about it.

Tucking the phone back into her purse, Jessica found Amy in the living room. She was watching a game show. The girl looked up when Jessica walked in.

"Just one last question," Jessica said, "then I'll be out of your hair."

"What is it?" Amy asked.

"After Peter was killed, what happened to his clothes?"

"Beth gave everything to the Salvation Army when she gave them that ratty old armchair of his." She watched Jessica for a second, then asked, "Why?"

"Do you know what he was wearing when he died?"

Amy frowned and spoke slowly. "He always wore the same thing to the barn. Aunt Beth almost had to fight with him when she wanted to wash his work clothes. He had on ragged bib overalls with red paint stains on them." She stared at the television for a second. "His shirt was. . .blue flannel with the pocket torn off and holes in the elbows."

"What about his shoes?" Jessica asked, cataloguing the list in her mind.

"He wore a pair of brown work boots."

"Did he wear a cap or a hat?"

"He didn't have one on when he was killed. Why do you want to know?"

"Just curious," Jessica said. She headed toward the door. "Thanks for seeing me, Amy. I'll let myself out."

Stretched out on the double bed in a Hyatt hotel room, Dan punched his home phone number into the phone. This was an unexpected detour. He'd purchased a toothbrush and a travel-sized deodorant stick from the hotel gift shop. That was the total of his baggage.

Aunt Elinor liked company, but she also liked to be warned. The phone rang a couple of times before she picked it up.

"Yes?" his aunt answered.

"Hi, Aunt Elinor, it's me."

"Dan, can you believe this, snow in October?"

Dan glanced out the window. Snowflakes drifted lazily down to the ground ten stories below. "It's pretty bad out here. Jessica says it's lighter out there."

"Some of it's staying on the ground, but I've seen worse."

"I think the city is going to be paralyzed soon."

"Vancouver would be," Elinor said. "The people in that city just can't drive in snow with their fancy sports cars and summer tires."

"All-season tires don't look good on Porsches and BMW's," Dan said, chuckling.

"I guess not," Elinor said. "Anyhow, I'm glad you called. I tried to page you, but you never answered."

"Sorry," Dan said. "I was having lunch with my lawyer, so

I turned it off. No medical emergencies for me for awhile."

"Lawyer?"

Dan could almost see Aunt Elinor's ear stretching to the phone.

"Beth's nephew is suing me for wrongful death."

"Oh, Danny, it just doesn't get any better for you, does it?"

"Not really."

"Well, I hope I'm not about to add to your grief."

"Why?" Dan asked.

"A Dr. Corbin called. He said it's urgent he talk with you right away. Dan, please tell me that's not bad news."

"It's not bad news, Aunt Elinor," he said, a grin in his voice.

"Who is he then? What does he want with you?"

"He's head of the College of Physicians and Surgeons disciplinary committee."

Her tone went up an octave. "I thought you said this wasn't bad news. That's bad news, Danny."

Dan chuckled. "You told me to tell you it's not bad news, so I did."

She sounded exasperated. "Don't tease me at a time like this."

"What else can I do? It's better to laugh than to cry, isn't it?"

"Danny, you know I'm praying for you," she murmured.

"Suit yourself," Dan said. "I think you'd better pray for Mike. Who knows where he is or what he's up to."

"Don't remind me. That boy has aged me ten years. Maybe twelve."

"Auntie, you look good for your age, and you know it. But, if you want to look better—and assuming I can still practice medicine—just say the word, and I'll have guys in their thirties chasing you."

"You know I don't approve of plastic surgery," she said. "God made us the way we are, and we should accept it."

"Remember to throw out your cosmetics when you get off the phone."

"That's different," she said.

"How? You're artificially changing your appearance."

"Dan, let's not have this argument again. You've got enough on your plate. . . . Wait a minute. Did you say Jessica's coming over?"

"That's why I called. She's over at Beth Martin's place, and she has my car. Within an hour the bridges and tunnels in Vancouver are going to be shut down. I told her she could spend the night with you. You don't mind, do you?"

"Of course not. It'll be nice to have a woman in the house for a change."

"Great," Dan said. After a short pause, he went on. "Well, I guess I should give Dr. Corbin a call."

"I'll take good care of your Jessica for you."

"My Jessica?" Dan rolled his eyes. "We won't even go there. Bye, Aunt Elinor."

"Bye, Danny."

He hung up the phone and pulled the telephone book out of the desk drawer. If he were in Langley, he could use the weather as an excuse not to visit Dr. Corbin. But he wasn't in Langley. He was within walking distance.

Chapter
Fourteen

Waiting to be ushered into the registrar's office at the College of Physicians and Surgeons of British Columbia, Dan Foster flipped through a back issue of an obscure medical journal.

Sitting in that waiting room, Dan felt very mortal. The college had the power to take away his medical license and turn twelve years of study and hard work to ashes. One thing was certain; Dr. Corbin hadn't summoned him for a social visit.

Dan tossed the magazine onto the pile on the oak table beside him and leaned back in the soft loveseat. The waiting room reflected the office it served: professional but not extravagant. Light blue, crush-pile carpet covered the floor. Native American art hung from the paneled walls. The registrar's secretary sat behind an oak desk. Wearing a gray suit, her blue-black hair cut painfully short, she projected an image of intense efficiency.

The window behind the receptionist showed that the snow was letting up a bit. Cleaning up the mess would take time. Cars had to be towed. Roads had to be plowed. With an inadequate fleet of snow-removal equipment, that would take time. He'd definitely be in the city overnight.

"Weather's improving," he commented to the starched secretary.

She glanced out the window. "Maybe," she said, her manner brusque, her face stiff.

A solid wooden door opened and a stooped, gray-haired man stepped into the room. "Dr. Foster?" he asked. His voice held a trace of British accent.

For now, Dan thought. *Once you're finished with me, I'll be Mr. Foster again.*

"Please come in," Dr. Corbin said, his manner cordial. If not for his bent-over frame, he would have been Dan's height. He had leathery skin and a hawk nose that could've benefited from Dan Foster's attention.

Dr. Corbin stepped aside to let Dan enter the office. "Terrible weather," he said as Dan passed him. "It's got me stranded in the city tonight."

"Me, too," Dan said.

Walnut paneling and a matching desk set the theme of the inner office. The gleaming surface of the desk was bare. Dr. Corbin closed the door, stepped around him, and offered his right hand to Dan. It contained only three fingers. Dan shook hands with him, and Dr. Corbin motioned for him to occupy a leather chair.

"You know," Dr. Corbin said, moving to his seat, "this hand of mine is a constant reminder to me of how serious my duty is. Because of it, I can truly say, I understand what it's like to lose the ability to practice medicine."

Dan felt a sudden surge of panic and swallowed it back.

The older man didn't waste time. "I've asked you to come today," he went on, "because of a malpractice complaint against you."

Like a five-hundred-pound bomb dropped from a fighter jet, the word exploded in Dan's brain. *Malpractice. Mal*—from the French word meaning bad. Bad practice, malpractice.

Dan cleared his throat. "May I ask who filed the charge?"

Dr. Corbin nodded. "The complaint came from Dr. Cruch."

How could Cruch do that? Beth's case hasn't even been closed yet.

Dr. Corbin's calm voice went on. "Before you blame Dr. Cruch, keep in mind that it's a doctor's ethical duty to report incompetence."

"Don't I even get some kind of hearing before everyone makes up their mind?"

"Absolutely," Corbin said. "And that's why I've called you in. There's going to be a panel consisting of two doctors, a lawyer, and a layperson to hear the particulars of your case. A lawyer will represent the college, and you are advised to have legal council represent you. Just like a regular trial, both sides will present their cases. The panel will decide on innocence or guilt and set the punishment." He paused. "Any idea who your attorney might be?"

"Arthur Stoll."

Dr. Corbin's face tightened.

"When's the hearing?" Dan asked.

Dr. Corbin rubbed the bridge of his nose. "Normally these things take time, but since we have an excellent file from the RCMP, we're going to move quickly. It's best for all concerned. The hearing will be two weeks from today. Nine o'clock."

Aunt Elinor opened the door before Jessica could knock. "Ms. Meyers," she said, "come right in before you turn into an icicle!"

Jessica hurried inside and slipped out of her coat.

"Let me take that," Elinor said.

"Thank you."

"You know, if you ever get stuck again and need a place to stay, you're always welcome to stay in my apartment, even if

I'm not here. You just punch the code into the keypad on the door, and it unlocks. The number is 7469."

Jessica started to dig a notepad out of her purse.

"Oh, don't write it down, Dear. Your purse is the first place they look for stuff like that. Just remember it."

"I'll try," Jessica said.

"It's easy to remember. Seventy-four is the year Nixon resigned and sixty-nine is the year men landed on the moon. Just be careful. Three wrong numbers and the lock won't let you try again for ten minutes."

"I will be," Jessica said, smiling at Elinor. "And this is very kind of you."

Elinor was a small woman. Her head barely came to Jessica's shoulder. Wearing a silky purple-print caftan, she looked like a tiny version of Eva Gabor, with gray hair in a spiky cut and fine lines around her eyes and mouth. It wasn't hard for Jessica to imagine this little lady standing by her kitchen window and tossing her china outside like the woman in that 1960's sitcom, *Green Acres.*

"I really appreciate you letting me stay over, Ms. Foster," Jessica said. "The roads around here are pretty clear, but according to the radio, Vancouver has gone into its usual melt-down during snow."

"Call me Elinor," she said. "Could I interest you in a cup of tea?"

"That sounds wonderful. In spite of this heavy sweater and my coat, I'm chilled clear through."

"Then come along, Jessica."

Jessica followed her past the kitchen door and continued down the hall to a door at the end. Gliding through it, she held the doorknob and waited for Jessica. "We'll sit in here. It's much more comfortable than that bachelor's hangout the boys live in."

Jessica entered Elinor's domain and paused on the threshold. She'd never seen decorating quite like this.

Wide ruffles in a pink floral print surrounded almost every flat surface. Ornate silver picture frames, stacks of odd-sized books, and a massive collection of trinkets covered the tables, the mantel, and the wide breakfront hutch. Maroon and indigo paint splashed and globbed across a silver canvas hanging over the fireplace. On either side of the painting hung two Rembrandt prints of little girls in their gardens.

"Now, to make that tea," Elinor said.

"Why don't you take it easy and let me do it?"

"Oh, I couldn't do that," Elinor said. "Imagine what a poor hostess I would be."

"Imagine what a poor guest I'd be, letting Dan's aunt wait on me like a servant. You just sit down in that comfortable lounge chair. I can find my way around a kitchen."

"Well, thank you, Dear." Elinor eased herself into the lounge chair and waved a hand toward the dining area. "There's a basket of tea bags on the table," she said. "Make your tea however you like it, then join me for a nice chat."

Jessica made her way to a short counter that had a microwave on top and a tiny fridge beneath. A narrow silver sink stood near the microwave. She lifted a curved china cup from a wooden mug tree and filled it with water, then ran her finger over the closely packed basket of tea bags.

"Tell me," Elinor said, "how does it feel to be a TV star? Do you get a lot of fan mail?"

Jessica said, "Most of my fan mail consists of people telling me where I made a mistake in my newscast. Not very exciting." She selected Earl Grey and tore open the wrapper.

"You mean you've never had a fan fall in love with you?" Curled up in the lounge chair, Elinor sounded like a teenager eager for some juicy gossip.

"Oh, yes," Jessica replied. "When I get those, that's when I start worrying. In this day and age, that kind is dangerous."

Elinor looked shocked. "Oh. . .yes. . .I see what you mean."

Stirring sugar into her cup, Jessica moved to the sofa. It felt soft and cuddly when she sat down. That wasn't surprising. Everything about Elinor showed that she loved comfort.

"Dan just got a call from Dr. Corbin. He's the head of the clinic's discipline committee or something like that," Elinor told her. "I'm so worried that Dan will lose his job."

"I'm doing everything I can to make sure that doesn't happen. And Dan has a great lawyer."

"Does he?" Elinor asked, delighted. "Is he expensive?" When Jessica didn't answer, she went on. "Of course he is. All good talent is expensive." She nodded as though coming to a decision, but she didn't say what it was.

Jessica pulled Kurt's matchbook from the pocket of her slacks. "Have you ever heard of this place?" She handed it over to Elinor. "I want to check out this bar if I can find it."

"Coyote Bar and Grill," Elinor murmured, thinking. "I know where that is. It's about six miles south on Fraser Highway and down Echo Road." She shook her head. "You don't want to go there, Jessica. It's a rough place. I don't even like to drive past it."

Jessica accepted the matchbook back from her. "How about the local Salvation Army store? Is that near here?"

Elinor stared at her. "You mean you want to go out again in this weather?"

Jessica got up to look out the window. "The snow's easing off. There's hardly any on the road at all."

"You're right. It doesn't look that bad," Elinor said, stretching to look out the window to her right. Beside the window an easel held a half-finished canvas showing a blue vase of daffodils melting and sliding off a cast-iron table. "What on earth do you need to go to the Salvation Army for?"

Jessica pressed her lips together. "I'm looking for the clothes Peter Martin wore the day he died."

"What do you want with that old skinflint's clothes?"

Jessica told Elinor about the urine and killer-bull theory.

"That sounds so crazy it's almost believable."

"While I'm out," Jessica said, "I can get us some Chinese food for supper."

Elinor's expression lit up. "Say, there's a terrific Chinese buffet near the Salvation Army. It's not a mile away. Let's eat there when we're through."

"We?" Jessica asked.

"Of course, Dear," Elinor said. "It's not every day I get to solve a murder and help my nephew at the same time. Just give me a minute, Dear," she said to Jessica, her silk caftan billowing out as she disappeared into her bedroom.

Jessica relaxed on the couch, a little overwhelmed at her hostess's sudden enthusiasm.

Two minutes later the little lady reappeared dressed for the elements. "Let's go then."

The two women left the house in Dan's car. Five minutes later they were walking into the Salvation Army store.

"What are we looking for?" Elinor asked as they pushed through the glass door. Narrow and deep, the store was cluttered from wall to wall. No other customers were in the store.

Jessica waited to answer Elinor until they were out of earshot of the bored checkout clerk. "We're looking for a pair of ragged bib overalls with red paint stains on them, a threadbare blue flannel shirt with the pocket torn off, and some brown work boots."

"Then let's start looking," Elinor said.

An hour later, the women had Peter's boots and overalls, but they couldn't locate his shirt. Each of them had been through the shirt rack twice over.

Finally, Jessica approached the cashier. "Do you have any more flannel shirts?" she asked.

"There's a bag of them in the back," she said, her words coming from far back in her throat. "We get so many that we can't put them all out at once."

"Would you mind if I look through them?" Jessica asked.

Elinor came up behind her. "We're looking for one particular design," she said. From the flushed and eager look on her face, Aunt Elinor was having the time of her life.

Glancing from Jessica to Elinor and back again, the girl slowly nodded. "Go through that door and ask for Don," she said, pointing toward the back.

When they finally got their hands on the bag, Jessica took it to an empty table in a corner of the storage room, unknotted the top, and dumped it out. Two pairs of hands pawed through it until Elinor came up with a scrap of blue.

"Got it!" she cried. Immediately she clapped a hand over her mouth and glanced toward the spot where Don used to be. "Sorry," she whispered.

Jessica laughed. "Don't worry. I'm having a ball." She held the shirt up. It had a wide brown stain across the middle. And there was the torn pocket. She sniffed the cloth and smelled only fabric softener. She scooped the shirt into her stack and smiled at Elinor. "Let's go eat, Partner," she said.

Chapter
Fifteen

After eight hours in a strange bed in a strange room, Dan felt like he'd been chasing sheep all night. During brief snatches of sleep, he dreamed of the hearing in Dr. Corbin's office. He didn't think anyone could be sentenced to death for incompetence, but that's what the committee in his dreams did. Fortunately, he escaped the nightmare before the sentence could be carried out.

He showered at dawn and put yesterday's clothes back on. They were a little rumpled, but they were all he had. Today was only Thursday. He felt like it should be a Sunday. This week was stretching out longer and longer. So much had happened in the last five days.

At eight o'clock he checked out of the Hyatt and went in search of breakfast. After ten agonizing minutes in line with a dozen other caffeine addicts at Starbucks, Dan finally got his turn.

"And what will you have, Sir?" a slim young man asked, his small hand hovering over the empty cups stacked before him.

"Make it a Venti house blend and a blueberry muffin."

"Right away." The man turned as he spoke, both hands in constant motion.

Dan dug a five-dollar bill from his pants pocket. When his order appeared on the counter, Dan gave the boy the five and didn't bother to wait for his change.

Pushing through the line to find a seat, Dan felt a grinding emptiness in his midsection, the ache of the unemployed. He glanced back at the kid behind the counter. Working at Starbucks couldn't be that hard. Maybe he should apply.

Dan squeezed into an empty seat at the coffee bar. A lady with big hair and crow's-feet at her eyes sat at his left, a yuppie in a sharp business suit to his right. Both read folded newspapers.

Dan kept a sharp eye on the window before him, monitoring traffic coming from the east. Jessica should be coming along soon. Finding a parking spot in Vancouver after a snowfall ranked right up there with finding out what happened to Jimmy Hoffa. It just didn't happen.

He sipped his coffee and let his weary eyes close as warmth traveled down his throat. At least fifteen minutes would pass before the caffeine did its thing, but psychologically, the effect was immediate. The sharp taste of Starbuck's strong brew assured him that relief was on its way.

He finished the muffin and washed it down with more coffee. Cup in hand, Dan left the shop and stepped into the brisk weather. Crystal clear blue sky hung over the city. The temperature still hovered below freezing, but with no moisture lurking above, Vancouver wouldn't see any more snow today at least.

Downtown Vancouver boasted tall office towers and wide condos. The people bustling past him were mostly white-collar workers—sharply dressed and prepared to do battle in the world of commerce. In the evening, some of them would travel to the many bedroom communities surrounding the city. However, a significant portion of them—the stereotypical yuppies—would stop off at their condo, change, and return to enjoy the many restaurants, playhouses, and clubs that made up Vancouver nightlife.

Dan spotted his car approaching in traffic. When the right-turn signal began blinking, the blast of several horns sounded loud and long. He stepped off the curb between two parked cars. The instant Jessica stopped the car, Dan pulled open the door and climbed in. Jessica pressed the accelerator, and the car surged forward to fill in the gap in traffic that her stopping created.

She glanced at Dan. "Did you sleep in a hotel or on the street last night?"

"For the good it did me, I should have saved the money I gave the hotel and gone to an all-night movie theatre instead. I couldn't sleep a wink."

Jessica reached over and tapped his nearly empty coffee cup. "Drinking that stuff, it's no wonder."

"Hey, I only use it for medicinal purposes to kick start me in the morning. I switch to decaf after three o'clock." He leaned his head back against the headrest. "My insomnia may be due to the impending loss of my medical license, lawsuits from irate family members, and constantly looking over my back to see if that psycho Carrington still wants a pound of my flesh."

She patted his arm. "Have faith," she said. "The truth is out there."

Dan faked a shudder. "Ooh, faith and the *X-Files* motto all in one sentence. Scary."

"The faith part comes from talking with your aunt last night during our slumber party—she's a great lady, by the way. The *X-Files* comes from watching your TV before I finally went to bed last night."

"Well, you've got it right. I feel like God is on my case because I told Aunt Elinor to shove her religion. This whole situation seems so weird, it's like an *X-Files* episode."

"According to your aunt, God doesn't set out to hurt people. He uses circumstances to draw us to Him. It's the devil who's responsible for the bad stuff."

Dan focused on Jessica. She flashed him a quick smile.

"This is an *X-Files* episode," he said. "You're not Jessica, are you? Has Aunt Elinor changed you into one of her kind?" Dan looked shocked. "Oh no, Jessica has gone over to the dark side."

Jessica laughed. "Uh, that would be the light side, and no, your aunt didn't convert me, though a lot of what she said made sense."

"And a lot of it is nonsense."

Jessica glanced at him. "You don't like your aunt, do you?"

"I don't exactly dislike her, but we do have issues."

"Like what?"

"It's a long story," Dan said.

"Well, it's a beautiful day, albeit cold. Let's head over to False Creek and get some fresh air. You can tell me about it. Then we'll plan our detective attack for the day."

Rocky Wiebe stood in a wide field and stared at a rear view of the farm. Soon it and the other properties would belong to him. How quickly his fortunes had changed. His latest scheme of selling shares in a mining property in Quesnel hadn't panned out. One of the idiot investors actually drove up to the central-interior town and checked the property out.

They found nothing but an overgrown field. The mining equipment Rocky described to him was nowhere to be found. Rocky couldn't answer his phone anymore because of angry investors who wanted their money and a chunk of his hide at the same time.

Soon he'd have the money to pay back the investors, and their threatened complaints to the police would fade like chills after a nightmare. He still didn't know what to do with the farmland. The last thing he wanted to be was a farmer.

Developing the property was out of the question. The area had severe restrictions on farmland. Greasing the palms of certain officials could get him around some of the regulations, but Rocky wasn't sure he wanted to go that route. Peter had kept his affairs close to his chest, and now Rocky understood why. If done right, leasing to the right tenants could bring in cash, lots of it.

How fortunes could change. One day he was flat broke, next day he was heir to farmlands and a fat bank account besides. All that, plus his take from the malpractice suit against Beth's doctor. Rocky had no delusions about himself. A hustler and con man, his conscience had become mute long ago.

Still, he was sorry Aunt Beth was gone. Everyone who knew him had eventually cast him off, yet Aunt Beth had never turned her back on him. One day he'd fix up her grave and maybe even put a plaque on a post by the farm's driveway.

"Counting your chickens before they're hatched?" a feminine voice asked.

Rocky turned around. "Who's that with you?"

"A lady shouldn't be alone when dealing with scum like you."

Like the rest of the city, False Creek had once been virgin forests with towering fir trees, inhabited by native peoples. Now stylish condos spread across the land, lush green parks lazed along the river's banks, and a red brick walkway followed the water's edge.

On the walkway that morning, Jessica wrapped her coat tightly around herself and gave a little shiver.

"Sure you want to go for a walk?" Dan asked. "That breeze is icy."

Jessica looked across the creek at the Coastal Mountains, the perpetual backdrop for the city. Snowcapped peaks above evergreen trees told the city that skiing would start soon. The tangy smell of the ocean hung in the air. Pulling in a tingling breath, Jessica realized that she needed to get out more often. Sometimes she forgot how beautiful the city was.

"Yes, let's walk," she said, starting out. "We'll keep moving to get the blood flowing. I need it, and so do you."

Near a clump of trees she glanced at him. "So, what's with you and your aunt?" she asked. "She gave me the impression you weren't too thrilled when she moved in a couple of years ago."

"Elinor actually lived with us once before. Our mom died a few years after our dad. Elinor came to Langley to attend Mom's funeral. I was twenty, Mike nineteen. I was closest to Dad, so Mom's death didn't hit me like it hit Mike. Elinor was great with him, helping him with his grief. In fact, Elinor is the one that gave Mike religion. It helped him, so it can't be all bad, I guess. He's stayed close to her ever since."

"And how did she come to live with you permanently?"

"Elinor used to live in one of those upscale seniors' complexes. You know, security gates, fences. Well, a couple of years ago some punks jumped the fence and kicked in her door. They trashed her place. Thank God she wasn't home. As it was, the poor woman was traumatized."

"I don't doubt it," Jessica said.

"Mike flipped, of course. He packed Elinor up right then and there and brought her home. I tell you one thing; if Mike ever finds those guys, they'll learn hurt in a whole new way. Later, Elinor paid to have that apartment built."

"Nothing you've said explains your feelings about her."

Dan looked up toward the mountains. "She's rich, you know."

"I got that impression from her apartment," Jessica said. "And she's the only senior citizen I know who drives a silver Camaro."

"She paid for all of Mike's education. Every cent."

"That's great."

"I got nothing."

"Why not?"

"Because I made the mistake of telling her I wanted to be a plastic surgeon. She spouted some Bible verses at me and told me if I wanted to waste my talents in pursuit of big money, I was on my own. I tried to explain to her that's not why I wanted to get into plastic surgery, but she wouldn't listen."

Jessica cocked her head and looked over at him. "And why did you pick plastic surgery?"

"When I was sixteen, I was at a parade. A big flower-covered float came down the street with a banner announcing it contained the parade princess. All the guys straightened up to get a look at the coming beauty. Instead of a cute babe, there was this girl of about fifteen with a badly burned face. She waved as if she were a beautiful princess. Some of the guys from the crowd called out, letting her know it wasn't so. I can still see the tear trickle down her cheek while she kept on waving. I swore if I could do something for people like her, I would."

"Hence all the charity work you do for kids?"

"That's right," Dan said. "I had to work and take student loans to pay for my education. When I finished medical school, I was in debt over eighty thousand dollars. I didn't expect her to pay the whole shot, but some help would've been nice.

"While other students were busy studying, I was working the nightshift as a hotel clerk. I missed scholarships by fractions of a grade point. I would have won those if I hadn't been so strung out on caffeine all the time.

"Aunt Elinor thinks I spend my time satisfying people's vanity. But she never meets the Chelseas in my practice. In a perfect Christian world where people accept everyone for what's on the inside, Elinor might be right. But in this world, where so much value is put on the outer appearance, I'm proud that I can help put some of the less fortunate on stronger footing.

"I don't deny I do vanity work. Women who want to look younger, those who want a shorter nose, a longer nose, higher cheekbones, lower cheekbones, thin lips, fat lips. I figure, hey, if they can afford it, I'll do it." He stared at the creek's ever-moving waters. "The money they pay for vanity work makes it possible for me to help those who really need my skill, people like Chelsea."

Jessica slipped closer for a quick hug. "And people like me," she murmured into his shoulder. "How could I have faced another day if you'd become anything instead of a surgeon?"

His somber expression in place, Kent Olund of the FBI sat at the head of a short table in a conference room in a downtown Seattle office building. Alan Hart, a white-haired senior agent from the DEA, sat to Olund's left, and fresh-faced Jerry Gosdin from the Treasury Department sat to Olund's right. Doodling on a notepad while he listened to the others talk, Mike sat at the foot of the table with Louise Crossfield on his right. Mike was the lone Canadian at the meeting.

The lettering on the office door read *Cascade Shipping Company*. Mike suspected that the CIA was the real occupant and that this group was borrowing the room for their meeting. Mike and Louise couldn't be seen walking into a federal building housing the FBI and DEA.

"Corporal Foster," Kent Olund said, "you want us to hand $280,000 to these drug dealers for a hundred kilos of grass?"

"That's correct, Sir," Mike said. He and Louise wore their street attire. All the rest wore gray suits and silk ties.

Gosdin from the Treasury cut in, his eyes eager behind round black glasses. "We may never see that money again."

"That's also correct, Sir," Mike said. He leaned back in his chair and smoothed his red hair down in the back.

"You think it's worth the risk?" Olund studied Mike.

"Absolutely."

"What's your opinion, Agent Crossfield?" Hart from the DEA asked.

She laid down her pen. "I'm convinced that Mike's plan is the only way we're going to get these guys."

On the long drive back to Seattle after their meeting with Garret, Mike had managed to break down Louise's hostility and get her on board with him. After breaking through her gutsy façade, he was surprised to learn that she was actually a likable woman, a dedicated eight-year veteran. Still, without the approval of this board, Mike's plan would be dead in the water.

Hart said, "You're talking about more than a quarter of a million dollars walking across the border because of a drug dealer's claim that he has contacts. We don't know who the contacts are and if they're the people we want."

"First of all," Mike said, "that's Canadian dollars. With the exchange rate, we're looking at 180,000 US."

"Still a lot of cash," Gosdin put in. He constantly scrawled numbers on his notepad.

"Sure, it is," Louise said, "but let's not forget where that money came from. We got it from other drug dealers. We're not talking about the taxpayers' dollars."

"Granted," Gosdin said, "but that's just the beginning. You're going to want another two million later on." He wrote a two and six zeros in bold black ink.

"It takes big dollars to catch big fish," Louise said.

"It's not the money that bothers me," Kent Olund put in.

"What's your concern?" Gosdin asked, looking toward the head of the table.

Kent Olund looked directly at Mike. "Corporal Foster, if

this goes wrong, you have a very real chance of being killed."

When Mike met Olund's gaze, he had to admit his plan was reckless. But it was the only chance they had.

Chapter
Sixteen

When Jessica released him, Dan took her hand, and they moved down the bricked walk. "So, now you can understand why I harbor a bit of resentment toward Elinor."

"But you don't hate her?"

Dan shook his head. "Not anymore, but for awhile I came pretty close. Now I just chalk up her opinions about my work to ignorance. Besides, being forced to work for my education probably made me a better man." They walked a few steps in silence. "What do you think of Elinor?"

Jessica smiled. "She made me feel very welcome." She laughed. "We had a blast at the Salvation Army and dinner. I like her."

"That's good," Dan said, putting an end to that line of conversation. In a moment he asked, "How did your visit with Amy turn out?"

Jessica's lips formed a slight curve. "I learned why you're so willing to believe in her. She's a very attractive, likable girl. Unfortunately, she's also a great actress."

"No she's not. She's a nurse."

"I saw her picture on the wall. She starred as Lady MacBeth in high school. That's a tough part to play. If she can pull that off, she can probably pull off a part as the grieving young girl who lost the only family she had." She lost her smile. "I'm sorry, Dan, but I don't trust her."

"You honestly think she could've switched those pills and killed Beth?"

Jessica shrugged. "You didn't do it, and no one else came near those pills on the way from the clinic to the farm."

"Except for the ten minutes while Amy was inside the grocery store."

"If that really happened. A big if."

"What's the *if* about?"

Jessica released her hand from his. "Dan, everything we know about what happened that day is at Amy's word. Despite how innocent she appears, you've got to accept the fact that Amy is the primary suspect."

"What about Kurt? He had access to the house, and he just up and disappeared."

"Sure, Kurt is a possibility, and we should try and find him. Just don't let Amy fool you; that's all I'm asking."

"Fair enough," Dan said. "I know we have to be objective about this. I consider Amy a friend. Shortly after I met Beth, I took Amy to dinner a few times. We never had anything serious between us, but it's hard for me to think of her as a suspect."

They didn't speak for a long moment.

"I did find out what happened to Peter's clothes," Jessica said as they reached the end of the walk and turned back.

"What happened?"

"They went to the Salvation Army. Elinor and I went over there and found them. We were too late, though. Everything except the shoes had already been laundered. Poof! No evidence."

Two steps later, she went on. "I did get a lead on Kurt, though." She opened her purse, removed a package of matches, and handed them to Dan. "I found these at Kurt's place."

Dan looked at the package. "Hmm, the Coyote. That's interesting."

Jessica glanced at him, teasing. "You know the place? I didn't figure you for that type."

Dan chuckled. "Not personally. I fixed a guy's face after he met a broken beer bottle there. I've heard Mike mention it a couple of times. It's a tough place."

Jessica shivered in the chill. "That's what your aunt said. I'm glad I took her advice and didn't go over there alone."

"So am I."

"We can probably go tonight," she said. She shivered again as a sharp breeze cut past them. "I have to do the newscast tonight. We could go over right afterwards."

Dan touched Jessica's arm, and she looked up at him. "I'd like to go alone."

Jessica tilted her head to look up at him. "Dan, I was an investigative reporter for years. I can handle tough bars."

"I know you can. But the truth is, you have a famous face. Famous faces tend to close mouths in the Coyote. I should do this alone."

She looked down. Finally, she nodded. "Okay," she said. "But promise me you'll be careful."

"Oh, you don't have to worry about that," Dan told her, stepping out. He didn't mention that his patient went to jail because the guy who'd held that bottle was dead.

"There's one more thing," Jessica said as he moved ahead.

He turned back. "What is it?"

"Beth's will is being read today at the law offices of Gary Barker. You need to go."

"You're not going?"

She fell into step with him. "I can't. I didn't go into work yesterday, so they need me to come in early today. You can handle it, Dan. Just make note of who gets what. Amy swears she's getting nothing. She says she isn't going, but I'll bet you dinner little Amy will get plenty."

Gary Barker's reception area offered four stackable vinyl chairs against a green plastered wall. A pudgy girl with curly brown hair sat behind a worn reception desk. She wore headphones, her fingers flying over a keyboard. When Dan entered and announced himself, all she did was nod toward the chairs.

He glanced at his watch. One minute to one o'clock and no one else was there yet. The outside door opened, and a female voice said, "Well, I didn't expect to see you here."

The hairs on the back of Dan's neck stood up. He turned to see Corporal Carrington close the door behind her. Dressed in a black civilian pants suit, she looked surprisingly average. She walked past Dan to stand in front of the receptionist. "Tell Mr. Barker that Corporal Carrington of the RCMP is here." Reaching into her purse, she produced a business card.

The receptionist paused her typing long enough to take the card and glance at it. She nodded toward the seats.

Carrington chose the chair closest to the door, leaving two empty spaces between her and Dan. Once again the door opened, and there stood Amy.

She smiled awkwardly at Dan. "Hi," she said.

"Hello," Dan said, trying to hide his shock. Had she lied to him and Jessica?

Amy took the seat beside him.

"Jessica said you weren't coming," Dan said, keeping his voice low.

Amy quirked her mouth. "I wasn't, but the lawyer phoned me last night and said I had to come. I don't know why."

One chair away from Amy, Carrington crossed her thick legs and flipped through a hunting magazine.

The center of three doors opened behind the typist. A thin, bearded man stepped out. He wore a black suit and a white button-down shirt with a black tie. The lawyer came near and held out his hand. "Rocky Wiebe? I'm Gary Barker," he said.

Dan stood to take the man's hand. "Actually, I'm Dan Foster. I was a friend of Beth's. I was hoping I could sit in on the will reading."

"You don't need permission. You're one of the beneficiaries."

Dan could sense Carrington's immediate interest. "You're kidding," he said. "This is the first I've heard of this."

"I'll bet," he heard Carrington mutter.

"I've been trying to contact you since yesterday with no success."

"I got trapped in Vancouver last night," Dan said. "The snow. Sometimes my aunt answers the phone; sometimes she doesn't."

"That explains it." He turned to Amy. "Ms. Creighton?"

"Yes," Amy said and shook the lawyer's hand.

He turned to Carrington. "I take it you're with the RCMP. You have a copy of that court order?"

She opened her wide purse and produced a document. Barker slipped narrow reading glasses from his pocket and scanned the document. "Seems in order," he said. "That's your ticket in, Ms. Carrington." He glanced at his watch. "I'd like to wait for Mr. Wiebe, but I have another appointment at one-thirty. He can meet with me at a later time if he wishes." He gestured toward the left door. "Please, come with me."

The three of them followed Gary Barker through the door on the left. They entered a conference room with a table and seating for eight. A lonely file folder rested at the head of the dark wood table. Amy and Dan took seats to the right, and Carrington sat at the opposite end from Barker. She took a pen and a small notebook from her purse and prepared to write.

Dan cleared his throat and tried to act unconcerned. He could feel dampness on his palms and tried to dry them on his pants legs. If Beth had left him anything valuable, his motive for hurting her was established. For the first time in his life, he hoped someone had overlooked him.

Barker took his seat and slid the last will and testament of Beth Martin out of a file folder. He opened the document, put on his glasses, and started to read:

"This is the Last Will and Testament of Beth Martin of. . ." He read the opening statements common to every will, including the part where he was executor. He paused and looked over the rims of his glasses and said, "This is actually quite a simple will." He returned to the document. "In accordance with my promise to my husband, Peter Martin, I leave all my lands and properties to my nephew, Rocky Wiebe, with the proviso that he produces an heir within five years. To Dr. Dan Foster, as I promised him, I bequeath $200,000. To my ward, Amy, I leave the balance of my estate. In the event that Rocky Wiebe does not have an heir at the end of five years, Amy will receive my land and properties."

Promised him? Dan wondered. *What was that about? Beth never. . . Oh no.* He lost his breath for a moment. He'd thought she was kidding. Dan looked up to find both Carrington and Amy watching him.

"She promised you that money," Carrington said, her dark eyes boring into him. "You knew you inherited two hundred grand."

"It's not like that," Dan said. His collar felt tight. "Beth knew about my overseas work. She said if she ever could, she'd help me out. It's for that, not for me."

Carrington smirked. "Sure." She turned to Amy. "And you seem to have done all right out of this."

"I do not understand," Amy said. "Peter Martin said I

would never get anything."

"He certainly couldn't stop you from inheriting the life insurance money," the lawyer said, "which is a substantial sum. He actually tried to do a will where Beth didn't inherit the farm, but when I told him the income tax consequences of not passing it on to her, he came around. Right here in my office, he made Beth swear she'd leave it to Rocky. However, if Rocky doesn't meet the conditions, the place would be yours, Amy."

Carrington scribbled on her pad.

When Barker finished with the formalities, Carrington looked from Dan to Amy and back again. Lifting her shoulder bag and standing, she said, "In a criminal investigation, motive is everything." She gave a little nod and said, "Have a nice day," before she pulled open the door and stepped outside.

At the TV station, Jessica scanned the evening's news stories. The majority of the newscast was dedicated to the pandemonium caused by the previous day's snow—lots of car accidents, some serious but fortunately no deaths. She smiled at a light-hearted piece about a guy in a four-wheel drive who didn't realize that even though his vehicle gave him better traction going, it couldn't stop faster than any other car. He'd managed to skid right into a police cruiser.

With ten minutes to spare before a full meeting of the news crew, she pulled up the coroner's report on Peter Martin. This was her fourth time through it, but Jessica was sure that she missed something. Her mind kept nagging her, urging her to look for something more. The cause of death held no mysteries. The injuries were all consistent with being danced on by a bull. Nothing mysterious cropped up like hypodermic puncture wounds, drugs in his blood, or a wound created by something other than a hoof.

She started at the top of the report and whispered everything she read. Arthur Stoll taught her to do that when she really wanted to comprehend something. He told her to read aloud to keep her mind from wandering and missing important details. She wrapped her tongue around some pretty awkward medical language, but nothing new crawled out of those pages. As she read, she tried to correlate Amy's story with the report.

Near the end she drew up. The slicker. It was a rainy morning, and Peter had worn a slicker. She flipped to the list of his personal effects. No slicker there. What happened to it? She clicked out of the file and picked up the phone.

Amy answered on the second ring.

"Hi, Amy. It's Jessica Meyers. I'm going over the coroner's report, and there's no slicker listed here. Peter had on a slicker, right?"

"Yes," she said. "The paramedics cut it off of him when they came to the farm. It was torn up already and covered with blood."

"What happened to it?"

A long pause. "I can't remember. I think they just left it there on the ground." She paused again. "It wasn't a crime scene, Ms. Meyers, so nobody really cared about Peter's clothes. No one was collecting evidence or anything like that."

"Who took care of the barn after that?"

"Kurt did it. He never did more than he had to, so the slicker's probably in the barn somewhere."

"Would he have thrown it away?"

"Kurt? If you'd seen his house before he moved out, you'd know the answer to that question. I don't think he knew what a garbage can was made for."

Jessica glanced at the clock. Three minutes to airtime. "Thanks, Amy. I may be out to see you later. Would you mind if I look in the barn for it? My broadcast ends at seven, so I could be there by eight at the latest."

"Sure. I'll see you then."

Jessica said good-bye and hung up. Lifting her paper script, she darted into the newsroom.

When Dan arrived home after hearing the will read, all he wanted to do was collapse on the couch. He just couldn't handle a sleepless night like he could ten years earlier. Back then, he only needed an endless supply of coffee and the company of other young interns to make him invincible. Those days were gone forever. He figured he'd check in on Elinor, then take a quick nap.

He went down the hall and knocked on the door to the apartment.

"Come on in," she called through the door.

Dan stepped inside and found his aunt packing.

"Where you going?" Dan asked.

She paused beside her dining table jumbled high with clothes and painting gear. "I got a phone call from an old friend, Edith Gardener, who lives in Arizona." As she talked, her nimble hands folded clothes and dropped them into an open suitcase positioned on a chair.

"And?" Dan asked.

"Edith saw our snowstorm on the weather channel and thought about me. She needs another lady to fill out a house party." Her face took on a demure expression. "There's a widower coming, so Edith has seven when she needs eight." She turned back to her packing. "And I got a great deal on a ticket from the Internet."

She glanced at the clock on the microwave. "I have to leave for the airport in half an hour."

Her hands moved faster. "I was going to take a taxi, but

since you're up, would you mind driving me?"

He sank into the lounge chair. "Sure, Auntie," he said. *Maybe sometime you can actually do something for me.*

Elinor closed the bag and zipped it shut. "I've got to change."

Dan stood. "So do I. I'll be ready in twenty minutes." He closed the door behind him, bounded up the stairs, dashed into his bathroom for a split-second shower, and dived into fresh clothing. Running a comb through his hair, he arrived at Aunt Elinor's door as it opened.

Elinor stood, suitcase in hand, waiting.

"Oh, let me take that, Auntie," Dan said.

Five minutes later, Dan's Grand Marquis backed out the driveway and headed south.

"I'm sorry to leave you when you're having so much trouble, Danny," Elinor said.

"There's nothing you can do, Aunt Elinor," Dan told her. "Jessica and I are doing everything we can."

"Have you learned any more about the case?" she asked. "Any idea who might have switched those pills?"

"Not yet. I'm going over to the Coyote Grill later today. Maybe I'll find Beth's farmhand. The way he just up and quit doesn't sit well with me. I think he knows something."

"The Coyote?" she asked. "Dan, that's a terrible place. Why don't you wait until Mike gets done whatever he's doing and let him go for you." She put her hand on his shoulder. "You're a big strapping fellow, but face it, you're no bruiser like your brother."

He smiled. "Don't worry. I may work in a plush office, but that doesn't mean I'm helpless. I'll be fine. And as for Mike, he could be gone a week or months. I can't wait that long."

"Then promise me you'll be careful. And listen, if for any reason you need my help, you call me at Edith's." She handed him a slip of paper. "There's her number."

Sure could've used that offer in the last year of medical school. He slipped the paper into his shirt pocket. "Thanks, Auntie," he said. "There's no need for you to worry, though. I'll be fine."

Chapter
Seventeen

Dan stayed at the airport long enough to make sure he saw Elinor's plane took off safely, then found himself held up in rush-hour traffic on his way back to Langley. When he got home, he slept deep and hard and woke up after four o'clock in the afternoon.

Feeling more refreshed than he had in a long time, Dan showered and changed. He carried his dirty clothes basket down to the laundry room. With the habit of a longtime bachelor, he checked his pockets before putting his clothes in the washer and pulled out the scrap of paper with Elinor's number at Edith's on it. He tossed it on the coffee table on his way out to his car.

As twilight dimmed the sun, he drove into the parking lot of the Coyote Bar and Grill. The after-work crowd had already arrived, so the only parking space big enough to fit his full-size car was around the side of the building. After locking his car, Dan strode to the front door of the bar.

The entrance was very much like those found in Western movies. Four steps led up onto a wooden walkway fronted by hitching posts. In Langley's more rural days, it wouldn't have been out of place to see a horse hitched there. Now chopped-down motorcycles occupied that spot. Their black-leather-clad owners would be inside.

At the entrance Dan found two steel doors with multiple boot marks on them. Dan pulled the heavy door open and went inside.

Smoke immediately stung his eyes. The Worker's Safety Board had banned smoking inside public buildings, but the Coyote's patrons showed little interest in complying. Dan could understand why. No sane compliance officer would dare set foot in there to hand out fines.

Rhythmic country music blared. Heads turned toward him when he entered. The next moment the curious ones went back to their own business. Good thing Dan had borrowed his brother's work clothes. Mike's torn fleece-lined jean jacket, ripped blue jeans, and black boots fit right in.

Dan chose a backless stool at the polished wood bar and placed one of his boots on the brass rail. Dark wooden shelves lined the paneled wall behind the bar. The shelves held bottles of every shape and color. A big bartender with a small bullet head and a black T-shirt stretched around biceps the size of tree trunks sauntered over. "What can I get you?" he asked. His low voice started up from somewhere around his knees.

"Give me a root beer."

The bartender watched him for a moment, then went to the soda station and filled a tall glass. He returned and relieved Dan of three dollars for the beverage. Dan sipped his drink and covertly watched his bar mates. Kurt would fit right in with this crowd of bikers and coarse cowboys—two-thirds surly men and one-third harsh women.

Most of the people seated at the two dozen or so round tables had their heads bowed over thick white plates filled with food. Dan's stomach reminded him that he hadn't eaten all day. He signaled the bartender. "Can I get a menu?" he asked.

The bartender jerked his head upward toward a smudged

black chalkboard. Through a smoky haze, Dan read three options—steak, burgers, or fish and chips. "I'll have the fish and chips," he said. If the food hadn't killed the people who were already eating, it probably wouldn't kill Dan. He hoped.

How do you find someone who doesn't want to be found? he wondered. *Especially in a place like this.*

While he waited for the food, he turned toward the eating, drinking, talking crowd. They acted friendly enough to each other, but how would they react if Dan started wandering around asking if anyone had seen Kurt Fletcher? He might as well paint *cop* on his forehead. How did his brother do this?

A woman got up from a full table and walked toward him, an inviting smile on her heart-shaped face. She wore a tight red T-shirt that stopped an inch above the waistband on her jeans. Sliding onto the stool beside him, she murmured, "Buy me a drink?"

She was as thin and tall as a vaulting pole. Her bleached hair and sunken sallow cheeks made her look unreal. The guys at her table had their heads turned, watching.

While in Rome. . . He smiled at her and said, "Sure. What'll you have?"

"Double scotch." She reeked of cheap perfume and stale cigarettes.

"Double scotch for the lady," Dan called to the bartender. He nodded and reached for a short glass. Dan felt like he was trapped in some sort of B-grade detective movie.

The bartender placed the scotch on the bar. "Thanks," she said to Dan. "My name's Cindy."

"Dan," he said, lifting his root beer for a sip.

Cindy dug a package of cigarettes out of her purse and lit one. She made a point of sending the initial cloud of smoke into his face. Dan forced himself not to react.

"The guys were wondering where your partner is."

"Come again?" Dan asked. "What partner?"

She grinned. "You guys never come in here alone. We figure your partner has to be good, because we can't spot him anywhere."

Dan gulped and tried to smile. "You think I'm a cop?"

"Well, duh," she said. "You look as comfortable as a lobster in a pot of boiling water. This definitely isn't your thing."

"I hate to disappoint you," Dan said, "but I'm not a cop."

"Get serious." She picked up her drink and sipped.

"No, really," Dan said. "Believe it or not, I'm a plastic surgeon."

She shook her head. "Get out of here. You? A plastic surgeon? No way."

The bartender dropped Dan's plate of fish and chips in front of him. There was enough grease floating on the bottom of the plate to do a lube job on his car. Dan touched the plate. "Where else can a guy get good food like this?"

Cindy's thin laugh broke through the pulsating music for a moment. "Oh, there aren't too many places you can get food like this, but I hardly think a *plastic surgeon* came to the Coyote for greasy fries and soggy fish. Why don't you just admit you're a cop? Your cover is blown, Honey. Take a hike."

Dan's smile disappeared. "I'm not a cop."

She shifted her weight to look at him better. "Right. You're a plastic surgeon."

"That I am."

Her hard eyes drifted over his flannel shirtfront. "Prove it."

"How?" Dan asked. "I can't perform a liposuction for you or do a silicon implant."

She took a drag of her cigarette. "Tell me how you'd give me a perfect figure."

Dan scratched the side of his face. "Well, I could do it with cutting and implants, but that wouldn't be my first choice."

"There's another way?"

Dan reached over, took the cigarette from her mouth, and butted it out. "Quit smoking."

She gave him a look that showed she doubted his sanity. "That'll give me a great figure?"

"No," Dan said. "But it's going to help you gain weight. You've got to be at least twenty pounds underweight." He looked pointedly at her bare midriff. "In fact, by the way your ribs are showing, I'd figure you to be fifteen to twenty percent underweight. Your skin is pasty, and your eyes are dull. Good indications of malnourishment. My guess is that despite everything I just said, you think you're fat."

Cindy fidgeted and wouldn't meet his gaze. She reached in her shirt pocket for her pack of cigarettes.

"Tell me honestly," Dan said, "do I sound more like a cop or a doctor?"

"Doctor," Cindy said.

"I came here looking for a guy by the name of Kurt Fletcher. He's a regular here. He's about fifty years old, missing his front teeth, always looks like he just got off the farm. Dark hair, unshaved face."

Cindy shook her head. "Don't know him. Thanks for the drink. I've gotta go." She slipped off the stool and rushed back to her friends.

You idiot, Dan thought. A diagnosis of her eating disorder in the Coyote Grill was probably the last thing Cindy wanted. Even if she knew Kurt, all he'd managed to do was wire her mouth shut by making her feel threatened. He spotted an empty table directly across from the big-screen TV bolted into a corner. Currently it was broadcasting the opening to a hockey game.

At this point no one in this bar would tell him about Kurt even if they knew the man. His best plan would be to blend in and wait to see if Kurt showed up.

Taking his plate and his root beer with him, he moved to the table. On his way Dan passed close to Cindy's table. Muttered profanities came his way. Counting on his size to dissuade any further abuse, he ignored them. He was almost the same size as Mike. Unfortunately, though, he couldn't punch his way out of a wet piece of tissue paper.

The table sat next to the wall where Dan could rest his back against the rough oak paneling. He sat down and settled in for a long wait. To Dan, hockey was strictly a spectator sport, and tennis was strictly for playing. Watching a tennis match made him fall asleep every time. Eyes on the screen, he leaned back and relaxed. The fish and chips weren't all that bad when doused with ketchup.

It was a good game, especially since the Vancouver Canucks were winning. The hours dragged on with no sign of Kurt Fletcher. At midnight Dan yawned and decided to head home.

The night air was chilly, and he buttoned his coat around him. He turned to the left and walked around the corner of the bar to get back to his car. The lighting around the back was poor. He dug his keys out of his pocket and started to insert it into the door lock. Footsteps rushed toward him. Dan looked up and his nose exploded in pain. He staggered backward.

When Jessica pulled into the Martin farm, the clock on her CD player said it was nine o'clock. A late-breaking story had kept her at the station much longer than she'd expected. She shut off the motor and stepped out into the front yard. A halogen light mounted on a pole illuminated everything in a pale white. She could see her breath in the crisp evening air. No lights shone through the house windows.

Had Amy already gone to bed? Jessica stared at the house and wished she'd called before she left Vancouver. She'd left the studio in a rush because she was late, and she forgot to get Amy's phone number. Otherwise, she would have called from her cell phone while she drove.

Jessica approached the front door and saw a yellow sheet of paper taped to it. In a hasty scrawl, it read:

Dear Jessica,

I got a call from the hospital after I talked to you. A nurse got sick, and I have to finish her shift tonight. Feel free to look around without me. The barn's light switch is on the left side of the wide doors.

Thanks,
Amy

Jessica returned to her car and retrieved a flashlight from the glove box. The beam cut into the darkness surrounding the side of the house as Jessica walked around to the back. The moon was a sliver overhead, the stars brilliant against an ebony sky. She felt like she was the only person alive in the middle of deep silence. The cold kept crickets and frogs quiet this time of year.

Other than the beam from her flashlight, total darkness engulfed the back sector of the yard. All the cattle were gone, so there was no need for any lighting here. Jessica's light scanned the area and fell upon Kurt's cabin. No sign of life there, either. She shifted toward the barn.

Her running shoes crunched across grass, then gravel. She kept the beam close in front of her, watching for holes and old cow pies. Her heart pounded in her ears, and she felt blood rush to her head.

Suddenly, the hair on the back of her neck stood on end. Jessica spun and shot the beam behind her. Nothing. Just nerves. Who wouldn't be nervous walking in the dark on property where two murders had taken place? She shivered and hurried toward the barn as though the dark cavernous building offered her safety.

The wide wooden doors stood open. She used her flashlight to find the light switch on the wall and flipped it on. Brilliant light filled the interior for a split second, then died. What a time for the fuse to blow. Playing her flashlight around, she could see stalls across one wall of the barn. Hay bales filled the other end. The rest of the barn was used for grain storage. To the left was a closed room with a heavy hasp and lock on its thick wooden door. A huge tractor stood in the middle of the barn.

For a long moment, Jessica stood there debating. Did she really want to venture inside in the darkness? What if she fell over something or had something fall on her? Then she thought about the long trip home and another drive out here tomorrow. Maybe the slicker was somewhere nearby. It would be a shame to be so close to it and walk away.

Flashing her narrow beam around, she saw thick dust over everything. Scuffling and squeaking brought her up short. Rats were something she hadn't counted on. After a moment, she pressed on.

Jessica wandered along the wall looking for anything that could contain a slicker. She spotted a cloth bag tossed up against the wall, partially hidden by a rake and a hoe. She crouched down and pulled the bag open. Gasping, Jessica stumbled back, dropped the flashlight, and crab-crawled away from the bag. The indignant screeching of mice filled the air as they scurried away in several directions.

Breathing in short, soft gasps, Jessica dropped to a crouch and held her hand against her chest, waiting for her pulse to settle down. After awhile the humor of her predicament struck her, and she started to giggle.

"Sorry, guys," she called. Standing, she retrieved the flash-light and shone it on the bag. She gave the bag a kick. When no more mice popped out, Jessica opened it and shone the flashlight inside. About four inches of grain lay on the bottom. A bonanza in mice dollars.

She continued searching along the wall and found only a couple of more mice-invested feedbags. Next, she moved to the stalls.

Starting from the corner of the barn, she pulled doors open and went over the interiors with her flashlight. Each one had an earthen floor piled with manure. She came up empty there, too. She looked back at the bales of hay and wondered how long they'd been there. Had Beth purchased more hay after Peter died? Was there hay cut on the farm afterwards? She couldn't think of a single reason for the slicker to be buried under the bales of hay and turned away.

Next she moved to the most obvious choice. If the slicker wasn't in the barn, it must be in the locked storage room. The heavy rusty lock was as big as her palm. The hasp was an old iron one. She hated to admit defeat, but she needed help with this. She'd see if Amy would give her the key in the morning.

The sound of roaring motors drifted in from the distance. Several cars made a flashing red and blue glow in the driveway coming toward her. Had someone seen her sneaking around and called the police? This was great. Just great.

Her first impulse was to run and hide. But why? Her Porsche sat in the front yard. In short order a patrol car swung around and stopped in front of the barn. Its headlights dwarfed her little flashlight. Jessica shielded her eyes.

Two car doors opened, and a deep voice shouted, "RCMP. Place your hands above your head!"

Chapter
Eighteen

Dazed, Dan slumped against his car. His attacker wore a ski mask. He had a wide torso and massive fists covered with thin white gloves. The thug moved in on Dan and fired half a dozen punches to his midsection. Dan grabbed onto him, trying to tie up his arms, but the man started pounding on his ribs.

"Back off!" a woman's voice commanded.

The man stepped away from Dan but kept pumping his fists in the air. Gasping and wheezing from his bruised ribs, Dan's eyes stayed on those powerful hands. He finally realized that he was looking at surgical gloves. His attacker wore a glittering ring. Dan stared at it. Why would someone wear a ring outside his glove?

"Remember, he won the fight," the woman said.

Bent over and holding his ribs, Dan peered in the direction of the voice. She stood in the shadow of the bar, her figure impossible to make out. Two men stood beside her. They all wore ski masks. What was this, a warning to stop looking for Kurt?

Dan pulled himself off the car. The attacker whistled a jab past his ear. "Come on, Doctor," he taunted. "Don't make this too easy."

Clenching his teeth, Dan moved away from the Grand Marquis. He put his hands up and squinted past his bruised cheeks. He dabbed at his streaming nose with the sleeve of his jacket and wished he'd paid more attention when their Dad gave him and Mike boxing lessons. Circling his attacker, Dan briefly wondered why no one from the Coyote came out to see what was going on—but only briefly. Even if someone could have heard noises of a fight over that pounding music, would they care?

Dan threw an awkward jab, which his attacker easily knocked to the side.

"Smarten up," the woman called. "We haven't got all night."

Nodding, his stance a picture of arrogance, the man beckoned for Dan to take his best shot.

Adrenaline power surged from Dan's legs and up through his shoulder. He rocketed a right haymaker at the man's face. At the last millisecond the man lowered his head, and Dan connected with the massive bone of his forehead. Howling in agony, Dan grabbed his hand.

For good measure the thug landed two more crunching blows to Dan's nose. Blood covered his lower face and shirt. Dan swayed, trying to stay conscious.

"That should do," the woman said. "Time to go."

Two more men bore down on Dan. He tried swinging at them, but two of them grabbed his arms and pushed him against his car. Dan started to call out. A sharp blow to his face, and a man's tenor voice hissed in his ear. "Shut your mouth, Doc, or you'll wish you had."

A black cloth came over his eyes. Strong hands twisted his wrists behind his back and bound them with something plastic that cut into his flesh. He felt a sharp pain behind his knees and fell to the asphalt parking lot. His feet were similarly bound.

Dan heard the familiar sound of his own car door opening. Hands grabbed underneath his armpits and around his legs.

They lifted him from the parking lot and shoved him into the car, wedging him on the floor between the back and front seats, and the door swung closed.

God, he thought, *I'm not ready to die.* The next moment everything went black.

In the wide beam of the police cruiser's lights, Jessica raised her hands over her head as instructed. Car doors slammed, and two silhouettes approached her—one a man, the other a woman. Another car pulled in behind them and two men got out.

"I thought that was your car," the woman said. It was Anna Carrington. "You can put your hands down."

Jessica dropped her hands to her sides and let them hang loosely. Carrington had her dead to rights. If there was ever a time to play nice, this was it.

Carrington flicked on her flashlight and swung the beam over the inside of the barn. "What's so interesting that you had to come out in the dark to find it?"

"I. . .have permission," Jessica said, fumbling at her coat pocket. She pulled out Amy's note and handed it to her.

Carrington read it under her flashlight beam and handed it back. "That's good, Meyers, but it doesn't tell me why you're here in the dark."

When Jessica didn't answer, Carrington shone her light on the locked door. "What's in there?" she asked.

Jessica kept silent.

One of the other officers, the smallest of the four, said, "Where should we start, Corporal?" Carrington towered over him by at least three inches.

"You and Jamie take this place apart. John and Steve can work on the house."

"What are you doing?" Jessica asked. "That's illegal."

Carrington smiled. "We have a warrant, Jessica. The will provided Amy with a tidy motive, so we got a search warrant to find evidence of Nardil."

"In the barn?"

Carrington touched Jessica's elbow. "Would you mind stepping outside with me for a moment? We need to talk." They walked toward the brightly lit police cars, and Anna Carrington held open the front door of the first one. Jessica got in, grateful for the warmth she immediately felt inside the vehicle. Carrington got in on the driver's side.

As soon as her door closed, Corporal Carrington said, "Contrary to what you might believe, I want to find out the truth behind this mess. Up until this afternoon, my whole investigation added up to one conclusion—medical malpractice. Hardly worth the RCMP's time. We were just about to close the file when I had an impulse that I should attend the reading of Beth's will. I called for a court order and went there on my own time. Ask Dr. Foster. He saw me there.

"In the lawyer's office I discovered that Amy Creighton did benefit from her aunt's will. Dr. Foster was named, too, but I don't think two hundred thousand is enough to get a successful plastic surgeon to kill a patient. . .unless he was deeply in debt. We're checking that out, too."

As she spoke, Anna Carrington slowly dropped her professional hard line. She turned to Jessica, pleading in her eyes. "We both want the same thing, Jessica. You know things that I don't know. You could help Dan by sharing information with me."

Jessica hesitated. Normally she could read a face with flawless precision, but she was having a hard time with Carrington. The corporal appeared sincere, but then so did the wolf in *Little Red Riding Hood.*

Anna Carrington went on. "Amy Creighton is our primary interest at this point. If you have something that can help us, now would be a good time to start talking. I'll be honest with you. If Ms. Creighton comes up clean, our attention turns back to the good doctor."

Jessica weighed her options. Telling Carrington about the slicker wouldn't hurt Dan. It could only help him.

"I should also mention," Carrington went on, "that if you withhold evidence or information, you are obstructing justice and could be charged."

Jessica touched the scar on her face. Did she dare take a chance on this woman? If she could help Dan, she should. Besides, there was no way she'd ever get to that slicker now that the police were involved. If she did manage to come back later and find it, who could examine it for cow urine beside police forensics?"

Finally, Jessica came to a decision. She spoke slowly as though feeling her way along. "A few weeks before Beth Martin's death," she said, "I met a young woman at the Cranfield restaurant in Richmond. She told me that Peter Martin's death wasn't an accident. It was murder."

Carrington's dark eyes narrowed. "Peter Martin was trampled by a bull. I've never heard of a bull as a murder weapon. She was pulling your leg."

"That's what I thought until I talked to a veterinarian friend of mine. Apparently, a bull can be agitated by smearing a victim's clothes with the urine of a cow in heat. That would drive even a docile bull into a rage."

Carrington's expression grew stern. "Don't mess with me, Meyers. What are you pulling here? I want the truth."

"I am telling you the truth," Jessica said. "I'm here looking for the slicker Peter Martin wore the day he died. It disappeared after the paramedics took him to the hospital. The last anyone can remember, it was left in the barn after the ambulance left here. I figured it must still be here somewhere. The only place I haven't searched is in that locked room."

She bore in on Carrington. "Don't you understand? If the slicker has cow urine on it, someone murdered Peter Martin. That person may have also killed Beth. This is bigger than money from a will or professional negligence. Grow-ops are big time, and we may be right in the middle of it."

Anna Carrington stared at Jessica, her olive skin turning from red to blue in the strobing lights. After a moment, she said, "We have to search everywhere that could hold a Nardil capsule. I guess a slicker would fall into that category. If it's there, we'll find it."

"You mean you'll have it tested?" Jessica asked.

Carrington reached for her door handle. "We're going to check every avenue, Ms. Meyers," she said. "Even a crazy theory about cow urine."

Dan's first waking impulse was to turn on a light. He touched his face and realized he wore something over his eyes. He fumbled with the cloth and pulled it off. Blinking, he tried to focus against the darkness of night. He was outside and lying on some gravel. The rustling of trees sounded around him.

Now that the excitement was over, his throbbing nose got his full attention. Dan gently examined it with his fingers. Definitely broken and pushed to the left. His ribs ached, but their complaint paled compared to his nose. They were probably only bruised.

He reached into his pocket for the penlight he always carried with him—a doctor's habit. The tiny beam was good for close work, but it was a pitifully weak replacement for a flashlight. He shone the light on his feet. A plastic tie bound them together. Nice guys. Rope he could untie, but without a knife, how was he to free his legs? Gravel dug into his hands and thighs as he dragged himself off the road.

He searched the shoulder until he found two rocks the size of large potatoes, one smooth and one with a jagged edge. Stretching his feet as far apart as the restraint allowed, Dan slipped one rock underneath the plastic. He slammed the jagged rock on the plastic strip. Nothing happened. He slammed it again and again until it fragmented enough so he could pull it apart with his ankles.

Dan stood and gasped. His abused muscles had been forced into a cramped position for too long. He'd be doing great if he could walk at all.

Looking around, he saw he was on a forestry road with trees towering on both sides. Using his tiny light, he determined that some of the trees were cedar. He could smell pine, too. The cedar trunks were so thick, he doubted he could wrap his arms around them.

There was only once place they could've come, considering the time they'd driven and these old cedars. The only place large enough for his kidnappers to dump him without being noticed was Golden Ears Provincial Park.

Of course, knowing where he was didn't help him walk out of there. Dan hobbled in the direction he thought his car had gone. As he moved, the stiffness in his ankles went away. It wasn't long before Dan managed a nice, easy stride. If only his face felt that good.

He wished he could whistle to chase away the stillness of the night, but his smashed lips wouldn't cooperate. Even a full-grown man possessed the fears of a child alone in the dark. A crash in nearby bushes made him jump. He shone his penlight toward the trees and two green dots glowed back at him. Didn't bears hibernate? Sure they did. His mind went back to a documentary he'd watched recently. Unless it was a garbage bear.

He let his light go out. "God," he whispered, "if You're still up there, I could use Your help more than ever."

At the farm, Jessica stood beside Anna Carrington watching the officers dismantle the storage room. A brilliant bulb on an orange cord hung from the rafters above, giving the men enough light to work. They'd been at it for half an hour and still no slicker. Jessica's legs grew weary, and she moved to a bale of hay to sit for awhile. This was taking longer than she'd expected.

Anna Carrington came to join her after a few minutes. Sitting down, she said, "You know, it's still not easy for women in the police force."

"I'm sure it isn't," Jessica said. "It's not easy in the media, either. Or anywhere else."

"We've made some progress," Carrington went on, "but women officers still have guys making crude remarks, and if a single girl won't go out with any of them, they'll accuse her of being a lesbian." She pushed back her wiry hair. "It doesn't help that I look the way I do. If I were five feet three and a hundred and twenty pounds. . ."

"You'd have more apes after you," Jessica told her. "It's not easy on either side of the spectrum."

In the light spilling from the storage room, Jessica looked at Anna Carrington and saw something she'd never seen before. Vulnerability.

"It took a lot of hard work for me to make sergeant. That story you did nearly broke my career."

"I wasn't wrong, was I?" Jessica spoke softly to take off the edge.

Anna moved a little closer. "We're off the record, right?"

"Of course. This is girl to girl."

"You weren't wrong," she murmured. "I pushed it too far."

"Is that what you're doing now?"

Anna hesitated. Then she nodded. "At first, yes. It wasn't just because you were involved. The thought of nailing a plastic surgeon appealed to me. He's the guy who creates all those women who look down their noses at me."

"Women like me?"

When Anna didn't answer, Jessica said, "I'd be lying if I said you were wrong. When you're pretty, everyone treats you special. After awhile you begin to think you really are special. You start looking down on everyone else. I'd still be that way if it hadn't been for the car accident." Jessica's voice quavered.

Anna watched her, waiting for her to go on.

"When I had the car accident and I knew my face was mangled, I wanted to kill myself. My whole worth was wrapped up in my skin. Without it, I had nothing. No one hires a disfigured news anchor. If it hadn't been for Dan Foster, I probably would have done myself in. He didn't just save my skin. He taught me there's more to life than this. . .this shell. Since the accident, I've tried to treat everyone the same." She met Anna's gaze. "I haven't been fair with you."

Carrington shrugged. "Same here." She touched Jessica's coat sleeve. "Why don't we call a truce and find out what really happened here?"

"Got something!" one of the constables called from inside the room.

Both women hurried to see what it was. Anna Carrington slipped on latex gloves as she moved. She waited for the photographer to get a shot of the brown lump on the dirt floor. Then she very carefully lifted it, and yellow vinyl fabric showed under the coating of dust. One of the officers held a brown paper bag under it, and Carrington dropped it inside.

Jessica peered over her shoulder.

"A slicker," Carrington said. "And does it ever stink!" She closed the bag and handed it to a young blond constable. "Tag it and send it to the lab."

"What do I tell them to look for?"

"Cow urine," Carrington said.

His jaw sagged. "Cow urine?"

"We're especially interested if any pheromones are present."

Anna turned to Jessica. "Unfortunately with the Missing Women's Task Force taking priority on all lab time, this slicker will have to be sent out. It'll probably be two months until we get results."

"It's a start," Jessica told her. She wanted to cry or dance around the barn. This was finally progress. She reached for her cell phone to call Dan but changed her mind. Anna Carrington had just turned into a real person. Jessica wanted to keep a low profile. She'd call Dan when she got home.

Anna turned to the other constables. "Finish here. I'll help the guys searching the house." She turned to Jessica. "You want to tag along?"

"Absolutely," Jessica said, smiling widely. "We're on a roll."

As they left the barn, Anna's cell phone beeped. She pulled it off her belt and flipped it open. "Carrington here." Her forehead creased as she listened. "I'll be right there." She closed the phone and said to Jessica, "I've got to go."

"What is it?" Jessica asked.

"Rocky Wiebe is dead, and Dan Foster's car was spotted in the area."

Chapter
Nineteen

Dan watched a wide dark form scramble out of the forest and soon recognized the shape of a black bear. Grizzlies would hunt down a man and kill him, but blacks were usually timid. Ninety-nine percent of the time, they ran away when they encountered a human—unless it was a "garbage bear." That type fed at dumpsites or carelessly stored trashcans. Those bears didn't fear humans. They also didn't hibernate because they had a steady supply of food.

It was late October, and this bear should have been getting drowsy. The animal turned toward him, stood on its hind legs, and sniffed. Watching the shadowy form ahead of him, Dan didn't dare breathe. Finally, it dropped down on all fours and waddled to the side of the road, where it started rooting around.

At least the animal doesn't feel like eating me, Dan thought. On the other hand, the only way to his car was past this furry creature. Dan didn't want to push his luck by walking past it. He looked toward the dense forest, considering his options. He could stay put and wait for it to move on. Or, he could go into the forest and work his way around it. Dan much preferred the first option but realized that before long the bear might get annoyed at his presence and decide to do something about it.

Dan edged sideways toward the trees. The bear looked over its shoulder, grunted, and returned to its digging. Dan slipped behind a cedar tree and waited, trying to breathe again while he had the chance. He might have to run for it in a minute.

The bear made no move toward him, and Dan continued into the forest. The thick canopy above him cut the moonlight into tiny fingers.

Easing forward, he held out his penlight and felt his way through the trees. Too long at this and his light would go out. He didn't trust this used triple-A battery to last more than fifteen minutes.

The moon and the road were in the same direction. Every few steps, he'd cut the light and stare overhead. As long as the slivers of moonlight stayed to his right, Dan was on track. A dozen paces later, he rested his hand on a large cedar and felt his way around it. He started forward, snagged his foot on a root, and crashed to the forest floor. He threw out his forearm to protect his face, and his broken nose smashed toward his forehead.

His scream echoed through the trees. He clenched his teeth and moaned, not wanting to give the bear a reason to come and see what he was up to. After a moment, Dan pulled himself to a sitting position, clamped his arms around his bruised ribs, and rocked in pain.

He lost track of time. Tears streamed down his face. After awhile he pulled himself off the ground, and the world spun in a dim, uneven blur. He settled on his haunches and let his head hang between his knees. Blood dripped from his nose to the earthen floor.

He took deep breaths and waited for the nausea to pass. After a couple of minutes, he touched the end of his nose with the back of his hand. The blood flow had slowed to an ooze.

He stood and waited a moment to make sure the worst of the nausea had passed, then took a couple of deep cleansing breaths, extended his hands, and continued onward. After a few minutes in the trees, he felt confident that he was well past the bear. He turned toward the speckles of moonlight and stumbled half a dozen times before he emerged onto the road. He looked up at the moon, never so glad to see its ghostly glow.

Looking to the right, he saw no sign of the bear. He left his light out and continued down the road. His eyes had adjusted to the darkness enough to stay on the gravel. If he strayed into the weeds along the road, his shoes told him so. Compared to bumbling through the woods, this was a breeze.

Dan's workout routine was now paying off. Despite his physical challenges, he could still move along at a good clip, probably around three miles an hour. That meant only an hour stood between him and the luxurious comfort and warmth of his car. Once, he tried jogging, but his nose didn't like the bouncing and he had to slow down.

Until now he hadn't had time to think about the whys of his predicament. If those thugs had wanted to scare him and keep him from looking for Kurt, the beating would have been enough. Why tie him up and dump him in a provincial park? Besides that, nobody said, "Stay away from Kurt or you'll die." He worried that he was caught up in something more far-reaching than Beth Martin's murder.

Dan's mind ran through various scenarios as he walked. Nothing made sense. That ring was important somehow. He'd seen that signet ring before. In the dim light behind the Coyote, he saw twinkling diamond chips in the shape of a "W."

At a bend in the gravel road, he nearly wept with relief. The flashing red and blue lights of a police car lit up the forest. They had parked behind his abandoned car. Two officers bent over the smashed front fender. As Dan watched, a camera flashed.

Dan lifted his arm, opened his mouth to call out, and then

froze. Why were the police out here taking crime-scene photographs? Was he the prime suspect for another crime?

Instinctively, Dan pulled the same maneuver he had with the bear. He held still, waited until the officers faced the other way, then he backed away, hoping the curve would hide him. Two steps later, a flashlight beam washed over his face.

"Hold it right there!" a constable called out.

As if on cue, Mike and Louise opened the front doors of their car and stepped out to the parking lot of the Crystal Springs Motel on Ellicott Road, near the border. Unlike the dingy broken-down hovels where drug dealers supposedly met, this motel couldn't have been more than three years old. The building had two levels, with doors opening onto an outside walkway. Its neon sign offered clean, quiet rooms and a family-friendly TV in every one.

"Room 234, right?" Mike asked, his stride loose and smooth.

"Right," Louise said. She held onto the strap of her shoulder bag as though it were a lifeline. Her shoes made sharp taps on the macadam. She didn't look happy.

Mike held a scuffed aluminum briefcase. They took the stairs on the left end of the building, turned right at the top, and spotted room 234 halfway down. Mike delivered three solid raps on the green metal door, paused, then rapped twice more.

He heard movement behind the door. The deadbolt clicked, and the door opened. Their contact, Garret, filled the doorway. "Come on in," he said. He had dark circles under his sunken eyes. If possible, he looked even more emaciated than he had at their first meeting.

In spite of the no-smoking symbol on the door, a haze floated in the room. A man of average build sat at a round table littered with fast-food breakfast containers. He had jet-black hair slicked tight against his angular skull. His dark blue business suit would put a Wall Street trader to shame. With narrow feminine hands, he popped a butterscotch drop into his mouth and let his lifeless blue eyes look them over.

Without getting up, he held his hand out for Mike to shake. "I'm Benny," he said. His voice sounded soft and nasal.

Mike ignored the offer of politeness and sat on the edge of a queen-size bed. Garret sat on the other bed.

"I'm Arnie," Mike said.

"Patti," Louise said, giving the drug dealer's hand a quick shake. Still clutching her bag, she moved to the door.

"You got the money?" Benny asked, pointedly eyeing the briefcase.

"You got the pot?" Mike countered.

"You're not seeing what I have until I see the money."

"And you're not seeing the money until I make sure the room's clean. If you break our agreement in any way, we're outta here."

Benny flung out a limp hand. "Suit yourself."

Mike pulled open the drawers on the built-in dresser, ripped off the bed covers, and looked between both beds' mattresses and box springs while Louise checked the bathroom and the tiny closet.

Mike moved close to Garret and said, "Against the wall!" He slowly obeyed, and Mike patted him down.

"You, too," Louise told Benny.

Benny dragged himself out of his chair and took Garret's place while Louise checked him out.

"Now our turn," Benny said, turning around.

Garret took Mike, and Benny took Louise.

"Careful with those hands, or I'll break them," Louise told Benny. He hesitated, then carefully patted Louise down.

Benny returned to his chair. Garret opened the door that joined their room with the next one.

"Hold it right there," Mike barked. "We haven't checked that place out."

Hands wide, Garret retreated, carefully watching Mike while Louise did the honors in the adjoining room.

"It's clean," she called through the open door.

Mike looked in Garret's direction. "No fast moves," he said, nodding toward the doorway.

The man hitched his jeans around his skinny hips and edged through the door. He returned with a green canvas duffel bag.

Benny nodded toward the briefcase. "Open it up. I want to see the money."

"That's not the money," Mike said. "The cash is locked in the car."

Benny stiffened. "What's in the briefcase?"

Louise eased toward the door as Mike opened it. Inside was his portable laboratory kit.

"What's that for?" Benny asked, his icy eyes darting from the case to Mike's face. Garret moved closer, ready to spring.

"I've got to check the quality of your pot."

A look of disdain twisted Benny's slim features. "Smoke it. You'll find out all you need to know."

"What do you think this is?" Mike demanded. "I'm strictly professional. I don't do drugs. I don't even drink."

Benny went rigid.

"You're a cop," Garret said. His fist shot out. Mike side-stepped the blow and rushed forward. Like a striking cobra, Mike's fingers locked onto Garret's throat. Garret slapped at Mike's thick arm. He kicked at Mike but couldn't connect.

Still seated, Benny simply waited. He didn't seem to want to take on Louise.

"Let's get this straight right now," Mike said while Garret choked and turned purple. "I am not a cop, DEA, FBI, CIA,

NSA, ATF, customs agent, sheriff, sheriff's deputy, or any other of this country's law-enforcement agencies. I'm a guy who likes to make money. Like you." He shoved Garret onto the bed, where he gasped and coughed a few times.

Mike turned to Benny, his words fast and hot. "What's it going to be? Does Patti go to the car and get the money, or do we leave?"

"Get the money," Benny said, his lifeless eyes on Louise.

Louise left the room. While she was gone, the three men watched each other in an uneasy standoff. Five minutes later, she rapped the signal on the door, and Garret pulled himself off the bed to open it. Louise came in with a brown leather briefcase. She laid it on the bed and opened it. Garret and Benny leaned forward. Their eyes roamed over the wrapped greenbacks with the satisfaction of men who'd just been served at a five-star restaurant.

While Benny and Garret counted the money, Mike worked on the marijuana. The THC levels of Mexican pot usually ran about 0.4 to 1 percent. BC Bud, grown with hydroponics, could go as high as 15 percent. The sample before him hit 13 percent. It had definitely come from British Columbia.

"Well?" Benny asked, overdone boredom in his voice.

"You're under arrest," Mike said.

Both men froze.

Mike laughed loud and long. "Just kidding."

Benny swore. "Don't ever joke like that, Man."

"Hey," Mike said, "you called me a cop, so I'm letting you know how it feels. Now that we all understand each other, let's get down to business." He closed the aluminum case and snapped the fasteners. "This is good stuff. We're going to distribute it to our people down South. I've got no doubt we'll be coming back for more."

"How much more?" Benny asked.

"Like I told Garret, about a thousand kilos. If you can handle it?"

"Absolutely."

"And that's delivered," Mike said, handing the case to Louise.

"Not going to happen," Benny said. "Our Canadian partners are going to want to handle a deal this big themselves. You'll never get them to cross the line. If you want a shipment that big, you're going to have to go to Canada and get it."

"Then if we're going to take the risk of crossing the border, we want a break on the price," Mike said.

"I'll see what I can do," Benny said.

The flashlight blinded Dan, and panic nailed his feet to the road. For an instant he felt tempted to let the policemen arrest him. He needed medical attention, food, and rest. Right after that, he realized a single week in prison would make him regret surrender. He couldn't bear to think of months or years in a tiny cell. He spun away and dashed around the curve.

"Stop!" one of the constables shouted.

Dan charged into the forest.

The policemen held powerful flashlights that gave Dan few options. He had to get deep into the woods and hide.

Like a pinball, he bounced from one tree to another, hardly feeling the pain in his hands and shoulders. In this situation his penlight would only give away his position. He had to move ahead like a blind man. Hands outstretched, Dan rushed forward and slammed into a fallen cedar about chest high. Glancing back, he saw flashlight beams moving along the road.

He took five steps forward and fell. Crunchy leaves broke the fall. What was this?

Shielding his penlight with his shirt, he looked around.

He'd fallen into a narrow ditch full of leaves. Letting the light go out, he burrowed down. The top leaves were dry and loose, but after a few feet they became damp and mushy. Like a chipmunk, he continued to dig. He curled into a tight ball and pulled leaves over himself. This was a simple solution, and if the cops didn't look too hard, he might get away with it.

He forced himself to breathe slowly. Even so, to Dan's ears each expiration sounded like a whale blowing. He'd hardly gotten covered when rustling leaves and crackling twigs told him the police were coming his way. He felt his throat go dry, but forced down the panic rising inside him. Now, more than ever, he had to stay cool.

"Do you think that was him?" a man asked.

"Fits the description," a woman answered.

"He could be anywhere in these woods. Maybe I should radio for backup."

"And leave me out here alone?" she asked. "Not a chance. They said he slit the guy's throat with a scalpel."

Dan stifled a groan. Mixing up medication was bad enough. Now they thought he'd brutally murdered someone.

The man spoke. "If we both go back, he'll have a chance to get farther away."

Their footsteps stopped close by.

Dan tensed, forcing every fiber of his being to remain still. He held his breath and closed his eyes so they wouldn't reflect the light. The beam flashed across him and moved on.

"We can't go too much farther, or we'll end up lost in the woods," she said. "It's too dark to tell which direction is the road."

The constable's voice took on a sly tone. "Hey, that wouldn't be so bad, would it? Being lost in the woods all night with me?"

"Get a life, Murdoch!" she blurted out. "Let's move over that way. It's closer to the road. He wouldn't want to get lost in the woods, either, would he?"

As they trudged away, the male officer said, "There probably isn't another patrol car within thirty miles of here. If we can't find him, we'll let the Abbotsford detachment know about this. They can decide how much manpower they want to commit to finding this guy."

An eternity later, their footsteps receded. Dan released his breath. He couldn't stay here all night. More police were sure to come at dawn. He peeked over the rim of the ditch. Judging from their lights, the officers were moving away from his car. If he could get back to the car without being caught, he had a chance. He always kept a spare key in his wallet. He touched his back pocket. The wallet was still there.

Keeping on all fours, Dan crawled out of the ditch and aimed toward the moonlight. The constables were specks of light in the distance. He didn't dare stand up and risk crashing into a tree or tripping over a branch.

Sometime later, he edged out of the woods. The cops' voices drifted to him from down the road. They were too far away for him to make out their words. As quietly as possible, Dan crawled to his car. The police cruiser stood ready to chase him. How far could he get before they caught up to him?

In a flash of inspiration, he pulled out his penlight and used the back of it to let the air out of the patrol car's tires until it sat on four flats. The cops said the nearest cruiser was thirty miles away. That was his only advantage.

Pulling out his wallet, he found the key. Why had those thugs left him his wallet? Nothing made sense.

He returned to his own car and opened the driver's door. The door chime sounded like an air horn in the quiet night. A shout came from the distance. He jumped into the car, fired up the motor, and slammed on the accelerator. Gravel flying, the car fishtailed, then sailed ahead.

The road was dark. He strained to see until he realized that he was driving with only his daytime running lights on. Pulling the light knob fully out, he followed the winding gravel road at speeds he'd never attempted before. The car jumped and rocked when he hit the paved section. Glad to be on safer footing, he kicked up the speed, his full concentration on handling the car along the winding road. At this pace he'd be out of the park in no time. Ten minutes later, he reached the highway.

He turned right, hoping to find a phone before more police arrived. There was an APB out on him for sure. Five miles down the road, he spotted a telescoping pole holding a bright service-station sign and headed toward it. At that moment, he also saw red strobe lights on an approaching vehicle.

Chapter
Twenty

Jessica stared at Anna's cell phone like it was a scorpion ready to strike. Rocky was dead? And Dan was suspected in his murder? This was the absolute limit. How much more bad news could there be?

Anna spoke into the phone. "Any other details yet?" The women stood in the yard outside the Martin barn. "Okay. I'll head over there." She flipped the phone shut and looked at Jessica. "I have to go to the crime scene."

"Dan couldn't have done it," Jessica blurted out before Anna could say anything more.

"I'm afraid we have to go by the facts, Jessica. You have to admit that you're not exactly objective about Dan Foster." Anna's face didn't hold its usual contempt. She was simply stating a fact.

"I don't suppose you'd let me come with you."

Anna slipped the phone to her belt holder and appraised Jessica. "It would be highly irregular to let the media in on a crime scene."

"I wouldn't go as media. I'd go as Dan's friend."

Anna tapped her cell phone case, thinking. "Promise me you'll just observe—nothing more."

Jessica crossed her heart. "Promise."

"Everything you see and hear is off the record. It won't show up on the news."

"Everything's off the record. I just want to help Dan. Messing you up won't do that. You have my word of honor."

"Okay." Anna's tone said that Jessica was on probation. "I have to come back here anyway, so we'll take my car."

They got into Anna's police cruiser. Jessica shivered and chafed her arms, willing the car's heater to work faster. Anna shifted into reverse, turned around, then shoved it into drive, and headed toward the house. She stopped near the front steps.

"I'll be back in a second," Anna said, reaching for the door latch. "I'm going to check on the guys and let them know where I'm going."

After Anna left, Jessica closed her eyes and tried not to despair. What would happen to Dan now? He was supposed to be looking for Kurt this evening. Why did he go over to Rocky's place?

Anna Carrington's briefcase rested on the space next to Jessica. It would be too easy to open it and read her notes. She could even see the front door, so she'd know when Anna came out of the house. Jessica reached over to snap open the clasps, then stopped.

Idiot, she scolded herself. *This woman could be a great ally, and you're going to betray her trust right out of the starting gate.* Jessica put her hands on her lap and locked them together in case they got any more dumb ideas.

A moment later Anna came through the front door and walked up to the car. As she got in, she glanced toward her briefcase, and Jessica breathed a silent sigh of relief. If she'd moved it even an inch, Anna would have known, and she'd read about the crime scene in the morning papers like everyone else.

The police cruiser pulled out of the driveway and down the road.

"No lights and siren?" Jessica asked.

Anna smiled. "He's dead now. No hurry."

Anna shared the same dry humor as news people. Because they dealt often in tragedy, they protected themselves with humor. If Rocky Wiebe's mother were alive, she wouldn't find the comment funny at all. As it was, Jessica couldn't think of a single person who would mourn Rocky's passing.

They drove through the business section of Abbotsford, through a residential area, and into the country. Anna slowed down in front of a small house with a small lawn. Yellow crime-scene tape circled the yard.

In front of the house, three police cars had their lights dancing in the darkness. She parked on the road and switched the motor off.

"This is where Rocky lived?" Jessica asked, leaning forward to see better.

"Looks like it." She caught Jessica's coat sleeve. "Remember our deal. Don't touch anything. Don't say anything. And most important, don't *write* anything."

Getting out of the car, Jessica saw a clapboard house with a basement. She couldn't tell the color of the siding under the flashing multicolor lights. Anna held up the plastic tape, and they ducked under it.

Yellow light streamed out the open front door. As they entered, Anna pulled surgical gloves over her hands. She paused to examine the splintered door frame. Finally satisfied, she stepped over the threshold. "Hello?" she called.

A broad-shouldered constable with a bulbous nose appeared in the hallway. "In here," he said. He stared at Jessica. "What's she doing here?"

Anna gave a small wave to show the topic was unimportant. "She's helping me, Tom."

Tom disappeared back through the doorway, and Jessica

followed Anna into the tiny living room. Too bad she hadn't made peace with Anna a lot earlier. A formidable enemy, the corporal was also a valuable ally.

Framed by his own blood, Rocky Wiebe sprawled on his back in the middle of the hardwood floor. Years of working as a reporter hardened Jessica to a sight that would send most people gagging. Anna Carrington took it in stride as well.

While Anna knelt beside the body, Jessica tucked her hands into her pockets and looked around. End tables lay upside down, lamps broken. An easy chair lay on its back staring at the ceiling. Evidence of a ferocious fight was strewn about them. Two constables were in the room. Tom examined the body while a man of East Indian descent took dozens of pictures.

Jessica stayed near the entrance, making good on her promise of keeping out of the way. Tom reached into his crime kit and picked up a couple of plastic evidence bags. "Here," he said, handing them to Anna.

She lifted a bag in each hand, showing them to Jessica. One held a bloodstained scalpel and the other a ring, also bloody. Anna handed them back to Tom, then lifted Rocky's right hand. "Is this the hand the ring was on?"

"Yeah," Tom said. He was checking out Rocky's shoe soles.

"Hmm," Anna said.

"What?" Tom asked, looking up.

"Nothing," Anna said.

Jessica studied the hand from a distance, wondering what the "hmm" was about. Something didn't ring true about the hand, but with her neurons rapid firing over the night's events, she couldn't put her finger on it.

"Where are the other guys?"

"Two are out back checking around the yard, and two are in the basement."

"What's this about a report that Dan Foster's car was in this area at the time of death?" Anna asked, letting the dead man's hand fall to the floor.

"Someone called in a hit and run a couple of miles from here. She got the plate number. The car is registered to Dan Foster."

"Maybe the plate was stolen," Jessica blurted out. Anna shot her a warning stare.

"The description of the car matched his," Tom said. "We've already put out an alert on the car. He really crunched up the front of the girl's car."

That's insane, Jessica thought. The horrors kept growing until she began to wonder if she was hallucinating. This couldn't be real.

"Who called this in?" Anna pointed at Rocky's body.

Tom jerked his head toward the body. "He did."

"No kidding."

"911 says the call came from here. The caller said his name was Rocky Wiebe and that Dan Foster was breaking into his house."

"He actually said *Dan Foster?*"

Tom flipped open his note pad. "I wrote it down. He said: 'Dan Foster is trying to break down my door. He killed my aunt, and now he's after me because I'm suing him.'"

"I'd like to hear the actual tape of that. How long did it take for the first car to get here?"

"Twelve minutes."

"So, in twelve minutes Dan Foster broke in, traded punches with Wiebe, slit his throat, then took off and hit this girl's car?"

"That's the way it looks," he said.

"That's not enough time, is it?" Jessica asked.

Anna turned to her, apology on her face. "Actually, it is. It's not a strong door, and there's no deadbolt. A man Dan Foster's size could easily kick it in within a minute. Dan Foster is much larger than Wiebe. He'd have no problem taking him down in a couple of minutes, killing him, and leaving."

"And trash the room, too?" Jessica asked, looking around at the mess. She turned to Anna. "I know Dan," she said. "He isn't capable of this."

Anna nodded sharply. "Let's step outside, Meyers."

Jessica followed Anna to the front porch.

"Look, Jessica, I have to deal with the facts in front of me. So far we've got a 911 call. . . ," Jessica started to open her mouth, and Anna held up her hand, ". . .which I concede could have been made by anyone. We also have Dan's car in the immediate area. To be honest, if that blood on the ring matches his, he's going to need a good lawyer."

"Why would Dan kill Rocky because of a lawsuit? They hadn't even gone to court yet."

"I've got some questions, too, Jessica. This isn't over yet." She paused. "But you should know, this can't get much worse for Dan." She nodded toward the house. "These guys have everything under control. We might as well go back to the farm."

They climbed into the car, and Anna turned onto the country road.

"Dan Foster isn't a violent man," Jessica said. "I mean, if push came to shove, I can probably kick his butt myself. He's a healer, not a killer."

Anna flipped the signal switch and turned onto the main road. "Jessica, how many murders have you covered in your career?"

She closed her eyes while she mentally counted. "It's got to be at least twenty."

"Think about the guy accused of killing all the missing prostitutes out at the pig farm in Port Coquitlam. What did his friends and family say about him?"

"They couldn't believe he did it," Jessica said. "I know where you're going with this, but I truly do know Dan. He could never do this." While she defended him, her brain ticked off the reasons she had to doubt Dan Foster. He lied about his other drug mix-up. He never told her about his fiancée or his breakdown. A cold chill came over her. Dan's fiancée had died. She only had Dan's word on what happened in that cave.

She touched her forehead. *Please, God, don't let it be true.*

"I hope you're right," Anna went on. "Meanwhile, you have to accept that I'm obligated to make decisions according to the facts. If the evidence points to him, I'll arrest him."

"I understand," Jessica said, feeling small and helpless. Her mind rushed down a dozen different trails and came to a dead end each time. There had to be a way out of this.

The rest of the trip passed in silence. Anna stopped next to Jessica's Porsche and turned to face her. "I have to ask this. Technically Dan is a fugitive. Do you have any idea where he might be?"

"Other than his home—no."

"Okay. Well, I'm going to go into the house and see how the guys are doing. If anything comes up that I can share with you, I will. I hope you'll do the same."

Jessica looked at Anna for a long moment, but she said nothing. Still watching her, Anna opened the door and got out of the car. She jogged up the steps and went into the Martin home.

Moving slower, Jessica crawled out and walked over to her car. She leaned against the hood and looked up at the night sky. *How did things ever get to this? Even if Dan had mixed up the drugs, he was only guilty of malpractice. He was supposed to be looking for Kurt Fletcher. Why would he end up at Rocky Wiebe's house in a violent rage? Did he find Fletcher and learn something that pointed to Rocky?* The only way to know was to find Kurt Fletcher.

"Jessica."

She looked up and saw Anna's silhouette in the doorway. "Yes?"

"You'd better come in and have a look at this."

Dread slammed her in the stomach. What now? Taking in Anna's somber expression, Jessica hustled into the house and followed Anna inside. The corporal led her into a bedroom. Based on the pictures of Amy's nursing graduation, two diplomas, and several photos of her and Beth, Jessica surmised that this was Amy's room. Against the wall, a floorboard had been lifted, exposing a hole.

Anna held out a blue leather-bound diary. "We found this under the loose floor board. It's Amy Creighton's. Read the last page."

Her hands shaking, Jessica took the diary and flipped to the last entry. It was dated for Thanksgiving Day.

Dan came over for Thanksgiving dinner today. I knew our relationship was progressing nicely, but I didn't think it had reached this point so fast. After dinner we went for a romantic walk. I'm sure he's going to pop the question soon. He's just nervous. He's been a bachelor for too long. By this time next year, I'll be Mrs. Dan Matthew Foster. I can't wait!

Jessica dropped the diary like it was a hot coal. "This isn't true! She must be obsessing."

"The constable who found it said there's lots more in there. Amy talks about the dates they've had, long conversations over dessert." Anna placed her hands on Jessica's shoulders. "If Dan Foster and Amy Creighton are lovers, we have all the motive we need to charge him with the murders of both Beth Martin and Rocky Wiebe. If we find cow urine on that slicker, then possibly Peter Martin, too."

Flashing red lights rushed toward Dan. He tensed his foot over the gas pedal, ready to command the horses under the hood to whip him away. Of course, flight would be futile. They'd just radio ahead and cut him off. Just then an ambulance zipped past him.

Dan went weak with relief. He still had some time.

He slowed the car and cruised past the service station. It was a truck stop with a gift shop and restaurant. He didn't dare pull into the immense parking lot; the police might drive by and see his car. But somehow he had to get inside the restaurant and use a phone. It was his last chance.

Moving down the road, Dan rubbed his palm over the steering wheel and thought about how much he loved this Grand Marquis. He pressed down the accelerator and shot a couple of hundred yards past the service station entrance, then pulled off the road. Beyond the wide shoulder lay an embankment that led down into a bushy area. Dan checked the rearview mirror to make sure no one was coming. The last thing he needed was a heroic rescue.

Aiming the car toward the edge of the road, he stopped, killed the lights, and opened the door with the car still in gear. Keeping his foot on the brake until the last moment, he lunged out of the car and watched as his pride and joy skidded down the embankment and into a thick stand of brush.

He took a couple of steps and felt violently ill. At the very least, he was in mild shock. He'd lost a fair amount of blood. He had to find a phone and get some help before he collapsed.

He trudged out of the forest and decided to walk on the grass strip below the highway. No point in taking a chance on being spotted by another police car or for that matter a concerned motorist. He must look terrible with a broken nose, bruised face, and blood all over his clothing.

Dan moved slowly, not wanting to tax his system and risk

passing out. Fifteen minutes later, he crawled up the embankment and stood at the outer edge of the truck stop's parking lot. Like a friendly face, a payphone hung on the brick wall of the service station.

Only a couple of semi's occupied the parking lot, so Dan crossed without encountering anyone. He reached the payphone and dug out a quarter. He wanted to call Jessica, but he didn't want to have his call on her phone record. He still had options, though. His good deeds were about to pay off.

Slipping the coin into the slot, he froze. He knew who to call, but he didn't know the number. Like most payphones, the phone book had been removed long ago. Calling directory assistance wasn't an option. The police could trace that back and find him. With no other choice, Dan hung up the phone, retrieved his quarter, and headed into the restaurant.

Warmth and the sweet sense of safety inside the building made him want to crawl into a corner, sip hot coffee, and wait for the police to come and arrest him. He was tired and so sick. How could he keep on running?

He thought of the odds against him. He thought of Jessica and all she'd sacrificed to help him. He couldn't give up. He was going to hide, get better, and find out who was trying to frame him.

He shambled to the cash register and lifted his hand toward the peroxide blond standing there. Her nametag read *Beth,* the name that had started his troubles.

Her features hard and worldly wise, Beth looked him over from his bloodied jacket to his smashed face. "How does the other guy look?" she asked.

Dan touched his throbbing nose. It felt as big as a football. "Better than me," he said, his words slurred. "I need to borrow a phone book."

"911," she said.

Dan peered at her. "Huh?"

"We have 911 out here," she said. "They'll send an ambulance and a wrecker. Her expression became guarded. "You did have a car accident, didn't you?"

She didn't know about his being wanted, so the cops hadn't been here yet. They must've hightailed it down the road thinking he was still on the highway. That meant it wouldn't be long before they came back.

"Yeah, I did," Dan said. "My car went over the embankment and hit some brush, but I'm not hurt bad enough for an ambulance. I'm just going to get a friend to pick me up. I need to look up his number."

She pulled a phone book out from under the cluttered counter and handed it to him. It only contained the pages for Maple Ridge.

"You don't happen to have the Surrey phone book, do you?"

"Actually, I do," she said. The Maple Ridge phone book disappeared behind the counter, and the Surrey one took its place.

"Any chance I could get a coffee and two donuts to go?"

"No problem," Beth said as she moved away.

Dan shuffled to a nearby table and flipped through the yellow pages until he found the number he needed. Beth headed to his table with the coffee and donuts. Dan closed the book before she arrived. If she saw the category he had opened to, she could help the police find him.

Beth placed a closed Styrofoam cup and a bag in front of him. "Sure you don't want an ambulance?"

"I'm sure," Dan said.

"You look white as a ghost to me."

Why wouldn't she go back to her register and leave him alone? "I've always been pale. Thanks for the coffee." He dropped four dollars on the table, picked up his snack, and headed out to the phone booth again. He dropped the quarter in, started to dial the number, then stopped. Could calls from a phone booth be traced? In today's world of computers, there was a record of everything. He glanced at the trucks and hung up the phone. He had a better idea.

Circling around, Dan left his coffee and donuts by the edge of the parking lot, grabbed a rock, and approached the trucks from the side away from the restaurant. He climbed up the passenger side of the first truck and peered through the glass. No luck.

He got down, sneaked around to the second truck, and climbed up again. This time he saw what he was looking for— a cell phone plugged into the cigarette lighter, charging up.

With the rock in hand, Dan grabbed onto the door handle to steady himself. He swung his arm back and tumbled off the truck as the passenger door swung open. The air exploded from his lungs with an *oof,* but he had no complaints. This was his first real break. The driver forgot to lock the passenger door. He climbed back up on the truck and froze when a deep, throaty snore rumbled out of the sleeper. The man's partner had stayed in the truck to catch a nap. If the creak of the door opening hadn't wakened him, surely removing the phone wouldn't.

Dan reached in and unplugged the phone from the charger. It beeped. The snoring stopped. The man behind the curtain tossed around but didn't look out or speak. Dan eased himself out of the truck and walked halfway down the length of the trailer. He flipped the phone open and hit send. Making a note of the last number called, he pressed end, then punched in his friend's number.

One ring, two rings, three rings—rats!—the answering machine picked up. Waiting for the message to finish, he wondered what to say. The machine beeped twice and waited for his message.

"This is Dan Foster," he began.

He heard a screech, and a man's Latino voice came on the line. "Dr. Foster, I'm here."

Dan's knees went weak with relief. It took him a second to get back his train of thought. Finally, he said, "Remember when you told me to ask you if I ever needed a favor?"

"Yes, of course. Anything."

"I need you to come and get me. I'm in trouble, and I've got to hide for awhile."

"Where are you? I come fast."

Dan didn't know exactly where he was, but with what he did know, his friend assured him he'd be there soon. "Just park in the lot," Dan told him. "If there's a police car in the front, go into the restaurant, and drink coffee until they go. If there isn't, just wait for me."

"I be there, Dan. I never forget what you do for us."

Dan clicked the phone shut, opened it again, and punched in the last number the trucker had called. He broke the connection after one ring. No sense taking chances. If the trucker needed to call the last number, he'd just hit send and get Dan's friend.

Climbing back into the truck, Dan returned the cell phone and gently closed the door. He hoofed it back to the edge of the parking lot. Again, he saw flashing emergency lights. Picking up his breakfast, Dan returned to the darkness of the forest.

Chapter
Twenty-One

An hour later, Dan huddled in the backseat of a fast-moving economy car. He shivered uncontrollably as heat slowly drifted from the front to the back. He kept low in case a police car passed them.

The slim, dark-haired driver spoke over his shoulder in a thick Spanish accent. "Dan, you have to go to hospital. You are hurt."

"No hospital, Luis," Dan chattered. "It's just shock. I'll be fine as soon as I get warmed up."

"I have doctor friend. He keep secrets." After six years in Canada, Luis had made great strides in his mastery of the English language, but his Colombian accent still dominated his speech.

"No doctors," Dan insisted. "Besides, I am a doctor. I know what's wrong, and no one else can help."

"Who did this to you?" Luis demanded. "I'd like to find him and work on his face."

"I wish I knew." Dan's voice grew stronger. "I'm going to get well and find out."

"Luis will help you. I do anything to help you, you know that?"

"I know that," Dan said. Lying down as best he could on

the short seat, he cradled his head in the crook of his arm and tried to relax. Tremors still shook his shoulders and his jaw, but that wonderful heat was beginning to seep through his flesh. He wanted to burrow into the seat cushion and let warmth soak into him for hours and hours.

Several years before, Luis and his wife, Angela, had a farm in the Colombian mountains. They grew coffee beans until the local drug lord decided he needed more coca leaves. He *encouraged* them to change crops. Due to deep religious convictions, Luis and Angela refused. The drug lord didn't see it their way, and he killed the couple's only child.

Since their farm was far from civilization, Luis and Angela fled through the jungle, hoping to find help in the city. Not wanting the other farmers to gain confidence because of Luis's escape, the drug lord tracked them down and dragged them back. In front of the whole village, he used a hot poker to disfigure Angela's Madonna-like face and abuse her body so she could no longer have children.

Soon afterward, they made a second escape attempt. This time they got away. They'd entered Canada illegally by hiding in a cargo container all the way from Colombia. They had to be treated for malnourishment when they arrived, and Dan met them at Vancouver General Hospital.

When they were discovered in the container, Luis and Angela claimed refugee status, which entitled them to basic medical care under Canadian law. But basic medical care certainly didn't cover Angela's burn scars.

The physician that saw them asked Dan for a consult in case something could be done for Angela. What Dan saw broke his heart. As soon as Angela regained her strength, he set to work reversing the hideous evil done to her. Her scars were so deep that perfect restoration went beyond his skills, but he accomplished enough so Angela could hold her head high as she walked the streets of Vancouver. Dan never sent them a bill. Still, the scars on Angela's soul were beyond a doctor's reach.

Like most immigrants, Luis and Angela worked two minimum-wage jobs each. They saved every penny they could. After they received legal status, they bought a dumpy motel in Surrey. A perfect hideout for Dan, at least for the moment.

His shivering finally settled down, and Dan yawned and sighed. His eyelids drifted closed.

When he opened his eyes, a flashlight beam cut through intense darkness. Cool air and a strange dampness surrounded him. He felt a gritty, dusty feeling in his throat. Shining the beam around, he saw the same cave where he'd lost Denise. "This is so cool!" a woman said. Her voice sounded very familiar.

Dan searched frantically until his flashlight lit up Jessica's face. "Jessica?" he cried. "What are you doing here?"

She gave him a dazzling smile. "Why wouldn't I be here? You love exploring caves, and I love what you love."

Dan shook his head, confused. "This doesn't make sense."

She tilted her head in that teasing way he knew so well. "What doesn't make sense? You asked me to come, and I came. This is great." Something caught her attention. "What's up there?" She darted past him into the depths of the cave. That's when Dan heard the rushing sound of the underground river.

"Jessica! Wait!" He tried to chase her, but his feet refused to move. He heard her carefree laugh, then a wail and a splash.

"Noooo!" he screamed.

Hands pressed his shoulders, shaking him. Dan's eyes flew open. He stared wildly about before settling on Luis's weathered face.

"Dan, you have bad dream?"

Dan touched his own forehead. Sweat glistened on his fingers. "I m—must have," he stammered. The car's dome light shone in his face. "Where are we?"

"Home," Luis said, moving back. He had been leaning in the car's open back door. Dan blinked, rubbed his eyes with the back of his hand, and sat up. He felt like he'd just stepped off a roller coaster. "Just give me a second," he said, reaching out to grab the doorframe.

He took a few deep breaths, waited for his head to clear, then grasped Luis's strong hand to steady himself. Dan stepped out of the car and looked around. Two security lights lit up the parking lot.

Fifteen units in a single row with doors opening onto the parking lot, the Buttercup Motel had a flat tar roof and freshly painted cedar siding. Luis had parked in front of a small projection on the end of the row. It contained the office and living quarters of Luis and Angela Osorio.

"You stay with us," Luis said. He had the smooth flat-planed face of a boy.

Dan shook his head, and his throbbing nose made him instantly regret it. "No. Register me in one of the rooms. If the police find me, I don't want you and Angela to get into trouble."

"They not find you," he said, his hands urging Dan inside.

"I'm not willing to take that chance. You've had enough trouble in your life. If I weren't desperate, I wouldn't have called you. Let's go inside and register."

Luis was a few inches shorter than Dan. He put his skinny arm around Dan's waist to steady him. Dan didn't complain. He was in worse shock than he let on. If Luis knew how bad he felt, he'd phone a doctor for sure.

As they approached the building, the office door burst open.

Tiny Angela Osorio rushed out. When she saw Dan's face, she stopped and put her hands to her cheeks. Her dark eyes were as wide as moons. "Dr. Foster, what happened?" Her accent was heavier than Luis's. She had thick black hair held back with two dark barrettes.

Luis spoke to her in Spanish, his voice urgent.

Angela moved to Dan's other side and threw her thin arm around his waist. She was surprisingly strong. Together they led him into the office. Dan didn't resist when they guided him to a low couch.

"I have the bedroom ready," Angela said in halting English. "But he needs doctor."

"No doctor," Dan mumbled. "Put me in one of the rooms. I'll be okay."

Angela shook her head as though dealing with a naughty child. She let out a thick stream of Spanish. Midway, she switched to English. "You not stay in room. You stay in house with us."

"If they find me, you'll be in trouble. I'm a fugitive. The police think I killed someone."

The Osorios shook their heads in disbelief. "Impossible!" Luis said, still holding Dan's arm as though afraid to let him go.

"You can never hurt a. . .a bug. . .a roach," Angela added. "You good man."

"Thanks for your faith in me, but you'll get in trouble if they find me in your house. I'll pay cash for a room. That way you're safe."

Angela Osorio cried, "Safe! We don't care about safe! You are friend. You stay in the house."

Dan took a deep breath and tried to focus. The room kept shifting. "They can deport you."

Luis broke into a broad smile. "Not now. We Canadian citizens."

"Great," Dan whispered. He slid out of Luis's grip and everything went black.

The phone by Jessica's bed blasted out a high-pitched ring. She groaned. The clock showed four A.M. She'd been asleep exactly two hours.

"Hello?" she answered, lying against the pillow.

"Jessica? It's Anna. Amy Creighton was just arrested and taken in for questioning."

Jessica opened her eyes and sat up. "What?"

"We found her at the hospital working the night shift. I've got to go over to detention and question her now. I thought you'd want to know."

"Oh! I did. Thanks for calling me." She sat up and pushed a thick mop of hair from her face. "Can I watch the interrogation? You know, through the one-way mirror."

"Sorry, Meyers," Anna said, "no can do. But no one can stop you from visiting Amy later and asking her questions yourself—if she'll agree to see you." She paused as another voice spoke in the background. "Look, I've gotta go. The women's lockup has visiting hours from nine to noon. What you do about it is your business."

"Thanks for calling me," Jessica said. "I owe you one."

The line clicked to silence. Jessica fumbled her receiver back to its holder. As tired as she was, the next four hours passed in fitful dreams that left her exhausted.

At ten minutes past nine, she arrived at the police station lockup wearing a Canucks sweatshirt and jeans. She approached the desk with a cup of coffee in one hand and her identification in the other. The burly guard peered at her driver's license, then stared at her face as if he didn't recognize her.

"Please wait over there," he said. He jabbed a thick finger

at a wooden table with a chair on each side.

The waiting room was long and narrow with bare walls and floors. Half a dozen chairs and tables were the only furniture. The walls were stained, the cement floors pocked and flaking. Fortunately, Jessica was the only one there at the moment. She pulled out the straight-backed chair and winced at the loud, scraping noise it made. The room smelled of strong disinfectant.

Hopefully Amy would agree to see her. Jessica had to learn the truth about Amy and Dan. All Anna would tell her about the interview was that it was interesting. Anna also had the preliminary test results on the bloody ring, and it wasn't good.

After five minutes, Amy Creighton appeared dressed in an orange jumpsuit with her hands cuffed in front. Despite puffy eyes, blotchy cheeks, and tousled hair, she was still an attractive woman.

Bitterness rose behind Jessica's throat. Not once had Dan mentioned his feelings for her. She had no claim on him. She sized up the girl before her. Did Amy?

Amy pulled out the wooden chair across from Jessica and sat down. "Hi," she said, as though it was the saddest announcement she'd ever made.

Jessica smiled and slid the cup of coffee over to her. "Thanks for seeing me."

Amy looked at the cup but didn't move to open it. "My lawyer said I shouldn't talk to anyone, but he doesn't have to live in there." Amy glanced at the steel door she'd just come through.

"What's going on with you?" Jessica asked. "Are you having trouble in there?"

Amy spoke in a low monotone. "If you're a drug dealer, a husband killer, or even a hooker, that's okay. You're one of the family back there. But if you killed the woman who took you in when no one else would—well, they just don't like you.

Guilt or innocence isn't an issue."

Jessica reached for Amy. The girl shrunk back, so she withdrew her hand. "Have you been abused?"

"Just verbally," Amy said. "Physical probably comes later."

"Say the word, and I'll see if I can get you your own cell."

Amy looked directly at Jessica for the first time. "If my lawyer couldn't, I don't see how you could."

Jessica smiled. "I have better connections than he does." At least she hoped she did. When this was over, she'd owe Anna Carrington more than she could hope to repay.

"I'll believe it when I see it." Amy sat a little straighter. "What do you want?"

"I need to know about the diary."

Amy exhaled slowly. "That stupid diary. Who could've known?"

"You realize what you wrote makes Dan look guilty. It could send him up for life."

Amy's bleary eyes gleamed. "Have they arrested him?"

"They're still looking for him."

"Are you still trying to clear his name?"

Jessica hesitated a long moment. She had to work up the courage to say the words. "With what I read in your diary," she said, "I don't think I can clear him. Corporal Carrington twisted the pathologist's arm, and he's already typed the blood on Rocky's ring. It's O-negative. Rare. And Dan's blood type." She shrugged. "Add that to the fact that your diary indicates you and Dan are lovers. Since Beth and Rocky both died, you inherit prime farmland and a lot of money. That's strong evidence against him. And you."

Amy looked away. "I wish my diary were true," she whispered.

Jessica leaned forward, straining to hear her. "What do you mean?"

"What you read in my diary was my secret dreams, what I *wished* would happen." She hesitated.

"I'm listening," Jessica said.

"When Beth first started doing Dan's books, she kind of pushed us together. She figured Dan needed a wife. I was twenty-five and a nurse. She thought I'd be perfect for him. As only Beth could do, she badgered Dan until he asked me out. She also made it clear that I'd better say yes.

"A week later, he took me out to dinner. We had a good time, at least good enough that he asked me out a few more times. I thought we hit if off pretty good, then Dan gave me that 'just-want-to-be-friends' talk."

Amy paused, then continued with resignation in her voice. "You see, this really started back when my parents died."

"When your parents died?" Jessica asked.

"Yeah," Amy said. "I never told anyone this, not even Beth. My parents didn't just go for a drive, they were escaping."

Jessica lifted an eyebrow. "Escaping? From whom?"

"From me," Amy said. "Dad was getting on my case about not cleaning my room and stuff, and I did an adolescent flip-out on him. Then when Mom took his side, I turned my guns to her. We had a big family blowup, and I threatened to run away. My dad, a pretty cunning guy, said, 'Tell you what, we'll run away instead.' He grabbed Mom, and out the door they went."

"But he was just kidding, right?" Jessica asked.

Amy nodded. "Sure. Twenty-eight-year-old Amy understands that, but the teenage girl back then didn't. I guess I've been overly sensitive to rejection ever since. When Dan dumped me, I figured if I couldn't have him in the real world, I could at least have him in a fantasy world."

"Hence the mushy diary," Jessica said. "What did the police say when you told them this?"

She sniffed. "They said it was a touching story, then charged me as an accomplice in the murders of Beth and Rocky."

"If it helps, I believe you."

Amy looked surprised. "Why would you believe me?"

She smiled gently. "A woman knows." Jessica never could believe that Dan and Amy were in love. The girl's story fit.

"I have a favor to ask," Jessica went on.

"What?"

She took a single sheet of paper from her purse and produced a black pen. "This is a letter authorizing me to go onto any of your properties. The key to this whole mess has to be tied in with them somehow."

She reached for the pen. "I'll sign it, but I don't own the farm."

Jessica smiled. "According to my sources, until you stand convicted, you do, because Rocky is dead."

"There's a house key hidden in a fake stone at the bottom of the step," Amy told her. "Just be sure you put it back." She grimaced. "Not that I'll need it again."

Jessica held the document while Amy positioned the pen in her cuffed hands and signed.

That afternoon, Jessica closed the door to Roger Pronger's office and leaned against it. "We need to talk."

Roger stacked some papers on his desk and pointed to a chair. "I agree. I've been waiting for you to come in."

Jessica sat and crossed her legs. "I have some problems with tonight's newscast."

Roger rocked back in his chair, a pen in his hands. "It's factual, isn't it?"

"It's factual, but it's wrong."

Roger ran his hand over his wide head. He glared at her. "Jessica, what will it take to convince you? They identified the

Wiebe murder weapon as part of the medical kit in Foster's car. The blood on the ring is Foster's rare type. Then there's the diary."

"The diary's off the record," Jessica shot back. "We can't report that."

"We won't, but it gives the guy a clear motive. And then there's evidence of guilt because of flight." He flung the pen to the table. "Those are hardly the acts of an innocent man."

"He's being framed, Roger. He ran because someone is closing a net around him."

"Who?"

"If I knew that, Dan wouldn't be hiding."

Pronger leaned forward, his stare boring into her. "Has he contacted you? If he has, you have to tell the police."

"I wish he had, but he hasn't."

Shortly after Jessica had left Amy that morning, Anna had called to tell her that they found Dan's car with blood on the front seat. According to the waitress at the truck stop, he'd looked pretty battered when he came to get some food. All the hospitals and clinics were watching for him. No one knew what happened to him after he left the truck stop.

Did he get somewhere safe? Was he lying in the woods unconscious? She couldn't bear to think about it.

Watching her carefully, Pronger went on. "Let me be sure I understand this. Beth Martin died from a drug reaction. Only Dan or Amy had the opportunity to switch the drugs. The diary indicates that Amy and Dan are lovers. Amy couldn't inherit because of Rocky, and Dan stands to lose millions because of Rocky's lawsuit. Then Rocky dies and Dan's car is spotted fleeing the area. Dan's blood is at the crime scene."

He paused to draw a breath and plowed ahead. "We haven't even talked about the bull killing Peter Martin. What do you see that makes this guy innocent? Spell it out for me."

"It didn't hit me until just before I came over here. There was no blood spatter on the finger the ring was on. I'm pretty sure Carrington noticed it, but for some reason didn't report it. Why was the rare blood type on the ring, but no more of it was anywhere else on Rocky's body? The ring must have been removed, coated with Dan's blood, and then replaced."

Pronger asked, "How did Dan's blood get on the ring then?"

"There's no positive proof it is Dan's blood on the ring. It's just the same type. Anna says DNA testing will take a couple of months. The RCMP lab is completely tied up with the Missing Women's Task Force Investigation. Rocky's ring was sent to the lab in Halifax."

"What if the DNA test says it is Dan's blood?"

Jessica started to tremble. "Then Dan might not be in hiding. Whoever did this may be holding him somewhere. He might be. . .dead."

Roger said, "He's not dead."

"How can you be sure?"

"If he was framed, as you believe, why frame someone and then kill him? The whole purpose of framing is to shift attention away from the guilty person. If they killed him, they'd have to hide his body. If Dan's body was found, the police would start looking for other perpetrators."

Wiping her face, Jessica's brain started working overtime. She'd let her fears overwhelm her professional cool. If she was going to help Dan, she had to stay focused.

"It's going to be tough around here, but take all the time off you need. Sooner or later this thing has to get resolved."

"Thanks," Jessica said. "You've been great, Roger."

He stood and moved back to his desk. "What's your next move?"

"I'm going to try and track down Kurt Fletcher. That's what Dan was doing when all this started with Wiebe. Something must have happened while Dan was on Kurt's trail."

"Who's Kurt?"

"The Martin's farmhand. He disappeared shortly after Beth died. According to Corporal Carrington, the police would like to talk to him, but they don't think he's terribly important to the case, and they don't have the resources to do a massive search for him."

"Where are you going to start?"

"The Coyote Bar and Grill."

Pronger tensed. "You mean the one in Langley?"

"The same," Jessica said. She lifted her purse strap to her shoulder and stood.

"You can't go there," he said. "People have been killed in that place."

"What choice do I have? As far as I know, it's the last place Dan went. It's the only lead I have to Kurt Fletcher."

Pronger held up a hand indicating for her to wait. He picked up the phone. "Look, let me make a call before you leave."

Chapter
Twenty-Two

D riving out of the city, Jessica glanced at the man in the passenger seat next to her. He was tough and lean, and his knees almost touched his chest. Her sporty car was designed for smaller people. Brush-cut blond hair, steely blue eyes, and a military bearing—Nigel Short didn't fit his name. This guy looked like a Chuck or a Bart or, well, a Rocky. Not a Nigel and definitely not Short. Jessica resisted when Roger suggested she bring Nigel along, but Roger had threatened to fire her if she didn't agree.

"What's it like being a professional bodyguard?" she asked.

"Depends on who I'm guarding." He glanced at her, and a smile flickered across his lips.

"I see. Is this a good assignment or a bad one?"

He moved his legs, trying to get comfortable. "This looks like it'll be a good one," he said, glancing at her.

"Speaking of the assignment," Jessica said, as she made a turn, "I want to go in alone. I have a feeling you'll scare people off."

"No problem," he said, looking straight ahead. "I'll enter five minutes after you do."

"I'd rather you didn't come in at all."

He didn't move. "I'll enter five minutes after you."

Jessica bit back a retort. Somehow she knew it would be futile to try negotiating with this guy.

A few minutes later, she downshifted the Porsche and turned into the Coyote parking lot. Seven o'clock and the place was nearly full. She found a spot in the front lot and shut the motor off.

Leaving Nigel inside the car, she headed to the entrance. She'd dressed in worn jeans, a fisherman-knit sweater, and a scuffed leather jacket, trying to blend in. She opened the door and winced as a wall of smoke closed around her. Looking around at the mass of glazed eyes and hardened features, she knew she'd never manage to blend with this crowd. She might as well forget the games and go for it.

Spotting the only empty stool at the bar, she wedged herself between a couple of biker types. Both gave her their full attention.

"Hey, you lost?" the left one asked over the pounding music. A heavy-set man, he had a full red beard and smooth features.

"I'm looking for a friend." She fumbled with her purse and tried to act normal.

"I'm friendly," the right one called out. He tapped his hand on the bar, keeping time with the music. He had a thinner build with a ferretlike face.

"So am I," said Red Beard. "Let me buy you a drink."

"No, thanks," Jessica said. "But you could do me a favor." She pulled two pictures from her purse. One was Kurt, the other Dan. "Have you seen either of these guys?" she asked.

Red Beard dropped his arm around her shoulders. He spoke close to her ear. "What's in it for me if I have?"

Grimacing at the alcohol on his breath, Jessica shrugged him off. "Have you seen them?"

"Let me have a look," Ferret Face said, leaning in.

Jessica showed him the pictures.

"Yeah, I think I have," he said. He puckered his lips and leaned uncomfortably close. "A kiss might jog my memory."

A wide hand covered Ferret Face's eyes and yanked his head back. In a conversational tone, Nigel said, "Knock it off." He pulled Ferret's head back until Jessica feared his thin neck would snap.

Red Beard slipped off his stool. "You're messing with the wrong guys," he growled, his fists up.

"I told you to give me five minutes," Jessica shouted over the music. "I was okay."

Nigel pushed Ferret Face into the bar. "I could see that."

"Take a hike," Red Beard told Nigel.

At a nearby table, four burly men stood to back up their friends. Nigel looked them over with open contempt on his face.

Just then, the bartender, a man the size of a buffalo with a dozen tattoos on his arms, came to their end of the bar. "Hey! Knock it off," he shouted. "No scrapping in here. Take it outside."

"Sure," Red Beard said, pleased. "We'll go outside."

Oh great, Jessica thought. Her bodyguard was about to get into a brawl.

"After I get a couple of questions answered," Nigel said. He slid the pictures toward the bartender. "You know either of these two?"

He didn't look at the pictures. "Never seen 'em."

Nigel brushed past Red Beard. He leaned over the polished wood and whispered something in the bartender's ear.

The man's eyes widened. He nodded. Nigel stepped back. The bartender turned toward Red Beard and Ferret. "You guys sit at a table and leave these people alone."

"What?" Red Beard demanded.

"Just do it!" the bartender shot back. "I'll bring you a couple of free drinks in a minute."

With parting glares, they slowly retreated to the table with their four friends. They sat down, but six pairs of eyes remained on Nigel.

"Now," Nigel said, in a low voice. "Do you know them or not?"

"One guy is Kurt Fletcher," the bartender said. "He's a regular."

"When did you last see him?" Jessica asked.

"It's been at least a couple of weeks. The other guy looks familiar, might have been in here a night or two ago."

"Any idea where we might find Kurt Fletcher?" she asked.

He shrugged. "All I know is he works on some cattle ranch."

Jessica laid a white paper rectangle on the bar and slid it across.

Picking up the card, his eyes lit up. "Hey, I didn't realize it was you."

"If you hear anything, you'll call her, right?" Nigel asked.

"No sweat. Nice to meet you, Ms. Meyers."

"Just out of curiosity," Jessica went on, "was Kurt a heavy drinker?"

He chuckled. "Are you kidding? Kurt can't drink."

"Why not?"

"Beats me. He just said he can't. He comes here to play penny poker."

"Okay, let's go," she told Nigel.

Six big men moved to follow them out, but the bartender glared at them, and they sat down.

As soon as Jessica and Nigel stepped outside, she asked, "What did you tell that bartender?"

Nigel looked down at her. "Ever heard of JFT2?"

"Sure. Joint Task Force 2. The Canadian equivalent of

Special Forces. That's the group that overran a Taliban position in Afghanistan. What about them?"

"I served with them for five years. The bartender had a Canadian Armed Forces tattoo, so I explained to him who I was. I told him what I would do if you didn't get your questions answered and if we didn't leave the bar safely."

"What would you have done?"

He smiled gently as though talking to a small child. "Jessica, let's just say that by the time I was done, the bar would have been a mess and an orthopedic surgeon would get rich putting those guys back together."

Jessica's smile died. Fear sent a chill through her middle. He seemed so calm and professional, so friendly. But Nigel was actually a fighting machine idling in neutral. She hoped she'd never have to see him shift into drive.

"Where to now?" he asked when they reached the car.

"Back to the city," Jessica said, sliding her key into the door lock. "I need to do some thinking."

Struggling up from deep unconsciousness, Dan opened his eyes and looked into the tanned face of a white-haired Hispanic man. He had a stethoscope dangling from his neck. A plastic tube ran from an IV bag down to Dan's left arm. He was in the hospital. Frantic, he looked around the room and saw a high chest of drawers with a picture of Christ and a burning candle in front of it. The walls were blue with pale blue curtains in front of a dark window.

Smiling at him, Angela stood beside Luis in the doorway. Dan relaxed. He was in their home.

"I said no doctor," Dan croaked. His throat felt raw.

"I am not a doctor," the man said, enunciating every letter. "I am a janitor."

Dan stared. "Why is a janitor wearing a stethoscope and running an IV into my arm?"

"You were in hypovolemic shock," he said. "I had to replace the fluid you lost from bleeding."

More awake now, Dan said, "For a janitor, you know your medical terms."

Luis stepped forward. "Miguel was doctor in Honduras. He is refugee now. His papers no good here, so he work as janitor. He helps people who can't go to doctors."

Dan moved to shift himself to a sitting position. Miguel reached under his back to raise his pillow for him to lean on. "How did you manage to get an IV?"

Miguel smiled. "I clean at a hospital. It helps."

"Did Luis tell you who I am, what I'm accused of?"

Miguel shook his head. "Luis told me you're his friend and you needed help. That's all I had to know. Once this bag is finished, you can remove the IV. Your heart rate is much better, and you have color again."

"Lots of color," Angela said from the door.

Dan felt his face. "It's bad, I know."

Angela handed him a mirror. Dan stared at himself, assessing the damage in terms of procedures and dollars. His nose took a sharp turn to the right, and he had the eyes of a raccoon. His upper lip was twice its normal size.

"You were too sick to straighten the nose," Miguel said. "I could do it now, but I think you need more rest."

"Don't worry about it," Dan said. "I'll do it myself later."

"I must go to my work," Miguel said, picking up a brown school satchel.

Dan caught his arm as Miguel turned. "Thank you, Doctor."

Miguel bowed. "You're welcome, Doctor."

"How do you know I'm a doctor if Luis didn't tell you who I am?"

Miguel grinned and saluted with two fingers. "We've met before."

"Where?" Dan asked, staring at the man's brown face.

"Cleft palates." With a parting smile, he left the bedroom. Angela followed him.

Dan leaned his head against the wall and closed his eyes. Cleft palates? Suddenly, he remembered. He'd met Miguel during one of his visits to Central America while Dan spent a week operating on cleft lips and palates. They hadn't talked long, and back then the doctor weighed twenty pounds more. Dan had no concerns about Miguel giving him away.

"How long have I been out?" Dan asked, gazing at Luis.

"Let's see," Luis said, checking his watch, "it's seven o'clock now. We got here around midnight last night."

Dan closed his eyes. He was already tired again. He'd been out for nineteen hours.

"Miguel was very worried about you when he first came over. He wanted to call an ambulance, but I talked him out of it. Instead, he stayed here with you all night."

"Boy, I owe him."

Luis shook his head. "The way he see it, he owe you. You do much good work in his country."

"Okay, Luis, move away," Angela called from the hall.

Luis stepped aside, and Angela entered carrying a tray with a bowl of chicken soup and two folded tortillas on it. She placed it on Dan's lap.

"Miguel say you must eat slow," she said, watching him.

Dan looked at her china-doll face and the muted scars on her cheeks. Lots of new technology had come out since he'd worked on Angela's face. When this was over, she was coming back in. He could do much better now.

"Thanks, Angela."

She kissed his forehead. "You eat and get well. We be back

later." She and Luis left him alone.

Slowly sipping, he finished half the soup and one slice of bread.

Later, Luis came back for the tray. "Angela is taking care of customers," he said. "Can I get you something?"

"I need some things from the store," Dan told him. "Could you get me a pen and paper so I can make a list?"

Luis disappeared for a moment. He returned with a pen and a note pad. Dan scribbled for a few minutes and handed the list to Luis. In Dan's current state, his handwriting looked like a drunken man's scrawl.

"There's money in my wallet," Dan told him, nodding toward the black fold of leather on the nightstand. "It's Friday night, so the stores are still open. Go to New Westminster to get these things. That way, if the police get onto us, the search area will still be too large for them to find me."

Luis looked at the list. He held it in front of Dan and pointed to one of the items. "Where I get this?"

"You can pick that up at any hunting store."

He looked worried. "But why you need it?"

Dan sighed. "Because I can't fight worth beans. You can tell that by looking at me."

"Okay, I buy this for you, but I pay. You no pay."

"You've done enough for me, Luis. Take the cash from my wallet. Make sure you pay with cash."

Angela came in and peeked around Luis's arm to read the list. "What you going to do with that?"

Feeling weaker by the moment, Dan slid down flat on the bed and adjusted the pillow under his head. "I'm going after the people who did this to me. But first I'm going back to sleep for a week or so."

After another fitful night's sleep, Jessica set out on a Saturday morning stroll. She crossed Denman Street on her way to the beach. Her right hand clenched her cell phone in her coat pocket. She squeezed it as though she could force Dan to call her through sheer willpower. At this point, she was willing to try anything. Even prayer. She hadn't used that word since summer camp when she was fifteen years old.

"Please, let him call," she murmured. A shrill beep and the cell phone jumped out of her pocket. Jessica's heart raced. She didn't know God worked that fast. She flipped it open and pressed it against her ear. "Where have you been?"

Roger said, "After I left the office last night, I went to dinner, then home. Why?"

"Sorry, Roger. I thought. . ."

"I was Foster."

"Yeah." Her mouth felt numb. She wanted to cry.

"Sorry. I was just calling to see how last night went."

"Your bodyguard friend is certainly capable, but he needs to work on his people skills. He almost got us in a fight with six giants."

"No kidding. Well, six isn't too many for Nigel. Did he get you any information?"

"Not what I needed, but I got some answers."

"At least he's effective," Roger said. "So what now?"

"That question kept me up most of the night. Right now, I'm not sure."

"I've got to go," he said. "If you need anything, call me."

"Thanks." She returned the phone to her pocket.

Keeping up a brisk pace, Jessica made her way to the shore and sat on a wooden bench facing English Bay. The snow was already gone. A stiff breeze blew in from the ocean, and she knew she couldn't stay there long.

She watched two tugboats guide a freighter into the bay.

Without the aid of the tugboats, the freighter would never be able to navigate among the other ships in such close quarters. Trapped by its own momentum, the ship couldn't steer well enough to avoid a collision.

This nightmare seemed like that ship. An evil momentum had built up. Without some powerful intervention, that momentum would strip Dan of his freedom. Anna told her that once Dan was caught, they'd charge him with first-degree murder. If convicted, that meant no chance of parole for twenty-five years. Without some way to refute the evidence, he would be convicted.

They had him dead to rights: blood, witnesses, and—unless you believed Amy—motive. Jessica felt the overwhelming frustration of helplessness. Dan was going to be flattened under a steamroller called the justice system. Before that happened, she had to find out who was driving that machine.

Chapter
Twenty-Three

In Luis's small bathroom, Dan lifted his head from the sink. He toweled his wet head and looked into the mirror at his black hair. With his new hair color and his smashed-in face, he hardly recognized himself.

He stuffed cotton up his nose, cradled it in his fingers, and twisted sharply. He howled and dropped to his knees, sucking in deep breaths while hot tears streamed down his face.

The bedroom door snapped open. "What happen?" Luis asked, rushing inside. His dark hair was uncombed, his shirt-tail hanging out.

Dan blinked up at him. "I was just trying to straighten my nose. I don't recommend trying this without a good shot of Demerol."

Luis reached forward and helped him to his feet. Examining Dan's face, he said, "It looks better."

Dan turned toward the mirror and tried to clear the tears from his eyes enough to see his face. "Still a few degrees to star-board. I'll get someone else to finish the job later. Meanwhile, I've got to get going."

"You take my car," Luis said, holding out his keys.

Dan took a step back and held up both hands, as though

warding him off. "That would connect you to me if I got caught. Just give me a ride out to Scott Road. I can get a car there."

Luis looked alarmed. "You steal one?"

Dan just smiled.

Jessica parked her car in front of the Martin home and trotted up the front steps. Yellow police tape barred the door. Armed with written authority from Amy, she found the key and unlocked the door. Ducking under the tape, she went inside. She somehow suspected Anna wouldn't consider a letter from Amy enough to bypass the police tape. Oh well, life was full of risks.

The house was icy. Pulling on her driving gloves, she moved through the rooms. The police had done most of the heavy work. The couch stood away from the wall, beds had been moved, drawers lay open. According to her last phone call to Anna, the police found nothing besides the diary and slicker —no Nardil stash, no smoking gun.

Jessica's attention finally settled on the dark rolltop desk in the living room. Like a gaping mouth, the top stood open, and the Martins' personal papers were strewn about it. Jessica pulled up the wooden desk chair and sat down to do some reading.

She removed her gloves for easier handling, and in minutes her fingers ached from cold. First, she looked over tax returns for the last three years. Peter showed a reasonable profit from his farming operations, a quarter of which came from leasing the other two properties he owned. Pulling a pad from her purse, Jessica made a note of the addresses. His expenses seemed reasonable, but then what did she know? She was a reporter, not an accountant.

Jessica scanned some personal correspondence and found nothing. In a cubbyhole, she found a stack of bank statements and cancelled checks—checks to suppliers, utility companies, other farmers, and Kurt Fletcher.

Kurt Fletcher? Jessica turned over the check. She saw Kurt's account number. And another interesting detail.

A blue Malibu was a long drop from a blazing red Porsche, but Jessica's Boxter didn't make a good stakeout car, so she rented the Malibu instead. She now had a clear line of sight to the Royal Bank located in a nearby strip mall. She took a sip of coffee and returned the paper cup to the car's drink holder. In this world of debit cards, staking out Kurt Fletcher's bank was a long shot. He could deal with any bank to draw out money, but she suspected Kurt wasn't a debit card kind of guy.

After going through the past three years of Peter Martin's cancelled checks, Jessica had discovered that most of them indicated Kurt took cash back from his deposits. A rough calculation indicated he typically deposited about half his pay. Since the Martins provided the cabin, his only personal expenses were food and entertainment. One look at Kurt told the world that clothes weren't a high priority with him.

According to the bartender, Kurt didn't drink, so Jessica calculated he could have accumulated as much as twelve thousand dollars over a three-year period—unless his card playing at the Coyote became a pricey proposition. Also, he could've emptied his account after he fled, but judging by the company he kept, that wouldn't be a smart move.

Growing bored, she wondered how often he came to the bank. She flipped on the radio and found a pop music station. Minutes dragged into two hours. The coffee was long gone, and she was starving. A small deli sat two doors down from the bank. If she got in and out of the deli in less than five minutes, even if Kurt went into the bank, she'd be back in time to catch him coming out. Opening the car door, Jessica slid out and jogged toward the cluttered restaurant.

She pushed open the door and could almost taste the scent of homemade soup. A quick glance at the menu board told her today's special was ham and coleslaw on a bun with Thousand Island dressing—an offering called a Sammy's Deluxe. Figuring specials always came faster, she decided to order that.

Jessica waited behind a large blue-haired lady with a massive patent-leather purse who seemed to want just a little of every type of meat and cheese the deli sold. Jessica kept an eye on her watch as the minutes peeled off. Three people lined up behind her.

It quickly became obvious that she'd never be able to get her order and pay for it before five minutes were up. Disgusted, she took a step toward the door, then forced her face to remain neutral when Kurt Fletcher walked in. He was dirty and unshaven as always. Turning her head away, she got back in line and ordered her sandwich to go.

Lunch bag in hand, she passed him on the way out. At the door, she glanced over her shoulder to make sure he wasn't watching her. She rushed to the car and strapped on the seat belt. She started the motor and waited. Kurt emerged from the deli with a bag in hand. He wore a dingy pair of khakis and a stained sheepskin coat. He paused to pull a knit hat on his head and turned toward the bank.

Continuing past it, he headed for the road alongside the strip mall. He stepped onto the sidewalk and set off walking. Should she follow him on foot? No, if they got to a quiet street, he'd spot her.

Waiting until he turned right, she eased the car into the parking lot and followed him. She turned the corner, pulled off the road, and kept her eyes on his bobbing black hat. His figure diminished in size to the point where she couldn't make out his stumbling gait anymore.

Back in the street, she drew within a hundred yards of him and pulled over again. Eventually, he crossed over to turn left. Jessica pulled up so she could look down the street.

Halfway down, Kurt disappeared down a driveway. Jessica waited for a break in traffic and shot after him. She passed the house just as Kurt disappeared into a side entrance. Stopping fifty yards past it, she got out of the car. It was a well-kept, two-level home with yellow aluminum siding and a gray asphalt roof. Likely, it had a basement suite where Kurt was staying.

She hesitated half a block away. What should she do now? She could knock on the door and demand that Kurt explain why he left the Martin farm so suddenly. If he were innocent, he would have a reasonable explanation. If Kurt were guilty, she'd be face to face with a killer.

Jessica pulled her cell phone from her pocket and punched in Anna's number. At the very least, this would show Anna that Jessica knew how to share. As she waited for the first ring, she headed back to the Malibu.

Fifteen minutes later, Anna's unmarked car pulled up behind Jessica's rental. Jessica got out and found Anna finishing a ham sandwich.

"Congratulations," the police officer said, smiling as she chewed. She swallowed and asked, "How did you pull this off?"

"I checked on the back of Kurt's cancelled paychecks to find his banking information, then I staked out his bank."

Anna brushed crumbs off her hands. "Good work." She looked up and down the street. "Which house is he in?"

Jessica pointed. "Three sixteen. He went in the side entrance. I'd guess he has a basement apartment."

Two marked police cars rolled up and parked behind Anna's Crown Victoria.

Moving away, Anna told Jessica, "Wait here, and we'll talk to him."

Jessica called after her, "I found him. I get to talk to him."

Shaking her head, Anna turned back. "That's not the way it works. We go in, make sure it's safe, and then you can listen while I talk to him." Without waiting for a response, she left Jessica on the sidewalk and headed toward the house with two tall constables beside her.

Jessica gave them a thirty-foot head start, then straggled along behind. She waited on the street while they went to the door. While Anna knocked, a shadow caught Jessica's peripheral vision.

Her head snapped to the left. Kurt Fletcher's cowboy boots kicked up dirt as he ran through a flowerbed and headed down a side street.

"He's running!" Jessica shouted.

She dug her running shoes into the grass and started pumping her legs. Cowboy boots weren't great for running, and Jessica started to close the gap. She picked up speed when she hit the sidewalk.

Thirty feet, twenty feet, ten feet. A voice behind her called for Jessica to back off, but she couldn't stop now. Finally, she drew even with Kurt and drove the heel of her hand between his bony shoulder blades. He tumbled forward onto the sidewalk. Jessica awkwardly flailed her arms and tried to stop. Blowing and gasping, she planted her feet and bent over to grab her knees while the three police officers swarmed the fallen man.

With a heavy knee pressing into his back, Kurt's hands were twisted behind him and bracelets slapped on. Once he was secured, Anna jerked him around to face her. "Never run!" she panted. "I hate chasing people, and now you've put me in a bad mood." She looked like a wild woman with her black frizzy hair coming loose and waving around her face, her blunt features rosy from exertion. She had enormous black eyes filled with rage that could have burnt a hole in the prisoner.

Kurt's eyes widened. He shied back from Anna. "I. . .I didn't do anything," he said, his loose lips working up and down.

"Sure you didn't," Anna said, moving back. "Beth Martin dies, you take off, and then run when the police show up at your door. All actions of an innocent man."

"It's not what it looks like," Kurt rasped. He was trembling. One of the constables helped him to his feet. "I can explain."

"Then explain," Anna said. She had her shoulders back and a hard line to her jaw.

"Out here?"

Anna shoved Kurt toward one of the constables. "Take him back to his home." She walked over to Jessica.

"What a fiasco, Meyers! Don't ever do that again! If you got hurt, it would end my career." She shook her head, over-whelmed by Jessica's stupidity. "I can just see the headline." She raised her hand as though underscoring text. "Famous news anchor killed due to RCMP incompetence."

"Sorry," Jessica said. "I saw him getting away, and I reacted."

"Well, let *us* do all the reacting from now on," Anna said. She drew in a heavy breath and let it out fast. That seemed to calm her.

The women walked to Kurt's suite. Inside, Kurt sat on a rocking chair with two police officers standing over him. He looked like a kindergartner between two tenth-grade bullies.

Across the room the sofa sleeper had its mattress stretched out. It had knotted sheets and blankets on it.

Anna found a chair in the kitchen area. She brought it in and sat across from her prisoner.

"Explain," she ordered.

"It's my blood pressure," he said.

Anna smirked. "What? It's off the charts because of your little run?"

Blood pressure, Jessica thought. "You take Nardil," she said.

Anna looked up at her, then at Kurt. "Is that true?'

He nodded. "When I heard Beth died from Nardil, I figured that would make me a suspect, so I took off."

"Big deal," Anna said. "Being a suspect doesn't make you a criminal. You would've had a chance to explain yourself. Besides, you had nothing to gain from Beth's death."

"I figured with my criminal record, you'd railroad me into jail."

"You have a criminal record?" Jessica turned to Anna. "Did you know this?"

"Sure," Anna said. "There's nothing major on his record—shoplifting, possession of pot, that kind of thing. Nothing to connect him with these murders."

"I didn't think you'd see it that way," Kurt said.

She leaned in, staring at him. "I would've seen it that way if you hadn't run. Now I'm not so sure."

His sallow face grew red. "I had nothing to do with Beth's death." He raised his trembling right hand. "I swear."

Anna made a point of standing and walking over to Jessica. "What do you think?" she whispered.

Jessica eyed Kurt and murmured, "He's hiding something."

Anna whispered, "I don't have enough to hold him. Dan Foster is still number one on the charts."

Jessica suddenly had an idea. If Anna didn't arrest Kurt, Jessica could bring Nigel back to talk with him. Seems everyone liked to talk to Nigel.

At Scott Road, Luis pulled to the shoulder, and Dan got out. "You want me to wait?" Luis asked, leaning toward the open passenger door.

"No, thanks," Dan said. "I don't want you to know what I'm up to. The less you know, the better for you."

Luis shrugged. "Okay."

"Thank you, my friend," Dan said. "You saved my life."

"If you still need help, you call," Luis said. He put the car into drive. Dan shut the door, and Luis drove off.

Heading down Scott Road on the Surrey side, Dan felt a sudden stab of fear when a police car cruised past. It didn't miss a beat. Walking on, he flexed his shoulders and tried to relax. He shouldn't be so worried. Dan Foster hardly recognized himself today, especially with his dark glasses. Good thing it was a sunny day.

Waiting at the intersection of Eighty-fourth and Scott for the light to change, he crossed to the Delta side. Scott Road was the border between the municipality of Delta and the city of Surrey.

As teens, he and Mike decided to cross over Scott Road and play a game in Delta where they'd knock on a door, then run and hide. They had a lot of fun rapping on doors. Some people tried to find them, some yelled out at them, and others shrugged and went back inside. Unfortunately, somebody phoned the police.

They were hiding in some bushes and laughing over another victim staring out at the empty street when a Delta police car pulled up behind them. One shout from the cops, and the boys took off like rockets. The police chased them. They ducked into some bushes, but the officers continued after them on foot.

In a flash of brilliance, they decided to cross into Surrey. Mike had reasoned that since Surrey was covered by the RCMP, the Delta police would have no jurisdiction, and they'd get clean away.

With the gall only teenagers possess, they stood on the other side of Scott Road and laughed at their panting pursuers. It turned out Mike was wrong. An hour later, their parents picked them up at the police station. There were no charges, just a stiff warning. Dad hadn't seen it that way. He was an old-fashioned parent who didn't have any problem spanking his teenagers before grounding them.

When he'd covered two blocks on Eighty-fourth, Dan stood in front of Play It Again car rentals. The lot contained about thirty cars, all twenty years or older. Play It Again specialized in classics and older cars.

He hesitated outside the door, suddenly overcome by misgiving. Did he have any right to drag other people into his problem? On the other hand, he had no choice. He was innocent.

He pushed open the glass doors and entered a wide, well-lit waiting room. A tall counter separated the office from the front where he stood. The next moment, a petite woman with sad brown eyes walked out. Originally a redhead with long wiry hair, she was now a brunette with a short cut. She looked like a college student, but Dan knew she was over thirty-five.

Dan met Marisa through his brother, Mike. She was originally from the Maritimes. After several years of dealing with an abusive husband, she got on a bus and fled to Ontario. He tracked her down and put her in the hospital. He told her not to tell the cops about him, or he'd kill her.

When she'd healed a bit, she fled to Saskatchewan. There, she discovered her picture on the Internet with a reward offered for information leading to her whereabouts. Marisa had nowhere to go. She knew it was only a matter of time before her demented husband showed up again.

She went to a local pastor and explained her plight. He phoned Mike's pastor, who called Mike. As a result, Dan lasered off her freckles. He also did a nose and chin job on her, completely altering Marisa's appearance. Mike found her a new identity.

Marisa looked up at Dan and asked, "Can I help you?"

Pulling off his sunglasses, he tried to smile. "Hi, Marisa."

She stared at him for five seconds. She moved closer for a better look. Suddenly, surprise lit up her face. "Dan! The police are looking for you!" She peered at a spot over his forehead. "What did you do to your hair?"

"The police think I killed someone. I didn't do it, Marisa. Someone—I don't know who—is setting me up." He touched his head. "You don't like my hair this way?"

She frowned, then grinned. "It's awful."

"You're just flattering me," he said. His lopsided smile faded. "I need a car. I'll pay cash and sign a phony name so this doesn't come back on you. If the police ever ask, I'll tell them you didn't recognize me."

"I can't do that," she said. "You can pay cash, because they're probably tracing your credit cards, but you must sign your real name. I can't lie, Dan. I'm a Christian now."

"You have to protect yourself," he insisted. "They'll be able to prove you aided and abetted a fugitive. You could go to jail."

"The news says you are a person of interest, not a fugitive. There's no law against helping a person of interest."

Right, Dan thought, *I'm only a person of interest until they catch me, then I'll suddenly become a criminal.* Lifting a blue pen from the counter, he asked, "Where do I sign?"

Marisa brought out a form and slid it in front of him. Dan filled it out, and Marisa handed him a set of keys. "I'd still watch my back if I were you," she said. "The news doesn't always tell it straight."

Chapter
Twenty-Four

L ate in the afternoon, Dan put his rental car in park and stared out the windshield at the Coyote Bar and Grill. The source of his latest troubles.

He'd spent most of the day wandering around and trying to figure out what to do next. He drove past the Martin farm and spotted yellow police tape. Too risky to go in there.

He swung by a few of Jessica's favorite haunts, hoping to connect with her, but no luck. Dan still considered a call to her cell phone too dangerous.

He could only think of one plan of action—go back to the Coyote and see if he could spot Cindy, the anorexic girl who'd accused him of being a cop. He figured that she and her friends attacked him, and he had only one way to find out if he was right. He touched the gun hidden by his leather jacket. This would even up the odds somewhat.

He got out of the car, and his black boots clicked against the asphalt. His disguise was much better after a visit to a Harley-Davidson shop in Vancouver. He'd considered the risk of being recognized, but if someone like Marisa couldn't spot him right off, chances were strangers wouldn't, either.

He pushed open the door and scanned the bar's dim

interior. No sign of Cindy and company. Settling into a corner booth, he looked up at the hockey game on the big-screen TV.

After about five minutes, a tall, masculine-looking waitress stopped by his table. She had a wad of gum in her jaw. "What can I get ya?" she asked.

"Fish and chips," he said and tossed a ten on the table. "And the biggest cola you've got."

"Sure," she said, pocketing the bill.

As the waitress delivered his soda, a cheer erupted in the half-filled room. The Canucks just popped one into the net. Dan lifted his glass and drank a third of it.

He took his time over the fish and chips and watched the game. In the third quarter he looked up to see Kurt Fletcher pass him and sit at the next table. Kurt signaled to the waitress. Dan waited until Kurt ordered, and then he moved to a seat across from the grizzled old man.

Kurt stared at him, focusing his eyes. "I know you?"

Dan eased open his leather jacket, exposing the butt of the handgun. "Yes, and we need to talk."

Kurt held up his hands. "Hey, I don't want trouble."

"There won't be trouble as long as you cooperate."

Kurt's eyes narrowed as he peered at Dan's face. "Hey, you're. . ."

Dan reached toward his waistband. "Don't say it out loud."

"What do you want from me?" he asked, his rubbery lips working up and down.

"Why did you run away after Beth died?"

"I already told the cops about that. Jessica Meyers tracked me down and turned me in."

"Then tell it again," Dan said.

"I ran because I take Nardil. I'm an ex-con. I figured the cops would assume I'd killed Mrs. Martin. They'd throw me in the can and lose the key."

"Didn't you know they were blaming me for that?"

Kurt squirmed. "If I came back, they might decide to throw *me* in jail instead of a well-connected doctor whose brother is a cop. You know how high-class lawyers are. They can talk a judge into anything."

Still watching Kurt carefully, Dan considered his story. It was almost believable. Problem was, Dan didn't know what to do next. Man, he wished Jessica were with him. One thing for sure, he had to hang onto Kurt for awhile. If he let him go, Kurt would run to the cops. He'd tell them where Dan was and what he looked like.

Using the side of her fist, Jessica banged on Kurt Fletcher's apartment door for the fourth time. She turned to Nigel. "I can't keep this up. The upstairs people will come to see what the noise is all about."

"Either he's out or he's not answering," Nigel told her. "He's had plenty of time to come. There's only one way to know for sure."

Jessica stepped back. "Do it your way."

He pushed his hands into a pair of black leather gloves and smashed the glass door panel with one punch. Reaching inside, he turned the lock and opened the door.

"Don't turn on any lights," he said, carefully removing his arm from the broken window. He pulled out a small flashlight. "Stay here, I'll look around."

As brave as she liked to think herself, Jessica decided to let the former commando do the dangerous work. If Kurt lurked in there, Nigel could handle him. She'd only make a good hostage for a desperate man.

Forty-five seconds later, Nigel returned. "He's gone."

Where would he go? she wondered. Of course. Kurt wasn't

hiding anymore. He'd go back to his usual haunts. "Let's go," Jessica said, heading out the door. They quickstepped fifty yards down the street to Nigel's black Crown Victoria.

"What's next?" Nigel asked when they stopped by the car.

"The Coyote Bar and Grill," she said, reaching for the passenger door handle. "It's probably old home week over there."

Jessica pulled on her seat belt, and Nigel shifted the car into drive. Moving into traffic, he constantly checked his mirrors, as if expecting an attack. Sudden unsignaled turns seemed to be part of his stock in trade. Jessica watched his every move, fascinated. He almost did a macabre sort of dance when he was behind the wheel.

At the Coyote, he parked near the corner of the building. "We go in together," he said, turning toward her. It was the first time he'd spoken since they got into the car.

"Absolutely," Jessica agreed. He smiled at her, and she noticed how attractive he could be.

As they got out of the car, two men came from the bar and stepped onto the porch. The first one came down the steps and crossed the light. Immediately, Jessica recognized Kurt.

"There he is!"

Nigel sprinted forward. With a startled jerk, Kurt and his friend looked toward them.

"Hold it right there, Fletcher!" Nigel called.

The second man sprinted around the side of the building. Kurt stood still, watching Nigel come closer. Jessica considered chasing the other man, but he was a big guy. She didn't think she could reel him in even if she hooked him.

When Jessica drew near, Kurt whined, "Haven't you done enough already? What do you want—a story for your TV station?"

Nigel grabbed Kurt's arm. The skinny man winced from a powerful squeeze on his biceps. "Talk nice," Nigel said.

"I've got some questions," Jessica said.

Pulling away from Nigel's viselike hand, Kurt said, "Aw, come on. I told you everything I know."

"Not everything," Jessica insisted. "You'll have to come with us."

The instant before he started running, Dan saw that the big man dashing toward Kurt could easily be one of his kidnappers. With a woman's form standing in the shadows, Dan faced too big a risk to wait around and make sure. They'd recognized Kurt, and Dan decided to run before they figured out who he was, too. He might not be much with his fists, but his legs were in great shape.

Each time his foot struck the asphalt, his nose felt the jolt. He ignored it and ran on. More than his nose would hurt if they got hold of him again. The Coyote bordered a farmer's bare field. Dan did a quick shuffle as he slowed down at a barbed wire fence.

Grabbing onto a fence post, he steadied himself to climb over the wire. One good thing about leather, it didn't snag easily. But denim did. A barb ripped his pants leg as he jumped down. He was glad the barb let go when he reached the other side.

He set a healthy pace crossing the field. Unfortunately, fields were notorious for gopher holes. One mistake and he could end up with a broken ankle. If the lady and her goon weren't chasing him, the best thing to do was put distance between him and the Coyote, circle around, and wait until they were gone. With any luck he could return to his car in an hour or so and drive away.

Keeping away from the farmhouse, he jogged to a corner of the field. Again, he climbed over barbed wire, taking a little more care. This time he got across without getting hung up. He flung himself to the ground and drew in deep, gulping breaths. Finally, a chance to rest.

As his breathing quieted, he heard a car. Then he saw the wide spotlight.

Dwarfed by Nigel in the backseat of the Crown Victoria, Kurt stared with bulging eyes from him to Jessica. She sat in front and leaned over the seat to glare back at their prisoner.

"You sure you told us everything?" she asked.

"Yes," Kurt said, nodding furiously. "Everything!"

"You want us to believe you went into hiding just because you take Nardil? Give me a break!"

"It's the truth," Kurt whined, holding his forearms up to cover his chest and lower face.

Nigel grabbed Kurt's elbow and squeezed. "Tell her the truth!" Nigel growled.

The old man howled, and Nigel let him go.

"You'd better come clean, or I'll get out of this car and leave you two alone," Jessica said. Everything she was doing was based on bluff. She'd made it clear to Nigel that no real harm could come to Kurt. They could end up in jail for this charade.

"I don't know why you won't believe me," Kurt said, pressing himself back into the corner. "It's the truth! You've got to believe me!"

Jessica took a stack of cancelled checks from her purse. She turned on the dome light and passed them back to Kurt. "Take a look at these," she said.

He flipped through the checks. "They're my paychecks."

"Look at the backs."

He flipped through them again. "What? I don't see anything."

"You always took cash back when you deposited your pay-check. Then, the week before Peter Martin died, you started depositing the whole check. What were you living on?"

Kurt's sallow face sagged. His Adam's apple bobbed, and he turned his whiskery face away. "I got lucky at cards the night before."

Jessica pulled on the door handle. "I don't have time for this." She nodded toward Nigel. "Give me a shout when he's ready to talk."

As Jessica opened the car door, Nigel began his squeez-ing routine.

"Wait!" Kurt screamed.

Jessica closed the door and watched him. "So, explain the money. Who paid you off and for what?"

"No one paid me off. I really did win at cards."

"Then why did you run?" Jessica asked. "And give us the truth. I don't want to have to get out of this car again."

Kurt nodded, shifting as far from Nigel as he could. "About a week before Peter died, I met a guy in the Coyote. We got into a conversation and started talking about Peter and the farm."

"What kind of talk?" Jessica asked.

"Normal stuff. What kind of cattle we ran, how the jobs were split up between Peter and me. . ."

"Cut to the chase," Jessica interrupted.

"Anyway, I caught the same guy at the farm. He had Mr. Martin's slicker, and he was doing something to it."

"What was he doing?" Jessica asked. "What did you see?"

"I couldn't tell. He was holding it and looking at it. He looked up and saw me." His Adam's apple moved in his scrawny neck. "He grabbed me and told me not to tell anyone he was there. If word got out, he'd kill me."

"What did he look like?"

"He was a big guy. He could have broken me in two with

one hand." He looked at Nigel. "He was bigger than you. He had dark hair, cut like someone in the army would wear."

"You may have been witness to evidence in a murder. Peter Martin was murdered. You've got to tell the police," Jessica said.

"You're making that up to scare me. A bull killed Peter. It was an accident."

"Then why did you run?" She moved in on him. "It wasn't the Nardil, and it wasn't Peter's accident. What made you run?"

Kurt's eyes widened. "When Beth died, I started getting suspicious. I remembered the man in the barn, and I figured I might be a risk to some important people. I got scared." He glanced around. "I still am."

"And yet tonight you came back to the Coyote. Weren't you afraid you'd run into them here?"

"The police paid me a second visit." Kurt turned to peer into the darkness as though searching for someone. "And a lot of good it's done me," he said in a raised voice.

Nigel jerked open Kurt's jacket and grabbed a small microphone. "He's wired!" Nigel sank back.

At that moment, Jessica's cell phone beeped.

Dan flattened himself in a shallow ditch near the field. Two seconds later, the searchlight swept over him. He heard loud engines racing down the road and looked up to see flashing red and blue lights against the night sky. Who called the cops?

His heart thumped, and he couldn't breathe. He had to think. . .think.

The cars stopped close to his position. Soon, they'd start searching on foot. They'd find him for sure. This wasn't a dark forest where he could bury himself. His best chance was the field. Unless they decided to shoot him, he might be able to outrun them.

Dan slithered out of the ditch and dragged himself toward the barbed wire fence. The more seconds he could buy before they spotted him, the better. He glanced over his shoulder. Half a dozen officers gathered around one car. They weren't moving yet. His only option was to slide under the lowest strand of barbed wire.

It helped that the country road had no streetlights. The bulkiness of his leather jacket made him take it off. He'd never fit under the wire with it on. Keeping as quiet as possible, Dan wiggled out of it. Cold knifed through him. Dropping the coat to the other side of the fence, he flattened himself and turned his head sideways, pushing with his hands.

His chest was under the wire when he heard a gruff voice call, "Okay, let's go!"

Beams of light spread out along the edge of the road, and Dan's luck ran out.

"Look there!" a female voice shouted. "Feet!"

Dan shoved with all his strength. His T-shirt snagged the barbed wire. With fumbling fingers, he yanked it off the barb and scrambled the rest of the way through. A flashlight beam struck his eyes from ten feet away. Jumping to his feet, Dan dug his toes into the ground and sprinted for all he was worth. No time to stop for his jacket. No more caution about gopher holes. If he got caught, he'd have lots of time to heal.

Curses, creaking barbed wire, and general mayhem broke out behind him. He wanted to turn around and see how close they were, but he didn't dare. He'd learned in high school that even a quick glance could cost a race. This time the prize was his life.

Halfway across the field, his lungs started to burn, but he forced himself on. He sucked great gulps of air, and his bruised ribs ached. The Coyote drew nearer, and the sounds behind him faded. He might just do this. Heading for the bar was a risk, but he had no other choices left.

Flying across the field, Dan concentrated on the thickest fence pole. He put every ounce of strength into reaching that pole. Three feet from it, he jumped, grasped the pole, and vaulted over the barbed wire. He crashed on the other side, rolling into a heap. Ignoring the jolt to his nose, he sprang to his feet and ran for his car.

He charged up the side of the Coyote, around the corner, and into a row of flashlights.

"Hold it right there, Foster!" It was Anna Carrington's voice.

Dan flew into the arms of two massive constables. Using his momentum against him, they slammed him down on the warm hood of a police car. They had his hands cuffed behind him in seconds.

One of the constables ran his hands over Dan's body. He pulled the gun out of his belt and spun him around to face Anna Carrington. In the glow of six flashlights, she grinned at him. "Carrying a gun now, are you?"

"It's just an air pistol," Dan said, panting. He felt a wave of weakness, and his eyes blinked as he fought for control.

Anna looked at the barrel. "So it is." She handed the gun to one of the men. "Dan Foster, I am placing you under arrest for the murder of Rocky Wiebe. You have the right to remain silent. You have. . ."

A light caught Dan's eye. He looked past Carrington into the nearest patrol car. Sitting in the backseat, Jessica looked out at him. She was crying.

Chapter
Twenty-Five

When the police cruiser pulled away from the Coyote's parking lot with Dan inside, Jessica stared at its fading taillights until they disappeared around the bend. It was over. The police had him, and she could do nothing about it. She sniffed and swiped her fingers across her damp cheeks. As it was, she'd probably end up in the slammer herself.

The front door of the police car opened, and Corporal Carrington slipped into the front seat. Turning to look back through the wire screen, Carrington shook her head. "You really crossed the line this time, Meyers." She held up her hand and touched her fingers as she counted. "First, unlawful confinement. Second, assault. Third, interfering with a police investigation. Fourth, aiding a fugitive."

"Wait a minute," Jessica called out. "Aiding what fugitive?"

"Foster. Don't tell me you didn't know he was here."

"I didn't know he was here," Jessica said. "If I had known, I would have put him in my car and. . ." She stopped.

"I'll be good to you and overlook your last admission, but that still leaves the first three charges. In case you didn't realize it, we had a sting set up and you blew it. Big time."

"If you had told me that you were still interested in Kurt,"

Jessica said, "I would've stayed out of the way. You lied to me when you told me you had all you needed from him. Now I find out you questioned him again and found out someone else is involved in this mess. What happened to our friendly cooperation truce?"

Carrington looked away. "I'm not obligated to you, Meyers. What I've told you has been out of courtesy."

"Courtesy or convenience?" Jessica asked. "Why do I feel like our truce was really a sham? Why do I feel like you've been using me?"

Anna Carrington shrugged. "Believe what you want. Fact is your boyfriend is in custody for murder."

"And what about the guy Kurt was just talking about? Find him, and you'll find the real killer!"

Carrington sighed. "If he exists. We only have Kurt's word on that. We came here tonight to check out his story, but you got to him before we had a chance."

"Then try another night."

"Everyone in that bar saw what happened. You blew it for him. Kurt can never come back here."

"So that's it?" Jessica asked. "You're just going to forget it?"

Anna leaned forward until her wide nose almost touched the screened partition. "We've got well over a hundred officers digging up a pig farm trying to find the remains of fifty missing women. We don't have time to chase down red herrings. I had to throw a screaming fit to get tonight's detail. Fortunately, we caught Foster, so it wasn't a complete waste." She got out of the car and opened Jessica's door.

Stepping outside, Jessica said, "I don't understand you. Doesn't justice matter?"

"Sure it does. And Foster will get justice. He'll get a chance to explain to a jury how the pills that killed Beth Martin were in the hands of two people—him and his girlfriend, Amy. He'll get a chance to explain what his blood is doing on Rocky Wiebe's ring and what Rocky Wiebe's blood is doing on his scalpel. If he can convince them of his innocence, more power to him. As for me, I've got my man. Meyers, I think it's time you woke up and faced facts. You're in love with a killer."

Jessica opened her mouth, but Carrington cut her off. "If you cry for justice again, I'll give you justice. I'll haul you down to the station and book you. I can make it stick, too." She eased into the driver's seat. "Now I'm going. I've got a prisoner to interrogate."

At the police station, Dan blinked under the intense glare of the flashbulb.

"Now turn sideways," the constable said. He was a thick pug-faced man.

Dan turned and another light flashed. He was now officially on record as a criminal.

"Okay, come with me." The same officer took Dan's elbow and guided him to a counter containing inkpads, a stack of printed note cards, and a box of tissues. The constable made impressions of his fingerprints, then handed him a tissue.

He led him into another room, a spartan affair with a long table and four chairs. Two thick-necked constables stood there with Anna Carrington.

"Good evening, Dr. Foster," Carrington said. "Now strip."

"Are you serious?" Dan looked across the four faces watching him.

"Absolutely," she said.

"I want a lawyer."

"After your booking is finished."

Dan stood his ground. "Not a chance. Not in front of you. I don't have to. It's not legal."

"Fine," Carrington said. "You want to do it the hard way, we can arrange it."

"Strip him down," she told the two constables. They advanced toward him, and Dan backed up against the wall. He lunged sideways, and they grabbed his arms. Dan twisted and kicked. The pug-faced cop jumped in, and they pulled him to the floor. One held his legs, the other his arms, and the pug-faced guy pulled at Dan's belt.

"What's going on in here?" a familiar voice boomed from the doorway.

Three heads turned toward the door. It was Bernie Thorpe, Mike's partner.

"Get off of him!" Bernie shouted, coming inside. Red-faced and glaring, he looked as though he'd like to kick someone.

Carrington said, "Let him up."

Trembling, Dan got to his feet and tried to get back some measure of dignity. "Am I ever glad to see you," he told Bernie.

Bernie turned his attention on Carrington. "This is Mike Foster's brother!"

"Which is why he isn't getting any special treatment," Carrington said. "He's responsible for at least two deaths. If we give him special treatment because he's Foster's brother, the media will be all over it."

"Tough on them," Bernie said. "You're not going to treat Mike's brother like some punk off the street."

"You've got no authority in this case."

Bernie nodded. "That's right, Carrington, I don't. But if you persist on treating Dr. Foster this way, you're going to learn just how well regarded Mike Foster is in the RCMP. Do your job, Carrington, but do it with respect."

"Do you mind if we question him?" Carrington asked, her voice dripping sweetness.

"Has he been read his rights?" Thorpe asked.

"Yes."

Thorpe turned to Dan. "Do you want to answer questions?"

"Not without my lawyer," Dan said.

"There it is," Bernie said. "Get his lawyer down here, and he'll talk to you."

"It's ten o'clock at night," Anna said. "No lawyer is coming down here at this hour."

Thorpe shrugged. "Then you'll have to lock him up until tomorrow. And don't put him in the holding tank. Give him his own cell."

"Whatever," Carrington said, shrugging.

Bernie Thorpe turned to leave.

"Bernie," Dan called after him. "Where's Mike? Why hasn't he come to help me?"

"Dan, all I can tell you is your brother is in one of those need-to-know places. You'd like to know, but you don't need to know. But if you're religious like he is, I'd suggest you pray."

"What does that mean?" Dan asked.

Bernie shook his head. "I can't say any more," he said and left the room.

"Well," Anna said, "it looks like your life of privilege is going to last a little longer." She turned to Pug Face. "Put him in a cell."

Cold fear washed across Dan. A small cell. A locked door. Like a cave. "Hey! Put me in with everyone else," Dan said. "I don't mind."

A cruel grin crept across Anna's face. "What's the matter? Don't like closed-in spaces?"

"Well?" Pug Face asked, grabbing Dan's arm. "Which is it?"

"Put him in his own cell."

"Don't do this!" Dan said, sweat covering his face.

Anna Carrington folded her arms. "Give me a reason not to."

"Like what?" Dan asked.

"Like talk to us now."

"Without my lawyer?"

Carrington shrugged. "You want a favor from me, then I need a favor from you. Your choice."

The thought of being locked in a six-by-eight cell made his throat go dry. What would a locked cell do to him? He couldn't find out. "Okay, okay," he said. "We can talk."

Carrington pointed to a chair, and Dan sat down. "Get a tape recorder," she told Pug Face. Two minutes later, he returned with a gray machine. Carrington set the microphone between them.

"This is Corporal Anna Carrington of the Royal Canadian Mounted Police," she said. "I am interrogating Dr. Daniel Foster in investigation of the murder of Rocky Wiebe." She looked up at Dan. "State your full name."

"Daniel Matthew Foster," he said.

"Have you been advised that you can have a lawyer present while we question you?"

"Yes," Dan said.

"And you waive this right freely and of your own accord?"

Dan looked at her, his eyes narrow. "Yes," he ground out.

"Fine. Why did you kill Rocky Wiebe?"

"I didn't kill him. Give me a lie detector test, and I'll prove it."

Carrington's heavy lips twisted. "Really? Please, explain how your blood ended up on his ring. Explain why the weapon used to cut his throat was a scalpel from the set in your doctor's bag. Why were your knuckles bruised and your face punched in?"

"Okay," Dan said. "I will."

He related the whole story to Carrington. From trying to find Kurt in the bar, being questioned by Cindy, and then being beaten outside. Her expression remained blank as he told her about being bound and taken for a ride in his car before being turned loose in the forest.

Anna looked up at the other two constables. "Wow! That was really good. What do you guys think?"

"Best I've heard in a long time," one of them said.

"It's the truth!" Dan shouted.

Carrington smirked. "Come on, Doctor. Some thug put on Rocky's ring, punched you in the nose, then put it back on Rocky's hand?"

"Yes," Dan said. "They must've taken the scalpel out of my car and used it to kill him."

Carrington nodded. "Tell me, Doctor, why would someone go to all this trouble to frame you for Rocky's murder? You see the problem I'm having? No one benefited from Rocky's death except you and Amy Creighton. According to Amy, you are lovers."

The breath left his lungs as though he'd been punched. "Amy and I are *what?*"

She looked over her shoulder at the other two. "He should go to Hollywood."

They both grinned.

"That's ridiculous!" Dan said.

"Is it?" Carrington asked, leaning toward him. "Her diary's so hot you can almost see steam rising off the cover. Every page is about you and her—what you said, where you went, what you did." She stabbed at him with a long index finger. "You deny dating her?"

Dan swallowed and drew in a slow breath, trying to focus as a hot wave washed over him. He couldn't afford to lose it now. "We. . .we dated a few times. . . . It was. . .nothing serious."

Carrington suddenly shouted, "We've got your sweetheart locked up in this very jail!"

"Jessica's in jail?" Dan asked.

"Nice try," Carrington said. "You knew I meant Amy."

"Amy's in jail? For what?"

"She's named as coconspirator with you."

The room began to spin out of control. "This is crazy," he muttered, rubbing his eyes.

"Not as crazy as your story," she said. "I suppose next you're going to tell us one of the guys attacking you was a one-armed man." The three RCMP members all laughed at Carrington's reference to *The Fugitive*.

"Look," Dan said. "Someone else must have had a reason to kill Rocky. I was just an easy target to frame."

"Sure," Carrington said, shifting in her chair. "We've spent enough tape on that. Let's move on. We want to know how you managed to escape after your car crashed and you left the truck stop. You were wounded. Someone had to help you."

"I can't," Dan said.

"Failure to cooperate is a no-no. Your private cell awaits you, Foster. Don't forget that."

"I can't," Dan insisted. "Believe me."

Carrington watched him, considering. She switched off the tape recorder. "Fine, have it your way." She looked at the two constables. "We're done. Put him in a private cell."

"Wait a minute!" Dan said. "That wasn't the deal."

"Tell us who helped you."

His mouth went dry. His hands trembled. He couldn't go into a small cell. He just couldn't. Then, Luis's concerned face flashed through his mind, Marisa's trusting smile.

"Well?" Carrington demanded, leaning over him.

Dan closed his eyes. Finally, he muttered, "Put me in a cell."

Carrington searched his face for a long moment. "Put him in the holding tank," she said. "He'll probably claim cruel and unusual punishment if we don't." She stared at him and went on. "After a night with the scum in there, you're going to wish I'd put you in a private cell like Thorpe wanted."

Half an hour after leaving the Coyote, Jessica sat at her favorite table at Denny's and stirred sugar into her coffee. Nigel sat across from her. Before going to the bar, they'd parked Jessica's car in this lot. When they returned for the Porsche, they decided to come inside for a few minutes to regroup and consider their next plan of action.

"You seem to be well-known here," Nigel said, trying to make small talk. In the five minutes they'd sat here, Jessica hadn't said two words.

"Dan and I come here a lot," she replied. Her makeup was smeared, her face troubled. She'd give almost anything to have Dan across from her instead of Nigel.

He laid his spoon on his coffee saucer and said, "Maybe I'm out of line for asking, but what are you two?"

Jessica turned up the right side of her mouth in a half-grin. "I wish I knew. It's safe to say we're close friends. Why do you want to know?"

"Couple of reasons. One, you're putting a lot on the line for him. From what I've read in the papers, the guy looks as guilty as sin."

"I have information you don't."

"Like what?"

"I know Dan Foster. He couldn't kill anyone. This has to be a frame-up."

"It's hard to argue with that," Nigel said.

"Look," Jessica said, "you don't have to baby-sit me any longer. I'm just going to take some time to relax before I head home."

He scanned the dining room. "I'd rather stick around," he said. "I think we were followed here."

"By whom?" Jessica asked, stiffening.

Nigel nodded toward a place over her shoulder. "By him."

Jessica turned to see Kurt heading for their table.

"What do you want?" Jessica asked when he reached them.

He sat down without waiting to be asked. "I've got to talk to you."

"Open your shirt," Nigel told him.

Kurt swore, then unbuttoned his grimy flannel shirt. When Nigel nodded, he fiddled with his buttons, trying to refasten them and getting them off track. He finally blurted out, "I came to tell you to be careful."

"Well, duh," Jessica said.

"No, I mean it," Kurt said. "Carrington is playing you for a fool. I heard her joke with the other cops about how you trusted her."

"I kind of put that together on my own," Jessica said.

Nigel spoke up. "Mind you, Carrington did let us go."

"She didn't let you go because she wanted to," Kurt countered. "She was going to charge you until I said I'd refuse to testify if she did."

"Why are you doing us favors?" Jessica demanded. This wasn't adding up.

"She promised me twenty-four-hour protection if I wore that wire. Now she says I'm on my own since the sting went south." His eyes darted about the room. "You're my only hope. I've got to get outta here. If they find me, they'll kill me."

Jessica looked at Nigel. "Can you make him disappear for awhile?"

"Sure," Nigel said, "but Pronger is only paying me to keep you safe, not all your friends."

"I'll take care of the extra cost," she said. "He may be Dan's ticket out of this mess."

Mike Foster waited in the dark at the side of the road in front of his hotel while Louise pulled the car close to him.

He got in on the passenger side.

"They called?" she asked.

He nodded. "Half an hour ago. Garret said to meet him at the same place as before."

"We were supposed to make the next contact. You think they made us?"

"I doubt it," Mike said. "Garret sounded more nervous than anything. I think something has gone wrong on their end."

"Well, I've arranged for backup anyway," Louise said. "My mom wouldn't like to trade in her dearly beloved for a fancy funeral and a folded flag." She stopped at a red light, flipped open her cell phone, and called in their destination.

"Why didn't you ever marry?" Mike asked. "If you don't mind my asking."

"Who said I didn't," she shot back.

"Sorry," he said, embarrassed. "I shouldn't have asked."

"He was a test pilot. He died in the line of duty."

"Forgive me for mentioning it."

She sent him a sad smile. "It's okay. We were together only fourteen months. One thing about being single, it gave me a lot of freedom to do this job. Being an undercover cop gives me something to live for. Something to do that's worthwhile."

Pretending to lean back and doze, Mike watched her profile. For the first time he saw the woman behind all the jewelry and the tough-guy bluster.

Half an hour later, they parked outside the bar near Mt. Baker.

The lot was crammed. The ski hill had opened early and hundreds of ski-wearing, pole-carrying fanatics infested the mountain and nearby businesses.

When Mike and Louise entered the bar, they came nose to nose with a dozen or more drunken skiers trying to line dance to pulsating country music. Shoving them aside, Mike spotted

Garret's hollow face in a back booth.

Finally, the last man chugged past, and Mike ran interference with Louise close behind him. Twenty steps later, they slid into the booth across from Garret.

Both Mike and Louise leaned forward so they wouldn't have to shout. "What's happening?" Mike asked.

Looking worried, Garret said, "We've got a problem on our end."

"Oh great," Mike said. "Are you saying after all the time and money we've put into this, you can't supply us?"

Garret looked away for a second. "We can supply you, but we need to do it sooner rather than later."

"Why?"

"We have to relocate our operations. We do it all the time. It just happens we have to do it sooner than usual."

"What's the problem?" Louise asked.

"Cop trouble."

Mike slumped back in his seat, mouthed a curse, then leaned forward. "You think we're crazy enough to make a buy with the cops sniffing around? Do we look insane to you?"

"They're not sniffing around," Garret said, his gaunt face anxious. "Look, we run a very careful operation. That's why we're still in business. Things are happening that could eventually lead the cops to us, so we're clearing out. We're willing to sell you the stuff at a third off, just to move it quick. Are you game or not?"

"If you deliver," Louise said.

Garret shook his head. "Not a chance. They'll burn their stash before they'll transfer it across the border. You'll still have to pick it up."

Mike looked at Louise. "We need to talk," he said. "Let's go outside."

Dodging the gyrating line dancers, they made it to the

door. For privacy, they headed for their car. "What do you think?" Mike asked, shutting the door behind him.

"Sounds like your people are closing in for an unrelated sting, and I don't like it at all."

"I could talk to my people. See what's going on," Mike said.

Louise shook her head vigorously. "No way. The three RCMP that know about our operation now are three too many for my liking. Those Canadian growers have to be getting help, and it could be your people."

"I highly doubt it," Mike said. "RCMP has a tradition of loyalty, but it is ultimately your call. What do you suggest we do?"

Louise sucked air through her teeth. "I'm wondering if this is some kind of setup to get us across the border, where they can kill us. They have the death penalty in Washington State—especially for killing a cop. Do it in Canada, worst you get is twenty-five years."

"Your people have been cleared to operate on the Canadian side of the border. They'll be watching us the whole time. If something goes wrong. . ."

"They'll get there in time to pick up our bodies."

"Thanks for the encouragement," he said. "Do you want to abort the mission?"

Louise Crossfield hunched inside her black jacket and gazed through the windshield at the sky. Her multiple earrings twinkled in the beam of the security light. "I didn't get this far by being afraid of a risk. But let's talk him down to half off. If we give in too easy, we might make them suspicious."

"You got it," Mike said.

Driving home from the restaurant, Jessica couldn't get Dan off her mind. If only there were some way to get him out of jail. Bail would probably be out of sight. Beyond anything Dan could handle, even with Jessica's help. Elinor talked about her investments but said something about them being all tied up. The elderly woman might not think much of Dan being a plastic surgeon, but surely she'd help him with bail. The sooner Elinor began untying her investments, the better.

Jessica put on her turn signal and got off at the first exit. She pulled into a gas station and called Elinor's number on her cell phone. She let it ring ten times. No answer. She punched Dan's number with the same result.

Where was Elinor? Out? No. Elinor mentioned over dinner that she didn't like to drive at night. A creepy feeling ran up her neck. What if someone knew about Mike being gone and Dan in jail?

Jessica pulled back into the street and gunned her Porsche for Langley. Visions of Elinor as the victim of a home invasion or a heart attack flashed through her mind. Giving little heed to the traffic signs, Jessica parked in Dan's driveway in short order and hurried up the sidewalk. Thankfully, the porch light was on. She knocked long and loud. No answer. Now she was really getting worried.

Let's see, she wondered, *was it moon landing or Nixon first?*

Jessica punched a number onto the pad. Nothing happened. She reversed the order and the tumbler clicked open.

"Elinor!" she called, closing the door behind her. "Elinor? Are you there?"

She hurried to Elinor's apartment and knocked again. Still no answer.

Jessica slowly opened the door and looked inside. The place was empty. No Aunt Elinor.

Jessica returned to Dan's living room. If Elinor was gone, she couldn't help Dan. There was no way to tell where she might have gone. Who would know? If only she could phone Dan and ask him.

She glanced down at the coffee table and saw a scrap of paper with a light, feminine scrawl in black ink. She picked it up and read:

Edith Gardener
(Elinor's friend in Arizona)
(602) 555-1919

Jessica blinked and read it again. She lifted the receiver from the phone beside the couch and punched in the number.

The holding tank at the Abbotsford police station wasn't attractive to see, hear, or smell. Moving through a dozen dirty, unshaven men, Dan found a bare mattress on the floor and eased himself onto it. He folded his arm under his head and closed his eyes. Maybe if he faded into the gray block wall behind him, no one would notice him.

"Hey, Stud," a voice drawled. "What happened to you?"

Someone nudged Dan's ribs, and he opened his eyes, dreading to see what would happen next.

A leather-faced man with a drinker's red nose sat down beside him. "You look like you got run over by a train."

Dan nodded. "He was about as big as a train."

"What'd you give him for it? Busted ribs? A busted nose to match yours?"

Dan sat up and the stranger settled down beside Dan on the mattress, easing his back against the wall.

"Well, actually," Dan said, hesitating, "he didn't get anything but a bruised fist from pounding on me."

"You're joking."

Dan felt his nose. "Wish I was."

"Looks like we've got all night. How 'bout I give you some

pointers in case you meet up with that dude again?" He raised his fists. "When someone comes at you, the first thing you do is protect your face like this, see?"

Dan nodded, watching closely. He raised his fists to match his teacher's. Maybe the night wasn't going to be so bad after all.

Chapter
Twenty-Six

Sunday brought nothing but frustration for Jessica Meyers. First, officials told the news anchor she could visit Dan in the afternoon. Then when she showed up, they said he wasn't there. He was at the courthouse being officially charged in front of the Justice of the Peace. By the time she got to the courthouse, Dan had already left.

Finally, she caught Arthur Stoll at the Abbotsford police station. He couldn't find Dan, either. Arthur went ballistic and started making phone calls. He did manage to twist the prosecutor's arm and get a bail hearing for Monday afternoon.

At six o'clock, Jessica finally went home. She was too exhausted to wait anymore. She'd already lost too much sleep over the past forty-eight hours, and tomorrow would be another long day.

Early Monday morning, Jessica's Porsche turned into the entrance of the 8-Seconds Ranch. She stared at the sign over the driveway entrance.

What a strange name. A quarter of a mile down the drive between parallel white-rail fences, she parked in front of a humble log house. With all leads exhausted, Jessica decided it was time to check out the other Martin properties. Maybe she'd find a clue to solve Beth's murder.

She turned off the motor. Seven o'clock was probably too early to pay a call, but she had a lot to get done before Dan's hearing at four-thirty that afternoon. Besides, these guys were ranchers. Ranchers always got up early.

A tall, solid man with a seamed face sauntered around the side of the house. He wore blue jeans, a fleece-lined denim jacket, and a black cowboy hat. His leathery skin testified to years of outdoor living. Jessica opened her door and got out. The man's eyes ran over the Porsche before he looked at her.

"Hi!" she said, smiling.

"Nice car," he replied, leaning down to eye the dashboard through the driver's window. "Must've cost a few bucks."

"Not as much as you'd think," Jessica said. "This is only a Boxter. The 911's are the pricey ones. But, yes, it did set me back a few bucks."

He stood and peered at her face. "You're Jessica Meyers. The news lady."

"That's right."

"What can I do for you at this fine hour, Ms. Meyers?" he asked.

"Sorry to bother you so early."

"Been up since five."

She pulled out the permission paper Amy signed for her and held it toward him. On the drive over, Jessica had made up a story to explain her visit. She hoped he'd buy it.

"I'm sure you know that Beth Martin's ward, Amy Creighton, is in jail. Her defense is going to cost a fortune. Her lawyer figures she'll be able to use these properties as collateral for a loan. She asked me to visit and, well, find out what you do here. I'm afraid she doesn't have a clue, and the bank has to be told something."

The cowboy slowly read the document. He handed it back

to her and extended his hand. "I'm Anthony Clark. I guess you'd like a tour."

"If it wouldn't be too much trouble."

"Not at all. Late fall is always slow around here. Most of the big rodeos are over."

"Rodeos?" Jessica asked. "What do rodeos have to do with ranching?"

Anthony cocked his head to look at her sideways from under the hat brim. "Didn't you see the sign on the way in? We're called the 8-Seconds Ranch."

"I wondered about that. What does it mean?"

"Why, we breed some of orneriest critters in the province."

"I'm still not getting it."

"Come on," he said. "I'll show you."

Jessica followed Anthony Clark around the side of the house. This wasn't much different from Peter Martin's setup—a large barn, a hay shed, and holding pens. In the pens, massive bulls grazed on hay. The only difference was the property had a full-sized rodeo arena complete with four chutes.

Jessica walked to one of the pens with her guide. Anthony placed his foot on the bottom rail and folded his arms across the top rail. Jessica did likewise.

"These babies look pretty calm, don't they?" he asked.

Doubtfully watching the big beasts, Jessica nodded.

"When you put one of them in a chute and wrap a strap around his groin, you'll get the ride of your life. If you stay on him for eight seconds, you win." A grin crept across the rancher's face.

"Hence, the name of your ranch!"

"That's right," he said.

Jessica glanced at her watch. At the speed this man talked and moved, she'd still be taking cowboy lessons at four this afternoon. She looked around and wondered how to hurry him along.

He nodded toward the arena. "We test each bull ourselves to be sure he'll make the grade."

"And if they don't, they go to the hamburger factory?"

He rubbed his hand over his mouth. "The lucky ones get sold to farmers for breeding stock. The rest have probably graced your dinner plate at some time or another." He glanced at her, his brow pulled down. "Unless you don't eat beef."

"I eat beef," Jessica said, glad she could make him happy.

"Good for you," he said. "You know, it's kind of tragic in a way. Samson, the bull that killed Peter, was one of ours. We were ready to send him to the butcher when Peter dropped by and saw him. You could say Peter saved Samson's life. That old reprobate repaid Peter by killing him. Strange thing, that."

"Samson wasn't ornery enough for you guys?"

"Not by a long shot," Anthony said. "He was a lover, not a fighter. Peter must've done something pretty stupid to aggravate him."

"I guess so."

Anthony gave her a two-hour-long tour of the entire ranch. His openness and willingness to answer questions gave Jessica nothing new to go on. If this guy was hiding something, she couldn't see it.

At ten-thirty Jessica turned into the driveway of the other Martin property. This one took Jersey Delight for its name. Whatever happened to the good old standbys like Double X and Triple Bar? The new millennium had reached the farming community.

This wood-sided ranch house stood close to the road. Jessica stopped in front and got out of the car. She walked up worn wooden steps onto the small porch and knocked. No answer. She knocked again, heard some stirring, some curses, and a chain being unlatched. Finally, the door peeked open. In the crack Jessica saw a woman in her thirties with platinum hair that needed a wash and a brush in the worst way.

"Yeah?" the woman muttered, one bleary eye to the crack.

"Hi, my name is Jessica Meyers."

"So?"

"I have a letter from the owner giving me permission to inspect the property." She held up the document for her to read.

The woman looked it over. "You can't come in here without giving us twenty-four hours' notice. It's in the lease."

"I don't need to come into the house," Jessica said. "I just want to take a look around the property. Amy needs to borrow against the property to pay for her defense, and the lawyer needs to know what kind of shape it's in. I can look by myself."

The woman chewed on her cheek for a second. "Hang on a minute. I'll come with you."

The door closed. Jessica waited on the edge of the porch. Five minutes later, the woman emerged wearing a cloth jacket and jeans. On her feet were men's work boots. She glanced down at Jessica's white jogging shoes. "It's messy back there," she said.

Jessica looked down. "They can be washed."

"Suit yourself," she said, setting out.

"I never caught your name," Jessica said, catching up to her.

"I didn't throw it."

They trudged into the back lot toward a massive barn. At the end closest to them stood twin stainless steel tanks almost as tall as the barn roof and, nearby, a power pole with a large transformer on it.

"What do you raise here?" Jessica asked.

"Milk."

Thirty cows stood in the fields behind the barn. Jessica

paused and gazed across the pasture. Piles of manure littered the landscape, a few with steady streams of steam rising. Odd, but not too odd. Composting manure gave off heat and steam.

"Did Peter get his milk calves from you?" Jessica asked.

"A few," she said. "What do you want to see?"

"Could I take a look inside the barn?"

"Sure." She led Jessica to a side door. They stepped inside onto a concrete floor. Milking stations ran down both sides, at least a hundred of them.

"So, can I ask your name? Or do I have to look it up in the rental records later?"

"It's Sylvie."

"Do you run this place by yourself?"

"What does that have to do with the place's value?" Her voice had a stiff, nasal tone.

"Nothing," Jessica said. "Just curious."

"I have help," she said shortly and moved on.

"How long have you been here?"

Sylvie's thin mouth formed a frown. "You want to look at the barn or learn my life history?"

"Just trying to be friendly."

"Well, don't bother," Sylvie said. "I was up all night with a sick cow, and I don't feel like playing twenty questions."

"Sorry," Jessica said. With Sylvie close on her heels, she walked around the barn. The milking machines looked interesting enough—four suction cups dangling from a contraption that fed into a pipe leading to plastic tubes overhead. Those emptied into the giant milk tanks at the end of the building.

"Anything else?" Sylvie asked after ten minutes had passed.

Jessica glanced at her watch. She might as well go home and freshen up before Dan's court appearance.

On the way out, Sylvie said, "Next time, call before you come. We're entitled to our privacy."

In a conference room at the courthouse, Dan rapped his fingers on the table between him and Arthur Stoll. Arthur overflowed the wooden chair where he sat flipping through a thick file in front of him.

"What's going to happen to me?" Dan asked.

Arthur peered over his reading glasses. "You want the truth?"

"Yeah. What else?"

"More than likely, you're going to prison."

Dan felt like he'd just caught a javelin in the chest. "You're joking, right?"

Arthur took off his glasses and looked Dan in the eye. "I wish I were. Carrington has a good case here. You've got plenty of explanations, but no physical proof to back you up. It didn't help that you talked to them without me present."

"I had no choice," Dan said.

"Explain that for me."

Dan sighed. "I'm claustrophobic. They threatened to put me in a small cell if I didn't talk to them."

Arthur tapped his pen on the table. "That might be useful when the time comes."

"When what time comes?"

"At some point we're going to have to make a deal with the Crown prosecutor. Paint it the right way, and Carrington's actions could be made to look like torture. They won't want that to come out in open court. We'll probably get this bumped down to second-degree murder."

"Second-degree murder! I'm completely innocent. Why would I settle for that?"

Stoll shrugged. "Because first-degree murder means life without parole for twenty-five years. You can get out doing fifteen for second-degree murder. Might even be able to get this down to manslaughter if we can paint it as a fight that went bad. That carries ten years."

Dan rubbed both hands through his short black hair. "But there was no fight. I wasn't even there. Are you on my side or not?"

Stoll closed the file and locked eyes with him. "I am on your side, Dan. Part of that is giving the truth to you straight. Sure, I could give you a sugarcoated pacifier to suck on and make you feel better. Would that do you any good?"

Dan shook his head, and Stoll went on. "All I can do is chip away at the Crown's case hoping to find a flaw or to find a version of events that lessons the severity of the crime."

"You're telling me to lie? To say I had a fight with Rocky and accidentally killed him?"

"I can't tell you to lie," Stoll said.

"Then what should I do?"

"Between now and the trial, you're going to have to find out who killed Rocky Wiebe. The cops have you, and they're not going to look any harder. Your brother's a cop. Maybe he can help."

"He's undercover. No one will tell me where he is."

"Then I suggest you hire a private investigator."

"How much does that cost?"

"A thousand bucks a day for a good one. Shouldn't be too hard for a plastic surgeon."

Dan rubbed his weary eyes. "Look, Arthur, there's something you should know. I don't have a lot of money."

Stoll's bushy eyebrows rose. "Are you kidding? With the money you make? Why not? You got some kind of habit I should know about?"

"Yeah," Dan said, looking at his hands clasped on the tabletop. "I've got a real bad habit. I'm a sucker for a hard-luck case. I do a lot of free surgery for people who really need it but can't afford it. Sometimes I can get other doctors and nurses to volunteer, but often I have to pay them myself. After paying off all my student loans, there hasn't been a lot left."

"How much can you raise?" Stoll asked.

Dan shrugged. "Fifty thousand, give or take."

"That'll hardly cover my fee."

Dan held out his hands. "What can I say?"

"Can you borrow the money? You have friends, relatives?"

"My aunt could probably spring it, but I'm not sure when she'll get here. I got a message saying Jessica called her, but Aunt Elinor's having trouble getting a flight."

"I pulled a few strings for today's hearing. Bail hearings don't usually come up this quick. I can keep my retainer down to the cost of what I've done so far, but you're looking at nothing less than five hundred thousand for bail. Can you raise that?"

Dan thought back to all the people he'd helped since he started in practice. As much as he hated to, maybe now was the time to call in favors. None of them could help him on their own, but together there was a chance. "Get the best deal you can," Dan said. "If Aunt Elinor can't come through, I'll try to get the money somehow."

"Okay," Stoll said. He reached for his shiny briefcase and dropped the file inside.

A knock sounded at the door, and a man in a sheriff's uniform poked his head inside the room. "They're ready," he said.

Arthur and Dan followed the sheriff through a passage that led directly into the courtroom. It had enough seating for two-dozen spectators, tables for the defense and the prosecution, and an elevated platform for the judge. The small room was full.

Looking refreshed, Aunt Elinor sat beside Jessica, her skin a healthy color from the Arizona sun. She wore a closely tailored teal suit with a wide-brimmed felt hat.

When he passed her, Elinor winked at him and reached out to squeeze his hand. "I'm praying for you," she whispered.

With smiles for Jessica, Dan and his attorney sat at the

table. Settling back into his seat, Dan felt a hand on his shoulder. He turned to find Jessica's face close to his. "It's going to be all right," she said. "I'm pulling for you."

"Thanks," he murmured. She'd never looked as good as she did at that moment.

Jessica sat down, and Dan looked at the Crown prosecutor. He was a thin man with a turkey neck, thinning hair, and a mousy face. "What's he like?" Dan whispered to Arthur.

"His name is Frank Kershaw. He's a lot like me. He hates to lose."

A door opened behind the bench and a gray-haired African-American judge entered the courtroom. "All rise," the bailiff called. "The court of the honorable Elijah Curtis is now in session."

Judge Curtis looked more like an ex-boxer than a judge. He had a broad forehead, a blunt nose, and a thick neck.

"At least you got one break," Stoll whispered. "Elijah Curtis is known for being a fair man. He gets furious if there's any hint of impropriety on the Crown's part."

Judge Curtis's booming voice filled the courtroom. "What do we have here, gentlemen?" He sorted through some papers. "Ah, yes. The Crown versus Dr. Daniel Foster for the murder of Rocky Wiebe. Application for bail." He turned his attention to Frank Kershaw. "Begin, Mr. Kershaw. Tell me why we should keep this man in jail."

"This is first-degree murder and a brutal murder at that. Dr. Foster fled from the crime scene and evaded arrest. We feel he's a flight risk. The evidence is solid. We have his blood on the victim's ring, we. . ."

Arthur stood. "Whoa a minute."

Judge Curtis turned to Arthur. "Yes?"

"They have the same blood type on the victim's ring," Arthur said. "Not a DNA match."

"Is that correct?" the judge asked Kershaw.

"Yes, Your Honor," he said. "We're waiting for DNA results. But it's a rare blood type, and his car was seen fleeing the area of the accident. Mr. Wiebe was suing him for ten million dollars. Besides that, Dr. Foster had a romantic relationship with a woman who inherits a fortune upon Rocky Wiebe's death. We request that bail be denied."

The judge said, "Mr. Stoll?"

"We hold that Dr. Foster is the victim of a frame-up, Your Honor. He was kidnapped, assaulted, and dumped in a forest at the time of the murder. He only evaded capture by police so he could clear his name. Incarceration would not serve justice. Furthermore, he is an established citizen. He owns a house. He lives with his brother, who is RCMP Corporal Mike Foster, and with his elderly aunt, Elinor Foster. We can bring forth many members of the community who will testify to Dr. Foster's good character and compassion for the needy. Jessica Meyers, the WTV news anchor, is willing to testify at this moment."

"His aunt is Elinor Foster?" Judge Curtis asked.

"Yes, Elijah," Elinor said, standing. "That's my nephew sitting there. Elijah, Danny is no killer. Something wicked is going on here. I guarantee it. You must let him go."

The judge let go a healthy laugh. "Elinor, I see you've lost none of your fire. Unfortunately, I can't declare him innocent on your say-so."

Elinor gave him an arch look. "And why not?"

Still smiling, Judge Curtis made a note. "Will you be responsible for him?"

"Absolutely," Elinor said.

"Okay then," the judge said, banging his gavel. "Bail is set at twenty-five thousand dollars."

"Are you kidding?" Kershaw burst out.

The judge sent a stone-faced look at Kershaw. "I don't kid

from the bench. If this lady will vouch for Dr. Foster, I don't need much else."

Elinor produced her checkbook. "Where do I pay?"

Stoll leaned over to Dan. "I think your fortunes are starting to change."

Chapter
Twenty-Seven

When court adjourned, Elinor offered to buy a celebration dinner for Dan, Jessica, and Arthur Stoll. They drove in separate cars to the Edgemont, one of the finest restaurants in Langley. As soon as the hostess saw Elinor, she led them to a secluded room and hurried away for their drinks. Watching the anxious care of the staff, Dan wondered if his aunt owned part of the establishment.

Never in his life had Dan been so glad to see Aunt Elinor, and never in his life had he felt so rotten for the things he'd said about her. According to Arthur, without Elinor, he'd still be in jail.

Arthur Stoll occupied the seat next to Elinor, and Jessica sat next to Dan. Watching Jessica's beaming smile, Dan couldn't be happier. He wished that the clock had a pause button like a VCR so he could park right here at this table for a few days and look at her.

Elinor glanced up from her menu. "Who fixed your nose?"

"Did it myself," he said, reaching up to touch the swollen projection on his face.

Her forehead crinkled. "It isn't a good advertisement for your services, I'm afraid. You need to take it into the shop and get it fixed."

Dan glanced at her, then looked back again. "Thanks, Aunt Elinor," he said. "A nose job is on the top of my priority list."

She reached over to squeeze his hand. "I've been too hard on you, Danny. I hope you can forgive me."

He looked at her. "I should be apologizing to you, Auntie," he said. "I've had a rotten attitude."

She smiled. "That's all in the past. We won't talk about it again."

"How do you know Judge Curtis?" Arthur asked her.

"I volunteer for Langley Hospice. Mrs. Curtis was a beautiful soul who spent her last days in that facility. She died from pancreatic cancer. During her illness and after she died, I spent a lot of time talking with the judge about loss, grief, and God. That poor man. It was such a difficult time for him. I think my talks and prayers helped him some."

"I'm sorry to hear you have such a close relationship," Stoll said.

"Why?" Dan asked. "It helped get me out of jail."

Stoll shook his massive head. "No, it helped you win round one. Right now Kershaw is digging into the connection between Judge Curtis and Elinor. Once he finds it, he'll ask the judge to excuse himself from the case. Even if Judge Curtis feels that his friendship with your aunt won't affect his judgment, he'll still want to avoid the appearance of conflict. He'll step aside. I've known him for fifteen years, and that's what he'll do."

"That won't matter," Elinor said. "This case isn't going to trial."

"It's not?" Stoll asked, turning toward her.

"God will help us find out who's framing Dan. And soon, I expect."

"I wish I shared your optimism," Stoll said. "Whoever these people are, they're good. The only mistake they've made so far is leaving no blood spatter on Rocky's finger. Suspicious, but not enough to overcome all the other evidence."

"They made two mistakes," Elinor said sweetly, closing her menu. "The first was Rocky's ring. The second was when they crossed paths with *my* nephew."

Dan chuckled. "Well, all I can say is I'm glad to see you, and thank you for coming to my rescue."

"Oh, don't thank me," Elinor said, patting his sleeve. "Thank God. Without Him, you'd be eating cold spaghetti in jail."

Dan lifted his eyebrows. "God?"

"When Jessica phoned me last night, I called the airport. Some kind of medical convention is going on in Vancouver, and we could only get a standby ticket. I sat in the airport most of Sunday. It was a trial, Dear, a real trial.

"Late in the afternoon, the girl at the desk signaled me to come and talk to her." She smiled. "I had told her how urgent it was for me to get home. That wonderful child told me she had someone call in a cancellation for Monday morning, and she was giving me that seat. So, I got in at a few minutes past one. Just enough time to get home and change out of my traveling clothes."

She turned to Jessica. "I understand you've been doing some snooping for Dan. What have you got so far?"

Jessica tucked a strand of strawberry-blond hair behind her ear. "Nothing besides what Kurt told us." She glanced at Dan. "As for the death of Beth Martin, Amy inherits everything. That makes her a suspect."

"Except for one thing," Dan said. "When Beth died, Amy didn't inherit the property. Rocky did. She had no motive to kill Beth, and I don't believe she was capable of doing it."

"That diary puts you in deep trouble," Stoll said.

"Why haven't they charged me for Beth's murder?"

"Well, for now they've got Amy Creighton for that." Stoll

began ticking off points on his fingers. "She had motive: the inheritance. She had the means: A nurse can get Nardil easily. And she had opportunity. But don't consider yourself off the hook. They'll keep sweating Amy to see if they can get her to turn on you."

The lawyer shrugged. "At some point in time, we're going to have to plea bargain if we can't find the perpetrators. During a plea-bargaining session, they'll offer to never pursue the Beth Martin matter if I agree to a harsher sentence on the Rocky Wiebe charge."

"So my goose is cooked unless we find out who did this?"

"'Fraid so," Arthur said.

"We'll get right on that first thing in the morning," Elinor said as the waitress came to take their orders.

Half an hour later, Dan leaned back in his chair. "I'm stuffed and exhausted. Not a good combination. I didn't sleep much last night. Jessica, would you mind giving me a ride home?"

Elinor started to open her mouth, then stopped, a twinkle in her eye. "Yes, would you, Jessica? I'd take him, but I so much enjoy my after-dinner coffee. Arthur will keep me company, won't you?" She smiled at the big man beside her.

"Certainly," Arthur said. He lifted his fork for another bite of blueberry cheesecake.

Dan and Jessica left the restaurant and settled into her car. She held the key but didn't put it into the ignition. The security lights around the parking lot obscured most of the stars. The night was very peaceful. He turned to her. "Thanks for everything," he said.

Looking down so her hair hid most of her face, Jessica shrugged. "I'm afraid I haven't done that much."

"You stuck by me."

"I guess so." She looked at him, and her eyes gleamed in the mellow light. "There's something I have to ask you. I have to hear it from your own mouth."

Dan nodded. "You don't have to ask. I'll tell you. There's nothing between Amy and me. Never has been. Just a few dinner dates."

She sighed. "I knew that from the first moment I read the diary." She hesitated. "I did find something this morning. Well, not exactly, but I had some suspicions."

"What?"

"I went to the farms Peter Martin leased out. At one they raise bulls for rodeos. The guy was friendly. He let me see whatever I wanted. He told me that Samson is a gentle bull. They couldn't use him for the rodeo, so Peter took him. The rancher couldn't figure out why Samson would attack Peter." Her voice grew more intense. "At the second farm, the woman couldn't wait to get rid of me."

"A woman?" Dan asked. "A woman was with the guys who pounded me."

"That's not all," Jessica said. "The place was kind of weird. It had way more milking machines than cows. Of the cows they did have, no more than a quarter carried milk. The rest were dry."

The hair on Dan's neck stood up as he remembered his conversation with Mike about grow-ops. "Jessica, this is all beginning to make sense."

"What is?" she asked.

"Let's talk on the way," Dan said, reaching for his seat belt.

"On the way where?" She slid the key into the ignition, and the engine roared to life.

"To call in another favor," he replied as the Porsche shot into the street.

Working with vengeance deep underground, the woman cut

leaves and buds from the stem of a marijuana plant and stuffed them into a newspaper-carrier's bag. In a closed room that looked like a cement-block cellar, she and two men stood around a table of rough lumber.

"Who would've thought he'd get bail today?" one of them said. He was longhaired and unshaven, a recent college graduate.

She glanced at him. "Someone pulled a few strings to get bail that fast."

"We're still safe, aren't we, Sylvie?" the other one spoke up. Medium height and medium build, he had short brown hair and wire-rimmed glasses. He looked like an accountant and, ironically, took care of laundering the money.

"According to my friend, yes," the woman said, "but we can't take any chances. Foster might be able to identify me. It was dark, but I wasn't wearing a mask."

"What are we going to do with Jack's sister?" Longhair asked, stuffing leaves into his bag.

"What can we do?" Sylvie asked. "Jack says he won't let us kill her. Do you want to argue with him? He's patrolling up top right now, if you'd like to start that 'discussion' again."

"My mama didn't raise no dummies," Longhair said.

"Mine neither," Shorthair added.

Jack was the gang's muscle, and he had plenty of it. A month ago, Jack's sister Rebecca had gone south on them. It was a shame. She'd been such a useful part of their team.

"I convinced Jack that we'd leave her where she is. I told him that we'd wait until we're in the clear, then we'd call the cops and tell them where to find her."

"But she knows who we are!" Longhair said. "She knows the whole operation."

The woman stopped clipping for a moment. "Don't worry about it, okay? Rebecca won't be a problem. Trust me."

Dan and Jessica parked at the side of the road about half a mile from Jersey Delight. Tonight, the moonlight was made for stealth.

"You look good in black coveralls," Jessica said, a grin in her voice, "but the combat paint on your face doesn't suit you, I'm afraid." She leaned a little closer to him. "You've got connections I never dreamed of. The clerk at that surplus store couldn't help you quick enough. I think he would've come along if you'd asked him. I've got a feeling there's a lot more to Dan Foster than most folks realize."

Dan touched her hand. "I'd better go. It's after midnight. Hopefully, they're all in bed."

She squeezed his fingers. "I'd rather stay with you."

"Not a chance," Dan said. "If this is a hydroponics grow operation like I think, then one of us needs to be able to get away quickly. You wait here. If I don't show up in an hour, call the cops."

She shivered. "Maybe we should call them now."

"And tell them what? Because some farmer has chosen not to milk all his cows, he's using the extra power to grow marijuana? If I could find Bernie Thorpe, I'd try it. He's the only one in that outfit I trust. But I can't reach him, and no one will tell me where he is."

He paused. "Even if the cops believed me, they'd have to get a search warrant and that takes time. I don't think we have time. You've been here sniffing around, and now I'm out on bail. They may pack up and run. If they get away, I'll never clear my name."

She tightened her fingers around his. "What if they catch you before you catch them?"

"Then I won't come back, and you'll have something concrete to tell the police."

She gasped. "That's not funny."

He gave her a quick hug and got out of the car. Moving off the road, he walked in the ditch that ran along the shoulder. Fortunately, there hadn't been rain for awhile so it was dry.

When he got to the ranch, he moved along the side of the property instead of down the driveway. Grow-ops were usually in the basement of houses. Sure signs would be aluminum foil covering the windows and condensation on the glass. If he found that, he'd have enough to take to the police.

A row of cedar shrubs lined the driveway. Dan crept up to them, peeked through the openings, and saw no lights on in the house. With any luck, the residents were in bed. He skittered across the driveway and rolled to the ground beside the basement. He came to the first window. No foil, no condensation.

Dan crawled all the way around the house, checking each window with his tiny new flashlight. No sign of a hydroponics operation anywhere. He suddenly realized that another thing was missing—a dog. Drug growers always had a pit bull or two kicking around. Either these people weren't drug dealers or they were smart enough to avoid the usual trappings of their trade.

The ingenuity of the dairy-farm cover told him he was dealing with some pretty shrewd operators. BC Hydro regularly monitored power consumption. Any property using too many kilowatts was flagged for the RCMP. A dairy farm could use tremendous amounts of power and raise no alarms. Since only a quarter of these cows were bred, the rest of their power allotment could be used for supercharged lights to grow marijuana, and no one would look twice at their bill.

With the house a dead end, Dan moved toward the rear of the property, dashing from shadow to shadow. He jogged to the barn and flattened his back against it. He slid along until he came to a door. He tried the handle. Locked. Why would anyone honest lock up a barn?

The end of the building had a couple of windows. Did he dare break in? Did he already have enough to bring the police? A locked barn wouldn't be enough, especially for Carrington. She'd figure he was grasping at straws and wasting her time.

He raised his gloved fist to punch the window. Before he could land the punch, a hand grabbed his shoulder and pulled him around. Half a second later, Dan's jaw crunched under a wide fist.

Grunting, Dan jammed his knee up, catching his assailant in the groin. The man gasped and doubled over. Next, Dan threw an uppercut.

Inside the dark Porsche, Jessica took a sip of coffee from her thermos mug. The warm liquid helped stave off the cold seeping into the car. She bundled her coat around her, hugging herself, and glanced at her watch. Forty-five minutes. Fifteen minutes more, and she'd call Anna's private number. Jessica prayed that she wouldn't have to make that call. Dan had to come back with evidence.

She heard footfalls coming fast and hard. Jessica squinted and made out a dark shape running along the road toward her. Dan! He made it, and he was in a hurry. She put her hand on the ignition key and waited. She couldn't fire up the car until Dan was safely inside. One turn of the key and the daytime running lights would turn on, giving Dan's position away. For all she knew, someone might be chasing him with a gun.

The figure drew nearer, and she breathed a sigh of relief. Commando Dan was only thirty feet away. He shifted direction toward the passenger side of the car, sprinted to it, and pulled the door open. The interior lights came on.

"Dan!" she cried. "I'm so glad to see. . ." A knife flashed against Jessica's throat.

Rolling his head back and forth, Dan felt like he was in a deep fog. He could hear a female voice. "Jessica," he moaned.

"My name is Rebecca Johnson," she said. Her voice was light, like a child's.

Dan opened his eyes and stared into total darkness. Thick, intense darkness. He sucked in deep breaths. His heart beat like a drum corps on parade. Struggling to his feet, he felt a concrete wall.

"Hey, take it easy," Rebecca called out.

Dan scrambled around in the darkness. His feet became tangled with Rebecca, and he tumbled flat on the earthen floor.

"Watch it!" she cried. Her hands groped across his face and found his shoulders, where she latched onto him. "Calm down!"

Dan scurried away from her and pressed against the wall. He was trapped; he couldn't get out. His throat felt gritty and dry. He couldn't breathe. The door opened, and light flooded in. Dan charged toward the light and collided with someone flying through the door. He stumbled backwards, falling to the floor with the newcomer on top of him. Darkness closed in on them again.

"Let me out!" Dan cried.

Familiar hands stroked his face. "Dan, it's me, Jessica."

His mind dashed about, wild with terror. *Jessica, yes Jessica, Jessica was his friend.*

"Take a deep breath and hold it," she said, pulling him into a sitting position.

Her arm was across his chest, her other hand rubbed his back. He sucked in a deep breath.

"Now let it out slowly. . . . Take another one."

As she whispered close to his ear, his fear started to drain away. With Jessica holding him, the panic slowly subsided, but it remained just below the surface.

"Welcome to my dungeon," Rebecca said.

"Who's that?" Jessica turned her head.

"I'm Rebecca. Am I ever glad you came along! Your friend really wigged out. He practically trampled me."

"Your voice is familiar," Jessica said. "We've met."

"If you're Jessica Meyers, we have."

"You're the girl at the Cranfield restaurant."

"That's right."

"What happened? Why are you locked up in here? I thought your brother was one of them."

"He is." Rebecca hesitated. "To be completely honest, I was one of them, too."

That didn't make sense, but Dan didn't trust his nerves to ask any questions. He just huddled against Jessica and listened.

"What happened to you?" Jessica asked.

"I'll give you the condensed version. We've been set up here for a couple of years."

Dan took a deep breath. He had to know. "Where's here?"

"Underneath the barn. When we leased this place from Peter Martin, it was nothing but a cattle operation. To keep him from getting suspicious, we told him we'd only take the place if he'd lease it to us for ten years because we were going to spend some money and make it suitable for dairy production. Under the cover of building a new barn, we excavated the floor, built an underground marijuana-grow operation, and covered it over with a concrete floor—which is normal for a dairy operation."

"No one can find this place unless he knows it's here," Jessica said. "When they brought me in, the guy pressed a switch hidden behind a board in the wall and some sort of hydraulic system moved a slab aside. The basement seemed bigger than the barn, is it?"

"Yes," Rebecca said. "For the size of operation we developed, we needed room, lots of it. The basement extends twenty-five feet wider than the barn."

"And no one thought it was strange the way you built this place?"

"We're part of a co-op," Rebecca said. "Anyone who worked on this place was already connected to us. We sure had a great thing going until Peter Martin got too nosy. He used to come around more often than necessary. At first I thought he just liked to flirt with me. But after awhile, we realized he was scoping us out, putting two and two together. Fortunately, instead of going to the cops, he asked for a cut."

"Hence the accident with the bull," Jessica said. "Someone smeared his slicker with the urine of a cow in heat."

"We weren't sure if the urine trick would work, but it was worth a try. If it didn't, we had contingency plans."

"Such as?"

"Farmers are accidents waiting to happen. Probably Jack would've pushed him off his hay pile or something. Not as good as being trampled by a bull, but it works."

"Who's Jack?"

"My brother."

"So why did you come to me?" Jessica asked.

"You'll laugh."

"Try me."

"Well, after Peter Martin died, I felt really low. On my day off, I went downtown to kill some time and try to get away from my problems. I was walking down Main Street, and I saw a poster for a concert that afternoon. It seemed like a good way to spend the rest of the afternoon. I play the keyboard, and I love music.

"So, I got a taxi to the city auditorium. It was a great concert. I was surprised when I realized it was a Christian performance. A man started giving a little speech during the intermission. It seemed like he mentioned God in every sentence. I tried to light out of there, but a nice-looking college guy named Derrick stopped me at the door and encouraged me to stay.

"He sat with me for the second half. After the concert, I sat in the lobby and talked with Derrick for more than an hour. He told me that Jesus died because He loved me. Can you imagine that? Me, Rebecca Johnson.

"Peter's death had really gotten me down. I knew I couldn't go on with my lifestyle. That night I turned away from the drug scene. The money no longer mattered to me." Sweet excitement filled her voice. "I found something better: Jesus Christ Himself.

"I tried to talk my brother into quitting the gang. He wouldn't do it, so I called you, Ms. Meyers. I couldn't let them get away with murder." She sighed. "They followed me to the restaurant. I think they would have killed me, but Jack wouldn't let them. They kept me in here so I couldn't blow the whistle on them."

"You've been in here since our meeting?" Jessica asked.

"Most of the time. They let me out for meals some days, but they don't like having me around. They say I preach at them too much. In a way I'm glad you are here. Except for when Rocky was here, it's been pretty lonely. But even then I was never alone. Like I said. I found Jesus at that concert, and He's never left my side since."

Dan found his voice. "Rocky was in here?"

"Yeah," Rebecca said. "But I think they killed him. He made the same mistake as Peter Martin. He figured out what was going on and asked for a cut."

"She can prove my innocence," Dan told Jessica, "if we get out of here."

"We'll get out," Jessica said.

"Kurt Fletcher said he caught one of you messing with Peter's slicker. Why didn't they take him out?"

"We sure considered it," Rebecca said. "Finally we decided it would be less trouble to let him live. What could he really say? Someone messed with a slicker. We doubted he was smart enough to put the slicker and the bull together, and we were right. Seems only Ms. Meyers managed that."

"Well, I had help on that one," Jessica said. "One thing I don't understand. Why did they kill Beth Martin? Did she figure them out, too?"

"Actually, we thought Dr. Foster killed her."

"What do you mean?" Dan asked. "Your friends didn't do it?"

"We had nothing to do with Beth Martin's death."

Chapter
Twenty-Eight

J essica awoke to a damp, musty smell that seemed to fill her whole head. She blinked a few times, trying to see, before she realized that she was still in total darkness. She felt a weight on her shoulder and soon realized it was Dan's head. He was asleep. Her muscle felt oddly numb with jumping pins and needles. She shifted, and Dan woke up.

"We're still here?" he asked, his voice groggy.

"I'm afraid so."

"I'd kind of hoped my dreams were reality, and this was the nightmare."

"It's definitely a nightmare, but it's also real. How are you doing?"

"Better," he said. "I can't say I'm happy, but I'm coping." He stretched his shoulders. "Elinor must be freaking out by now. At least she'll have the cops looking for us."

"Will they?" Jessica asked. "Think of it. What can she say? My nephew left with the girl I think he's sweet on, and he hasn't come home yet. With everything the cops have to do, do you think we'd be a priority when our absence could just as easily be explained as two lovers on a tryst."

"I never thought about it like that. In fact, she might be

stewing right now if she thinks that's what happened. Elinor has some pretty set ideas on propriety."

They fell into comfortable silence for a few minutes. Dan cradled her hand in the darkness. Finally, he said, "You know, I've always had this crazy idea that if I did all the right things and punched all the right buttons, I'd have a good life. I've lived that. . .gone above and beyond even. And look at what I've been through."

Rebecca spoke. "Lots of people have that idea, Dan. But it takes a power greater than ourselves to get through life. Good deeds won't see us through when everything falls apart. And, believe it or not, that happens to everyone at some point or another. All we can do is admit we're not good enough and ask for help. I wish everyone in the whole world could know Jesus like I do."

Jessica said, "That's very sweet, Rebecca," then they all fell silent.

After awhile Dan said, "There was sure a lot of activity on the other side of that door last night."

"Sounded to me like they were packing up and leaving."

"Which begs the question, what happens to us?"

Rebecca spoke up. "I think you guys are going to be okay. When we talked about taking Peter out, Sylvie was determined to have it look like an accident."

"Who thought of using cow urine?" Jessica asked.

"Unfortunately, it was me. I was a veterinarian assistant in Moose Jaw. When my brother gave me a call and asked if I'd help his friends set up this dairy operation, I figured, why not? Everything went fine for about twenty months. One night they were tossing around ideas for getting rid of Peter, and without thinking of the consequences, I gave them the urine idea."

"You realize this makes you—at the very least—an accessory to murder?" Jessica asked.

"I've thought of that," she replied, her voice sad. "I'm prepared to go to jail. I know I won't go alone."

"Your brother can't go with you to a women's prison," Dan said.

Rebecca chuckled. "My brother? No. I was thinking of Jesus."

"You figure they won't just up and shoot us?" Jessica asked.

"That wouldn't look like an accident."

"Or a frame-up," Dan said.

"Or a frame-up," Rebecca agreed.

The previous evening, Dan had filled Rebecca in on how Rocky had met his death. She was dismayed but not surprised at what her brother had done.

They heard a key scraping into a padlock and the snap of it opening, then light flooded in. A woman's silhouette filled the doorway. She had a revolver in one hand and a canvas sack in the other.

"Hi, Sylvie," Rebecca said. "I really wish you'd repent and turn to Jesus before it's too late."

"Shut up, Rebecca," Sylvie Stanton said. "This is why your brother won't come and say good-bye to you. You just can't shut up."

"Are you sure?" Rebecca asked. "Or does it hurt his conscience too much to see me like this?"

"Whatever," Sylvie said. "Here's the deal. We're going now. This place is a bust. We can't operate here anymore. Once we're safe and sound, we'll tell the cops where you are. It might be a few days, so here's some food." She tossed the sack into the room.

"What about us?" Jessica asked.

"You stay here until help comes. How hard the cops look for us depends on how heinous the crime. Shooting you or the doctor would give them all the more reason to stay on our trail.

We've got enough heat as it is." She looked toward Rebecca in the corner. "I don't suppose you'd agree to come along and keep your mouth shut."

"My Lord won't let me do that."

Sylvie shook her head. "It's your choice."

The door closed. The padlock snapped shut.

"Wow!" Dan said. "I was sure they'd kill us."

"So was I," Jessica replied. "Don't start celebrating yet. Something isn't right. They've already killed two people. Why leave behind three more who can identify them? It doesn't add up."

"Despite his faults, my brother does love me," Rebecca said.

"Yeah. Enough to mix you up in this," Jessica said.

"If you knew the old Rebecca, you wouldn't say that. I wasn't exactly a pristine flower."

Dan spoke up. "I know this sounds hokey at a time like this, but I'm hungry." He shuffled away from Jessica. The bag rustled. "Muffins and bottled something," Dan said.

A cap twisted off.

"Bottled water," he said. "Anyone want a muffin and water?"

For the next few minutes, Dan played waiter in the dark.

After a drink, Jessica lowered her bottle and sniffed. "Does anyone else smell smoke?"

There was a pause. "Yeah," Dan said slowly.

"Rebecca, how does air get in here?" Jessica asked.

"Near the top of the wall there's a vent from the other room."

Jessica stood with her nose upward until she found the vent. She coughed. "Definitely smoke."

"Oh no," Rebecca said. "She's lit the outer room on fire."

Two thousand feet above the ground, DEA pilot Brian Westmore turned to his passengers, Mike Foster and Louise Crossfield. "Strap in," he said. "This runway isn't exactly up to par."

The Beech 1900 aircraft lowered its flaps and lined up with the gravel airstrip. The plane tilted left then right as the pilot made final adjustments. The plane shuddered, then rolled down the runway, the turbo props roaring in reverse pitch to stop in thirty-four hundred feet—three hundred feet less than the plane's minimum runway requirements.

With brakes applied, the plane shuddered some more and eased to a halt.

Louise looked pale. Mike felt pretty good. He'd done a fair share of flying with RCMP bush pilots, so little fazed him. He looked out the window and saw a truck stacked high with hay at the end of the airstrip.

"Time to get this show on the road," Louise said.

The pilot opened the door, and they climbed down onto the runway. Clouds hung overhead, making for a gray day. That didn't help Mike's mood much. Bernie met with him the previous night and filled him in on Dan's troubles. It was all Mike could do not to charge up to Langley and throttle Anna Carrington. His brother a killer? What a joke! He took a deep breath, forcing himself to concentrate. This scum had to go off to jail so he could move on to helping Dan.

Garret stood with his four Canadian partners. Mike had been banking on the fact that with so much money involved, none of the partners would trust each other. They'd all want to come.

A woman sauntered up. Her hard face had been pretty at one time. She had deep lines around her mouth and a tough set to her jaw. "You got the money?" she asked.

Mike nodded.

"Guns?"

"Absolutely," Mike said. He reached into his pocket and pulled out a Glock. The five of them froze.

"We agreed on no guns," she said, staring at the weapon.

Mike laughed. "You're crazy if you think we're going to show up unarmed with this kind of money at stake. You could rip off the money, and that would be it. Now, I've got a gun, and I'm putting it away. If I was going to pull a fast one, I'd do it right now."

The woman was tense, like a rattler about to strike, but she uncoiled when Mike holstered his weapon.

"I'd like to see the money," she said.

"Not a problem," Mike said. He nodded to Louise, who disappeared into the aircraft and returned with a briefcase. She handed it to the woman, who took it to the hood of the old farm truck and opened it. She flipped through the money, snapped the briefcase shut, and set it inside the truck.

"Let's get this done." She nodded to her partners, and they began moving bails of hay off the truck bed, breaking them open, and pulling out plastic bags of marijuana.

"If you don't mind," Mike told her, "I'd like to do some tests to make sure this stuff is the same as the sample."

"Suit yourself."

He grabbed a couple of bags and disappeared into the aircraft with them. Instead of doing the test, he got ready for the next phase of the operation. He couldn't suit up before in case they wanted to search him. Mike emerged from the plane, and Louise looked over at him. "It's fine," he told her.

He hung around the plane until it was almost loaded, then sauntered to the boss lady. "Is this an abandoned airstrip? It's in pretty good shape."

"Actually, it's a training strip owned by a local flight school," she said. "We don't exactly have their permission to use it, so we shouldn't drag this out too long."

Louise wandered over beside Mike.

"So, where are we exactly?" he asked, looking overhead.

The woman's face tightened. "Why do you want to know?"

"Just curious," he said. "It's a pretty area. I might want to come back here sometime. We flew over Abbottsford, right? That would put us not far from Mt. Lehman Road."

"What are you doing, Arnie?" Louise asked, using his undercover name.

"Just trying to figure out where we are."

Louise stood with her side touching his. She stared closely at his face, then backed away, drawing her weapon. "He's a narc! I can't believe this."

The gang leader jumped away from Mike like he was on fire. "A cop? What do you mean he's a cop?" she shrieked

"Look in his left ear," Louise told her.

Mike winced when she yanked down his ear lobe and the electronic transmitter fell out.

Louise's lower lip trembled. "We've spent three years together. . .and you're a cop? I mean we. . .we. . ."

Mike held up his hands and backed away from Louise. "Hey, don't take it personal."

"Personal. I thought you loved me!" Louise screamed.

Her Beretta fired four times. Mike jolted with each shot. He stared down at his chest to see red ooze seeping through his shirt. He crumpled to the ground, his face slamming against the gravel.

"What are you doing?" Mike heard the woman dealer shout.

A boot drove into his side. Mike didn't react. He just kept his breathing slow, his body motionless.

"Filthy pig," Louise said. "He'll never double-cross me again."

"Oh good for you," the woman said. "I'm glad you're happy, but you just made us all accessories to murder of a cop."

"What do we do now?" one of the men asked.

"I don't know," the woman said. "I'll have to call and find out."

Call, Mike thought. *Call who?* He thought they had the whole gang. He heard a cell phone snap open.

"It's me," the woman said. "Arnie is a cop. How come you didn't know. . . . Yeah well, Patti just put four into his chest, so what do we do. . . ? I'd rather not. Sure there isn't another way. . . ? Yeah okay. . . We'll meet you there then." The cell phone snapped shut.

"What did she say?" one of the men asked.

"She said to get on the plane and head into the US. She hasn't heard anything, but that doesn't mean we're in the clear. They don't tell her everything. The cops could be on their way even as we speak."

"But I thought we never wanted to go to the US," the man said.

"You want to stay in Canada and stand trial for murdering a cop? Assuming the cops don't just shoot us and save the trouble of a trial."

"Let's go," he said.

Fire!

The word exploded in Dan's mind like a mortar shell. *We're trapped! We're going to die. . . .*

Dan clamped his hands over his eyes. He'd failed once in a crisis. He couldn't let that happen again. He scrambled to his feet. With hands extended, he walked toward the door and felt along the wall until he found it.

"What are you doing?" Jessica asked.

He barely heard her. All his energy focused on that door. He backed up five paces. With a primordial scream, Dan charged into the darkness and slammed into the heavy wood.

"Dan, what are you doing?" Jessica yelled.

"You're not going to die!"

He backed up, took a deep breath, and slammed into the door. The frame creaked, and his shoulder felt a terrific jolt. He crumpled to the floor, holding his shoulder, and looked up to see light peeking through where he'd loosened the frame.

"Let me try," Jessica said, behind him. She cried out and the shadow of her foot slammed into the door. She sent rapid-fired sidekicks to where the door joined the frame. Wood and metal began to rattle.

There was enough light now so they could make out each other's shadows. He reached for Jessica and moved her aside. Dan backed up to the other end of the room. He barreled down on the door, planted his other shoulder into it, and the frame splintered. He tumbled head over heels into the barn basement.

Covering his eyes with his hands to protect them from the light, he blinked and forced his eyes to open a crack. A thick layer of gray smoke billowed against the ceiling and spread out.

Jessica dropped to her knees beside him. "What are we going to do?" she gasped.

Dan tried to stand but pain shot up his ankle. He howled and fell over. "I've twisted my ankle." He looked around. At the far end of the room, two wooden planting benches were smoldering. The flames would easily jump from bench to bench. The fire wasn't widespread yet, but the prisoners had nothing to fight it with. They needed water.

Dan looked up. Plastic pipes ran along the concrete ceiling, a convenient watering system for the grow-ops. He pointed to them. "That plastic can't be too strong. Pull them down over the fire."

Needing no more encouragement, the women found chairs and dragged them to the other end of the barn basement. Jessica and Rebecca got on the chairs and together used their strength to pull down a water line. It broke at the fitting and water flooded the burning bench. They repeated the procedure three more times, dousing the flames. Finally, Rebecca rushed to the far wall and turned a valve to stop the water from flooding the basement.

Her hair tousled, her face covered in smoke, Jessica rushed back to Dan. She threw her arms around him, and he cried out in pain. "Watch out for my shoulder!"

She eased off and smiled. "Sorry. I'm just so glad to be alive."

"I can't believe Sylvie did this," Rebecca said. "She tried to burn us alive."

"I knew she couldn't leave us untouched. She did this so that when your brother asked questions, she could blame the fire on bad wiring or something."

Dan looked around the basement. "You know, I think I banged myself up for nothing. Look at this place. Concrete floor, concrete walls, concrete ceilings. The fire could only burn the benches. It couldn't have reached us. What on earth was she thinking?"

"Oh no," Rebecca said. She suddenly shouted. "Be quiet! I've got to listen!"

They held their breath, waiting.

Finally, Rebecca said, "I can't hear the ventilation fan. Air is pumped in here from outside and vented out through the manure piles beside the barn. I don't hear the fan."

Jessica grabbed Dan. "She wasn't trying to burn us alive."

"She was burning up all our air," he said. "She was suffocating us."

"We've got to get out of here," Jessica said. She turned to Rebecca. "How do we get out?"

Rebecca pointed to a short staircase leading to a concrete panel covering a square opening in the ceiling. "That panel moves by hydraulics."

"Great," Dan said. "Where's the switch?"

She pointed again. The switch and the wires running to it were in the corner, burned beyond recognition.

Mike pulled himself off the ground as soon as the plane's droning motors died away in the distance. The one wildcard in his plan was whether one of them would decide to put a bullet in him for good measure. A DEA sniper was off in the trees somewhere for that contingency. Fortunately the sniper hadn't been needed. No loss of life.

He looked to the sky. In five minutes they would be in US airspace. Another ten minutes and they'd land at an airstrip near Bellingham, where swarms of DEA agents were waiting. The DEA had gotten their wish—Canadian drug dealers with a major amount of drugs on US soil. Sylvie's gang would go to jail for a long, long time. But there was another one out there. Maybe with a little negotiating, they could get Sylvie to give her accomplice up.

Two unmarked police cars roared toward him and skidded to a stop. Bernie burst out of the first one. "You okay?" he asked.

"Sort of," Mike said. He ripped off his shirt to expose his chest. Four welts were turning dark purple. "Where's that little jerk?" he ground out.

A short, round fellow got out of the second police car, his face beaming. "It worked."

Mike rushed over and grabbed his shirt. "You said it wouldn't hurt. Look at me."

The special effects artist shrugged. "Sorry. I guess I didn't put enough padding behind the blood pads. Looked real, though, didn't it?"

Mike shook his head and let the man go. "Yeah, it worked. Thanks, I guess."

Bernie looked at the damage without bothering to comment.

"Are you ready to go back to work?"

Mike gave him a hard look. "I've got some time off. I want all the files on my brother's case. Something about that situation stinks, and I'm going to find out what it is."

"Carrington will be ticked off if you stick your nose in."

"If she doesn't like it, she can call Inspector Bernier. See how far she gets with him."

"Come on," Bernie said. "I'll give you a ride home."

They got into the unmarked car. Bernie turned it around and headed toward Langley.

"I feel rotten about my brother," Mike said. "How could someone do this to him? He's a classic do-gooder, right up there with Mother Teresa."

Half a mile later, he went on. "You know, all that time in the motel I never once thought to watch the Canadian news. A doctor accused of murder won't even make the back page of the papers in Washington State."

"It's just as well you didn't," Bernie said. "If you had, you would've broken cover. As it is, you took down a major grower."

"It'll be interesting to get the DEA report on this one," Mike said. "We still have to do some more cleaning up on this operation—find out how they got set up, who they networked with. This thing is far from over."

Sparks flew, and Jessica yanked her hands back from the wires. "Well, that didn't work," she said. She turned to Dan, who sat on the floor and rubbed his ankle. "Any ideas?" she asked.

His breathing sounded loud and labored. Injured and being the largest of them, he needed more air than the ladies. "Get another wire from the lights and try again," he whispered, his words slurred.

Jessica felt lightheaded. Rebecca sat in a corner, praying for all she was worth. To conserve the remaining air, they'd decided that only one of them should move about. Jessica trudged to Dan and sat beside him. "You okay?"

He looked up at her, his eyelids lazy. "Huh?"

"You okay?"

His hoarse breathing was rapid and shallow.

"Lie on the floor," she said.

"Gotta tell you something before I die."

"We're not going to die," Jessica said. She helped him lie back before he fell over and hit his head.

"Gotta tell you. . .love you." Dan's eyes fluttered and closed.

"I love you, too," Jessica whispered, touching his bruised face.

She looked up at the opening in the ceiling, and her vision blurred. She knew she couldn't hold on much longer.

Chapter
Twenty-Nine

"Wake up!" Bernie's voice called from the driver's seat beside Mike.

Mike shook his head and opened his eyes. He sat up and looked out the windshield. The day was overcast. Scattered houses flew past them with wide yards between.

"We're almost there," Bernie said. "I guess you fell asleep."

"Last night was kind of long."

"It wasn't that bad. I got to bed by midnight. What happened to you?"

Mike rubbed his face. "Louise and I stayed up until four talking."

"About what?"

Mike shrugged. "Everything and nothing. Probably just prebust nerves."

"Want to grab a coffee?"

"Yeah. Actually, I'm kind of hungry, too."

Bernie drove through Langley and pulled up in front of the Whitespot restaurant. Bernie picked up the microphone and informed dispatch where they were, then the two men crossed the parking lot into the restaurant.

There were just a few patrons. They grabbed a booth by the

window. A waitress came and poured them a couple of cups of coffee, took their orders, and left. Mike took a sip of coffee and sighed. "I think I've died and gone to heaven."

"Doesn't take much to please you, does it?" Bernie asked.

"Not right now it doesn't," Mike said. "Being undercover isn't all the movies crack it up to be. Sleeping in motels and eating restaurant food all the time can get boring fast. I'm glad this one didn't last too long, especially after what happened to Dan." Mike clenched his fists.

"Things will work out for your brother," Bernie said. "I've got some vacation time coming, too. I'll use it and help you."

"Thanks," Mike said. "I appreciate it."

The waitress delivered their food, and they passed the time with Mike giving Bernie the details of the operation. He just pushed his plate away when Anna Carrington entered the restaurant. Mike gripped the edge of the table.

"What is she doing here?"

Bernie looked back over his shoulder. "She's either one brave woman or a fool."

Corporal Carrington scanned the restaurant, then headed straight to Mike and Bernie. She flashed an awkward smile when she drew up to the table.

"Hi," she said. "I heard on the radio you were here. How did the operation go?"

"Cut the pleasantries," Mike said. "What's the matter, need another Foster to torture?"

Anna held up her hand. "Hear me out," she said. She slid into the seat beside Bernie. "Look, sooner or later our paths are going to cross, so I think we need to get the air cleared on your brother right away."

The waitress stopped by and filled a coffee cup for Anna.

"Sure," Mike said. "Everything's clear to me already. You got tunnel vision and dragged a truly decent man through the

mud and worse. I tell you, Carrington, if you botched this—
and I'm willing to bet that you did—you'll find yourself cleaning up behind the horses in the RCMP Musical Ride."

"Step back a minute," Carrington said. "You need to see
the evidence we've got before making a decision."

"I don't need to see anything," Mike said. "I know Dan
and. . ." Mike's cell phone beeped. "Excuse me," he said. He
took it out of his belt clip and flipped it open. "Mike Foster."

"Hi Mike, it's Louise."

"Hey, how did it go at your end?"

"Not too good, I'm afraid."

"What happened?"

"When my people came out in the open, the big guy
grabbed me and put a knife to my throat."

"Are you okay?"

"Yeah. But he isn't. A sharpshooter took him out."

"Louise, that's horrible. You're sure you're okay?"

"Well, actually I'm not." Her voice wavered. "I think I'm
going to put in for a transfer. This is starting to get to me." She
took a deep breath. "Anyhow, the reason I'm calling is they
want to make a deal."

"What kind of deal?"

"They want us to agree to ten years on the drug smuggling
charge and guarantees that they'll never be extradited back to
Canada."

"That's odd," Mike said. "You'd think they'd want to come
back here. Our prisons are so much nicer. Unless they've done
something here that's worse than drug smuggling. What are they
offering in exchange?"

"It seems they're part of a drug co-op. There are four more
grow-ops being dismantled as we speak. If we don't act now,
they'll be long gone."

"What about their other partner, the one she talked to on

the cell phone?" Mike asked. "Is she in the deal?"

"Only Sylvie knows who she is, and she says it's a non-negotiable issue. Unfortunately Sylvie managed to bust her cell phone onto the tarmac, so we can't use that to trace the other woman. So, do we make a deal to get the others?"

Mike rubbed his unshaven face. "Boy, Louise, that's a tough one. Tell them we want the location of their grow-op before any deals are made. If they've done something worse, we'll probably find it there."

"Okay," she said. "I'll call you back."

"What's that all about?" Bernie asked.

"The perps want a deal. They're willing to give up some of their partners in exchange for ten years and no extradition to Canada."

Carrington fumbled with her coffee cup and spilled some on the table. Mike tossed her a napkin.

"Louise is going to tell them no deal unless they give us the location of their own operation first. I want to make sure we don't have bodies out there before we agree to anything."

"Good plan," Bernie said. "With what's going on at the pig farm, we'd look ridiculous if we made a deal like that and then found a bunch of bodies somewhere."

Mike's cell phone rang. "That'll be Louise." He flipped it open. "Mike Foster."

"Hi," Louise said. "They said they cleaned the place up before they left, so you won't find any pot, but they said you're welcome to look around all you want."

"Did they actually say I was welcome to look?" He looked at Bernie, who had the last bite of butter pecan pancake on his fork. Carrington seemed to be transfixed by her coffee cup.

Louise said, "Not too bright, are they?"

"They just saved me the trouble of a search warrant."

"I got another bit of good news," she said. "Sylvie's cell

phone might not be broken."

"Really?" Mike asked.

"Yeah. It looks like it was just the battery pack that popped off. One of our guys has managed to fix it up with another pack. I'm thinking the phone is either ripped off or a pay-as-you-go phone. These guys are smart; I doubt we'll be able to trace anything with it. I was thinking I'd just press send and see what happens? Okay with you?"

"Sure," Mike said. "Why not. I'll wait while you do it."

He could envision Louise standing on the tarmac of the Bellingham airport with a cell phone to each ear. "It's ringing," Louise said. "Once."

A shrill beep emerged from Anna Carrington.

"Twice."

Another beep from Carrington.

"Aren't you going to answer that?"

"Three," Louise said.

Carrington pulled the phone from her jacket pocket and flipped it open.

"Hello," he could hear Louise say.

"Hello," Carrington said into her phone.

"Who is this?" Louise asked.

Mike's eyes narrowed on Carrington's phone. "Man the coffee here stinks," he bellowed.

Carrington flipped her phone shut. She shrugged. "No one there."

"She hung up," Louise told Mike. "Uh, but this is really weird, Mike. I heard you complain about the coffee in both phones."

"It's not that weird," Mike said. "I'll call you back." He flipped his phone shut. He tapped his coffee cup. "I have to go to the little boy's room."

Mike slid out of the booth, walked even with Carrington,

and grabbed her arm.

"What are you doing, Foster?" she yelled as he pulled her onto the floor.

"Mike, knock it off," said Bernie. "This is going too far."

Carrington was a strong woman, but not anywhere near as strong as Mike. He flipped her face down on the floor, pinned his knee into her back, and twisted her arms around behind her back. "Give me your cuffs," he said to Bernie.

"Foster, you'll go to jail for this."

"No, Carrington, you're the one going to jail. You're under arrest for trafficking in narcotics, for starters."

"Mike, do you know what you're doing?" Bernie asked.

"Oh absolutely, Partner. Just trust me."

Bernie handed him the cuffs. "Okay."

Mike snapped the bracelets on her and removed Carrington's weapon. "Louise heard me on both cell phones. The only way that could happen is if she was talking to one Corporal Anna Carrington."

Bernie looked down at Carrington.

"I want a lawyer," is all she said.

After leaving Anna Carrington in the custody of Inspector Phil Bernier, Mike called Louise back, filled her in on what happened, and got the address of the grow-up. Thirty minutes from the restaurant, they pulled up into the driveway of the Jersey Delight, where three other cars already waited.

Mike and Bernie got out of their cruiser. "Grab the universal door opener," Mike told Bernie.

Bernie opened the trunk while Mike walked up to a corporal, a slim fellow with the first signs of crow's-feet by his eyes.

"Hey, Mike," the corporal said, shaking his hand. "Glad to see you made it back okay."

"Good to be back, Ward." Mike turned to the other two—a redhead with a paunch and a man of Asian descent. "Okay, guys, this is the deal. We believe this house was used as a grow-op. It's supposed to be deserted, but we're going to treat it as if there's someone with a gun on the other side of every door."

Bernie walked up behind him, a three-foot battering ram in one hand and two bulletproof vests in the other.

"Which is why you're going to put this on," Bernie said, handing Mike a vest.

In uniform, the other officers already had their vests on as per standard procedure.

"No argument there," Mike said. He strapped on the vest and said, "Let's go."

Mike and Bernie approached the front door of the house with Ward and the constable while the redheaded officer moved off to cover the back.

Bernie set the battering ram in place. Mike drew his weapon and stood to the side. Bernie slammed the ram just above the deadbolt lock, and the door splintered open.

"Police!" Mike bellowed.

They charged into a living room littered with cigarette butts, beer cans, and empty fast-food wrappers. Mike entered a small bedroom on the right, and the other officers broke off in different directions. In less than a minute, they were certain the house was empty.

Back in the living room, Mike told Ward, "Bernie and I will search for evidence here. You take the rest of the guys and check the barn."

Ward grabbed the ram and left with his men.

Two minutes later, Mike and Bernie entered the basement through a doorway in the kitchen. The wooden stairway was steep. It creaked under their combined weight.

"Might be time for me to lay off the pancakes," Bernie said.

Mike glanced back at his partner's paunch. "I'm not saying a word."

Bernie chuckled. "Next time I'll order five instead of six."

They stopped at the bottom of the stairs and looked around. The area was dry and surprisingly clean. A dozen tables lined the walls. Each table had a six-inch raised edge and was filled with Heydite—small pieces of shale rock used as growing medium for marijuana. A garden hose was attached to the tap by the laundry tub, and a few grow lights rested on the floor.

"This is a red herring," Bernie said.

"No kidding," Mike replied. He walked to the nearest window, pulled out his pocketknife, and snapped it open. He dug the blade into the wooden window frame. "No sign of rot whatsoever," he said.

Bernie went over to the electrical panel and opened it. "No tampering here. If they were growing pot down here, they'd have bypassed the meter to avoid detection by BC Hydro."

"Let's see what the guys found in the barn," Mike said.

They hustled up the stairs and outside. One of the barn doors hung on one hinge. The barn smelled of white lime and grain.

Ward walked over to Mike and Bernie. "Nothing here," he said. "We've been over it twice."

Mike took his time scanning the walls and the floor. "You checked everywhere?" he asked.

"I've even got Reg looking in the milk tanks."

"What about a basement?"

Ward shook his head. "We checked. There isn't one. This is a concrete slab."

Mike rubbed his forehead, trying to think. "I can't believe they grew all that pot in a small basement. Even with partners."

"Maybe they did," Bernie said. "These people are pretty ingenious sometimes."

Mike shook his head and walked away from the others. He looked over the milking stations, scanned through the utility room. Nothing there.

Maybe it was just a milking barn. He opened the wide doors at the end of the barn, put his hands on his hips, and gazed toward the cows munching hay in the pasture. *Lord*, he prayed. *There's something here. I know there is. What is it?*

"What do you think?" Bernie asked, coming close behind him.

"I guess the basement of the house is it." Mike shook his head, disgruntled but not sure why. "We might as well go. I've got business to take care of, and I'm standing here wasting time." He turned to Ward. "You want to secure the house as a crime scene? The forensic guys can check it out when they get a chance." Mike looked at his partner. "Let's go."

Jessica stroked Dan's face. His lips were faintly blue, the veins in his cheeks stood out. Feeling weak, she lay on her back beside him. The remaining air was low against the floor. She took his limp hand and looked up. Rows of powerful grow lights ran along the ceiling. Thankfully they were turned off. Six incandescent bulbs lit the room. Water pipes ran above the lights. The part of the ceiling that wasn't under the barn had four vents. Why was no air coming down through the vents?

Rebecca said the vents came up through manure piles. Sylvie must have blocked the vents after she lit the fire. Jessica sat up, and the room spun. She took five deep breaths to get as much oxygen as she could. She crawled to Rebecca and shook her, but the girl had passed out.

She looked about and spotted the dangling plastic pipes that saved their lives. Maybe they'd do it again. Pulling a chair to the fastened end of one of the broken waterlines, she climbed up and grabbed onto it with both hands. She pulled, but it held fast. Her lungs sucked for air, and her vision turned red, but Jessica kept yanking and jerking again and again. At last, the flexible pipe broke away from its fitting. Jessica tumbled to the floor with a twelve-foot section in her hands.

She climbed up on a table and reached for a vent cover in the ceiling. Cutting her hands, she pulled the shiny metal off and cried out in frustration. A baffle system lay inside it. She couldn't shove the water pipe directly into it.

Sobbing, she rasped out, "God, help me. Please!"

Sinking down on the table, she saw a three-foot length of four-by-four lumber—a table leg from one of the burned tables. Most of the table burned away from it. Jessica slid off the bench and lowered her head to keep from passing out. She took some deep breaths and retrieved the leg. It had a couple of short, charred boards nailed into one end, but she didn't bother trying to remove them. The bottom end was all she needed.

Returning to the vent, she knelt on the table and rammed the leg upward into the vent's opening. Made of light tin, the baffles buckled. Moving like a person in a drunken stupor, she fed the plastic pipe into the duct. It knocked against an obstruction. She sucked on the pipe. No air.

Grunting and sweating, she slammed the pipe against the barrier and prayed they hadn't propped a cement block or something else heavy against the opening. As she worked, her blood smeared the white plastic. She tried again, praying that the pipe wouldn't break. Unexpectedly, a cool stream of air came down the pipe.

Like a drowning woman, Jessica put her mouth to the pipe and clamped her nose shut, so the air would go directly into her lungs. She breathed deeply. In and out. In and out. The air tasted like manure—and the sweetest thing Jessica could think of at the time. It took a couple of minutes before the oxygen worked its way through her lungs to her bloodstream.

This tiny draft wouldn't let in enough to refresh the whole basement. She had to get Dan and Rebecca to the air. She looked at Rebecca, slumped against the wall with her head rolled to one side. Jessica would need her help to move Dan.

She dragged the girl's slim form to the bench. Rebecca moaned but didn't wake up. The air pipe was too high to do her any good.

Jessica grabbed under Rebecca's armpits and lifted. The girl was like a rag doll. She simply flopped over. Gasping and praying, Jessica leaned Rebecca against the bench, grabbed the back of her pants, and hoisted her up. Positioning the girl's head near the pipe, Jessica pulled in a dozen breaths before turning to Dan.

Using the same technique, she grabbed under his armpits and tried to drag him. His legs felt like they were glued to the floor. With a bone-jarring jerk, she managed to move him four feet. Then she had to return to the pipe for air. It took eight tries before she moved him to the bench.

She leaned Dan against it and slapped Rebecca's face. A moan, but no response. "Wake up!" she screamed in the girl's ear but only got another moan.

Jessica's hands were trembling. She couldn't lift him even in good circumstances. Oxygen starved herself, this would be impossible. Dan's lips were purple, his breathing irregular. *Please God,* she cried in her heart. *Don't let me get so close only to see him die.*

Mike and Bernie sauntered back toward their car. Mike felt like a little kid was hanging on his leg, trying to get his attention. Something wasn't right here. He stumbled when they reached the edge of the driveway but quickly regained his balance.

"You okay?" Bernie asked.

"I guess so." He sounded morose. He might as well call Louise and tell her to make the deal. He flipped open his phone and dialed.

"Louise Crossfield," she said.

"Hi. It's Mike."

"Find anything?"

Suddenly he jerked his head around and looked at the cows. "I'll call you back." He flipped the phone shut. "Let's go back to the barn," he said and started jogging.

"What is it?" Bernie panted, running to catch up.

"There aren't enough cows for the amount of milking stations."

"Which means they're not using much power," Bernie said, falling into step.

Thirty seconds later, they burst into the barn. The other officers looked up when they came in.

"What is it?" Ward asked.

"This place has to have a basement," Mike said. "There aren't enough cows for the milking stations."

Ward looked around, his gaze intense. "If there's a basement here, I don't know how you'd get into it."

"Neither do I," Mike said.

"You want a jackhammer?" Bernie asked.

"Yeah," Mike said, "Call the public works department and get a crew over here."

"That concrete looks thick," Bernie said. "This is going to take awhile."

Looking down, Mike moved along the wall until he stood by the utility room. He looked at the milking station adjacent to it. "Why is this one on a raised platform?" he asked.

Bernie walked over and gave it a kick. "Good question. You think it moves?"

Mike squatted for a closer look. "I'm not sure." He stood up and stared at the wall of the utility room. He paced the length outside, then entered the room and paced the inside length. A full pace different. "Bernie!" he shouted. "Get me the battering ram."

Seconds later, Bernie rushed in with the ram. Mike slammed it against the wood frame wall. The wood splintered, revealing a hydraulic motor with an arm that reached through the wall. "Take a look," Mike said, standing back.

Bernie peered inside. "My, my. These guys are slick."

"Stand aside," Mike said. Using the ram, he smashed a hole big enough for him to squeeze into the hidden compartment. The motor had a manual switch, and Mike flipped it. Above the motor's whine, he heard a grating sound.

"Mike! Get out here!" Ward called.

Mike banged his head on the way out of the hole and stumbled out of the utility room holding his forehead. He caught sight of Bernie's head disappearing down the opening in the floor. Mike followed him. Halfway down, he stopped dead in his tracks.

Five paces away, Jessica Meyers leaned over his brother. She seemed to be giving him mouth-to-mouth resuscitation.

"Hurry!" she cried. She leaned over a table, sucked air from a pipe, and returned to Dan, blowing into his mouth. Mike took a breath and nearly choked on the stale air. Suddenly his adrenaline kicked in. He charged down the stairs, scooped his brother up in his arms, and rushed out of the basement. He did not stop until he could lay Dan on the grass outside. He tilted his brother's head back and opened his mouth.

Leaning on Ward's arm, Jessica staggered outside. She sank to the ground and gasped, "He's still breathing, but he needs oxygen. They lit a fire down there to suck out all the air."

Bernie emerged with a young woman in his arms. She was

waving her arms and saying, "I'm okay, I'm. . .okay," in a slurred voice.

Mike turned to Jessica. "They trapped you down there and lit a fire?"

She nodded and covered her eyes with her hands.

Ward spoke into his radio. "We've got three victims here. Send paramedics."

Mike flipped his phone open and hit redial.

"Louise Crossfield," a voice answered.

"No deals, Louise. In fact, I want them back here, stat."

"Back in Canada?"

"That's right," Mike said. "They're wanted for attempted murder—minimum."

Dan stirred and moaned softly. His nose throbbed something awful. Kicking his right foot, he realized that he was in bed. He drew in a long, deep, beautiful breath and opened his eyes to a hospital room. Beside him, Jessica sat in a chair reading a book.

"Jessica?" he croaked. "What happened?"

She dropped the book and came immediately to his side, taking his hand. "A miracle happened, Dan. A great big miracle. Your brother's task force was on the trail of Sylvie's gang the whole time. They arrested them in the US a few hours after they left the farm. Then, Mike came to collect evidence."

"Mike's back?" He reached up and touched a stiff plaster over his nose. It pounded like a toothache.

"He found us. Mike carried you out himself."

"Wow," he said, closing his eyes. "I thought we were dead for sure. He got there just after I passed out?"

Jessica lifted his hand to her cheek. "Something like that," she told him. "Do you remember what you said just before you passed out?"

He winced, trying to recall. "It was something about a wire." He looked at her. "Wasn't it?"

She bit her lip. "Uh, yeah."

His eyes closed as a spasm hit him. "My nose is hurting something fierce. Can you get a nurse? I need some Demerol or something."

"Just press the button connected to your IV drip," Jessica said. "You're on self-serve, Dan. You don't remember the nurse telling you about it?"

He looked confused. "No. What's going on, Jessica? I'm missing a big block of time."

"The doctor said that sometimes oxygen deprivation blocks out short-term memory."

"How long have I been here?"

"This is your second day. We came to the hospital from the barn. They kept Rebecca and me overnight. Rebecca went into custody, and I went home for twenty-four hours."

She perched on the edge of his bed. "I've got some good news for you. First, you've been cleared of Rocky's murder."

"I figured that would happen if Rebecca told what she knew."

"She sang like a meadowlark. Mike figures she'll probably get a suspended sentence for cooperating with them."

"What about Beth Martin's death? Rebecca said the gang had nothing to do with that."

"That's the second thing I wanted to tell you. Mike picked up the copy of the security tape that Corporal Carrington promised us. He brought it to your home last night." She yawned. "The three of us were up late last night staring at the screen in your living room. Mike watched the people. Elinor watched the room itself, and I watched the pill bottle."

"For six hours?" Dan asked.

"We took some breaks to rest our eyes. Anyway, Elinor

noticed that the wall clock jumped five minutes at one point."

"The tape had been tampered with," Dan said.

"Right!"

"But all that does is raise doubts about my guilt, not prove my innocence."

A deep voice spoke from the doorway. "This may be what the doctor ordered." Mike walked in with a videotape in hand.

"Hey, Bro," Dan said, weakly.

"He can't remember anything since the barn," Jessica told Mike.

Mike came over to the bed. Moving awkwardly, he hugged Dan close. His voice choked with emotion, he said, "Sorry I wasn't there for you."

"Hey, you were there when it counted," Dan replied, his voice muffled. "Now let me go before we both start crying and ruin our reputations."

Mike pulled back and swiped a meaty hand at his face. "The test results came in from the slicker." He grinned. "There was cow urine on it. However, too much time had passed for the test to show any pheromones. So, the test was pretty worthless."

"Well, at least your influence got the test done a little faster than two months."

"Bringing down a criminal organization gets you some pull," Mike said.

"Still, it's too bad it doesn't prove anything," Jessica said.

"Don't let it bother you," he said. "With Rebecca's testimony, we don't need the lab results to make a case. We've still got the goods on both murders—Peter's and Rocky's. And get this, Guy Jones—one of Sylvie's gang—is also turning over. Sylvie and Anna Carrington are going up for a long time."

"Carrington!" Dan straightened up. "She was involved?"

"Yep," Mike said. "She was protecting them, feeding them information. That's why she was so interested in framing you. Anything to keep the RCMP from looking in the right direction."

"But why?" Dan asked. "Why would an RCMP officer throw in with drug dealers?"

"Well, it seems Sylvie Stanton and Anna Carrington grew up together. I think when Carrington got busted down to corporal, she started to think more about herself than the force. We may never know her true motive. We can only guess."

Dan ran his hand through his hair. "What a nightmare." He looked at the tape in Mike's hand. "What have you got there?"

Mike moved over to the TV/VCR combo already set up in the room. "On the security tape we noticed a patient in the bed next to Beth. Her husband had a camcorder. This is his video. I got his name from your former office and paid him a visit."

At that moment, Aunt Elinor walked in with a box of donuts and a cardboard tray holding three coffees. "You're awake," she said, smiling at Dan. She set the food on a stand and moved closer for a hug.

"Now that we're all here, let's find out what's on this tape," Mike said. He pressed play on the VCR. The swollen face of a Japanese woman filled the screen. She kept waving her hands, trying to get her husband to stop. The volume must have been turned down, because there was no sound. Suddenly, the camera appeared to be set on a table, causing the view to rest—albeit not perfectly—on Beth Martin.

The bodies of a man and a woman crossed the screen, then disappeared.

"Camera angle is all wrong for a head shot," Mike said.

"That's Amy and me," Dan said. "I recognize the clothes."

They returned to camera range. Dan walked out the door, and Amy soon followed him.

"Lord, let him leave the camera there," Mike whispered.

Beth Martin slept. Five minutes passed. Ten minutes. Aunt

Elinor moved to the lounge chair, and Mike perched on the air-conditioning unit. Jessica sat on the edge of Dan's bed.

Staring at the video, Dan clenched the sheet in his fists. How much longer before the man realized he'd left his camera on?

The Japanese man suddenly appeared in the field of the camcorder as he left the room.

"Wow, that's a break," Mike said.

Another ten minutes passed. The door opened, and a man in a white physician's coat entered. He wore black pants, but they could only see up to his shoulders.

"Bend over," Mike said. "Let us see your face."

Wearing surgical gloves, he lifted Beth's pill bottle. He dumped her amoxicillin capsules into his hand and dropped them into his pocket. Reaching into his pocket, the unknown man pulled out another bottle and poured its contents into Beth's bottle.

Dan slammed the bed with his fist. "That's him! That's the scumbag that killed Beth."

When the killer extended his arm to put the pill bottle back, his sleeve slid up.

Mike hit the pause button. "Gotcha!" he cried. "See those moles? They're as good as a fingerprint. We've got him."

Dan slumped in the bed. He shook his head. "This is unbelievable."

"What?" Mike asked.

"Yes, what?" Jessica and Elinor chimed.

"I know who it is," Dan said. "It's Dr. Cruch. I've seen his arms and noticed those moles before. I told him he ought to have them checked." He put his hand to his head and groaned. "I never dreamed his jealousy would go this far. I should have seen the signs and stopped him."

Jessica bent over him. "You can't blame yourself for what happened. You had no way of knowing Cruch was so twisted."

Mike ejected the tape. "I'll see you later, folks. I'm on my way to arrest a murderer. Believe me, it'll be a pleasure." He dashed out of the room.

Elinor turned to Dan, her features sagging with fatigue. "Don't blame yourself, Dear. Sometimes we have to trust the Good Lord for the answers. That's why He's God. He can handle all the why's and what-if's." She leaned over him for another hug. "I was so worried about you." Her voice cracked. Holding her hand out to Jessica, she said, "Do come by and see me, Dear." She patted the blanket covering Dan's foot and walked out.

Still sitting on the edge of the bed, Dan reached for Jessica's hands. "I was so afraid I'd lose you," he murmured, squeezing. "Every time I get close to someone, they go away."

"I thought I was going to lose you," she said. "It's no wonder you can't remember so much of what happened. Your lips were blue by the time Mike found us."

"I don't know if you'd call it destiny, or God, or what," he said, his eyes half closed, "but it seems like someone was watching over us. Both of us."

"You felt that? I felt it, too."

Watching her face, he smiled softly and said, "One thing I do remember. We had a date last Friday night. You stood me up."

She laughed. "*I* stood *you* up? Sorry, Dr. Foster, but I think that was a mutual situation. I was at the Coyote Bar and Grill looking for Kurt Fletcher."

"I was roaming around the woods looking for a bear." He grinned. "Not!" He pulled her hand to his lips. "Can I have a rain check for this Friday night? I should be sprung from this place by tomorrow."

"Why wait until Friday?" she asked, her voice gentle. "We can go anytime. Anytime at all."

Would you like to offer feedback on this novel?

Interested in starting a book discussion group?

Check out www.promisepress.com for
a *Reader Survey* and *Book Club Questions*.

About the Authors

Rosey Dow is a best-selling and award-winning author. Her novel, *Reaping the Whirlwind*, won a 2001 Christy Award for excellence in fiction. A former missionary and lifelong mystery buff, Rosey now makes her home in the South, where she writes and speaks full time.

Andrew Snaden coauthored the novel *Betrayed* and has also written articles for several publications. A native of Canada, he makes his home on an eighty-acre farm, where he works as an accountant.